# The Pendulum's Path

# The Pendulum's
# Path

*To Derek,
Dave Shields*

Dave Shields

Copyright © 2001 by David Shields.

Library of Congress Number: 2001118729
ISBN #: Softcover 1-4010-3027-0

All rights reserved. No part of this book may be reproduced or transmitted in any form or by any means, electronic or mechanical, including photocopying, recording, or by any information storage and retrieval system, without permission in writing from the copyright owner.

This is a work of fiction. Names, characters, places and incidents either are the product of the author's imagination or are used fictitiously, and any resemblance to any actual persons, living or dead, events, or locales is entirely coincidental.

This book was printed in the United States of America.

**To order additional copies of this book, contact:**
Xlibris Corporation
1-888-7-XLIBRIS
www.Xlibris.com
Orders@Xlibris.com

*For Elle and Carly,*
*I love you more than words can ever express.*

# Chapter 1

I often wish we hadn't walked the dog that day.

The cold broke records for Salt Lake City in late November. The slight breeze stung exposed skin and even pierced through clothing. Six inches of snow from the day before remained mostly untrodden. Frost sheathed bushes and trees. Sara, Ranger, and I followed the familiar quarter-mile path from our home, crested a final rise, and looked down upon the three acre clearing where we loved to play. A duck paddled quick circles in the last bit of open pond water. A thick ribbon of mist revealed the path of the meandering brook that filled the small reservoir. Normally, even in winter, Brigham Park teemed with people and their pets. Today it was virtually empty. Not a soul visible and only one van in the lot, a rusted powder blue Ford I'd never seen before.

When I paused at the top of the steep railroad-tie staircase, Sara cuddled close, tucking her shoulder beneath my arm. I felt a shiver descend her spine. I glanced at her. With her beautiful face concealed beneath two swirls of an Aztec print scarf and her long blonde hair tucked under the hood of her coat, all I could see were her eyes. Exotic deep blue, but softened by highlights radiating from the hidden center, like deep water on a sunny day. Would our child inherit that color?

I felt a burning awareness of the confidence she'd placed in me by carrying our child. Her upbringing taught her much more skepticism than mine. We were deep into our courtship before she ever spoke of her hopes or dreams, even though I'd opened up to her from the very first. But eventually she told me everything, including how her mother had trained her for her entire life to doubt the intentions of anyone who wanted to get close. As a result, the process of earning Sara's faith, bit by bit, and the knowledge that she gave it at that level to no other, made it the most valuable gift anyone had ever shared with me.

Ranger tugged at his leash, yanking me from my daze. His breath escaped in charging white clouds.

"You're certain it's all right for you to be out in this cold?" I asked Sara.

She stroked our retriever's golden hair. "Make up your mind, Tom. You talked me into coming. Now you're trying to talk me into going back? Maybe you're getting cold and want to use me as an excuse."

She knew that wasn't true. "No, just experimenting with being overly protective. As a father that will be my main responsibility, won't it?"

"Your idea of parenting scares me. We need to get you a book. You have less than six months to study up on this."

I chuckled. "No, I'm not studying some book. That's your answer to everything." Even though I'd grown up fatherless I was confident I knew what it took to make a good parent. All my life I'd watched dads, paid close attention to everything they did. I'd developed a sort of expertise. Since adulthood I'd often dreamed of the relationship I'd have with my kids. "I don't need an instruction manual. It might take me a while to hit my stride, but I will. Bear with me."

"Yeah, right. The moment we get home I'm getting on the Internet and buying every child-rearing manual I can find." Her muffled voice emerged from the many layers of clothing. She gave me a quick hug, then nodded at the stairs. "Take Ranger on ahead. Use the railing, the steps look slippery."

"Now who's overprotective?" I started down, one hand holding the leash, the other in my pocket. Ranger lunged forward. I windmilled arms and legs in a fight for balance as we careened down the steep slope. When I hit level ground I pitched face first into the snow. My ears and cheeks went numb. I rose to my knees, blew out a mouthful of ice, and removed my powder packed sunglasses. As I cleared the lenses, I glanced toward my wife.

"Very impressive," Sara called.

I climbed to my feet and brushed myself off. "They don't teach those moves in any book."

"Believe me. I can tell."

Unclipping the leash, I spanked Ranger's flank. He loped away. "At least there won't be anything putrid for him to roll in today."

Sara smiled as she eased her way down the steps. Near the bottom I reached out for her gloved hand. Together we crossed the snow-covered parking lot. Ahead, Ranger circled the rusty blue van, nose to the ground, pausing to give each tire an extra sniff. The van looked out of place to me, sitting alone where there were usually half a dozen shiny SUV's. Various tracks made it impossible to tell which way the occupants had gone.

After a moment Ranger looked toward the park, sniffing the breeze. I tucked the leash into my coat pocket and looked in the same direction. No sign of anyone. "If his brain were half the size of his nose, we'd have something special," I said, laughing.

"Be nice. He'd never say such a mean thing about you." Sara poked the side of my nose with her finger.

"My schnoz-to-brain ratio is the opposite of that mutt's, if you're trying to imply something. But now that you mention it, what *does* Ranger say about me?"

Her sly smile crinkled the corners of her eyes. "He says you're handsome, sensitive and trustworthy."

"Very perceptive. Maybe I've underestimated him."

The dog leapt through the snow ahead of us, dodging this way and that, frolicking with invisible friends. He scooted low to the ground, burying his snout in the snow, then looked back toward us with a powder-enshrouded face.

We laughed, then Sara's smile faded. She bit her lip. An

increasingly familiar expression of uneasiness overcame her face. "What is happiness, Tom?"

I chuckled and pinched her cheek. These unanswerable questions of hers seemed somehow tied to her pregnancy. I suspected she pulled them from women's magazines, and I worried that she'd compare anything I said to the "correct" answer written upside down at the end of the article. "How about you tell me?"

"I wish you'd at least try."

"Normally I would, but right now my brain is frozen." I wondered what topic she would come up with next, for she seldom tolerated silence when there could be discussion. To Sara conversation, or rather, conversation with friends, might have outranked breathing in importance. While, prior to getting married, I enjoyed spending days at a time alone in the wilderness, she'd always hated being by herself for even a moment. She discouraged my trips to the back country. Since our wedding I'd gotten used to a lot more time together, and a lot more talking.

I looked ahead. A thick curtain of fog rose above the serpentine creek. We entered the mist and crossed a bridge, our echoing footsteps accompanied by water gurgling through encroaching ice. For a moment we couldn't see beyond arm's length. Then, I sensed shadowy figures beyond. I stepped from the cloud to see a man and two dogs emerging from the park's wooded fringe. Ranger bounded toward them like a dolphin leading a skiff to open seas. The stranger grabbed his pets' collars, then crouched low, as if preparing to kick my dog in the face the moment he came within reach.

"Ranger! Sit!" I yelled, already sprinting in his direction.

To my surprise the dog sat in full stride. He slid to an uncomfortable looking halt only a few feet from the group. I hurried to his side and grabbed his collar, not confident his good sense would last.

While the man struggled to restrain his dogs, I looked him over. He wore an overstuffed goose-down parka which made it impossible to judge his size. The tightly drawn hood revealed only a small circle of his leathery face. Two thick brows, the color of storm clouds, loomed over ultramarine eyes. Heavy crow's feet made the features seem deeply set. His lips hid behind a scruffy salt-and-pepper mustache and beard. Similar countenances filled inner-city bread lines across the nation.

The dogs were both mutts, medium-sized and rambunctious. The stranger spoke to them in an urgent whisper. "Daddy shouldn't have brought you here. We should've gone to our usual spot in the hills. Sorry Moxie, sorry Bailey, I know you're upset."

Their tails wagged vigorously, and they strained at their collars. They didn't look upset to me.

The man's gaze met mine. "The way he charged like that. You can't tell what'll happen . . ."

The words blurred. His voice was soft, yet a disturbing whine predominated it, like a pre-adolescent boy trying to talk his way out of punishment. A deeply buried memory stirred. I'd once known this voice, but from where?

He cleared his throat, and the sound brought everything back. Uncle Martin. I'd last heard his characteristic cough at age twelve. Images that might have lain dormant forever returned. My bloodstream felt carbonated. I battled my nerves. Here before me stood the black sheep of my family. I'd long since quit thinking I'd ever see him again. Now that we stood face to face, staring across a gap of two decades, now that I suddenly knew he was alive, I felt unprepared.

My face must have twisted in concern, but the man misread my expression and tried to explain himself. "It's not that I don't trust dogs. Trustworthy dogs are as common as trustworthy people are scarce. I'd rather trust a coyote than—"

"Are you Martin?" I remembered how much he disliked being called "Uncle," so I avoided the term. My question billowed through the icy air in a gossamer cloud.

He glanced at me, then away. His eyes didn't return to my face. Apparently my voice didn't reawaken memories in him.

Why should it? I hadn't even been through puberty the last time we spoke.

Then, cautiously, as if it were more a question than an answer, he said, "Yes? People used to call me that."

"What's your name now?"

"My new name?" His tone suggested he couldn't remember that one either. "Just call me Martin. Who are you?"

I extended my bare hand. "I'm Tom." He still didn't recognize me, so I added, "Thomas Lewis."

His crumpled expression transformed into a grin. "Thomas Lewis? Little Tommy?" Ignoring my hand he moved closer and looked me up and down. "You grew up." The pungent odor of halitosis wafted toward me in strong bursts at each cloudy exclamation. I worked my frozen fingers back into my glove.

I felt my wife's arm slide into the crook of my elbow from behind. "Martin, my wife, Sara. Honey, let me introduce you to Martin Crump."

Out of the corner of my eye I saw her nod, probably recalling no more than a few passing references to this man, the youngest of my mom's two brothers. "It's a pleasure to meet you," she said.

Martin nodded shyly, his gaze on the snowy ground.

"How've you been?" I asked.

"I've been."

He said no more. Overhead, geese honked as they beat their way south in a rippling vee.

I wracked my brain for something safe to say. "Nice dogs."

He glanced at the animals. They were sniffing one another's privates. "Yours too."

I seized the opening. "Ranger's a great dog. Doesn't mind as well as I'd like, but we—"

"Dog's shouldn't have to mind. People don't."

I looked toward him quickly, hoping to better understand his odd words with the aid of his expression, but he turned away. I followed his gaze to the dogs, already play fighting.

I took Sara's hand and started walking in the direction Martin must have been headed when Ranger interrupted. The biting cold made motion a necessity. Martin fell in step at my side.

"What breeds?" I asked.

"Bailey's half lab, half chow. Moxie's part collie, part something else. I'm not sure what."

I wasn't either. Moxie personified mixed breed. Her confused expression indicated a shortchange when vital genes had been dealt. "Looks like she might have shepherd in her," I said.

Martin regarded the mutt. "I hope not."

Sara and I shared a puzzled glance.

Moxie looked over her shoulder at me, flipped her tail up, and caught the end in her mouth. She stared straight into my eyes, teeth clamped on the furry appendage. She may as well have said, "If you think I've been shortchanged then how about that? I solved the ultimate canine puzzle."

Martin swatted the tail from the dog's mouth as if the habit annoyed him.

Sara smiled. "Tom and I spent last weekend with your brother, Joe."

Martin kicked powder into the air. "My brother– the big shot." He spat, as if removing a bad taste from his mouth. The little ball of saliva rolled down an undulation in the snow. It picked up a furry looking coating and stopped. He said no more. That single statement apparently exhausted his interest in the subject.

I stared ahead, letting the white to gray monochrome of the winter scene blur in my mind. Surely Martin remembered how much I'd once admired Uncle Joe– that I'd looked up to him like a son to his father. And though that sort of emotion was now ancient history, our recent visit to Joe's Santa Barbara home had rekindled my love for the man on another level.

"Tom, how long has it been since you and Martin have seen one another?" Sara's question brought me back to the present.

Before I'd even begun the mathematics, Martin spoke. "Four days short of twenty-one years."

I looked at him in amazement.

He continued. "The last time I spoke to my sister, and therefore the last time I saw Tommy, was Thanksgiving Day, 1975. When I left her house that day everything worth saying had been said."

"You haven't spoken to your family in all that time? Why not?" Sara asked.

"Lot's of reasons." He hesitated, as if trying to buy time to recall them. He looked to the frigid sky and seemed to discover the remainder of his thought in a cloud. "I'd had enough of her trying to force me to live my life her way. I said to myself, 'I don't need this. I know what this is about and I don't need it.'"

Sara crinkled her brow. "What was it about?"

He snorted. "Tommy could tell you." He looked at me as if we were soldiers who'd defended the same hill.

I shrugged. "No one ever told me why you disappeared."

He shook his head. "Figures."

"So what happened?" asked Sara.

Martin's tone sharpened. "My, aren't you a nosy one. Emma wanted to gloat, okay? She's certain if I'd followed her advice things would've turned out better."

I knew the rebuff would dampen the fun of discovery for Sara. I wondered what sort of advice my mom might have wanted to dispense, but I'd rather ask her than him. We walked silently for quite a ways.

Sara squeezed my hand. I looked at her and she mouthed her next question.

She'd owe me big for this. "What advice?" I asked hesitantly.

The visible fragments of Martin's face reddened. "Emma has all the answers, Tommy. How can you not know that? She's always shoving them up everyone's nose. Well, I have a news flash. Her lifetime of good luck has come at my expense."

I squeezed Sara's hand and mouthed back, "Thanks a lot." I certainly hadn't wanted our exchange to follow this course. After all, Mom's greatest weakness was being too compassionate, everyone knew that. She volunteered for the homeless, attracted stray kittens like a lint magnet, once even rescued a mouse from a spring trap and nursed him back to health. She'd practically raised her own mother, for God's sake. I could sooner believe the Pope had been baptized Mormon than give weight to Martin's version of events.

His ridiculous claim revealed something fascinating, though. Beneath his crusty exterior flowed molten emotion, no matter how disconnected from reality. Our silence was broken only by the sound of snow crunching beneath our boots, until I asked, "Where do you live?"

"Why do you want to know that? Don't I have a right to my privacy?"

I put up a hand, feeling frustrated. Couldn't he discuss anything calmly? "Forget I asked. Sheesh."

"It sounds like something Emma would ask."

I shook my head in disgust. "Anybody might, don't get so riled."

"Wouldn't Emma love to know what I'm up to? Did she send you here to spy on me?"

Sara tugged at my arm. When I looked her way, she flicked her head toward home.

He'd piqued my curiosity, but I wouldn't force Sara to remain in a situation she didn't like. "Listen Martin, we've got to go. If there's a way to get hold of you I'd like to talk more. If not, I guess that's the way it has to be."

He didn't respond as he continued walking at my side. I noticed the dogs. They wrestled in the snow, grabbing at each other with lethal looking fangs. Their communication looked so much more dangerous than ours, yet it was really the other way around.

After a long moment Martin spoke. "I don't see why it's any of your business. If you must know, I live in the Avenues."

One glance at his worn clothing and I knew he was lying. He

couldn't afford the Avenues. A lot of good such a vague address would do me anyway.

He cleared his throat, as if starting fresh. "The city has sure grown. Did you realize there are over a million people in this valley?"

I looked at Sara hopefully. It sounded like an honest effort at friendly conversation. Maybe we could start again. She lifted her eyebrows, and I took it to mean she'd give him another chance.

I nodded toward the Wasatch Front. "Maybe they like the view."

Martin grunted, apparently unconvinced.

I looked at the faces of the imposing wall of mountains, covered in a fresh layer of white. "We've been to the top of many of those peaks, hiking and skiing. Ranger's even been up several, including Mount Olympus there. I've gotten us into, and fortunately back out of, some pretty tight spots. Do you like to hike?" I'd taken two or three more steps awaiting a response before Sara halted. I looked at her, then followed her gaze back.

Martin's eyes weren't on the peaks, but instead on a spot inches forward of his boots.

"Are you all right?" Sara asked.

He nodded, keeping his gaze down. "It's a surprise to run into a familiar face, never happens. Not until today. That's fine by me. I've had it with being judged by people who won't forgive me for what happened decades ago."

I looked at him, trying to interpret his seemingly heartfelt words. "What are they judging you for?"

His gaze stayed on the ground. "It's impossible to avoid those people . . . too many of them. All thinking they've earned the right to judge me; well they haven't. They don't know a god damned thing. So what if it bothers them I'm independent. Why should I care?"

He stroked his mustache. "Just me and the dogs. That's how I like it. I get out like anyone, though. Shopping and whatnot. I look at the people and wonder, what right do they think they have to be here?"

I studied a row of poplar trees, naked of leaves, sheathed on this day in a biting frost. The uppermost twigs scratched at the sky, pleading for more hospitable air. How could he be so obsessed with the opinions of strangers and so uninterested in his own family? With unlimited topics to discuss we couldn't even talk about the weather without conflict. I had so many questions, if only he would share his answers. I had so many answers, if only he would ask the obvious questions.

"But what were they judging him for?" Sara whispered, mulling the still unanswered question.

A rapid twitch convulsed an inch below his left eye. Then he stuck a finger past me into her face. "Mind your own business."

I swept his arm away. "That's no way to treat a lady, Uncle Martin. We're leaving now."

The motion threw him off balance. He stumbled backward. A new expression, oddly like curiosity, overcame his face. "Uncle?"

I recalled his inexplicable contempt for that word, and half-heartedly wished I hadn't used it. It no longer mattered, though. I'd had it with this frustrating exchange. I grabbed Sara's hand and started away.

"Tommy!"

I looked back.

"I'm not your uncle. Your life is a lie."

# Chapter 2

Martin averted his eyes and took nervous steps toward the parking lot. "Moxie, Bailey, come!"

I wanted to let him go, but couldn't. I took a long stride and cut him off. "Of course you're my uncle."

He kept his head down as he stepped around me. "No. It's a story they made up. Said it was for your own good."

I wanted to hold him by the shoulders, stare into his eyes, and straighten things out— but how would he react? Instead I grasped at the sleeve of his parka. My fingers clenched nothing more than goose down in a polyester casing. The gesture slowed him, caused him to turn squarely toward me. The look that flashed through his eyes sent a dose of adrenaline surging into my veins. Instinct overruled good sense. "What the hell's wrong with you?" I asked.

He gaped, then spoke slowly. "That's easy. I'm surrounded by humanity— deceit. All I want is to live an honest life, and that's brought me more trouble than you can ever know. I won't be a party to lies, white or otherwise. When I hear one I correct it. Consequence be damned."

"If you're so honest, then tell me who you think you are?"

He shut his eyes. His lower lip trembled, half fighting to conceal his answer, half battling to reveal it. "I'm the man you once knew as Uncle Martin. I can't say more." He stood, waiting for me to get out of his way.

I dropped my arms and he stepped past, headed toward his van, dogs at his side.

Ranger, lying on his back, lolled over and watched them leave. Even he knew something had gone wrong.

Sara brushed up against me. "That guy's wacko."

"Yeah, he's sailing in a leaky boat without a bail bucket. We can't just let him wander off, can we?"

"You're kidding, right? Let him go. He doesn't want our help. All I can say is, thank God."

Despite his insults, despite his madness, the severity of her words surprised me. I looked at her face, noticed her clenched jaw. A change had come over her; I saw her for the first time as a protective mother, a lioness who wouldn't allow her cub to be harmed.

"If we ever see him again it'll be way too soon," she added.

I managed a noncommittal grunt. Never would I have guessed our reunion could turn out so badly. No one even said "Goodbye."

For the remainder of the evening and throughout the night, Martin dominated my thoughts.

As we lay in bed Sara spoke sleepily. "Is there anyone he didn't have contempt for? I mean, your mom sending us to spy? Give me a break."

"Yeah, that's a good one. He pretty much nailed your previous opinion of my Uncle Joe, though."

She chuckled. "Key word: 'previous.' I was very impressed with Joe this time around, and you know it."

I ran a hand down her thigh, enjoying the smooth texture of her bare skin. "Yep, I know that. Joe's something else, isn't he?"

She rolled onto her side, facing away from me, and drew me into a spooning position behind her. Over the three years we'd slept in the same bed this had become our subtle sign that the time had come for sleep. I was ready too, but my imagination wouldn't relax.

In my mind's eye I traveled back in time and place to the previous weekend in a quaint little Santa Barbara restaurant that happened to be my Uncle Joe's favorite. My uncle, Aunt Heather,

Sara, and I sat about a circular table. Joe dipped a piece of sourdough bread into a mixture of vinegar and oil as he spoke. "My doc said, 'This is a Come-to-Jesus meeting. I need to tell you how you're going to die.'" Joe put the bread in his mouth.

My muscles tensed, despite his apparent ease. I looked into his eyes. Sara had already commented on how alert he was, a trait she hadn't experienced in their two previous meetings when she'd judged him an arrogant drunk. She'd seen through him, even though I tried to cover his weaknesses and present only his best side. On this weekend, however, his jokes had been witty, his observations poignant. I felt grateful my wife could finally glimpse why, throughout childhood, I'd considered this man a god.

Joe swallowed. "Doc said, 'One day you'll notice your urine running red, you'll be plagued by forgetfulness and dizziness, you'll have no appetite, and you'll lose feeling and control in your extremities.'" He looked at Sara, then back at me. "I've already experienced every one of those symptoms. Some for over a year."

I shuddered.

Joe must have understood my reaction. "I'll spare you any more details. Let's just say I left his office feeling petrified, and I haven't touched a drop of liquor since. To paraphrase W. C. Fields, 'I've lived for days on nothing but food and water.'"

We laughed.

Joe added, "Seriously, I'll never drink again."

I hoped somehow he could keep that promise, but he'd made and broken it before. Still, something felt different this time, more resolute, more at peace. Maybe somehow the moon could enter a different orbit, the tides might be held back, and Joe would not be drawn once again into his pool of fermented spirits.

* * *

By the next morning I'd decided to swing by Mom's on the way to work and let her set things right. After all, Martin had taken pot-shots at her reputation; she deserved a rebuttal. The mere thought of talking with her seemed to make his bizarre words less threatening.

I drove the ten minutes to her house feeling confident she could clear up the confusion. I entered the always unlocked kitchen door of the tiny brick rambler where I'd grown up. The aroma of baking bread filled my nostrils and eased my tense muscles. I headed down the hallway. As expected, I found Mom in the study. A beam of morning sun streaked through the skylight, bathing her in a warm hue. Mom spent a large chunk of her life in this small but comfortable corner of the house, buried in the paperwork of her physician's billing service. Her formerly walnut colored hair, medium gray now, was cut to shoulder length. She wore makeup, but made no great effort to hide the wrinkles. That made me happy, because to me they spoke of her kindness and wisdom, rather than her age. The creased skin of many more smiles than frowns. She dressed meticulously, as always. It made no difference to her that, in all likelihood, she'd spend the entire day at home.

A pair of reading glasses rested precariously close to the end of her nose. I'd never seen her use them before. I watched her tap numbers into an adding machine. When she paused I spoke. "Aren't you ever going to trash that archaic device? What do you think the computer is for?"

Mom turned, a wide grin lighting up her features. "Well, hello Tom. What a pleasant surprise."

"I came by to make certain you're staying out of trouble."

She rearranged a stack of papers. "If you're looking for trouble you've found a dead end. Can you do me a quick favor? Then we can talk."

I nodded.

"Peek into your sister's room and make certain she's okay. She's unusually quiet this morning."

I walked toward Jill's room at the end of the hall. I turned her doorknob and peered into the dark interior. My eyes adjusted slowly, but after a moment I made out my sister's form beneath the sheets. She lay peaceful and motionless except for the methodical rise and fall in her chest. She looked so content, so beautiful, so complete. More complete, in fact, than when she navigated the halls in her motorized wheelchair, mumbling words that everyone but Mom and I found incomprehensible. Over the last several years she'd deteriorated in mind and body, but not in spirit. Her will to live might have been exceeded only by Mom's will to keep her alive.

Jill was dependent upon Mom for virtually everything. Mom bathed her, dressed her, fed her, and changed her diapers. Jill often got food down her windpipe, and Mom would sit up late into the night pounding on her daughter's back, helping her achieve some level of comfort. Outside their hearing, people would say that nobody in Jill's condition should be alive. They didn't speak these thoughts in secret out of any sort of contempt for Jill, but because my mom's determined aspect made it obvious to all that such negative talk wouldn't be tolerated.

Jill repaid Mom's devotion in a most unusual and fulfilling way— by expressing her love of life and gratitude to everyone who would accept it. Though Jill couldn't form words that even a longtime friend could understand, she could convey messages with her eyes and body language that were absolutely unmistakable. My sister understood that her mumbling and slobbering, her awkward gesturing and moaning, intimidated people. But they were all she could do to interact, so whenever someone took the time to stoop down to her level and look into her eyes, she rewarded them with the most appreciative and pleasant audience they could ever have imagined. Whoever had Jill's attention, knew that they had her full attention. I don't believe anyone has ever paid me greater respect by honoring my presence and truly hearing my message, than she.

Jill, more than anyone I've ever known, made the most of what she had. What might she have been if so much hadn't been taken away?

If only that rusty gray Buick hadn't crossed the median on a rainy Illinois night. Mom wouldn't discuss it much, but I'd learned the basics from others. We crashed head-on at forty miles an hour. Dad died instantly. Mom broke her left arm and two ribs. Jill's back snapped and her head smashed into the windshield causing paralysis from the waist down as well as severe brain damage. I wasn't scratched. The back seat was obviously safer, but in a way I regret having no scar to show for the moment that changed my family's fortune.

We moved back to Salt Lake where Mom started the billing service out of our home so she could be there to raise us. She never remarried, always claimed she could never love any man more than John Lewis, my father. Anyway, she didn't want the distraction of dating to hurt our family time. I grew up believing my mother's sole purpose was making my sister's life and mine as comfortable as possible. In retrospect, I took advantage of her way too much; but by the same token, I don't know what would have become of me if she hadn't been there.

I returned to the study in a thoughtful mood.

Mom didn't look up from her work. My calm return must have been enough to tell her Jill was okay. "What brings you by, Tom?"

I steeled myself to bring up the issue. "I ran into Martin yesterday."

"Who's Martin?" she asked without a pause.

"Your brother."

She lifted her head, her expression blank. "Martin Crump? You're kidding? What did he say?"

"Talking with him was like reading a supermarket tabloid. Lots of scandalous headlines, but no substance to the stories."

"He hates me, you know." She looked into her hands. "He's decided I'm the source of all his problems. Did he say anything about that?"

"He mentioned it."

"Martin was the cutest little kid. I've never seen another smile equal to his," she said more to herself than to me, as if flipping through photographs in her mind. "I used to tell him his teeth were as sparkly as a mouthful of diamonds. I adored that little guy. It's unbelievable he now holds so much against me."

"What happened?" I kept my tone as calm as possible.

She regarded me warmly, but her answer was cold. "Nothing about my childhood is worth remembering."

I waited for her to continue. She didn't.

"That's all you're going to say?"

"You've heard some stories."

"Bits and pieces. I have no context."

"How can it be so important, then? You've made it this far without their burden. Let me tell you something. I changed my thinking when I married your father. I quit looking back. I didn't like where I'd come from. John taught me to focus my attention on the present. For me, that's made all the difference."

I covered my eyes with my open hand and squeezed my temples with thumb and index finger, corralling scattered thoughts. "I'm not a child anymore." Meeting Martin made me realize I must understand my mother's family. I dragged my hand down my face and stared at Mom.

She held her mouth in a straight line, then said, "I'm not silent to protect you, Tom. The stories would dredge up terrible memories that I don't want to relive."

"You can't erase the past by pretending it didn't happen," I said, as if imparting some great lesson.

She didn't listen, just continued in a dreamlike voice. "I look at my life today, and I'm so satisfied with where I find myself." She counted off the positives on the fingers of her left hand, "– great children – nice home – good health – a job I love –

security —" She was silent, and I couldn't tell whether she stopped because she'd run out of positives or fingers. She stared at her hand, waiting, it seemed, to see what it would do next. Finally she formulated her conclusion. "I've made difficult decisions to get here. I'm not going back."

"So, this is something we can't even discuss?"

She shrugged. I didn't notice she'd been holding her breath, and I doubt she did either, until she let it out in a sudden rush. "Martin's the expert on this topic."

"Martin? Are you kidding? It's impossible to talk to the guy. He's a total lunatic."

"No, no. You misunderstand. I'm not suggesting you talk to him, definitely not. He's grown up to be a very strange man, and the more comfortable he becomes in your presence, the odder he behaves. From what you say of him it sounds like he hasn't improved. What I meant was that the difference between me and my brother is, I've done everything I can to leave our childhood behind, while Martin's done all he can to retain it. He reviews the stories endlessly. I don't know whether he's looking for a solution or an excuse. All I know is he has more facts than anyone else, and they've done him the least amount of good."

"Why would Martin know more than you?"

Mom hesitated. I knew she found my questions uncomfortable, but I deserved to know. She spoke with a sigh. "In our house, Martin was the fly on the wall. We kids shared stories . . . and everything else. Beyond that, my parent's spoke freely around Martin, as if he wasn't even there."

"Why?" I sensed her desire to turn the conversation in another direction, but she seemed to feel an obligation to answer, so I waited silently.

"To my dad that was the ultimate way of showing disrespect. Dad said Martin wouldn't amount to anything. He told anyone who would listen that all of his hopes and dreams rested in Joseph alone."

"Why not with you? You're the oldest."

"Tom, please don't push this way. I don't want to talk of these things."

I shrugged. "Grandpa died before I turned five. I never really knew him."

She nodded slowly. "I guess you'd say Dad held traditional views. He saw women as inferior creatures– for serving men and bearing children. To him, even siring a female was a sign of weakness. My birth proved he wasn't perfect. He never forgave me for it." Her glassy eyes held back tears.

"I'm sorry for bringing this up. It just seems so important. I'd always assumed I knew everything about you. Now I discover I know so little."

She sniffled. "That's not true. You know exactly who I am now."

We sat silently. It felt like we were waiting for something important to happen.

My gaze fell to my lap. "Martin says he's not my uncle." I'd wondered how I would bring it up, and now, there it was. It came out sounding like I believed it might be true.

"He said what?" Her urgent tone surprised me.

"I felt so sorry for him." I looked up. She'd gone pale. Why hadn't I kept my mouth shut?

"I don't know what to say," she croaked. Then she stood, and opened her arms. I stepped into them, but I didn't know why. The moment felt surreal. She hugged me tightly. "I couldn't have loved you more. You were always my son, simple as that."

The room darkened. A cloud must have passed in front of the sun. I retreated from her embrace, wished I couldn't smell her rose scent.

She shut her eyes and sucked in what seemed like a long and painful breath, then spoke in a low voice. "Despite what you're probably going to think, I've wanted to tell you this for years. I just couldn't face the pain. You were only a few hours old when Patty abandoned you. We never heard from her again."

"Abandoned me? Patty?"

"Patty is your birth mother. Martin, your genetic father."

"Martin is my. . . ?"

"He was sixteen when you were born."

I fought to interpret her words in a positive light as the room began to spin. "Listen to what you're saying. It's impossible! It's ridiculous." I fell into her small couch, then lay on my side.

When the sun re-emerged the room had changed, but in a familiar way. The shadows cast were those from my youth. Mom looked down upon me. Tears streaked her face. "Tom, please don't take it like this. Patty disappeared without a trace. Martin begged us to take you. John and I agreed. We adopted you legally, but as a condition John made Martin swear he'd never reveal the secret. John wanted to tell you— eventually. He simply felt you needed to learn what really happened from us, your parents, not from Martin or anybody else. We planned on waiting for the right time. Then John died."

I put my hands over my ears, wished I weren't hearing these confusing words.

She reached toward me but I pushed her away. "We'd always planned to tell you. Just delayed a day at a time. Then somehow it seemed too late. You've got to understand . . ."

Thoughts swirled through my mind like debris in a tornado. Who's "we?" Could it ever be too late to tell a person who he was? Then my focus turned inward. Could I possibly be a fit parent? Judging from the men in my family what were my odds? What sort of mother could abandon her baby?

Mom's words continued, her tongue flitting between her teeth. "The Thanksgiving Dinner when you last saw Martin ended in a huge fight between him and me. He said you must be told, that he couldn't go on living this "farce." I told him nothing would please me more than to introduce him as your father, but he had to get his act together first. He was using drugs, partying non-stop, blaming everyone but himself for his failures. I told him that until I felt certain you could be hurt by the lie or helped by the truth I wouldn't change a thing."

Every fond memory seemed altered. My head throbbed.

Mom wiped her eyes with a tissue. "Martin claimed his high ethics wouldn't allow him to lie, that he had no choice but to disappear from your life forever. Of course, I didn't believe him. He'd never followed through on a commitment in his life. I saw no reason he'd start with one as unreasonable as this—"

"But he did, and you never set the record straight."

Mom gaped, as if stunned I could speak. "Yes, he kept his word. What a moral giant to keep a promise like that. Can you imagine walking out on your son rather than telling a white lie for his benefit?"

"I can't imagine the two of you couldn't work this out."

She shook her head slowly. "I'll never be convinced that Martin's supposed lily white ethics are the real reason he left our lives. Blaming me seems like a convenient way for him to walk away from responsibility and leave the guilt behind."

I glared, feeling venomous.

"I've done the best I can for you, Tom. After Martin pulled his vanishing act I felt relieved you didn't know him as your father. Why should you feel abandoned when so many people loved you? I told myself you were better off not knowing. Eventually I forgot . . . nearly forgot . . . that it was ever even an issue."

"So, do you remember now?"

"Life gets complicated. I made my decision based upon a very difficult situation. I can't go back and make a different one. Why waste energy imagining how the world might change if I had? Until you bumped into him my choice remained the best possible. If he hadn't broken his word, it would still be today."

Broken his word? I sat up. "Martin didn't break his word. I couldn't understand his behavior at the time, but now I see he was bound by his word to you. You're the one who told me he's my father."

She tilted her head. "But . . . but he told you he wasn't your uncle. That's the same thing. He knew right where it would lead."

"That's not how it happened at all. I forced him into saying what little he said."

Mom stared at me. "It would have been better if you'd never known him."

I returned her gaze. "Why? Because I would have wandered past him yesterday in oblivion? It wouldn't have been better. It just would have been a different lie. How can I trust anything you've taught me when I uncover this by accident?"

She lowered her eyes. "Most everything you know is truth. We changed tiny details so things fit properly."

"This ought to be rich. Like what?"

Mom sighed. "Like– Jill is a month and a half older than you, not ten and a half months younger. We celebrated her first birthday twice, and you passed her up."

"Why did you do that?" I asked.

She just stared at me.

A light dawned, and with it, betrayal. "Damn it, Mom. That's not a little detail. It's a big one. And it didn't come as a result of Martin disappearing. He was around a lot back then. If you were confusing birthdays back in 1965 it could only have been to set the stage never to tell me who I really was."

"We thought we did it for your own good."

"Nice try." I stood and turned to leave.

"Wait, Tom." She walked to her filing cabinet and fingered her way through documents in the rear of a drawer. Soon she extracted a photograph. She stared at the four by six inch scrap then handed it to me.

I studied the image. A very young Uncle Martin with a wide grin rested his arm uncomfortably over the shoulders of a buxom girl. They were completely mismatched, she much more mature than he, and at least three inches taller. Her eyes captivated me, for they resembled my own. Almond shaped and hazel, unlike anyone else in the family.

"Her name is Patty Peatrie. She came into our lives like a whirlwind, and left the same way. When she disappeared your grandpa ordered the destruction of everything she'd touched. He said the only hope of recovering our family dignity was to forget her entirely. The picture you're holding may be the only thing he missed."

I shoved the photo into my pocket. "That's not true. He missed me." Her stunned expression brought me satisfaction. I turned and wandered down the hallway, feeling large and out of place in the shrunken home.

Mom called from behind, "Tom, don't leave like this."

I kept walking.

"Tom, please, let's discuss something brighter."

I reached the kitchen door.

"Tommy, don't go. Please."

I'd never heard her beg. I stopped. "All right. What do you want to talk about? How about this. I'll soon be a father. Can you think of any good practical jokes I can play on my child?" I stepped outside and slammed the door.

# Chapter 3

Outside Mom's house, I took in a deep breath of the crisp November air. I climbed into my Jeep Cherokee. I pounded my head against the sport-utility-vehicle's steering wheel and remembered a time I'd known exactly what sort of dad I'd wanted.

Memories came back so vividly that I could practically taste the salty air that had filled my five-year-old lungs as I stepped from Pan Am flight 164 in San Diego. I'd never been so aware of oxygen. Accustomed to the thin atmosphere of Utah, the humid mixture tasted to me like an exotic concoction. By the time I descended the stairs to the tarmac I could no longer contain myself. I left Mom's side and ran toward the terminal. She had Jill in her arms to keep her company, after all.

I sprinted past the adults. They seemed to think it a violation to stray from the red carpet pathway. Their comments reached my ears, but I didn't even turn to see their expressions as I flew by. I raced into the terminal ahead of everyone and took an anxious look at the large group at the gate. Out of the center stepped Uncle Joe. I spread my arms wide and ran to him. He freed me of gravity.

"Tommy," he said, "you've grown so much. I can't believe it."

I looked into his dazzling eyes and returned the compliment, "You've grown a lot, too."

"Why, thank you, Grasshopper." I loved the nickname, simply because Uncle Joe, the most important man in my life, had given it to me. He laughed a deep masculine laugh that felt like refreshing water as he swung me atop his shoulders. I put my hands on my uncle's head to steady myself, then looked around to find the crowd staring with envy. Because I could think of no other response to all the attention I thrust my fist into the air and yelled, "I love California!" The people roared their approval.

When Mom and Jill caught up we headed to the baggage carousel.

Uncle Joe spoke to Mom, "Emma, you'd never believe how good it feels to live so far away from Dad. Utah will always be the home of my heart, but the distance from Dad energizes me. It makes him seem so . . . insignificant."

My mind was on other things. From my vantage above the crowd I watched the herd of heads bob down the hallway. Periodically, one or another would look at me and smile. I smiled back politely. Why make them feel worse than they already must? After all, they were walking while I'd been chosen to ride upon the shoulders of a god.

I'd barely seen my uncle's face, but I could envision every perfect detail, everything in ideal proportion. His hazel eyes were full of magic and burned with confidence. I pushed my fingers through his thick corkscrew locks to test their consistency. The color, light brown, matched mine.

My mother, who walked at his right side, overwhelmed him with a staccato barrage of questions and comments. She never looked at anyone else with this sort of admiration. He responded to everything in an easy cadence. I enjoyed the sound and feel of his bass voice as it vibrated through his chest and shoulders.

At Mom's right shoulder walked another woman, obviously paying close attention to our conversation. Once I noticed her I couldn't tear my eyes away. She looked straight back at me as we floated along in a light and effortless, but also wordless, communication. She seemed familiar, but I couldn't remember where we'd met. She didn't seem to be the same pretty lady Uncle Joe kissed on the day I stood on the temple steps holding a lacy pink girl's pillow, but there was a similarity. That woman had long curly blonde hair which fell to the middle of her back, while this one had soft-looking short red hair. It hung straight down each side of her face before the ends curved in. The motion of her stride made the curls dance at the bottom of her jaw like quotation marks. Hers was a face worth framing in quotation marks if I'd ever seen one. No doubt she was a movie star, and that's why I thought I knew her.

I saw a flash of purple when she blinked, and I stared for a long moment hoping she'd do it again. When she did I confirmed that the lids were purple. I almost told her I liked it, but held my tongue not knowing if it was rude to notice such an abnormality. I kept inspecting her. She had a long neck and curvy body. I'd always thought my mother the prettiest woman of all, so it seemed strange to see her walking beside an even prettier one.

After we gathered our luggage from the carousel we walked to the parking lot and loaded everything into Uncle Joe's car. Just as we were about to back out he pushed a secret button that caused the roof to rise up and fold into the trunk. I gaped at the miracle, and jumped up on the back seat to inspect the sky at a closer range. Dusk began to fall and the wispy clouds took on fiery hues. I stumbled forward as the car reversed out of the lot. When Mom pulled me onto her lap beside Jill I felt secretly thankful. The miracle of California had filled me with helium and put me at risk of floating away.

Jill and I clasped hands as the wind whipped our hair. She made a groaning sound that I knew meant pure pleasure. We passed bizarre trees I'd never before imagined, golden beaches where I couldn't wait to leave footprints, breaking waves rolling from infinity, dazzling neon lights, buildings that really did scrape the sky, and so much more.

We checked into the hotel, and I'd been bouncing off the walls for an eternity by the time we heard a knock at the door.

"That will be Joe picking us up for dinner," Mom said. "Please answer it, Tommy."

I ran to the door and swung it wide. There stood another of those beautiful women peculiar to California, this one with a dark black beehive hairdo . . . and blue eyelids. Otherwise she looked so similar to the woman from the airport I could hardly believe my eyes. Before I could digest it all Uncle Joe stepped into the room. He carried a small blonde girl in his arms.

I glared at the child, wondering how she'd gained such a favored position.

Mom ran to take the baby. "This is Rachel? I knew the two of you would have beautiful children, but she's gorgeous! The pictures you sent didn't do her justice."

Children! I wondered if Rachel would fit into my recently unpacked suitcase. Maybe I could zip her inside and send it away. I turned my back as I went to measure.

Uncle Joe grabbed both my shoulders from behind and shook me lovingly. "Hey, Grasshopper. Meet your cousin."

I turned on him wearing a scowl. How could he go and have a child of his own?

"You don't like her?" he asked.

"Who's her mommy?"

"Heather is of course," he said, smiling at the black haired woman.

I looked at Heather, not certain whether she could be trusted. "What about the lady from the airport?"

She giggled, then smiled at my mother and uncle. "What lady from the airport?"

I decided I liked the redhead better, and I wondered why Uncle Joe would change dates in the middle of the evening.

I soon learned this was his habit. Each time we met with him a different lady stood at his side, each more exotic than the last. They were beautiful, exciting, and friendly, and together constituted the first women on whom I'd ever had a crush. I felt dizzy trying to keep track; and I couldn't figure out how the gorgeous blonde could know things I'd told the beautiful redhead, or the woman with the black bob could continue conversations begun with the flowing brunette. I tried to discuss it with my mom, but she only said she couldn't wait until the excitement of the trip wore off for me.

Finally I realized these women were communicating with one another . . . that they were sharing my uncle. It didn't surprise me one bit that so many women would want him, but I did become more impressed than ever with his magnificence. I fantasized non-stop that he was my father.

On the last day of our visit I made a frightening discovery. At my uncle's home I needed to use the toilet. Mom pointed me into the master bedroom, which led to the master bath. I walked past an open closet and saw something so startling I jumped back. There, arranged like soldiers along the length of the top shelf, stood a platoon of Styrofoam heads; and atop the heads rested the scalps of the various women who'd captivated me over the past week. I'd stumbled upon some hideous crime, but I didn't know exactly what it was or who to blame. At that moment I became anxious to leave California behind, and ecstatic we'd depart the next day. As I think back, how could I have ever been naive enough to be totally confused by Heather's costumes, and entirely oblivious to Joe's disguise?

I rocked my head away from the steering wheel and saw Mom staring at me through the kitchen window. How long had I been sitting here, daydreaming? I needed to get to work. Mom's concerned expression only made me feel angrier with her, and I looked away. I turned the key and the engine roared to life. I remembered how devastated I'd felt back when I realized that the man I'd admired as a father, Joe, wasn't as he appeared. Now I faced the possibility that the man who was my father, Martin, might be exactly as he appeared. The men of my family hadn't exactly excelled at parenting, and here I sat, about to become a dad in my own right. The thought paralyzed me with fear.

My determination to learn my family's history increased. I shifted into reverse and began backing. I looked over my shoulder just as a horn blared. The swerving car raced through my field of vision as I slammed on the brakes. I gripped the steering wheel and tried to clear my mind.

Once on the road I considered phoning Joe. Despite the failings in his personal life, he had great survival instincts. His incredible success as a real estate developer led to three terms as a United States Congressman representing California. He orchestrated his career masterfully, coercing the family, including me, into the role of co-conspirators to hide his alcoholism from the outside world. We lived under the aura of secrecy that surrounded Joe's habit. I'd rationalized my role in the affair. My uncle's intentions were good, and he'd positioned himself to accomplish great things. I could never have participated in bringing him down. But, having toiled in his campaigns, I felt relieved a year earlier when he decided to retire. With that announcement our fear of discovery passed.

It only now occurred to me that he'd probably been equally instrumental in hiding my past from me. He'd mastered spin. In fact, if I called him he might twist things around until I felt obligated to apologize to him. I decided to wait to contact him until I had things under a bit more control.

Somehow I reached the office. Other loan officers, their processors, and various clients milled about, hardly noticing my presence. Nevertheless, I hung my head as I walked toward my position near the rear of the building. I stepped into my office and reached for the handle to shut the door.

A voice surprised me. "Wanna see my new tattoo?"

I stopped and turned toward my loan processor's voice. Daisy sat in her cubicle across the hall from my doorway. "Please tell me you're kidding."

She shook her head, grinning confidently as she lifted the cuff of her bell bottomed pants. The colorful likeness of a mermaid rising from a frothy wave peeked out above her shoe. "I bought her with that bonus you just paid me."

Every day around Daisy Love held some sort of surprise. I certainly hadn't seen this one coming. I remembered the first time I'd heard her name. I'd laughed, but I soon understood that compact little sentence was the perfect introduction to her personality. "Those things are permanent. You know that, don't you?"

"No duh. What do you think of it?"

"I think, I hope you have enough of that bonus left for socks. From now on you'll have to wear them to work."

"Tom! They'll hide Aurora," she said, using an olive green fingernail to trace the outline of the woman on her foot.

"Exactly my point. Around these parts people still shy away from mortgage brokers with tattooed assistants. I don't mind what you do after hours, but at work we have to present a professional image."

She frowned. "I'm going to get more tattoos. They're addictive."

"And when you get one your clothing can't hide, I'll be hiring a replacement. It won't matter that you're the best loan processor I've ever worked with, that I admire your organizational skills, or that I'm glad we met and became friends. If you make decisions that negatively affect my ability to satisfy clients I'll be forced to let you go."

She frowned at me. "Some people have no appreciation for art."

"You've got that right." I stumbled to my desk, shoved aside client files, and inadvertently knocked my keyboard to the floor. I picked it up, also retrieving a ball point pen with the company name emblazoned on the side. Flipping open my day planner I turned to a blank page. "Positives," I penned atop the left hand side, "negatives," on the right. It's the method I used whenever facing a difficult decision. Then I stared at the walls and waited for inspiration. I found none in the meaningless landscape paintings hanging there. I looked at the wall behind me and the various plaques I'd earned. In the center hung my degree, a Bachelor's in History. It seemed so irrelevant to what my life had become. I tore the page from the day planner and threw it into the garbage can. I couldn't even figure out what I'd meant to decide.

The receptionist's voice jolted me when it came over the phone speaker. "Tom, your wife is on line two."

I picked up the receiver. "Hi, Honey."

"Hi. Do you have a moment?" I sensed urgency in her tone.

"I've got nothing but moments."

"What are you up to?"

I opened a file and flipped through papers. "Just trying to get my work done."

"Tom, your mom just called."

"Hmm."

"She told me about your little talk."

I tensed. "That was a little talk? I wonder what a big one would have been like."

"Okay, big talk. Tom, what are you going to do?"

"I'm considering a nervous breakdown."

She laughed, but it sounded forced. "Please don't do anything drastic. Be straight with me. How are you feeling?"

I shifted the phone to my other ear. "The only way I can calm my mind is to concentrate on other things, but everything outside of this one subject seems trivial. There's a stranger inhabiting my body, a stranger I know cannot be exorcised. I don't even understand my own reactions, Sara. I laid into my mom– even knew it was wrong as I did it– yet I have no intention of apologizing."

"I'm worried about you, Tom. This stuff doesn't change who you are. You shouldn't think it does."

I closed the file. "I wish I could be certain of that."

"Why don't you take the day off? We could talk this through."

"I've got two closings this afternoon. I have a pile of work I need to get focused on."

"But you'll be meeting me at Dr. Lowrey's office at four o'clock, right?"

I flipped my dayplanner open and looked at the four o'clock entry. "Ultrasound," it said in my sloppy handwriting. "Oh no, I totally forgot. There's no way I can make it. I'm way too far behind."

The line stayed silent for a long time. "So, what time will you be home?"

"It's going to be late. Maybe seven . . . seven thirty."

"Seven thirty?"

"I'll do my best to get home earlier."

"No. I know you have a lot to do. Just get home when you can."

We said our good-byes. I replaced the phone on its cradle, and looked across the hall at Daisy. What would it feel like to be so carefree? How I longed for her uncomplicated life. She'd shown up at the office one day two years previous in response to an ad for receptionist. Patrick, the owner, hired her on the spot. Within hours she'd put her imprint on everything. The phone messages were, for the first time, not merely legible, they were practically in calligraphy. What's more, every one of them featured at least one, and sometimes more than a dozen smiling flowers. These and many other embellishments were born at the tip of a fantastic little multi-colored pen she carried tucked somewhere deep beneath the auburn curls of her hair. In her able hands that absurd dime-store curiosity of a writing instrument took on the properties of a magic wand.

She and I had hit it off immediately. I soon learned she'd been in the midst of a cross-country journey from her hometown in Ohio to California, a state whose name she always said with reverence. Car trouble and dwindling finances stranded her in Salt Lake.

Before three months were up I asked Patrick if he would promote Daisy to my personal processor. This meant I'd become responsible for the majority of her salary and all of her bonuses, while Patrick's financial obligation would decrease substantially. I knew he'd agree to the plan, not merely because he pinched pennies, but also because he made it no secret that he loved seeing loan officers take on financial obligations. Whenever one of his commissioned sales people struggled he'd pull them aside and say, "I want you to take the day off. Spend it on the car lots, and don't come back here without a shiny new ride complete with payments you get nauseous just thinking about. That'll motivate you to get your act together."

Daisy took to the detail oriented nature of loan processing like an otter to a snowstorm, and in no time had my practice under such control I found myself wondering whether she thought she'd hired me. Every day with her was an experience. She constantly found tricks to play. Often she'd steal my leather bound day-planner. She thought it hilarious that I kept the big book with me at all times and could hardly function without it. When my desperate pleas finally resulted in its return I'd find numerous ridiculous notes and appointments filling the coming week, all entered in her colorful style.

In the midst of her work Daisy glanced in my direction and noticed my stare. She crossed her eyes and stuck her tongue out the side of her mouth.

"Could you come in here for a moment?" I asked.

She stood and made a show of strutting into my office. Then she sat down on a leather chair and pivoted both her legs over the armrest. She put her feet on the seat of the adjacent chair and looked at me with a smile, hoping, I think, that I would be annoyed at her lack of professionalism. "Can I get you something, Master?"

I pretended not to notice. "Daisy, you fascinate me. Did you know that?"

"I fascinate everybody. I even fascinate myself."

I laughed. "Are you really as comfortable with the world as you seem?"

"Of course. I'm centered. I've found myself."

"If I were to try to 'find myself', how would you suggest I go about it?"

"Wait a minute. Is this some kind of mid-day fraternizing."

I threw my pen at her. "I'm serious."

"It's just that you've never asked this type of question when I was on the clock before. I'm surprised. In a way, since I'm getting paid at the moment, this is professional advice. I have to take that more seriously than some gibberish I'd come up with over a beer."

"Sorry I asked."

"No, don't be sorry. Here it is, and the advice is well worth what it's costing you. Do what I do. Get in the car, drive until you have a reason to stop, then see what you can make of the experience."

"What if you had a pregnant wife who wasn't in favor of that strategy?"

She furrowed her brow. "Ooh. That would be tougher, but I don't expect that to happen, Tom."

"You're a lot of help. Sorry I called you in here."

"What are you really trying to ask?" She removed her feet from the chair.

"How about this? What's your honest impression of me?"

"My honest impression?"

"Yeah. For instance, I look at you and see a young lady who was headed in the right direction when her car broke down, only she was born three decades too late. You would have been perfectly suited to the San Francisco flower power scene of the 1960's. Your organizational abilities would have revolutionized the Hippie movement."

She blushed. "Do you think so?"

"Absolutely. As a matter of fact, had the cosmos gotten that one bit of timing right I believe there's a fair chance our Air Force would've wound up dropping daffodils instead of Agent Orange onto the jungles of Viet Nam."

"That's the nicest thing anyone's ever said to me."

I smiled. "Okay, so now you have to do the same for me, but it doesn't have to be a compliment. I want complete honesty."

"All right, but it is a compliment. I see you as the hardest working and most honest mortgage banker there could ever be. I wouldn't work—"

"That's how you see me? As a mortgage banker? Am I really that pathetic?"

She looked confused. "What did you think I'd say?"

"Mortgages are what I do, they have no right to become who I am. Do you want to know how I see myself?"

"Sure."

"As a university history professor who scales technical cliffs on his days off . . . who just happened to get sidetracked into a career and a family and has to put his dreams on hold for twenty years or so."

She laughed. "You're kidding? I didn't know any of that about you. When was the last time you climbed a cliff?"

"In college."

"How long ago was that?"

"It doesn't matter. I still hike all the time. You know that."

"There's a huge difference between hiking trails and climbing cliffs, Tom."

"You think I don't know that? What I'm trying to say is that I never meant to get into this business, and now I'm defined by it. How did that happen?"

She counted on her fingers and ignored my comment. "It must have been at least ten years ago you graduated from college. Tom, you can't call yourself a climber when you haven't been on a cliff in over a decade."

"Will you knock it off? You're not getting the point."

"You have a point?"

I stood and paced. "Yeah. Here it is. Just because I have to earn a living doesn't mean what I do for that living is all I'm about. Mark my words. You'll find yourself in my situation one day wondering how some of the tiny choices you made along the way turned out to have such a big impact on your life."

She shook her head. "If I was in that situation I'd quit my job and go find something I enjoyed doing."

"You won't be able to. There will be too many people counting on you. Do you want to know the most amazing part? It will be your success that trips the trap door shut. You've become accustomed to a lifestyle, your wife has become accustomed, your child hasn't even taken in its first lung full of oxygen yet, but already it's accustomed. You've become so specialized in your skills that you can't hope to make the same type of money doing anything else, let alone something you like, so you're stuck for life."

Her fingernails were between her teeth. She pulled them out just enough to talk. "You're scaring me, Tom. What brought this on?"

"I'd tell you, but I doubt you're prepared to hear it."

"Try me."

"All right. I found out this morning that my father is a psychotic transient bum who may have lived in a cardboard box for significant portions of the last twenty years and who doesn't want to see me now that I accidentally discovered him. How's that for a shocker?"

Her eyes opened wide but she didn't speak.

"Do you want to hear more?"

She nodded.

"Sara doesn't want me to have anything to do with him. My mother, who I just found out isn't actually my mother but my aunt, won't talk about it because the past was so horrible. It's as if the world has come loose from its axis."

"You're serious, aren't you?" I heard her concern.

"No Daisy, I'm not serious. From where I stand, serious would be a dramatic improvement. My condition is critical."

"So, what are you going to do?"

I went to my wall and gathered my framed degree and the offending plaques, then tossed them into the garbage. "I'll tell you what I'm going to do. I'm going to find myself."

# Chapter 4

As if to challenge my resolve the receptionist paged me. "Tom, Great Basin Title Company is on line one, Jerry Reiser is on four, and the sellers for the Tomkey transaction are on five. Which do you want first?"

"Don't take any of them," Daisy said, sparks in her eyes.

I sighed, then responded to the receptionist. "Give me line four."

Daisy laughed. "You're not going to find yourself, Tom. You're too responsible."

I remained swamped for the rest of the day. Sure, I wanted to change my life, but how could I do it at the expense of clients who'd put their trust in me to guide them through major financial decisions? How could I let my own family down when we needed money and stability the most?

I dealt with one problem after another. I calmed a crying woman whose mortgage had been rejected because the underwriter refused to count her child-support as qualified income. I told her not to worry, that we would repackage the loan, more fully document the child-support, and submit it to another investor. I spoke with an irate seller who said the reason his appraisal had come in under value was that the buyer, both realtors, and myself were in collusion to force him from his home at an unfair price. I reminded him that my fees as well as the realtors went down when the sales price was reduced so why would we want that? The logic made no difference to him and he continued to bawl me out. All the while, thoughts of the situation with Martin clouded and complicated every move I made.

Even on the drive home, well after dark, I couldn't find a free moment to deal with my concerns. I spoke on the cell phone with clients for the entire commute.

I flopped face-first onto my living room couch at 8:13 p.m.. "Do we have aspirin?"

"Oh, Honey." Sara hurried up from the basement, leaned over me on the sofa, and began massaging my shoulders. "Bad day?"

"Horrible."

She swatted me on the butt, then walked to the kitchen. "Did you come to any decisions?"

My head throbbed. "I'm sorry Sara. I need a moment to relax."

"I don't like what that job does to you. You're stressed so often. You really ought to think about a different career."

I thought about my garbage can full of plaques. "Yeah, right. Are you willing to lose your insurance and income?"

She brought the pills. "No. Not now."

"That's what I thought."

"As you know, better than anyone, uncertainty scares me. Relying on others frightens me more than anything. I've put more trust in you than I ever have anyone else in my life."

"I'm grateful—"

"Let me finish. I have confidence in you. I know you'll provide well for our family. Once we're through the childbirth you'll have my support in looking for another job."

"Let's just take it a day at a time."

"You should know me better than that. I don't take anything a day at a time. What I'm telling you is that I'm preparing myself in advance."

I laughed. "You mean that you're planning some spontaneity a few months from now?"

"Yes, that is what I'm saying." She smiled as she sat down on the arm of the couch. "Can I tell you about my day?"

"Please."

"At the beginning of the ultrasound Dr. Lowrey had some minor concerns."

I kicked my legs to the floor and sat up. "Concerns?"

She kissed my cheek. "Turns out everything's all right. Seeing the baby on the monitor blew me away, though. I have a complete human being growing inside of me."

"I can't believe I missed it."

"He gave me these." She handed over a small envelope.

I opened it. Inside I found three black and white pictures. I stared at the first one. It resembled a Rorschach inkblot. I could make no sense of it and moved on to the next. Same thing. Around the edges were all sorts of measuring marks and codes, none of which made any sense to me. I flipped disappointedly to the final image, and recognized an immediate difference. A tiny human hand . . . five perfect fingers, reached toward the camera. Then, behind the hand I noticed . . . a face, or at least a skull. One clearly visible eye socket seemed to be looking straight at the camera. The mouth was partially open, and the nose, though appearing in only the lightest outline of gray, was also in sharp focus. I imagined where other body parts should've been, and could now recognize the blurry outlines of some of those as well.

I held the image toward my wife. "This one's fantastic!"

She took it from me. "That's my favorite, too. "

"It's a real person, tiny and helpless." For the second time in this day I contemplated the question. Could I be a good father? It was way too late to have doubts.

"She . . . not it."

I stared at Sara, wondering if she planned to add anything. She didn't. The gears in my brain turned very slowly. "A girl?"

"A daughter." Sara's eyes became electrified. "I told you from the first that if it was a girl I wouldn't be able to resist buying all the cute clothes. They have much better things for girls than boys. I don't know how I can pass on any of them. I went shopping right after I found out, and I bought some of the most adorable outfits. Do you want to see them?" She pointed to a large collection of boxes and bags labeled Baby Gap, Gymboree, and even Nordstroms.

I could hear the money being sucked from our bank account. A wave of nausea made me feel fortunate to be seated. I wouldn't have boarded the loopdy-loop parenthood roller coaster ride if I'd known the track was damaged beforehand. I don't remember how I answered Sara's question, or even if I did. Nevertheless, she demonstrated the many features of some small and colorful pieces of clothing.

Normally Sara gets frustrated with me when my mind wanders while she's talking. This time I may as well have been on another planet, but her enthusiasm overflowed to the point that she didn't seem to notice. It seemed any response I threw out during her periodic silences could satisfy my obligation to the conversation. She just moved on to the next item. I don't even think she noticed I'd picked up the ultrasound picture.

As I studied the image-- the tiny hand and eye– I realized that over the past day or so my simple, airtight life had sprung some serious leaks. I was the son of Martin Crump. I still hoped he might be a respectable person, but I couldn't deny that he was a failure as a father and provider. Was I made of the same material? Would my shortcomings show now, just when I wanted to excel? Without intending to I whispered, "I don't know if I can do this."

"Do what?" Sara walked a sun dress across the room like a marionette, as if a baby toddled along inside the garment. She picked it up in her arms and gave the invisible little girl a hug.

I looked into her energetic eyes, and wished I hadn't spoken. It took a long moment to invent an excuse for my words. "Button up those dresses. They look so– complicated. I've been worried about handling a diaper, and now you add all this."

She smiled as she walked toward me; and I stood to accept her embrace. I tried to imagine her expression as her chin rested on my shoulder. She thought she was supporting me for my lovable insecurity. I accepted her consolation for what I knew to be my actual inadequacy. My doubts concerned career, endurance, earning power, heredity . . . Difficulties materialized like mirages on a hot asphalt highway where a day earlier there'd seemed so few.

I knew any mention of my fears would cause the enthusiasm to drain from Sara as if a plug in her big toe popped loose. She'd have every right to be frustrated. We'd discussed this all in advance— made the decision to become pregnant together. I had no right to even think these thoughts, yet they wouldn't go away.

"Oh Tom, I'm so excited. We'll soon have a daughter. Someone to care about, and teach, and love, and protect. We're a family, the three of us, more important to one another than anyone in the entire world. I want her to experience all the good things, and to keep harm far, far away."

I tightened my grip and buried my face in her honey-colored hair. It had felt so energizing to take those plaques off my office wall. Come morning, I'd be hanging them back up. It wasn't the time for finding myself. Still, Daisy had been wrong. I wasn't too responsible. I just had too many responsibilities.

# Chapter 5

On the next morning's commute, the rugged looking Rock's Climbing Gym sign jumped out at me. I'd driven past the building many times, but never investigated. Now, an idea occurred to me. I called the office on my cell phone to tell them I'd be late getting in, then pulled into the parking lot. Daisy was right on this point. I couldn't call myself a climber when I hadn't been on a cliff in over a decade. That could be fixed. More than repairing my vision of myself, though, I recalled how energizing it felt to solve the puzzle of an intricate cliff face. Like deploying chess men, each small movement had an effect on the whole. An incorrect foot placement at the beginning of a critical section might make it impossible to reach a difficult hand-hold several moves farther up the wall. Climbing, more than anything else I'd ever done, required single-mindedness. Scaling a wall might be the one activity capable of evicting thoughts of Martin Crump from my brain. My overworked imagination desperately needed the break.

I heard the music before I stepped inside. It was metallic and techy, it probably came from a synthesizer more complex than any I'd ever seen. I wondered how different this indoor version of climbing would be from the more natural version I'd once loved. Inside the building, the angular walls jutted this way and that. They were covered with colorful globs, reminiscent of wadded gum stuck to the underside of the typical high-school desk.

I walked up to the counter and paid for a lesson. The cashier regarded my double-breasted suit skeptically. I removed the coat and asked if I could hang it somewhere. She took it to a back room and returned with an armful of rental equipment. Everything looked less familiar than I'd expected it to.

"What's this music?" I asked.

"Sucks, doesn't it. What do you want to hear?"

"Maybe you could put in some Sting."

"I figured you'd be a fan of the oldies. I'll look around for one of his CDs."

"Where's my instructor?" I looked over a gym full of physically fit men and women.

She pointed toward a skinny, pimple-covered kid— eighteen years old tops. I watched him tend the rope for his current student, pulling it backward through the belay mechanism as the student moved toward him or allowing it to play out as the student moved farther away. In order to climb confidently it's critical to be comfortable with the person tending your safety line. The student lost his grip on one of the colorful globs that served as hand and foot-holds. The instructor immediately braked the line and eased his customer to the mat. I relaxed, now confident of his expertise.

I carried my equipment to a bench and sat down to sort through it. A bit at a time my memory of climbing technique returned. The bright pink crisscross webbed nylon was the harness. I determined which strap went where, stepped into it, and cinched everything tight. It looked ridiculous atop my navy blue dress slacks. Through the harness loop positioned right below my belly button I clipped a carabiner: an oval three by two inch hinged aluminum eyelet. The cashier had given me a dozen of them. I hooked the rest to the harness near my left hip where I'd be able to grab them as I climbed. Beside the carabiners I attached the bag of chalk for grip. I swapped my wingtips for black rubber-soled climbing shoes. They felt slipper-like, except that they laced securely to my feet. The helmet remained on the bench at my side as I uncoiled the rope, inspecting it for signs of wear.

It was sound. I tied it in a bowline to the carabiner in my harness loop.

My instructor finished with his student and headed in my direction. He looked me up and down. "You're up, Bishop."

Wise guy. I strapped on my helmet and stood.

He inspected the fit of my harness, removed the carabiner, untied the rope, retied it, and reattached it to my harness. "Your first time?"

I must have looked like some sort of clown. I removed my tie and shoved it in my pocket. "Actually, I've climbed before."

He regarded me skeptically. "Sure, the corporate ladder. This is different."

I smiled as I dipped a hand into my chalk bag.

We moved to the wall. He threaded my rope through his belay, and I removed a carabiner from my harness. I hooked it to a piton above me, flipped the rope through the carabiner's aluminum gate, and readied myself to climb.

The technomusic stopped abruptly, and "Don't Stand So Close To Me" from Sting's days with The Police replaced it.

Being on the wall felt instantly familiar. The dry aroma of the chalk triggered pleasant memories. I ascended quickly, attaching additional carabiners as necessary. A spiritual connection I'd forgotten, but had felt often while ascending rocky faces, overcame me. I know of no comparable sensation, a mixture of confidence and vulnerability. Space-walking astronauts must experience the same sensation in the extreme.

I experimented by using the hand and foot-holds in different ways— climbing with compression in the nooks, skittering across easier sections, using my hands and arms to move around overhangs. The spider-like sense of gliding about the wall, holding my body away for increased leverage, made me feel free. I moved fluidly, but I also became aware of a problem. My heart throbbed at maximum capacity. Sweat soaked my shirt. I gasped for breath. Finger muscles conditioned for years to hold only a pen wouldn't remain up to the task of lifting my body weight for much longer.

Even larger muscle groups weakened rapidly. My forearms and calves throbbed. When had I fallen into such terrible shape?

"I want to try to pendulum to that section of wall over there." I pointed to a spot on the other side of a fifteen-foot wide gap to my right.

"Go for it."

I rigged the line through a carabiner at the top of the wall, then moved to my left about eighteen feet without hooking in. I nodded to the instructor, and saw him put his weight into the rope, tightening it against the maneuver I was about to attempt. I took a deep breath then stood, perpendicular to the wall, and let myself fall. As I swung I ran, increasing my momentum through the arc. Traveling across the vacant space between walls I looked for something I might grab onto at the other side.

My measurement had been good, my momentum nearly spent as I reached the target. I grabbed at the wall with both hands and clung momentarily while my feet searched for stability. But then my right hand slipped and my body twisted. I fell backward. As I swayed my left hand was wrenched from its hold. I lost control, and barely pivoted in time to face the oncoming wall. I felt myself rise, and realized the instructor had been alert enough to tighten the line, reducing my momentum.

"Thanks," I said as soon as I'd arrested my motion. I hopped down the wall as he played the line out.

"Nice job. I thought you were going to hold on."

I nodded, but I felt failure, wished I'd nailed that last move. In my college days I would have held on easily. Obviously I wasn't what I'd once been. I began to unhook my harness, then realized my chalky sweaty hands would leave a stain on my crotch. I looked around for a towel.

The instructor pulled his tee-shire out in front and extended it toward me with a nod. "You're quitting?"

"I'm spent." I wiped my hands clean.

"You might not be half bad with practice. You paid for another half hour."

"So you get a break. My treat, but I'll make you a deal. Same time every Thursday morning."

He stuck out a hand and we shook.

I returned the equipment and headed for my Cherokee. Behind the wheel I drove with no destination in mind, and gradually my disappointment over my performance faded. My muscles throbbed pleasantly. The climb had been enjoyable, and I looked forward to making it a part of my regular routine.

As I sat at a stoplight reliving the moves I'd made on the wall, a heavily bearded man with a dirty blanket wrapped around him crossed in front of me. He reminded me of Martin. Just as I'd hoped, the mental effort had taken my mind completely off my concerns for the first time in two days. Now reality returned, but with a difference. At first I'd judged Martin to be crazy, but his odd behavior could be that of a disillusioned man forced to build his world around a lie. The random statements he'd made might not be the meanderings of a mad man, but the first opportunity to express to me, his son, ideas that had tortured him for years.

I tried to reconstruct our conversation in the park to see which of his phrases might be transformed in the light of my new knowledge. I wished I could remember his exact words more clearly. What he'd actually said, rather than the meaning I'd perceived, seemed all-important. I tried to see him, for the first time, as a man worthy of some admiration.

Then I pulled the photo of the stranger who was supposedly my biological mother from my wallet. I stared at her for a long moment, trying to imagine who she'd been, and who she'd become. But I felt nothing for her. I had no interest in a new woman to fill the maternal role. As far as I was concerned, Emma Lewis was the only mother I'd ever have. If Patty Peatrie didn't need me, then I didn't need her either.

My thoughts remained incomplete, half-evolved, but at least they had form. It would take some time, but I could deal with this. I steered in the direction of my office, confident I'd gotten back on track.

* * *

Thanksgiving was that Thursday. Months in advance the family had planned to eat dinner at my mom's house. There would be six of us. Joining Mom, Jill, Sara, and me, would be Grandma Crump and her current boyfriend, whomever that might be. She would have died, though, if anyone ever referred to her as Grandma to her face. She'd put a stop to that long ago. She went by Delilah.

Delilah would bee-bop to her grave in her battle to maintain a stranglehold on teenagedom. She still even had the sorts of emotional emergencies sixteen-year-old girls are prone to. Only last week she called my mother in tears because she'd attended a dance and seen another woman wearing her exact same dress. Such catastrophes were an everyday occurrence for my grandmother.

When Sara and I arrived for Thanksgiving Dinner the first thing I did was go to Mom. I found her stirring a pot on the stove. I set the casserole I'd carried in on the counter. Its steam rose and mingled with that from half-a-dozen other dishes. The smells caused me to salivate. I took in the feast, then turned my eyes to Mom. Her expression seemed hopeful, but wary.

"I'm sorry for how I acted the other day. I was hurt and confused," I began.

Tension vacated her frame as she again became the mother I knew and loved. "I understand. I'd been afraid you wouldn't come. Can we talk for a moment?"

The doorbell rang and Mom pulled me toward the recess near the kitchen door where the view from the front entrance would be blocked.

I turned to see Delilah arriving with a much younger man I'd never met. I bet he has no idea how old his date is, I thought as

I stepped out of their line of sight. "I love you, Mom. I don't know how I got so lucky."

We embraced. Her warm and familiar body felt comfortable. My life was returning to normal.

"Tom, I'm so proud of who you've become. You're my son and I love you. None of this other stuff changes anything."

"Yeah. For a while it didn't feel that way, but you're right. Sara said the same thing from the very first."

"Well then, it must be true. Martin and Patty left your life by their own choice. It's their loss."

I nodded. "We'd better join the party." As I stepped from the cubby hole I saw Delilah scurry around the corner. I wondered how much she'd overheard, but I didn't really care.

Thankfulness enveloped me during the meal. We ate crisp salad, potatoes with creamy gravy, vegetables, casseroles, succulent turkey, and Mom's famous stuffing. Everything tasted delicious. Laughter filled the air.

When I pushed my chair back from the table I felt completely satisfied. "I've got to walk some of this food off so I can fit in a slab of Jill's pumpkin pie."

My sister grinned from ear to ear and made some self deprecating sounds. She didn't do more than watch the pies get made, but we'd always given her credit for them. She'd swell with pride whenever anyone took a bite.

I stepped outside and carried the garbage cans to the curb just for something to do. Icicles dripped from the carport roof as unseasonably mild temperatures replaced the frigid air of only a few days before.

When I returned to the house it surprised me to find Delilah standing outside the door. "What were you and Emma discussing when I arrived, Tom?"

I shrugged. The cloud of sweetly scented air that followed her everywhere assaulted my nostrils.

She flipped open a compact and began to work on her

makeup. She put a lot of effort into trying to appear relaxed. I knew she never relaxed. "I heard names."

"That happens in a conversation," I said.

She scowled. "The names I heard were Martin– and Patty. How do you know about Patty?"

"What does it matter?"

"It matters. Tom, don't go digging into the past. There's nothing to be gained from it." She punctuated her last statement by jabbing at the air between us with her tube of fire engine red lipstick.

"What's that supposed to mean?"

"It means that no matter how much you may want to, you can't understand the reasons a particular decision was made. You can't imagine the pressures someone might have been under."

I studied her critically. "Is there a decision you wish you hadn't made, Delilah?"

"No . . . no, not me. I never did anything your grandfather didn't force me to. I just don't like seeing anyone get hurt. You most of all." Her gaze didn't waver from mine.

Her words didn't fool me. She did have something to hide, and I wondered what it was. As we stared at each other my hard-won denial faded into oblivion. Despite Mom's and Sara's determination to convince me otherwise, Martin's role in my life changed a lot of things. I needed to understand what had gone on in his family. Besides that, I'd spent a lifetime dreaming of a father. What sense did it make to deny his existence now that I'd found him? Martin had become the key to my concerns. If I ever hoped to truly understand myself I needed to figure out Martin first. Somewhere, buried in the past, lay the explanation as to what had gone wrong. I'd find it, and maybe I could make things right.

* * *

When we climbed into the Cherokee to leave I spoke to Sara. "I've decided to look for Martin."

She put a hand over mine on the ignition. I looked at her, the sparkle gone from her eyes. "Think about what you're saying. You don't need him. He's the ultimate dead-beat dad. How many times must he have turned his back on you? How many chances must he have had to make things right?"

Why couldn't she understand? I gritted my teeth. "It's more complicated than that."

"I have a terrible feeling about this— woman's intuition. Let's get on with our own lives. We have a child on the way . . . present day concerns to worry about. Can't you see Martin's the reason for this problem, not the solution."

"What I see is that he's the reason for my existence. He's my father. That puts our conversation the other day in a whole new light. If we'd known then what we know now, everything he said would've sounded completely different."

"Tom, think about what might happen if you bring Martin into our lives. He's unstable. That's not your fault, and there's nothing you can do about it."

"But he needs—"

"If Martin were to try to reconcile with you we'd deal with it at that time. For now, why complicate things? We've had a good day, right? We have so much to be thankful for. I'd been getting the impression you'd put this behind you."

"I just started thinking—"

"Now is the time to think about your own family." She patted her belly. "You're about to be a dad."

She couldn't have chosen a more terrifying phrase. Beyond that, why wouldn't she admit Martin was as much a part of our family as the child she carried? "I need your support, Sara."

"I'd be lying if I gave it to you. Please take more time to think this through." She nestled her head against my shoulder. I wondered whether she did it to avoid seeing the determination in my eyes.

I did think about it as I put an arm around her and pulled her to me, and certain feelings changed, but not the ones she'd hoped. I felt angry with her for not understanding, for transforming my desire to know my father into some act of betrayal. At the same time, I understood her. She'd explained her fear of abandonment, of uncertainty, early and often in our relationship. They were markers that defined her personality, and inexplicably, things I loved about her. "You want me to just forget about him?"

"It's the right thing to do. Think about it, please."

I started the engine, and we drove home in silence.

When Sara finally went to bed I lingered downstairs. I grabbed the White Pages and leafed through to the C's, then ran my finger down the page toward the listing for Martin Crump.

# Chapter 6

There was no listing for Martin Crump. Then I remembered he went by a new name. Had he taken it to hide from me? Probably, or at least to make sure no one stumbled across him while looking up his mother, Delilah. That didn't matter. I would find him anyway.

One thing I could do was keep my eye out at the park, though I doubted he'd ever return. Then I came up with a better plan. I'd search the neighborhood he claimed to live in. When morning finally arrived I dressed quickly, grabbed a bagel, and hurried out the door. Only as I swerved my way down Foothill Drive while shaving did I realize I hadn't kissed Sara goodbye. I didn't have time to turn back.

Once in the oak-lined Avenues my pulse slowed. I felt confident I'd find Martin on this first day of searching. I'd doubted him when he'd said he lived here, but he alleged complete honesty. So, in a way, I was putting my trust in him. If I couldn't discover him he'd probably lied about being honest, and if he had, maybe I didn't want to find him after all.

I'd always loved this neighborhood. I passed the Kearns' Mansion, product of one of the state's great mining success stories and now better known as the Utah State Governor's Mansion. The home, servants' quarters, livery stables, and various outbuildings covered more than an acre. I peered down the drive just in case, as if I might stumble upon some sign of Martin in quarters like these. Adjacent to the estate sat a simpler home, still large, yet not nearly so elegant. As I drove up the hill beneath the arching branches of a thousand leafless oaks the homes became generally smaller, but not uniformly so. At the top of the hill, I knew, were the modern mansions, peering over the valley with opulence and majesty. I wouldn't make it into that area today.

I noticed a two-story flat-roofed market. An American flag served as a drape in one of the upper floor windows. This was a likely place for Martin. I made a mental note. Here and there were high-rise apartment buildings erected in the sixties and seventies, sometimes displacing an entire block of what had once been gorgeous Victorian homes. A jumble of small and mid-sized houses of various architectural styles completed the neighborhood. Nearly every building on every street had been lovingly restored sometime in the last ten years.

Mormon chapels were scattered throughout, as in all Salt Lake neighborhoods, and I used them as navigational buoys. Having grown up a member of Utah's predominant religion I sensed the boundaries of the numerous wards. Each time I passed a chapel I considered going inside to ask around for Martin. I forced myself to resist. He'd ranted about his suspicions of the motives of church members, and I didn't want to do anything that might make him less inclined to talk with me once I found him. After an unsuccessful fifteen-minute search I headed to the office.

I returned in the evening to try again. My second foray found no more success than the first. I tried not to let it dampen my hope because the neighborhood was huge. I'd simply alter my commute whenever possible to take me though different sections. It wasn't that inconvenient a detour from my regular route to work anyway.

Every weekday morning except Thursday, my climbing gym day, I wandered the streets like a confused delivery boy. Evening after evening I returned for a second pass. I searched for over a month without uncovering a single trace. On a Tuesday in early

January I didn't find my way home until particularly late, my tardiness mainly the result of a surging workload at the office, but the time searching the Avenues hadn't helped either. I greeted Sara, feeling exhausted. "What a day."

"How so?" she asked, anger in her tone.

I knew I couldn't share my most pressing frustration. "I'm focusing on becoming more efficient, but it's hard. You know, spending less time learning about my clients' lives and just making their decisions for them. That's the difference between me and the 'big hitters.' Efficiency."

Her swollen stomach bulged beneath her flannel nightgown. "Oh, good. So now your goal is to become just another heartless mortgage broker? The world sure needs more of that." She stomped off to the bedroom. I shook my head as I followed her with my eyes.

I felt like an intruder in my own home as I gathered dinner from the fridge and ate alone on the breakfast bar. I'd been aware that my long hours grated on Sara, though I didn't understand why. Wasn't it a man's job to make a living? Did she think I could do that while cuddling with her?

By the time I found my way to bed the room was black. I climbed beneath the covers, then bumped into something. "I see you've added another pillow to your barricade."

"You try being pregnant and practically widowed."

It seemed like an overreaction. "I'm trying to do what's best for our family, Sara. Just like you are. Besides, you and I both know I'm not invited over the parapet you've erected here. It wouldn't matter if I arrived in bed at eight in the evening or two in the morning."

"It would too matter." Her words came through tears.

I hated it when she cried. "Hey, Sara, don't do this. You've made it obvious lately that you want your space. I give it to you and this is what I get?"

"Sure I need space, not solitude. I'm sorry that my hormones are out of control, but I need you by my side. I need you here to listen."

I moved pillows so that I could get near enough to drape an arm over her, reluctantly admitting to myself that I'd have to put my search for Martin on temporary hiatus. "I'm sorry Sara. It's a hard time for both of us. I'll do better." It felt so comfortable to hold her. I could have lain in that position forever.

Her sniffling told me she'd gained control of her emotions. "This is going to sound wrong of me Tom, and I don't want you to misunderstand. Could you put those pillows back where they were. I had them just right. It's so hard to get comfortable."

I sighed. As I rebuilt her fortress I tried to understand. She couldn't be blamed for wanting little to do with me, I reasoned. Withholding affection was simply her method of exacting punishment for my role in dispossessing her of her body. As her figure showed increasing signs of double occupancy I couldn't help feeling fortunate she could never play a similar trick on me.

"You're not mad, are you?" she asked.

I thought a moment. "No. Confused. We can talk later. We both need our sleep. I promise I'll be around more. Goodnight."

"Goodnight."

I lay there with my eyes wide open. The realization that we couldn't discuss my underlying concern, my search for Martin, made my mood especially somber. My lies to Sara were having far-reaching effects. Where once we'd understood each other so completely, now we often went to bed angry. Tonight wasn't the first time I'd found myself forced to twist facts beyond my original intent just to cover my tracks.

Besides that, interest rates were on the decline. Business increased despite my decreased marketing efforts. Everyone wanted to refinance. Low rates were responsible for a surge in new home sales as well.

I shut my eyes having reached the obvious conclusion. The time had come to give up the search for Martin.

\* \* \*

Business didn't just boom, it erupted. Daisy and I accepted plaques for leading the company in loan production for two consecutive months, and based on files in process it looked like many such honors were on their way. Daisy had initially expressed concern at my corner cutting saying, "It's not like you not to teach your clients about all the different loan products. Suddenly you're just making their decisions for them."

I had to save time somewhere. Hot business cycles never last long. I couldn't imagine turning clients away, neither could I afford to spend time with borrowers at the expense of my wife. Daisy couldn't argue with the results, anyway, and soon she was too busy to complain. What had all my extra attention to clients accomplished anyway? It just bogged things down. They always followed my advice no matter how much effort I spent educating them. Why waste both my time and the borrowers? The less friendly I became with my customers the more efficiently I dealt with their files. Money rolled in, and I began to believe that with a large enough bank account I could prepare for any eventuality, overcome any crisis, solve any problem. Enough money might even make me a good father. At the very least my earning potential proved that, at some level, there were major differences between Martin and me.

In early May a newlywed couple, Rick and Cindy Foster, arrived in my office for pre-qualification. I walked in ten minutes late because of an appointment with a realtor. Daisy and my clients were sitting around my desk laughing when I rushed in the door. I smiled, extended handshakes, and waved my processor out of my chair so I could sit down. "I need the most recent paystub for each of you, your last two years' W-2s, your current bank statement, social security cards, and statements of any outstanding loans including credit cards."

There was an edge to Daisy's voice as she left the room. "I've already photocopied everything you need. It's sitting right in front of you. Rick and Cindy came here very prepared. The credit report's there too. I just pulled it off the fax. I've also entered all their data into your computer."

I looked over the credit report. They had substantial debt, but at least they paid their bills on time. They had few assets, not even cars, to show for all their borrowing. To make matters worse, neither of them had shown good job stability, and their bank account held little savings. I manipulated numbers on the computer and soon discovered what I felt would be the best scenario. "Looks like what we're going to need to do for you is an FHA adjustable rate mortgage. If we went fixed rate I'm afraid I couldn't qualify you for anything worth looking at."

I printed off a Good Faith Estimate and reviewed the numbers quickly. "Let's get your signatures on the necessary documents and you'll be good to go." I slid one form after another in front of them. They signed as quickly as I could move the papers past. We were finished in no time. On the way out I walked with them to Daisy's desk so I could drop off the file to be set up.

"How does it look?" Daisy asked Cindy as we approached.

"I doubt we can afford a dog house," she said dejectedly, and for the first time I recognized how deep her emotion ran.

"You'll find something in your price range," I assured them, "and then in the future you'll be able to move up. The important thing is you're making the commitment to become homeowners. You won't regret it. Once you're settled in your first home all you need to do is make sure you don't allow your personal debts to get so out of hand again."

Daisy hugged the Fosters good-bye. I felt separated, like a tax collector barging in on a family reunion. It was obvious they'd really enjoyed the short time they'd spent together. They were still talking when I returned to my office and went to work on another file.

After a few minutes I heard Daisy. "What do you think you're doing charging extra fees to the Fosters?"

I looked up, "What's gotten into you?"

"I'm serious, Tom. Those two need every penny they can scrape together, and you're hitting them with junk fees. Do you have any idea how important this is to Cindy and Rick?"

"Those fees are standard. Everyone charges them. Just because I used to waive them doesn't mean I need to continue to. Even with the fees we're hardly making anything on the loan. It's not worth the effort we'll put into it."

"Oh, give me a break. In the time I've worked for you we've done at least twenty loans this size and smaller. When it came to helping someone get into their first home you used to waive fees every time."

"Thank you for telling me how to run my business, Daisy. Now, are you done?" I asked.

She glared for a moment then said, "Maybe I am. Maybe I'm done for good."

I'd never seen her so angry. I followed her to her desk, knowing I couldn't let the conversation end that way. "What was that supposed to mean?"

"What did it sound like it meant?" She dumped recycled paper on the floor and set the empty box on her desk. She gathered personal items and tossed them in haphazardly.

I hadn't realized we were yelling until I noticed the woman at the next desk staring at us. I looked around the room to see heads poking over cubicle walls. It looked like a gopher colony. "You're making a scene," I whispered. "Look, I'll do the loan for free if that's what you want. Just put your stuff back on your desk."

"You're missing the point, Tom." She wasn't whispering. "I used to love working for you, and now I hate it. I once felt good about what we did for people, and now I feel sick about it." She indicated the head protruding from the corner office, "You used to say you couldn't understand how Dennis could sleep at night after he screws his clients, and now you're becoming just like him."

I felt my face redden as Dennis sheepishly returned to the interior of his large office. "I still put my clients' interests first."

"Is that right? Then tell me, don't you think you said some callous things to the Fosters about their debt considering it's the result of Cindy's miscarriage?"

"Miscarriage?" I couldn't focus as I tried to recall my words. They escaped me.

She nodded.

"Daisy, think about what you're doing. I can't handle all this business without you. If you need a vacation, just say so, but don't threaten to quit when we're on such a roll."

"It's not a threat," she said. "Remember when I told you if I didn't like my life I'd walk away and find a new experience? Well, I'm walking. My decision is made."

I spun on my heel and threw my arms above my head in resignation, accidentally tossing the sheaf of paper I'd forgotten I held. I walked back to my office through a blizzard of documents, stepped inside, and slammed the door.

\* \* \*

At six-thirty I got home. My headache had been raging for over two hours. Sara greeted me with three aspirin tablets and a beer.

"When did you learn to read minds?" I took the pills from her and chased them with the beer.

"Daisy called."

"Did she let you know about all my crimes against humanity?"

"It does sounds like you're doing business a bit differently than you used to." She reached for my shoulders and massaged.

"I haven't heard you complain when you cash the checks."

She removed her hands from my shoulders. I knew my comment had caught her off-guard. I hadn't meant it to come out sounding nasty. Now I didn't want to look in her direction. I felt in no mood to explain. I walked into the kitchen looking for food.

After a while she said, "I bet you're sorry to see Daisy go."

I turned toward Sara, appreciative of her effort to avoid more confrontation. I tried to reciprocate. "That's a bet you'd win. I don't suppose she called you to say she'd rethought her decision?"

"No," she said in a long drawl. "She said she realized it was rash, but leaving the mortgage industry is 'sort of cosmically correct.' She says a phase of her life has passed, and that means a new one is beginning. 'With every death there is rebirth,' were her exact words, and you'll never guess how she's being reborn." Sara paused, apparently to build anticipation.

I wasn't in the mood for suspense. I tried to beckon the words from her lips by rowing the air away from her mouth with my fingertips. It didn't work. "Please, just say it."

"She's going to India." Sara enunciated the words for impact.

"India? Not funny. Tell me you have your fingers crossed."

She held both hands out, palms open. "It's God's truth, and there's a kicker. There's something that fits Daisy and no one else."

"My processor is relocating to the diametrically opposite side of the planet and you want me to believe something could top that? Wait . . . don't tell me . . . I'm getting a vibration," I cupped my hands in front of my forehead where they could capture as many psychic waves as possible. "It's coming to me. She's going to fly there solo on a hang-glider towed by pelicans."

"No, but you're not too far off. Do you want another guess?" she asked, enjoying having cornered the market on this information.

"Just tell me."

"Okay, here it is, but you're not ready for it." She gave me a teasing look.

I returned a scowl that must have finally convinced her I'd tired of the game.

"Her plane already left. She was afraid if she didn't go immediately she would chicken out. She called to say good-bye to you through me because she knew you'd talk her out of it. She also asked me to give you this." Sara gave me a peck on the lips.

She hadn't kissed me in a long time. It felt so nice to have her near me, if only for a moment. She backed away and I stared into her eyes. "First of all, Daisy doesn't kiss like that at all. She uses much more tongue."

Sara punched me in the shoulder.

"And second, why didn't you talk her out of it? I thought we were a team."

She looked puzzled. "It never crossed my mind. I just remember thinking, 'I knew this would happen one day.'"

"Damn it Sara, don't make light of this. You don't like it when I get home late. Without Daisy, you ain't seen nothing yet. I can't let my clients down just because she did. I'm screwed."

Sara smiled, obviously drastically underestimating what all this meant. "There's nothing that can be done. One day you'll laugh about all this. Why not now?"

I'd finished my first beer. I open the fridge and found another. I swigged it as well, then boosted myself to a seat on the counter. "I'll tell you, it's sheer poetry. Clients will call for her tomorrow and the receptionist can say, 'Please hold. Daisy is tied up with the Dalai Lama.'"

"She mentioned the Dalai Lama."

"Of course she did. He's her hero. She talks about him constantly. The main gist is he's a man who would never charge junk fees on a mortgage, the kind of man I used to be. The reason she's gone to India is she believes she can learn the meaning of life by . . . Oh, no, do you know what else? I'm sure she's financing this pipe dream with the bonus I paid her last week. Why couldn't she have just gotten something pierced like she usually does?" I banged my head against the cabinet.

"She mentioned that. She believes deep down when you gave her the money you realized you were buying her freedom. She wanted to thank you, and said she was certain you'd understand after you let go of some initial anger."

I couldn't suppress a laugh. "I bought her freedom for two thousand bucks?" And I thought to myself, I wish my own could come at such a reasonable price. Not only was that impossible, the consequences of losing Daisy would be disastrous. I couldn't get drunk enough to forget that.

I tried to focus my thoughts on how I would extract myself from my predicament, but my mind refused to stay on the topic. Daisy's emotional tirade forced me to confront the differences between who I'd intended to be and who I'd become. For some reason I kept seeing Martin's face. It occurred to me that, without realizing it, I'd tried to act the opposite of Martin in nearly every situation. Now I was someone I didn't like. After three solid months focused almost entirely on Sara and my job I suddenly felt reawakened to the pieces of my life I'd shut out. I regretted my abandoned search for my father, saw finding him as a key to bringing the other pieces of my life into alignment. By morning my failure to find him felt like a gaping wound, enormous and foreboding beside my minor business problems. There must be a way. I had to find Martin!

## Chapter 7

On the way to work I veered through the Avenues for the first time in weeks. After a while I realized I wore a broad smile. It was fun, even exciting, to be looking for clues again, and an unexpected notion occurred to me. This detour into the Avenues was the first time I'd strayed from my goal-oriented path in eight weeks. I thought about how businesslike I'd been with clients, and regretted it. As I traveled each day from "Point A" to "Point B" in the straightest line possible, making great strides toward my financial goals, I'd been missing out on my favorite part of life. I craved the unpredictable in the same way I looked forward to the juice of a just bitten nectarine running down chin and neck. This side trip reminded me why I'd been so prone to taking the scenic route my whole life. I was eager to revert to my old form.

The necessary clue was here somewhere. It had to be. I drove along the streets and avenues looking for something, anything, out of place. The preponderance of well tended gardens and manicured lawns annoyed me, as if they were meant to taunt. I felt the familiar dejection as I headed back toward the main thoroughfare, unsuccessful yet again. Tonight I would begin visiting the local wards. It was time to talk to anyone who might be of help, regardless of consequence. If Martin were nearby I would find him.

I braked at a stop sign. Down the road to my left I spotted a mongrel dog loping away from me. At least it looked out of place.

That was better than nothing. I turned down the street, and as I approached the mutt she glanced over her shoulder, then flicked her tail into her mouth. Moxie had to be the only dog on earth capable of such a trick. I looked at her closely— and saw the same confused expression and crooked smile I had that day in the park. I'd rediscovered Martin's trail.

I drove beyond the dog, and pulled to the shoulder. I watched her in my rear view mirror as she bounced toward me. She passed by. I pushed in the clutch, rolling behind her down the slight incline. At a fire hydrant midway through the next block she paused for a sniff, then trotted up a faint path I'd never noticed. Looking closer, I saw signs of the infrequent passage of tires over the grass.

The trail went between two homes, into the center of the block. No wonder I'd missed it. I jumped from the Cherokee and followed on foot, ignoring a "No Trespassing" sign posted on the trunk of the willow tree whose weeping boughs obscured the entrance to this unusual lot. I'd never even suspected the existence of a home with no frontage on the street. Careful to stay well behind, I watched Moxie disappear into the tall grass of an unkempt lawn. There sat Martin's van at the end of the drive. My heart raced.

I moved toward the ramshackle house and its rickety companion garage. The vegetation, emboldened by its success in the yard, appeared determined to take over both those structures as well. From what little I knew about my father this home matched his personality perfectly. The only thing that made the residence look slightly sound was its square walls when compared with the garage. The two buildings stood about ten feet apart at their bases, but at least eleven feet at their rooflines. The garage leaned toward the downhill side of the property at an unbelievable angle. I approached the house with an eye on the other building, certain it would collapse before I could ring the doorbell.

"When you figure out how to keep your cats in your yard I'll work on keeping my dogs in mine!" I heard Martin yell.

Instinctively I moved for cover, hurrying to the side of the house, then easing along it toward the conversation.

I couldn't make out the muffled reply of the irate woman who yelled back.

"Well I hope they do," Martin said.

I strained to hear the woman, when suddenly my cell phone rang. I fumbled for it on my belt, flipped the mouthpiece open, and crouched low, hoping Martin had missed the unusual noise.

"Hello," I answered.

"Tom? This is Patrick at the office. Why are you whispering?"

Just then Martin stepped around the corner and stared at me.

I straightened. "I'm not whispering." We stood about six feet apart.

"Whatever you say. I just called to give you a heads up. The

Fed raised the rate this morning. Things are going nuts around here. You better get in as quickly as you can."

"This is private property," Martin growled.

"Tom?" I heard Patrick ask.

I disconnected the call. "I want to talk to you, Martin." My voice came out in little more than a squeak.

"I knew if I let you know where I lived eventually I'd lose my privacy. You lied. You're just like all the others."

"I have a right to be here."

He scowled. "You have no right. This is my private land, and you are trespassing."

"What did you mean when you said we're related in the worst possible way?"

He grabbed a rake that leaned against the house and took a step in my direction. "Is there something wrong with your ears? I told you to get off my land. I meant now! You are nothing but a trespasser."

I backed away. How had I allowed myself to believe this conversation would go differently than our previous one? "You can't mean that."

"It's not an opinion. It's a fact."

"No. Here's a fact. You owe me an explanation. I'll be back to get it." I stared at him, then spat at the ground. Forcing myself to turn away was difficult, but we were headed nowhere, and Patrick wouldn't have called if the problems weren't serious. As I walked toward the road I felt Martin's eyes upon me, though I didn't look back. I rounded the willow, climbed into my Cherokee, and drove.

\* \* \*

The moment I opened the office door I heard the raised voices of loan officers, processors, and closers. A couple, somebody's unfortunate clients, sat in the waiting room wearing frightened expressions. I wondered what could possibly be going on. When I pulled a rate sheet off the board I knew. Yields had skyrocketed beyond my worst expectation. Someone said to me, "Don't bother reading those quotes. That's ten minutes old. They've gone up again."

I dropped the paper into the wastebasket and my sour mood worsened. I had a drawer full of loans, very few with locked rates. I went through Daisy's cabinet and pulled every purchase transaction where the rate was still floating, intent on locking the terms if at all possible. Maybe I could save some of them in time. The refinances wouldn't be worth bothering with at all. Thousands of dollars in income swirled around the drain.

When I reached my desk calls were ringing through, the receptionist apparently too swamped to page. With no time to waste I couldn't afford to pick up the phone and get sidetracked. I ignored the incoming lines and dialed my most reliable investor. I got a busy signal. I dialed three more large institutional investors and got three more busy lines. They'd probably just taken their phones off the hook in hopes the chaos would cease. I wasn't going to get through to any of them.

I picked up a ringing line. As expected, it was a concerned client. The questions he asked me would become all too familiar before the day was through. "Have you heard what's happening to rates? Did you get my loan locked? Where's Daisy?" None of the answers were the ones I wanted to give. The workload would've been overwhelming even if I had my assistant. Without her the ringing phone sounded like fingernails on a blackboard.

Then the really bad calls started arriving. On a locked transaction scheduled to close the next day the realtor called to inform me that the buyer had been hospitalized. On a very large cash-out refinance which I'd been fortunate to lock the day before, the appraiser gave me the bad news that his estimate of value had come in more than $100,000 below what the homeowner had expected. It went on and on. As if they'd been held in check by her mystic powers alone, problems arose in Daisy's absence. Even my cleanest transactions weren't immune from glitches. When one woman, a self employed borrower, called to find out how much income we'd been able to verify from her tax returns I spent twenty minutes trying to give her a useful answer before I realized that I'd have to re-compute the numbers when the environment was less hectic. What would have been a simple matter for my assistant to sort out became a disaster for me. I didn't know how to do her job, and even if I had, I couldn't understand her systems. Over the past two years she'd developed her own shorthand in four dimensions. She could pack unbelievable amounts of information into her jottings using colors and symbols. I'd encouraged her creativity. It always made me smile when I looked into a file and found vibrant notes interspersed with ornate etchings. I should have realized there'd come a day I'd need to decode her cryptograms.

Around ten o'clock I decided to hire a temp. She arrived in less than an hour. For no reason I could comprehend she immediately disassembled several files and mixed the contents together. I fired her before lunch. Other processors cautiously offered assistance, but they weren't Daisy, and their methods only frustrated me. With the rising rates adding to their own workloads they were only too happy to abandon me, and my lack of civility provided an easy excuse.

At one point Patrick stepped into my office and said, "I bet you wish you had Daisy right now."

I threw a paperweight at him. It was meant as a warning shot, but accidentally slammed his knuckle against the door frame. He wandered away with a hurt expression.

At home things went almost exactly as I had predicted when Daisy quit. Sara couldn't understand why I seemed to value my time at work over my time with her. I had no energy to argue the point, and took to sleeping on the couch.

It was a full week before I gained any semblance of control. I scooped up all the unsalvageable files and dropped them into a pile on Daisy's old desk. Then I walked to my office, shut the door, closed the blinds, and dropped into my chair. I flopped my head back and stared at the ceiling, blowing out a long breath. It was time to consider what I'd become, not just as a result of my seven-day meltdown, but over the big picture.

I didn't like what I saw. How could I? I'd compromised my ethics by increments until they'd reached gutter level. My self-esteem had dropped as well. My business was in tatters. And to top it off, the only recent sign my marriage still had a pulse was the kiss my wife had delivered courtesy of Daisy Love.

I rose from my chair and walked into Patrick's office to resign. He held the phone to his ear while he impatiently tapped his pen on a notepad. I sat down in one of the leather chairs facing his oversized walnut desk and waited.

When he hung up he looked squarely into my eyes. "You've just gone through the toughest week I've ever seen this business throw at anyone, and I've seen some brutal ones."

"I feel like I've been hit by a train."

"Lots of people run and hide when things get unpleasant. I admired the way you dealt with the problems head on. Your family should be proud of you."

His words caused me either to lose my nerve or come to my senses. I'm not sure which, but either way I couldn't resign. I stared at him with what must have been a confused expression while the incongruity of his statement sunk in. My overriding problem with Martin still loomed, more menacing than ever. How ironic that I'd be praised for my greatest shortcoming. I rose from my seat and headed to the door.

# Chapter 8

I sped all the way to Martin's house, practicing my tirade toward him against a defenseless passenger seat. Other motorists must have thought me insane and gave me wide berth. I skidded to a stop at the curb and stormed toward the house. I raised my fist to pound on the door when his distinctive voice came from my left. "What's your business here Tommy?"

I spun to look at the far end of the porch, and there he was, only a few feet away. He reclined in a lounge chair meant for the living room, not the patio. An astounding clutter filled the porch. A bookcase stood against the wall; knick knacks took any space not occupied by a tattered volume. I fought an urge to pick everything up and take it inside where it belonged.

A grandfather clock caught my eye just as the hour changed to six. The pendulum swung evenly as the clock emitted a series of impotent clicks in place of its expected chime.

"What business have you got here?" Martin repeated.

"You owe me an explanation."

He looked thoughtful, then whispered, "I don't owe anybody anything."

"Did you really mean it when you said we were related in the worst possible way?"

He slapped his forehead. "That again?"

"I know you're my father."

His features went wide. He uncocked the lever at the side of his chair and rocked forward. "You know what?"

"I know about Patty, too."

His mouth fell open. He took long, deep breaths, like a laborer who'd just thrown a heavy load from his shoulders. "Which means I've kept my end of a bargain I never meant to enter. It's been so many years. Come over here, Tommy."

I walked toward him. Moxie and Bailey sprawled near his feet. They watched me closely, noses working. Sitting on a TV tray beside his chair was a syringe and a vial. My train of thought scrambled away like a cat dropped into a bathtub.

He must have noticed my preoccupation. "Damn your grandpa. When the diabetes killed him I considered it the most blessed disease in the world. I didn't know he'd passed it on to me. Now I can see my own ending."

I glanced at him, but couldn't reply. His pale complexion indicated he might be right. I felt suddenly weak, as if I too carried the flaw. It took great effort to gather my thoughts. "What did you mean when you said we're related in the worst possible way?"

He nodded his head slowly, as if the voices inside had come to some sort of agreement. "There's no such thing as a good father. You already know that even if you're unwilling to admit it to yourself."

I clenched my jaw until it hurt. It took all of my will power not to explode. "Running from parenthood was your own choice. It doesn't mean you couldn't have been a good father."

My anger didn't faze him. He shook his head as if amazed at my naiveté. I watched the gears turn in his mind. "All right Tommy, do you have time for a story?"

I moved close so that I towered over him. He had to bend his head back to meet my eyes. "I want an explanation."

"That's what I meant. It's the story about why things turned out the way they have. It starts way back when I was a kid, and it's going to take some telling before you'll truly understand. I'm not going to attempt it with you looming over me like this, though."

I glowered at him as I backed off. He looked away. I settled down on a milk crate.

Martin cleared his throat, satisfied. "I've told this story before . . . many times . . . but never to another human."

I looked at the dogs. Moxie blinked.

"Pay attention, because the details are important," Martin said.

"How long is it going to take?"

"As long as I need it to. You need to learn patience." He looked at the sterile set up in front of him, removed a couple more items from a small medical kit, and continued preparations to administer the insulin. With the skill of a surgeon he dabbed alcohol on his upper arm, filled the syringe from a vial, and injected the drug into his tissues. Apparently he'd forgotten about me and his promise. By the time he looked back I realized he was again in control of our exchange. Finally he said, "So, you want to know why I'm this way? Why I'd abandon a family you think is so great. I'll tell you about my childhood, a typical Sunday with the Crumps."

I adjusted my position on the crate, wondering how much accuracy could be left in a tale so thoroughly handled. Impatience strained at my gut, but I'd go along for a moment. "Is it important that it's a Sunday?"

"Yes, because the way I was taught to see God has affected everything in my life. Now shut up and listen."

Martin's eyes fell shut, but otherwise his face took on the aspect of squinting, as if he were intent on bringing something into focus.

Somehow the seriousness with which he approached this task calmed me, made me willing to share the recollections, altered though they must be by fifty years of insight and self doubt. I recalled my mother's inadvertent advice: "Martin's the expert on this topic." Nevertheless, I prepared to filter his statements with the fragmentary things I knew about the past and the presumptions I'd developed about his mental health.

\* \* \*

The year was nineteen-fifty-one. Joseph was nearly eight and would soon be baptized. Martin was five, Emma eleven. Father was bishop of their ward, a position he held for years. He was still in his early thirties.

Martin sat on the wooden pew kicking the seat back in front of him. He was happy to be between his big brother and sister and wanted it to remain that way, but then Emma stood up, hand aloft. Martin felt an urge to pull her back.

When the deacon spotted Emma he headed toward her. He passed the microphone down the aisle, the warm black cord draping across Martin's lap.

Martin followed the wire's tangled route to the loudspeaker with his eyes. Then he gripped the line, wondering if he would be able to feel his sister's voice as it passed through. It had been Father's idea to use the microphone in church, and the experiment was working out better than anyone could have anticipated. Father was a real innovator.

Martin looked up at Emma. Holding the microphone, she looked like a movie star. Even without it she appeared stately on this day. She tilted her head. Her blonde hair reached the small of her back. The locks danced against the floral imprint of her new Sunday dress.

"She looks so mature, doesn't she Delilah?" Martin heard Grandma Pearl whisper to his mother. He knew his wiry old grandmother had labored late into the previous night making final alterations to his sister's clothing.

Emma inhaled, gathering herself to speak. Martin followed her gaze forward to their father. Bishop LaVar Franklin Crump– Martin felt the full name and title held a regal quality– presided over the congregation. The bishop didn't acknowledge his children, for he was asleep. The first counselor, edgy and attentive, sat to father's left. The second counselor, also asleep, sat to his right.

Martin inspected his father's circular face. The many lines around his mouth and near his eyes weren't so apparent from this far away, but the graying and receding hair was. Just the way a father should be, thought Martin.

"I would like to stand and bear my testimony that I know The Church is true," Emma said in pure tones. A satisfied smile lifted the corners of her mouth. She collected herself, then continued, "that it is the one true church, restored to the earth by Joseph Smith, a prophet of God. I know he also was given the Holy Melchezidic Priesthood by the angel John the Baptist who received it from Jesus Christ who received it from God; and I know that same Priesthood has been passed down to President David O. McKay, our living prophet who speaks for God. I am grateful for the guidance and teaching of our church leaders, for the examples they set every day. I am also very thankful for my family and all of the many blessings that have been given me. I say these things in the name of Jesus Christ, amen."

Martin looked at his father— still deep in sleep.

The deacon moved toward Emma to take the microphone, but the girl turned the other way. She looked at her family, as if trying to determine whom she'd inspired into following her example.

"Here, you take a turn, it's not hard," she whispered enthusiastically, extending the microphone toward Joseph.

The boy scowled. Emma, apparently frightened by the intensity of her brother's anger, and recognizing her miscalculation, pulled the microphone back to her breast. All three Crump children looked toward the podium where they hoped Father was still asleep. They weren't so fortunate. As if he'd been alerted to the sin by the Priesthood which resided so mysteriously within him, his eyes were wide open and his gaze rested upon his eldest son. Emma fumbled to hand the microphone back to the deacon.

Joseph reacted differently. He rose to his feet insolently, his gaze met Father's. "Hand it to me," he said defiantly and not at all in a whisper. The microphone amplified his words.

Tension filled the room, as if released in gaseous form from canisters hidden beneath the pews. The congregation craned their collective necks, wanting to know who had defiled the spirit of the gathering by speaking out of turn and in such an unorthodox tone. Many in the rear might have stood to have a better look if decorum hadn't bound them with greater force than curiosity could muster.

Martin's lower lip trembled, and although he sat just feet from his mother he moved toward his sister. He, and everyone else in the family, always looked to Emma for comfort.

Joseph could never resist jumping into dangerous waters, swimming against established current. He reached in front of his sister, his focus still on the stage, seemingly oblivious to the discomfort he created. Emma handed Joseph the microphone, then slunk down in her seat. Martin scrambled into his sister's arms.

She whispered, "If you promise to be quiet I'll sneak you a treat."

Martin nodded greedily.

Emma reached into her purse and pulled out a Tootsie Roll. The boy pulled at both ends of the wax-paper wrapper, causing the chocolate morsel to twist free. He shoved it into his mouth and chewed. Feeling comforted, he looked at Joseph in anticipation.

"I would like to bear my testimony," the eight-year-old said in a measured voice, "that I know The Church is true. I say these things in the name of Jesus Christ, amen."

Joseph set the microphone in his mother's lap. Her eyes lit up in terror. Joseph grinned devilishly. Mother never spoke in church, and all three children were well aware that she never wanted to. She looked at her son, then at the device, and finally toward her husband.

LaVar cleared his throat as he rose to his feet and stepped to the podium. He cast a stern glance at his wife, then tossed his chin toward the deacon crouched at the end of the row. Mother stretched the microphone past her three children and into the hands of the young man.

"My beloved Brothers and Sisters," Bishop Crump began in a voice even deeper than the one he used at home. "What an honor it is to preside over this congregation and hear such an expression of love for the Lord and His Church as we have here today. It is with immense humility that I take my turn now to stand before you and offer my testimony as to the truthfulness of this doctrine. As our true and living prophet, President McKay has told us, we now stand at the threshold of the Latter-days, the days of reckoning spoken of in the Gospel. It is time that we make certain our affairs are in order. Our nation is again at war, this time in Korea, and there can be little doubt that the Second Coming will soon be upon us. The world is turning, more rapidly than ever before, toward the shining example that The Church of Jesus Christ of Latter Day Saints represents."

A baby let out a wail. Martin turned to look, but most of the congregation did not. Such interruptions were commonplace.

Father didn't even pause. "Our missionaries in the field are experiencing unprecedented success as we prepare the way for Jesus Christ to return to this earth and cleanse it of sin. I often think of the work begun in that sacred grove in Palmyra, New York one-hundred-and-thirty years ago as Christ's one true religion was restored. I think of the persecution those brave men and women endured in the early days of The Church as they paved the way for the modern organization we have inherited today. Though the oppression which we Latter Day Saints continue to experience is very real, it is but a fragment of the abuse our forefathers endured in their quest to establish our community here in the Land of Zion. Throughout their prolonged journey westward these men of God persevered despite degradation and worse at the hands of jealous Gentile mobs whose motivation came at the behest of Satan himself." He paused for a long moment, allowing his message to sink in.

Martin noticed as his father's gaze paused lovingly, one by one, on the members of the congregation. The Crump family was the only group he ignored.

Then Father's eyes locked on Joseph. The bishop spoke again, more slowly. "Some members of the younger generation have not gained a proper respect for what has gone before." To Martin the intensity of the stare became unbearable, although it wasn't even directed toward him. He turned his head, then watched in awe as his brother looked unflinchingly into Father's eyes.

Father's tone took on heightened intensity. "As adults, it is our responsibility, indeed obligation, to impress upon our children's generation the need to remain aware, and even proud, of our tortured legacy. Not only does it set us apart from others; it tightens the bond within our own ranks. Let our capacity to believe in ourselves and our brethren, and our faith in the teachings of our church, be a light unto the world.

"Let no one be mistaken. There are dark days ahead. Our resolve will be tested, but the rewards of faith will be great. My beloved brothers and sisters of the Spring Creek Second Ward, I bear this as my testimony to you, and say that I know beyond a shadow of a doubt that we live in the latter days, and that this is the one true church, and I say all of these things, in the name of our Savior, Jesus Christ. A-men." Father stood motionless at the podium, as if weighed down by the gravity of his message. Finally, like a shepherd admiring his flock, he swept his gaze across the room.

After the proper pause he nodded his head in a subtle sign of satisfaction and cleared his throat. "Now, Sister Gooch will lead us in "We Thank Thee O' God for a Prophet" as our closing hymn, then I have asked Brother Moss to offer the prayer. Please travel home in safety, and to those of you we are not fortunate enough to see during the week, we will look forward to meeting with again next Sunday."

The chorister rose and the congregation sang one of their favorite songs:

> We thank thee, O' God, for a prophet
> To guide us in these latter days.
> We thank thee for sending the gospel
> To lighten our minds with its rays.

Mother spoke in a coarse whisper. "How dare you children make such a scene in church. Everyone's staring at us. I don't know how we'll ever live this down."

Martin glanced around. He couldn't see anyone looking in their direction.

> We doubt not the Lord nor his goodness.
> We've proved him in days that are past.
> The wicked who fight against Zion
> Will surely be smitten at last.

Mother gripped Joseph's and Emma's hands. Martin saw his siblings cringe in pain. "Emma, the moment the prayer is over, you grab hold of Martin's arm. I'm taking the lot of you outside to wait for your father in the car."

> Thus on to eternal perfection
> The honest and faithful will go,
> While they who reject this glad message
> Shall never such happiness know.

When the song ended Brother Moss stepped to the podium and prayed.

The congregation was just rising as Sister Crump and her children hurried from the chapel. Martin could barely keep up as they scurried out of the building and toward the car. When they reached the most prestigious looking automobile in the lot, a 1951 Lincoln Cosmopolitan, Mother opened the rear door and pushed the children inside. "Behave yourselves," she warned.

The door slammed behind Martin as he slid across the back

seat. He turned to see Mother pacing, wringing her hands. Through the side window he could see her midsection and arms. He felt happy he couldn't see her face because that meant she couldn't see his. When she stopped decisively he trembled. Then she bustled off toward the church. Martin scrambled to his feet, realizing a moment later that he was standing on the leather upholstery. Although he knew it was wrong, he had to watch Mother out the back window. Besides, both his siblings knelt beside him. Just because he was shorter didn't mean he couldn't be curious.

After Mother disappeared Joseph spoke first. "I hate the first Sunday of the month. I don't know why they call it 'Fast Sunday.' I'm starving. I think it's the slowest day of all."

"They call it Fast Sunday because we don't eat anything until after Testimony Meeting," Emma said. "The money we save goes as Fast Offerings to church welfare projects."

"Oh really? Gee, I didn't know that. Thanks for explaining." Joseph looked away. "The only thing I like about any Sunday is going for a ride in this car."

"Shhh. Don't talk that way. It's not reverent," Emma said. "You should be thinking of the Lord and all of the blessings he has given us."

"Pfff," Joseph waved her comments off with a swish of his hand. "I don't have to be reverent. We're not in church anymore. You're the one who caused this whole mess anyway. Why do you have to be such a goody-goody passing the microphone around?"

"You should get used to bearing your testimony. You're about to be baptized, you know. In just four more years you'll receive the Aaronic Priesthood. Those are wonderful gifts, and I thought you might like to show how grateful you were to receive them. Besides, I figured you'd like to try the microphone out. It's really marvelous. You can even whisper if you want, and still everyone can hear you clear as a robin's song. It sure beats yelling it out. You know, it was Father's idea to use—"

"Big deal. I've already heard that a million times. Why should I care?"

"Brother Pratt said in our Sunday School lesson today that we should be thankful for the Lord's gifts every day, not just when it's convenient to us," Emma said. "He said that Jesus watches us always, and that we would be blessed in the afterlife for our humility and thankfulness. He said you should never forget to smell the flowers or listen to the birds sing. I think it would be the same way for inventions and conveniences as for birds and flowers."

Joseph regarded her silently. Martin guessed that while Joseph enjoyed disagreeing with Emma, he didn't want to contradict the adult who was the runaway favorite of every child in the ward. Finally Joseph asked, "Did Brother Pratt say the part about inventions, or is that something you made up?"

"You know he would've said it. He just didn't get to that part because Mary Beth Eldridge chimed in as usual with a scripture. She raised her hand, jumped out of her chair, and just started reciting without even being called on. 'Blessed are the meek,' she said, 'for they shall inherit the earth.' I couldn't figure out what it had to do with anything, but it sure did make Brother Pratt smile. He's grade A, and would never make anyone feel bad for speaking out of turn or anything else."

Martin knew both his siblings loved Brother Pratt. He joined in as the three enthusiastically compared experiences.

After a while Joseph turned from the window and dropped into a seated position.

"Here come Mom and Dad," Emma said urgently, a split second later. She pulled Martin onto her lap. The little boy riveted his gaze on the seat back in front of him.

"I want to drive this car one day," Joseph said casually.

"What are you talking about? You're just a little kid." Emma's voice trembled with stress.

"I would steer with one hand, right at the top of the wheel.

The window would be down and I'd rest my other arm on the door."

Emma spoke through gritted teeth. "What are you talking about? Dad will be here any second."

"The wind would blow through my hair, and I woul . . ."

Martin heard the soft click signaling the spring in the door had been activated. The mechanism had also been rigged, somehow, to silence Joseph's speech. He remained casual, though, as if he hadn't noticed the words had quit flowing.

The door opened slightly, but no one got in. Moments later the door on the passenger side swung wide, and Mother scrambled through. She looked over the seat back and spoke in an urgent whisper. "He's in a good mood. You kids don't say anything to change that. Do you hear me?"

Martin listened to his father. He yelled good-naturedly to someone who must have been across the lot. Martin felt Emma relax. He saw no change in Joseph.

"We'll miss you at the Leadership Meeting on Thursday, Brother Pratt. I'll put in a good word for you," Father said. "Have a wonderful time with your family in Yellowstone, and don't let it bother you that there's a war going on." There was a playful sarcasm in his voice Martin didn't know exactly how to interpret. He'd only heard it when Father talked to other adults, but never when he spoke to Mother or Grandma Pearl.

Brother Pratt's muffled reply could be heard, but not interpreted. It was probably funny. Nearly everything Brother Pratt said was, and Martin smiled appreciatively. Father laughed as expected, then added, "I'll look forward to hearing about it when you return."

Father slid behind the wheel. He shut the door firmly and turned to look at his family. He smiled. Martin smiled back, and a quick glance told him both his siblings wore the same expression. He felt glad he'd misinterpreted the course this exchange might take. Emma hugged Martin tightly, and the boy laughed for no reason other than the pleasure of being loved.

Martin made brief eye contact with Father as the man's gaze passed from him to his sister, and then to Joseph. Martin saw Father's face turn red. Then the monstrous hand rose over the seat back. It slapped Joseph smartly across the cheek. Saliva splashed on Martin's face. Blood poured from the corner of Joseph's mouth.

# Chapter 9

"We never knew when Father might explode." Tears streaked Martin's face. "As a boy, I looked at my father and thought how perfect he was. I saw no faults, even at the worst of times. When he slapped Joseph, or Emma, or Mother, or even when he hit me, I never questioned why. He was my father. Whatever he did seemed like the thing that should be done."

"There's nothing unusual about that," I said. I remembered how I'd dreamed of emulating Joe. "Every five-year-old boy would describe his dad in the same way. Big. Handsome. Strong. Smart. The father defines the role for the son. How could a five-year-old's dad do anything that isn't father-like?"

Martin picked up the syringe and flicked at it distractedly with a forefinger. "I felt that way long after I was five. I saw the world through those same eyes at the age of fifteen. Years passed before I thought to question the way he raised us. I often wonder, if I hadn't allowed Father's opinion to affect me so deeply, how differently would my life have turned out?"

"Don't beat yourself up over something that can't be undone."

He paid no attention to me. "I accepted his god damn rules. They affect me every day of my life. I still catch myself doing things exactly as he would have, and I can't believe it. I hate him so much, but I act just like him. He's been gone nearly twenty-five years yet he has more daily influence on my life than any other person. How can that be?"

I shrugged.

His eyes narrowed. "You were coddled. You have no reason to regret your childhood."

I felt a spark of anger, but wouldn't be drawn into a fight. "I'm grateful for my childhood, although it wasn't perfect. None are."

"You had unfair advantages."

"One day I hope to give my own children every advantage I can. That's not unfair."

Martin scowled. "Think instead of your greatest weakness, because that's what you'll pass on."

My blood heated. It didn't matter that he knew nothing of my unborn daughter; his words were offensive. We'd made progress tonight. Before he could melt away whatever rapport we'd built I should leave. I stood. "I've taken up enough of your time for one night, Martin. Let's continue this later."

He straightened his chair and sat forward. "No, no! Sit down. I'll continue my story."

I smiled at the change. Everything had altered since he'd learned that I knew his true role in my life. I took the cell phone from my belt. "I have to call Sara."

Martin eyed the device, looking like he'd bitten into a lemon. "Another convenience for making people dependent on others. Such excesses are the reason America is no longer a great nation."

He sure could be a pain. I started dialing the number when the phone emitted two quick beeps—dead batteries. I flipped the mouthpiece closed in disgust. "You have no phone?"

He shook his head slightly.

"How much longer will your story take?"

"Awhile. It depends on how much I tell. If you stay you won't regret it."

I glanced at my watch. Now that he'd outlasted his pledge to hide the family secret, the finger in the dike had been removed. Rushing waters were bound to bring barriers down if I'd simply let them do their work. Under the circumstances, I couldn't bring myself to leave. "Please, tell me more." I sat.

He nodded, then squeezed his eyes shut in that odd manner of his.

I pondered his behavior, recalled what Mom had said about Martin acting more strangely as he became more comfortable, then decided to shut my eyes as well. If I were going to invest time listening to his stories, I might as well do so as intently as possible.

\* \* \*

"Don't do this LaVar." Mother's voice quavered. She reached toward Joseph. His blood stained her white blouse.

Martin wailed as if the blow had struck him. Emma gripped him in her lap and scooted to the remotest corner of the seat. Martin noticed that Joseph's face bore the same cool expression as before he'd been hit.

Father sounded frustrated. "You people are an embarrassment. Don't you realize that I am being judged based upon your behavior? Do you have any idea how much pressure there is on me? Would it be too much to ask that my son show respect?" he looked at Joseph. "Or act like a man?" his gaze turned to Martin. "Is there any reason my wife should be the weakest woman in the ward, or that my daughter. . . ? Oh, never mind. None of you understand, do you? I may as well be talking to myself."

"We're sorry, Dad," Emma said meekly.

Father started the car. "What kind of a testimony was that, Joseph? You sounded like a prisoner of war. Name, rank, and serial number. Isn't there a single thing you are humble enough to be thankful for? I faced the ward members on their way out of the building even though my own son made a mockery of the meeting. These people want to look to me as their example. What do you think they thought today?"

No one responded. Martin sat motionless on his sister's lap, forgetting to look out of the windows, not even seeing the things right in front of his face. The rare pleasure of riding in the big car was ruined for this particular day.

The moment the Lincoln stopped in the Crump driveway Joseph hopped out. He ran around the corner of the house.

Father watched him disappear. "Go inside and get supper ready, Delilah. I'll be in momentarily."

Martin felt the oddest sensation, as if he were abandoning Father in a time of need. Still, he climbed from the vehicle and followed Mother to the house, as he knew he must. On the stoop he glanced back. Father remained motionless, fingers wrapped around the wheel.

The aroma of roast beef, which had simmered for the entire day, filled the house. To Martin this was the smell of Sunday, especially sweet on those days they fasted. He followed his mother and sister into the kitchen. He dropped to his belly and scooted beneath the kitchen table where he went to work on a jigsaw puzzle. He loved lying in this spot while meals were prepared, smelling the odors and listening to his sister's voice. Today she didn't speak.

When he heard footsteps in the living room Martin tensed. Mother cocked her head, listening to the movement. The creaking recliner springs calmed Martin. It meant Father had settled in his favorite spot for a nap. Mother tiptoed to the kitchen door. She pushed it open a crack and peered out, like a mouse watching a cat. After a brief look she scurried back to the sink where her daughter cleaned vegetables.

She spoke in a hurried whisper. "You know I didn't want to marry him. He was mean from the start. It was your Grandma Pearl who made me do it. She said, 'This is the only good one you've ever dated. Finally you've met a man who will go somewhere.' She told me, 'You get this man to marry you if it's the last thing you do.'"

Emma sighed. "Mom, please. You've told me all this before. Why do you–?"

"I'd like to divorce him."

Emma stomped her foot. "Divorce? Mom, you're making no sense, and you know it. You were sealed to him in the temple for time and all eternity. It's God's will that we be joined as a family. You can't go back on such a promise. Don't even discuss it."

Mother scowled. "The things I've done for that man."

"Mom, please. Don't think about these things. Let's just get dinner made."

"You're the most precious thing in the world to me, Emma. You're the only one I can confide in. Do you think I have anyone else to turn to? I'm just trying to make certain you never make the mistakes I did."

Martin heard his sister's heavy exhalation. "Please don't say Dad's a mistake. I love him."

Mother's eyes widened with fright. "You're turning against me, aren't you?"

"That's not true. I can't settle some argument between you and Dad. I just want everyone to get along. Can't we do that?" Emma reached out and Mother embraced her.

"Don't cry Mom. It doesn't fix anything. We've got to put dinner on the table, so let's just get through it, all right?"

"All right," Mother said as she cuddled closer. She faced Martin, but her bloodshot eyes didn't look at him. Tear-streaked mascara accentuated each crease in her skin. To Martin, Mother had never looked so old.

The embrace continued for a long moment before Emma said, "I love you, Mom."

Martin imagined his sister's relief as Mother ended the hug. The older woman clutched her daughter by the shoulders and examined her at arm's length– the same way she would hold a cookbook when the quantity of the next ingredient was critical. It must have been her best range for focus.

Emma looked at Mother, then at the ground.

"I love you too, Emma. You mean more to me than you'll ever know. Thank you for saying those words. I don't hear them as often as I need to. We women have got to stick together." Mother now wore a determined grin, as if she lent her daughter support. Martin wished that were the case. He felt certain Emma did, as well.

As they completed dinner preparations only two sounds remained in the kitchen— one, the clatter of pans and dishware, and the other, Mother's occasional sniffle.

Eventually Emma looked at Martin. "Can you set the table?"

Martin scrambled to his feet.

Father arrived at the table while Martin arranged silverware. He took his seat. "Where's your brother?"

"I bet I know," Martin said, thinking of the tangled briar behind the chicken coop.

"Get him. I'm certain he's hungry."

Martin ran outside. He found his brother right where he expected— beneath the wild rose bushes in the space they called the clubhouse. "Supper's ready."

The look in Joseph's eyes revealed the pang in his stomach. "I'm not coming."

"Good. More food for me." Martin ran back to the house knowing his brother would follow. As he climbed into his chair and faced the overflowing table Joseph shuffled in the door.

The older boy slumped, avoiding eye contact with everyone. "I haven't eaten all day, except for that tiny piece of sacrament bread."

"Well, you're going to get something now," Father said. "This meal looks delicious. Emma, would you please offer a blessing on the food?"

The days events had to be put behind them. Emma was the

one to do it. Martin folded his arms and watched his sister. When she bowed her head he did as well.

"Our Dear Heavenly Father, thank Thee for this food, and bless that it may nourish and strengthen our bodies so that we will grow strong and healthy. Thank Thee for the many blessings Thou hast given us, for our home and neighbors, and for the love we share. Please grant us the strength to overcome hardship, and help us to remember the importance of our relationships. Help us to always be worthy of Thy blessings, and I say these things in the name of Jesus Christ, amen."

Martin lifted his head and looked at the others. The mood was still somber. As Emma dished mashed potatoes onto his plate he glanced at her. In her eyes he found the expression he'd been seeking. She looked back adoringly, then kissed him on the forehead. "I love you, Martin."

"I love you too, Emma," he whispered back.

The others piled beef, vegetables, and breads onto their plates. Joseph poured gravy on nearly everything.

Father cleared his throat. "Let's all forget about what happened in the car today."

Martin looked up, surprised.

"I am sorry for what occurred. I will tell you why I had to do it, then we can all forget about it. We will move on. Experiences like these ultimately strengthen our family." He waited for each family member to agree.

Martin watched the others nod, then nodded his own head.

Father continued in a satisfied tone. "Good. You know I would never do anything to hurt any of you; at the same time, as the patriarch and sole priesthood holder in this family, I cannot allow you to hurt yourselves. I have grave responsibilities.

"Satan tests us every day. We must remain vigilant of his traps. Often his schemes are difficult to recognize. That is why I fear the future. There are so many things in this world I wish I could change, but I am not certain I can even protect my own family. Joseph, your pride made you act disrespectfully– to me, and to the Lord. It hurt you to be punished. It hurt me even more to have to do it. Do you understand that?"

The boy stared at his plate. Everyone in the room knew that disagreement would end his meal. Still he hesitated until the silence became too long to bear. Then he said, "Yes, Dad."

"Good boy," Father said with satisfaction. "A man must demand respect in his own home. I know sometimes things do not make sense. That is just how it is at your age. The day will come that you will thank me for being strict. Take my word for it. If anything, I am too lax with you children. My dad ruled me with an iron fist." He glanced at each reverent face, apparently satisfied with how everything had turned out. Then he added, "Now pass me those potatoes."

Father wolfed down his food. Soon, he pushed back his chair. "I have work at the ward." He strode to the door, and was gone.

Mother didn't look up from her plate until the sound of the car faded from the driveway. Then she spoke. "Oh, I do love it when he leaves. The four of us make a nice little group, don't you think?"

"You're a different person when he's away," Emma said.

Mother glowed. "Who wants to go for a Sunday drive? Leave the dishes behind."

Dishes were never left dirty. Martin gawked at his mother, then hurried to the car before she could change her mind. He clambered into the 1931 Model A Ford taking his usual standing spot behind the driver's seat. Emma took her spot next to the door, and Mother sat at the steering wheel.

Joseph turned the crank. The auto sputtered reluctantly, then caught. Joseph hurried to his spot straddling the drive train, then they backed out.

"Where are we going Mom?" Emma asked.

"I have no idea." Mother fiddled with the gears.

"Wooooooo Hooooo!" Joseph yelled as the car gained speed and the wind swirled through his hair. "Go up! Go to the highest road this little clunker can reach."

They left the confines of their neighborhood, then traveled through the heart of Spring Creek. Even on weekdays the town was sleepy. It practically fell comatose on this Sunday evening. Mother guided the car to the foothills where the route steepened when it took on Mount Olympus directly. The under-powered vehicle labored beneath the weight of the family. Martin felt certain gravity would win the day.

"We have to jump out to lighten the load," Joseph yelled, his tone overflowing with the adventure of the moment. He reached past Emma to the door handle. In an instant he'd vaulted from his spot, and was on the road running beside the car. He looked at his sister. "Jump out, it's the only way she'll make it!"

Martin gaped at Joseph, then looked to his sister, certain she wouldn't do anything so rash. At that moment she leapt to the road.

"Push, Joseph, push," Emma yelled.

Martin looked out the rear window. The two children took positions side by side at the bumper. Clenched teeth spoke of straining muscles as they urged the car toward the junction with the Boulevard. Martin looked at the level crossroad ahead. It kept coming closer. As the grade mellowed the little car regained speed. The moment Martin could tell they would make it he patted his mother's shoulders and laughed.

She laughed with him as she braked at the Boulevard. "We made it. I never would have believed it was possible."

Martin looked back, but his brother and sister were nowhere to be seen. "Where's Emma?" he cried.

Mother exited the car in a flash. "The kids?"

Martin sprang to the ground and looked down the road. They'd vanished.

"Joseph . . . Emma!" Mother's panic increased. She grabbed Martin's hand and ran down the hill. Martin spotted the children lying beside the road at the same moment his mother's voice became hysterical. "Oh no! There they are. I've run over them somehow." She sprinted, dragging Martin. His legs churned at their maximum rate. He barely kept his balance.

Mother dropped to her knees. "What's happened? Talk to me."

Joseph's limbs were splayed at grotesque angles. His tongue lolled out to where it nearly touched the dirt. One of his arms had flopped across Emma's face, hiding her expression.

"Joseph, are you all right?" Mother asked.

Suddenly Joseph grabbed his mother's blouse with both hands and crowded his face into hers. "We're dead," he said in a goulish voice. He pulled her down to the ground.

"What? Is this some kind of trick?" Mother asked, still not comprehending the joke.

"I got you again," bragged Joseph.

Worry creased Mother's face. "Emma, this isn't like you. Are you all right?"

The girl smiled sheepishly. "When the car sped up we fell. Joseph made me play his game to make up for the testimony thing. I wanted to call out to you, but he wouldn't let me. I'm sorry."

Mother put her hand on her breast and drew labored breaths. "You nearly gave me a heart attack."

"I'm glad I didn't. Oh Mom, this is wonderful. Smell these flowers, feel this grass." Emma picked a daisy and tucked it behind her ear.

"I almost had a heart attack, too," Martin said.

Emma laughed, pulling the boy onto her lap. "What more could you ever want than we've got right here?"

Joseph assembled a bouquet and handed it to his mother. She held the flowers to her nose and inhaled. "They're beautiful."

"Look at the sunset." Emma's voice trembled with awe. Everyone turned west. The sun set the waters of the Great Salt Lake on fire. Color squirted everywhere. Cumulus clouds, chandeliers beneath a cobalt ceiling, took on vibrant reds and pinks at their underbellies, while their tops ebbed to black. At higher altitudes stratus clouds resembled scribbled yellow crayon. Warm light bathed the meadow where they sat.

"I don't want to look at my watch because I'm afraid I will see the hands are still moving at their same dreary pace. I don't want this moment to end," Emma said.

The sun slid downward, its movement made all the more obvious by comparison to its reflection in the lake. The golden lights collided, then swallowed each other and burned out.

Martin watched the valley darken and the incandescent lights of the city switch on; headlights and streetlights traced out roads. "The streets are so straight it looks like a checkerboard."

"That's the way Brigham Young planned it," Mother said. "Isn't it lovely how orderly the community is?"

Emma regarded the settlement. "How could the city ever stretch clear from Ogden to Provo the way Brigham Young prophesied? That's over seventy miles. Where would the farms go? I can't see how it would be possible."

Joseph's eyes lit up. "I can. "We just need more people, and they just have to build more homes. I can't wait until they do."

"Not me," Emma said. "I like things just the way they are. I can't think of one reason this valley would be better if it were filled to the brim. I can't imagine cars and factories and people everywhere. I know the prophet wouldn't have said it if he didn't have a reason, but I would just as soon it never happened."

Joseph looked smug. "It will anyway."

Martin regarded his sister thoughtfully. "I like it this way too. I don't ever want anything to change."

## Chapter 10

Martin had only a vague awareness he now lay in his own bed rather than in his sister's lap on the mountainside. Through drooping eyelids he watched Mother pull pajamas over Joseph's head. He regarded his big brother with cautious admiration. Joseph took risks— something Martin had never been able to do. When an idea occurred to Joseph he ran with it.

At that moment the older boy thrust an outstretched finger toward a spot behind his mother's back. "A mouse!"

Martin sprang up and looked at the spot. Nothing.

Mother let loose a scream that rattled the house. She threw Joseph onto the bed and hopped up behind him, then danced around as if they stood on a sizzling griddle. All the while she let out piercing yelps.

Emma skidded into the doorway. "What's wrong, who's hurt?"

"Get up here right now! This is the only safe place," Mother said.

Martin, ricocheting around the bed helplessly, vaulted into his sister's arms. She stumbled backward. He clung to her neck.

"Ooooohhh, Emma, Emma. . . . Get up here," Mother cried.

Emma set Martin on the toy chest, adjacent to the bed but at the moment much more stable. She swiveled her neck this way and that, trying to locate the source of the confusion. Finally she bent down and reached for the dust ruffle, apparently to peek at whatever demon might be hiding there.

"That's right where it went," Mother screamed.

Emma jerked back. "Where what went?"

"The rat," Mother said. "Joseph and I saw a huge rat run across the room."

Emma looked at Joseph. "Are you sure?"

"A big hairy one," Joseph said.

Emma reluctantly climbed onto the bed. Mother gathered her daughter into her arms as if reconciling with a rebellious child. Martin clambered to his sister.

"But Mother, I looked, too. There was nothing there. Joseph's playing another trick," Martin said.

"You shush! Don't tell me what I did or didn't see," Mother said.

Joseph broke into a triumphant grin behind Mother's back, then mouthed her reprimand to Martin wearing his sassiest expression.

Mother remained oblivious. "We can't have you boys sleeping in this room tonight. The rat could be anywhere. Its nest is probably up inside the mattress springs."

"If he'd gone up there he would have been crushed," Martin said.

A shiver ran down Mother's spine, and because they huddled together it transferred to the group. "Rat's are impossible to kill. Besides, where there's one there are bound to be many. It's too late to get rid of them tonight, though. We're all going to have to sleep in my bedroom."

"Why can't I sleep in my bed?" Emma asked.

"Your father will need a place to sleep. I can't have him barging in and waking the boys again once we calm them down. He'll have to use your room tonight. Now, the first thing we need to do is find a way out of this room, then we'll seal it off."

"Why don't we just go out the door?" Martin asked.

"I don't want any of you kids stepping on that floor. Do you hear me? Rats grab pant legs and climb right up." Mother scrutinized the children, apparently surprised they didn't understand this favorite rat pastime. "If we line up the furniture we can walk out on top of it, then we'll shut the door and stuff rags under the crack."

"That's a great plan. We can walk on this night stand." Joseph moved the table lamp onto the bed and dumped the other night stand items to the floor.

"Emma, twist the toy chest around so we can walk down it," Mother said.

Emma groaned. For a moment she tried to maneuver the big box while remaining on the bed, but when Mother turned to help Joseph untangle the nightstand from electrical cords Emma stepped to the floor and spun the chest to the required position.

Joseph strutted across the bed and down the toy chest holding the nightstand like the spoils of war. He set it where he could just reach a chair that he pulled into position at the end of the line thus creating safe passage to the sanctuary of the hallway.

"Right this way," Joseph said.

After everyone made the journey safely Joseph risked trips back to the bed. He bravely retrieved pillows, bedtime stories, and more. "What if Martin wets the bed? He'll need spare pajamas. I'll go get them."

Joseph was climbing onto the furniture again when Mother pulled him back. "We won't need extra pajamas. We have to seal the room." She pulled the door shut and began stuffing towels into the small gap beneath.

"Rats can squeeze through the tiniest of holes," Joseph said, already enthusiastic about this new task. He shoved rags under the door first with his hands, then with his feet for better leverage.

"It's time you boys get to bed," Mother said.

Joseph hopped to his feet. "Goodnight." He skipped down the hall and into his parents' bedroom.

Mother stood transfixed, mouth open. Finally, she looked down at Martin. "You, too. To bed."

Martin meandered down the hallway and into the bedroom. He climbed into the large bed beside Joseph. The thought of a rat attack felt so unnerving Martin couldn't sleep. Meanwhile, Joseph already snored. After fifteen minutes of lying motionless, but still feeling no signs of sleep, Martin climbed from the covers and crept toward the kitchen. He paused just outside the entrance.

Emma spoke to Mom. "Are you going to stay up to tell Dad what happened?"

"No, I'm too tired. I've written him a note." Mother handed Emma a slip of paper

"Dear LaVar, The mattress in the boys' bedroom is infested with rats so I put them in our bed." The girl looked at her mother, "The boys or the rats?"

Mother's brow wrinkled. "Do you think I need to explain that?"

Emma shrugged. She looked back at the paper and continued. "We'll have to throw out the bed in the morning. Emma will also sleep in our room tonight. Please spend the night in her room. Love, Delilah." Emma set the note down. "What are you going to do with it?"

"Tape it to my bedroom door. I already hung his pajamas on the knob."

The girl sighed. "Goodnight. I'm exhausted. Those boys better be asleep."

Martin hurried back to the room and buried his face in his pillow. He barely beat Emma and Mother. Joseph snored louder than ever.

"This will be fun. It's sort of like a sleepover," Mother whispered as she flicked on the reading lamp.

"What's so unusual? You sleep in my bed nearly every night," Emma said.

"You know this isn't the same. That's to get away from your father. Tonight he's not even here. We've just handled an emergency. We're celebrating. It's fun if you think of it that way. Besides, I've got something special."

"It's a school night. I've got to get some sleep."

"You know how much I love you, don't you?"

"Yes Mom, I know," sighed Emma. "Let's just go to sleep."

"This will only take a moment. You'll enjoy it, I promise." Martin heard Mother kiss Emma, then felt the older woman wiggle her way up to a sitting position. "In this box are love letters from the boys I knew before I met your father. I'm sure any day now a young man will begin taking an interest in you, and he will write you wonderful letters and poems like these. It's the most exciting time of life. Soon you'll be collecting drawers full of notes and memories. When you do, we'll have such fun sharing them. Here, let me read you some of my favorites."

Martin tried as hard as he could to sleep, but the tighter he shut his eyes the wider his ears opened. Mother read letter after letter. Between each she would explain how much she missed the author, recall her feelings at the time, and wonder what might have been.

Mother prattled on. "Charlie was the sweetest boy I ever knew. Beautiful green eyes and curly blonde hair. And smart . . . why my guess is he's a huge success about now."

"Then why didn't you marry him?" Emma blurted.

Martin held his breath. Just then the room lit brilliantly. What was going on?

"Oh, darn it. There's your father," Mother said. Martin realized the illumination came from the big car's headlights. Mother switched off the reading lamp. "Isn't it just like him to ruin our fun? Why does he have to come home, anyway? Stay quiet and we shouldn't have to talk to him."

Paper crumpled as Mother shoved the letters back into their box. Martin lay listening to Father's approaching footsteps, trying to imagine his reaction. A long silence followed, then the knob rattled. Martin tensed. When he heard the footsteps again, this time headed down the hall, he realized father had taken his pajamas and gone to Emma's room as instructed. Unbelievable. His heart pounded so furiously he couldn't make out Mother's excited whispers.

Martin remained completely still for a long, long time. He couldn't empty his mind, so he stared at the wall contemplating the moonlit shadows. While he never heard a sound from Emma, eventually he could tell from deepened breathing that Mother dozed.

\* \* \*

Mother jostled Martin as she climbed out of bed the next morning. "Did you have a good sleep?" she whispered.

He couldn't focus.

She lifted him to his feet. "You can help me make breakfast."

He followed her down the hall. She walked past the boys' bedroom and checked the rags, then peered into Emma's room. With a smile on her lips she motioned Martin to look inside. There slept Father, curled up in the undersized bed.

"He did as I asked." Awe and confidence mixed in her tone.

They moved on to the kitchen. Mother hummed a tune as she scrambled eggs. Martin watched in wonderment.

"What is this all about?" boomed a voice behind them.

Mother shrieked. It didn't compare to the screams from the night before, but it was shrill, nonetheless. Martin wheeled around, and there stood Father holding the note.

"Gosh darn it Delilah. Why do you have to screech every time I try to talk to you?" Father refused to use swear words, but he had substitutes that always got the point across.

"Why do you like startling me? A woman has a lot to be cautious of." As she spoke Mother ran her hands down her apron, as if searching for the confidence she'd felt moments before. Soon she collected herself. "I see you got my note. I'm glad you took it seriously. Joseph and I saw a rat in the boys' room. We got it sealed off, but I need you to throw out that old mattress and get traps in here this morning."

"Oh, that's what you need me to do, is it?" he said sarcastically. His features hardened. "Well, I won't do any such thing. You seem to think money grows on trees. I'm not going to throw our savings into the wind to replace a perfectly good mattress just because you're hallucinating. I had half-a-mind to get everyone up and put them in their own beds, but it was well past midnight and I could see it would not be worth the effort."

"LaVar, you can't ask your boys to sleep in an infested bed. I think we did well to get the room sealed off. You should be proud, not angry."

"Pfff. If there is a single rat in that room you can boil my shoe and I'll eat it for dinner. Let's go have a look."

Joseph wandered into the kitchen, rubbing his eyes with his fists.

"Tell your father about the rat last night," Mother said.

Joseph hesitated. "I . . . I . . . at first I thought it was a mouse."

"A mouse?" Mother sounded astonished. "That's bigger than the biggest mouse you'll ever see. It's definitely a rat, and I'd be surprised if it's alone. I'll bet there's a nest."

"Well, we'll know soon enough," Father said. "I've got to tell you Joseph, it disappoints me that you're a part of this. I'm not surprised the others in this family are taken in by such foolishness, but I expect more from you. Well, let's go take a look,"

Mother grabbed Father's hand and attempted to hold him back. "LaVar, I don't ask you for much, but if you get rats spread all over this house I'll . . . I'll . . . let's just please throw out that old mattress."

Father broke away easily. He spoke over his shoulder as he strode toward the sealed bedroom. "Only if the boys would prefer sleeping on the floor. Come on Joseph."

The rest of the family followed to see what havoc the rodents had wreaked.

Father turned the knob. The door wouldn't swing open because of the rags jammed beneath. He threw his shoulder into it and fell into the room.

"What the heck?" Father asked. "Are you sure you didn't lock some kind of deranged maniac in here?"

"We had to climb out on top of the furniture," Martin explained.

Father glared at him as if he'd lost his marbles.

The little boy continued with less enthusiasm. "So the rats couldn't crawl up our pants."

"Darn it, Delilah. What are you teaching these children?"

Mother brought her elbows in to her stomach and sucked on her knuckles.

Father mockingly tiptoed deeper into the room. He peered back at his family as he pretended to sneak up on the bed. "The element of surprise is still on our side." He reached under the mattress and flipped it against the wall. Stuff tumbled everywhere.

"YIIIII! Now do you see what I'm saying," Mother screamed, as if she thought the rats had done the flipping.

Father glared at her. "Delilah, get a hold of yourself. One day that ridiculous screech is going to deafen me."

"That was nothing. You should've heard her last night. I thought the windows were going to break," offered Martin.

Father shook his head in disgust. "No rodents yet. Let's take a look under the box springs." He flung them on top of the mattress. There'd been no rat. There wasn't even a hole for him to climb into.

"There's my slingshot!" Joseph bolted in and picked up the toy.

Father locked eyes with Mother. She seemed unable to look away. Words would only have weakened the harsh message, and since Father was a master at this sort of thing, he didn't use any. Then he simply walked out the door and down the hall to reclaim his own room.

When he'd gone Mother staggered to where the bed had been.

She crumbled to her knees next to the pile of toys. Her expression became hollow as she sorted through the items, one by one, hoping to find a rat. Martin stood behind her, not daring to break the silence.

## Chapter 11

A cacophony of barks and yowls yanked my eyes open. I hadn't expected the world to be so dark. Moxie and Bailey weren't in their places. "Sounds like they're after your neighbor lady's cat."

Martin opened his eyes, lips curled in disgust. He waved off my concern with a flick of his wrist. "Pfff. I hope they eat that damned pest for ruining my story. Where was I?" He shut his eyes again.

I pressed the illumination button on the side of my watch. "Oh, shit. We're going to have to pick this up another time." I sprang to my feet and took a long stride, then turned back. "How much longer until this story gets to the part about you being my father?"

"I already told you, the background is critical. You've got to know who we were in order to understand what we did."

It wasn't that I minded learning who they were. In fact, I found it fascinating. But so far we'd covered less than a twenty-four hour period decades long gone. At this rate I'd never learn my true origins. I prayed that the time spent becoming comfortable in one another's presence would eventually pay off. "I'm just anxious to learn what happened."

"If you'll be patient, you'll learn. Same time next week?"

A week? "How about same time tomorrow?"

He shook his head. "I can't just drop everything to tell you stories."

I looked around. What was left to drop? Clearly, yard care and housework didn't take up much of his time. I wished I could have mentioned that, but I didn't dare make a joke. Even though he'd warmed considerably on this visit, there were no guarantees things would stay that way if I let down my guard. For now, my only real option was to play by whatever rules he set. "Yeah, same time next week." I hurried to my Cherokee and sped off, anxious to get home to Sara.

Martin had told the tale ably, as if it were a favorite fable. His words revealed for me the structure of my family, something I'd never before seen– or even considered. I'd been somewhat aware that the family worked in a peculiar way, but oblivious to the reasons, having never even imagined any of my older relatives as young people faced with difficult decisions.

As I pulled onto our street and pushed the garage door opener, I stopped rehashing the stories I'd learned about my family's past. I imagined Sara cuddled in bed, recognizing the rumble of the garage door, and wondering why I'd stayed out so late. What could I say to forestall her anger?

I rehearsed my explanation. "I found Martin," I'd say. "You know how he is. He has such a fragile psyche, and I felt like if I didn't give him my full attention I might never get to speak with him again." I climbed out of the vehicle and walked toward the door.

I noticed a note taped to the knob.

*Tom,*
I started labor. You didn't answer your phone. Where are you? Mom took me to hospital. Come quickly, I need you!
Love, Sara.

My heart skipped a beat. It was too early for the baby. We had five weeks to go. Not only that, the dragon lady was at Sara's side instead of me. I scrambled back to my Cherokee and pounded the steering wheel while the chain drive hauled the garage door up. I backed out, then sped toward the hospital. Had I become completely incompetent overnight? How could a man like me be a father? How could I have been so thoughtless? What must Sara be thinking? It hadn't even occurred to me labor could come so soon. I couldn't help wondering which experience Sara was finding more painful— labor, or listening to her mother rag-on about me.

Once my tires jolted against the curb, I jumped from the vehicle. I sprinted toward the hospital entrance. Two women exited the building, one of them waddling. I didn't look straight at them until I'd nearly passed. "Sara! Are you all right? What's happening?"

I looked up at the other woman, my mother-in-law, Irene. In her expression, I read every name she'd called me over the past two hours. I looked to Sara, praying her face would never become capable of such contortion.

In her kind countenance I read some frustration, but mostly concern; and I wondered how she always managed such beauty. I'd heard it said many times that women are most attractive when pregnant, though I thought it a white lie. With respect to the woman I'd married, however, the statement was true.

"Is everything all right?" Sara asked. "I've been worried sick about you."

"I'm fine. The important question is, are you all right?"

"False labor," interjected Irene, "but it easily could've been the real thing, and you should've been here for her. Sorry isn't good enough. There's simply no excuse."

Sara sighed. "Mother, please. You promised."

"Irene's right," I said. "I should have been here."

"Where have you been?" Sara asked.

I put my arm around her shoulder. "I found Martin. We had a long conversation tonight."

She frowned. "Tom, I thought we'd agreed on this. Nothing good can come of spending time with that man."

I opened the Cherokee's passenger door. "Let me help you

in." I assisted her into position. The flurry of activity tripped up our burgeoning argument, just as I'd intended. I'd discuss everything, but not while Irene cheered on the sidelines.

"Thank you for all of your help tonight," I said without looking at Sara's mother. I shut the passenger door, isolating my wife inside the vehicle.

I hurried to my side, but couldn't make it before Irene tapped on her daughter's window. Sara hit the button and the pane of glass disappeared into the door. "You be sure to call me if anything else happens. I'm here for you."

I started the engine and backed out while Irene walked along beside the window. "Thanks again," I said as if the offer had been directed toward me. "I'd better get her home. She's sleeping for two, you know. You be sure to drive safely. Good-bye." We were rolling forward by the time I finished talking.

Sara slugged me on the shoulder. I pushed the button on my door panel to roll her window back up. "Don't be so obvious in your contempt."

"Obvious? Are you kidding? I got us out of there without a fight, and she's back there feeling satisfied that she told me off. The second you got frustrated with me her spirits rose. Did you hear the tone in her voice as we left? She practically sang. I'm happy I brought her such joy."

"I couldn't believe how quickly you got me out of there. That's no way to handle a pregnant woman."

"Hey, in times of war . . . you know. You may just owe me for saving your life. The way I see it, I pulled both of our butts into a foxhole under heavy fire."

She shook her head playfully. "I guess you're going to try to take credit for saving the baby as well."

"That's right, thanks for reminding me. Three people spared by one heroic act . . . an entire family. I'll probably be awarded a medal for that one day." I grinned, and she smiled back. Something in her expression generated within me the same electrical surge I'd felt on that hot summer night four years before when our eyes first met. "There's also something else, Sara, and I'm not trying to duck it. I let you down tonight. I feel terrible about that. I've been letting you down for some time, even after you brought it to my attention. I haven't been there for you, and I'm sorry."

She surprised me by continuing with my analogy. "I had to turn to the enemy for assistance."

I smiled at her, then laughed. "Maybe I shouldn't have been in such a hurry to get you out of there. I'd like your mother to overhear this conversation."

"Let her think it went badly. You can't deny her all of her pleasures. After all, I'm her only child, and you took me away. Furthermore, I agree with her. How could you ever hope to be good enough for me?"

I knew she meant to make fun of her mother's opinion, but the comment jolted me. I could only manage a forced smile in response. How could I hope to be good enough?

Sara eyed me in the temporary glow of a street lamp. We lost the light abruptly as we passed beneath. Soon, the radiance from another grew to take its place. Like a metronome beating cadence to our conversation, the light alternately built and disappeared. I felt my wife inspect my expression each time the car's interior lit. The delay became uncomfortable.

"Tom, what's wrong with you?" Sara finally asked.

I conjured an expression of incredulity and looked at her briefly with it, feeling thankful for my obligation to keep an eye on the road. "What's that supposed to mean?"

"I didn't want to say this. I don't even like to think it; but you've forced me." I heard in her tone something of her mother, as if the older lady's poisonous words were about to germinate. Sara's beautiful face hardened. "You're letting me down, Tom. I believe in you. Why aren't you willing to believe in yourself? Ever since—"

"Wait a minute." The pit of my stomach sank. "Where are

you going with this? Are you saying this is an issue of my character?"

"Did we or didn't we agree it's best not to bring Martin into our lives?"

"We didn't. We agreed I would take more time to think about whether or not I should get in contact with him. I did, and I came to the same conclusion as before."

"How much longer did you take to think about it?"

"What does it matter?" Clenched teeth emphasized my words. "I've got the right to get to know my own father. I knew how you felt about him so I just quit discussing the topic with you. It wasn't a lie, it was a courtesy."

Her eyes told me she wasn't fooled. For nearly a minute she didn't respond. It seemed an eternity. Finally she said, "Whatever happened to the man I married, the man I could trust?"

I couldn't have felt more pierced if she'd buried a dagger in my heart. Trust formed the foundation of our relationship. And I had violated it . . . but only under extraordinary circumstances. Still, she'd swiped her trust away from me, or at least suspended it. Worse yet, I couldn't refuse its return. I felt at her mercy.

Her eyes penetrated me as I puzzled through the situation, and I didn't welcome the pressure. I sensed her apprehension over my self-control, and I knew she had good reason.

I felt it slipping. "We left somebody on the curb who would be delighted with this little turn of events. Does all this come out of left field, or is it some idea Irene planted in your head?"

"This has nothing to do with my mom." Sara's voice broke. She pulled herself close to the passenger side door.

"Nothing to do with your mom?" I mocked, aware I was taking our relationship into uncharted territory. "I tried to apologize, but that isn't enough for you, is it? You want a pound of my flesh."

I gave her just a moment to answer, a moment she didn't seize, before I continued. "I can't tell you how thankful I am it was only false labor." The term rolled off my tongue, dripping with condescension, and the result sounded even more belittling than I'd intended. I didn't bother looking to see how much injury I'd inflicted. Like a bomber pilot preferring to remain ignorant of the damage his payload wreaks I kept my eyes glued to the road. There was some lesson to teach her, if only I could stumble upon the right words.

I plowed forward. "I don't have to apologize when things don't go exactly as you expect, Sara. I can't be held responsible for bends in the river. That isn't part of the marriage contract. Relationships don't come with money back guarantees if you're not completely satisfied."

I paused for a breath, or maybe to convince myself I was making progress. I hoped she would use the opportunity to defend herself. She didn't. Her silence disturbed me, and I decided I must force her into the fray. "Let me ask you a question, Sara. Do you think I'm deriving some obscene pleasure out of watching my life fall apart just when you'd like to see it fall together?"

She seemed in the midst of some breathing exercise. I waited for an answer through a number of heavy exhalations. Finally she pulled a tissue from her purse, dabbed at her eyes, then blew her nose. "Your question is ridiculous. I've always been supportive, and you know it. Sometimes I wonder if I care about you more than you care about yourself. Every day you go to a job you don't like. That can't be good for you. I've let you know you have my support to make a career change, and you won't listen."

"We were talking about Martin. How is this relevant?"

"It's totally relevant. I want the best for you. Just because I don't want Martin to come into our lives and harm you, or me, or the baby doesn't mean I'm not supportive. You have to look at the whole picture."

"The whole picture?"

"You know what I mean. Now it's my turn, Tom. Let me ask you a question. Aren't you sensitive enough to understand that the pain I felt tonight was real? Look at my body. It's not even mine anymore. Can you imagine how this feels?" Her voice quavered. I wondered if I were even capable of experiencing such raw emotion. "At first, you were the one who wanted a child so badly, but I'm the one who has to make the sacrifice. I've given up my career, my body, my goals . . . everything is on hold . . . and all so I can feel lousy and be treated like a burden. I was scared and lonely tonight, and all I wanted was you. I kept wondering why you weren't there. So when I find out it's because you've been hanging out with Martin, what do you expect me to do? Tell you I'm happy for the two of you? Well, I'm not.

"I've worked all of my life to put myself in a secure position. I accomplished that by relying on myself because . . . because I didn't know how to trust. Then you taught me. You'll never understand how much I admire you for that. You said you wanted to take care of me, and you backed it up with action. So I violated the major rule I'd built my life around, and became vulnerable to you.

"As a girl I dreamed of Prince Charming riding in on a white stallion and sweeping me off my feet. Of course, girls grow into women, and I'd given up on fairytales long before we met. You awakened something, though. You reminded me of my dream."

I recalled my many attempts to sweep her off her feet. This had never been part of the plan. A tear rolled down my cheek. I collected it, and any others that might try to follow with a forearm swipe across my face. I felt disgraceful. I pulled to the side of the road, closed my eyes, and thought about her words.

She continued. "I wasn't throwing darts at the phonebook trying to decide which man I should tame. You came along and told me of your immense goals. You were persistent, and eventually I bought in. So yes, I'm holding you responsible for the bends in the river, not because they're there, but because you promised to get us through them. I'm not asking for my money back. I'm asking for the man I married. It's not the earth-shattering insult you want to make it. It's just a simple little question of concern, and the answer you just gave only makes me miss the man I married all the more. Where is he?"

I let her words sink in, beginning to see things from her perspective. "I'm sorry, Sara. I never dreamed I could have become so confused. At the moment nothing's going right, but I'll get it back together. I promise."

She kissed me on the cheek. "I know you will. Just don't let it take too long."

\* \* \*

The following morning I woke early. I went upstairs and made breakfast.

Sara walked into the kitchen as I scrambled eggs. "Are you trying to earn brownie points?"

"I could sure use some."

She nodded agreement. "So, was the knowledge Wise Old Martin imparted to you worth what we went through last night?"

I wanted to make my experience sound as important as I could. "Last night Martin told me about his earliest memory. That brought a whole string of experiences to his mind, and he just kept on going. The stories I heard yesterday evening explain a lot. I think eventually I can understand why things came out the way they did."

She turned her back and walked to the kitchen table. "So, you'll keep seeing him?"

"I'd like to. I feel it's important to, but you tell me. I realized last night my relationship with you is far more important to me than understanding him. That is . . . if I have to choose between them."

She eyed me intently. I wondered if she was imagining fitting me with cement shoes. "What's the point, Tom? How can you believe what he says? You're really expecting a fifty-year-old psychotic to remember his childhood clearly? It's ridiculous."

I recalled once pegging him similarly, but I now knew there was more to him than the impression he'd created in the park. "There's no question he sees the world through a bent lens, but I already knew that. The important thing is I'm aware of the prescription and it's not hard to make a correction. His memory of his childhood is very good. I'm not denying there's something wrong with Martin. It's something terrible I don't yet understand, but it doesn't disqualify him from having viable memories."

Doubt dripped from her expression. "What, of value, has he told you?"

"He has a lot to say that's important to me. He knows my family's history. I don't. He knows the origin of many family traditions. I don't. He's my biological father." I searched for the slightest glimmer of understanding in her eyes.

She watched silently. Finally she asked, "How can you be so interested in discovering the past at the expense of the present?"

"I just don't want to repeat the mistakes."

Her expression revealed disgust. "Well, if you ask me, you were doing a much better job before you became so obsessed with avoiding them."

"The negative things that have happened recently aren't due to my curiosity about my family. That they're happening at the same time is coincidence, maybe even opportunity. If I can improve our lives by understanding my forebearers, won't we be better off? Doesn't that make sense to you?"

"Not much," she said.

"But a little . . . Sara, our life's about to change in a very important way. You've seen what miserable fathers the males in my family are. I believe John Lewis was a good man. He adopted me, but died before he could teach me anything about being a man. So who do you think I learned from? Nobody. Please, allow me this shot at understanding what they should've done. I'll learn from their mistakes. Isn't that better than making my own? I promise you, in the long run it'll pay off."

I saw the first glimmer of empathy in her eyes, but forgiveness wasn't there. "See Martin if you must. There's only one promise I want from you. Be with me when I have the baby."

# Chapter 12

Six days passed. I'd spent part of the week interviewing replacements for Daisy. The pool to choose from depressed me. The rest of the week overflowed with the dual tasks of originating and processing my own loans.

On the morning of my next meeting with Martin I handed Sara a gift. Her eyes lit up. She loved presents. She set it on her lap and admired the fine wrapping. "There's no way you did this," she said indicating the French wire ribbon bow.

I shook my head. "I paid a professional. Don't you love the way the gold satin looks against the salmon paper?"

She smiled. "It's unlike you to care about such things. What's going on?"

"I know how much you care. That's enough for me. Open it."

She slid a slender fingernail beneath the tape on the side of the package. "Salmon?" she laughed. "I thought that was one of those colors masculinity made you unwilling to recognize."

"I still think it's a better description of a fish than a hue, but I'm starting to come around. It might not be too late for me to learn to appreciate some of the finer things."

She carefully removed the paper, as if she planned on using it again, and opened the box. She lifted out a black leather overnight bag. "What's this?"

"Inside I've packed everything you could possibly need for an emergency trip to the hospital including a brand new robe, bath oils, baby powder . . . everything."

Her face shone with pleasure. "Why?"

Now the hard part. I swallowed. "Tonight's my evening with Martin, remember?"

She nodded.

"I've got to go. Please understand. I've attached a fresh battery to my cell phone and I've got another fully charged one in my pocket. My watch alarm is set to go off at eight p. m. just in case, I won't stay a moment later than that." I waited, nervous for her response.

"Thank you, Tom." The words sounded like a beautiful melody.

I kissed her on the forehead. "I'm off to work, then Martin's. See you tonight. I love you."

* * *

I arrived at Martin's right on time. I eagerly anticipated learning all I could, despite Sara's premonitions.

He was in his garage. When his eyes met mine he seemed startled. Then he checked his watch, set down his tools, and headed past me toward the house without a word. I noticed he'd been working on a big antique wall clock. His dogs fell into step behind, as if it was the most ordinary thing in the world to parade around the yard single file. He marched up the porch steps like a programmed automaton. I half expected him to grab a timecard and punch in. He then headed to the far end and sat down in his lounge chair. At that point his behavior changed to the opposite extreme. He wriggled and writhed like a worm evacuating rain soaked mud, as he settled in amongst the cushions. Meanwhile, the dogs twirled in ever tightening circles, zeroing in on the exact spots they'd lain the last time I visited.

I observed the gyrations, barely able to suppress laughter. I'd planned to ask him what he'd been up to and considered telling him about the impending birth of my daughter, but where would such small talk fit in? I got the overwhelming feeling he didn't care about events that didn't directly impact him anyway. He'd never even asked about my wife or my dog, and I remembered vividly his disinterest in his own brother.

The moment Martin was comfortable he closed his eyes and screwed up his face. This time it took only a moment to launch into his narrative of childhood events, almost as if opening some old novel to a dog-eared page.

So abruptly did the story begin that it seemed he'd started mid-sentence. I clambered for a seat, and had to settle for the same damn milk crate I'd perched upon seven days earlier. I closed my eyes, anxious to again intrude upon the lives of my closest relations, to visit them from a fourth dimension. Martin's story, or at least the story I experienced when what he said was mixed with my own knowledge, soon enveloped me.

* * *

For one year only, nineteen-fifty-two, Martin attended the same school with Emma and Joseph. Emma was a Spring Creek Elementary School sixth grader, due to graduate to Valley View Junior High the next spring. Joseph attended third grade, and Martin had begun first. It didn't take Martin long to learn his brother and sister's routine. Always the same thing for breakfast: hot milk poured over toast; and afterwards they'd take the same route to school, right past Grandma Pearl and Grandpa Mel's front door. Mother's parents lived in a whitewashed cottage three blocks from the Crump house. Martin loved them.

It didn't matter how quietly the kids approached, Grandpa's baritone always rang out, "Pearl, here come the kids." They'd round the big pine tree that shaded the house, wondering what had given them away. Of course, they'd never ask. The spy contest was a favorite part of the morning ritual. They wouldn't change it if they could.

Grandpa Mel, his tall frame bent forward over the porch railing as far as possible would say, "Well, my, my. Look how big you children are getting." Martin felt buoyant as he raced Joseph toward Grandpa's arms. The old man would lift both boys as Grandma walked onto the porch, drying her hands on her apron. She'd wrap a loving arm around Emma, and Martin would admire his sister's wide smile.

Despite the regularity, there was one particular day that stood out in Martin's memory. "You two are getting too heavy for me to lift," Grandpa said, struggling to straighten himself.

Emma pulled on Grandma's arm, and the old woman leaned down. "How did I look in the dress yesterday? I didn't get to see you after the meeting ended."

"You were beautiful, dear," the white haired lady said. "I told your grandpa that I couldn't have been more proud. He felt bad he didn't get to see you. Isn't that right Mel?"

Mel nodded. "Maybe you can bring the dress over here and model it."

"Grandpa, why don't you have to go to church?" Joseph asked.

The old man's brow furrowed. He looked at his wife, as if she might know the answer.

"Grandpa is an adult, and adults can do with their time as they see fit," she explained

"How long until I'll be an adult?" Joseph asked.

"You don't need to worry about that. Those kind of things have a way of taking care of themselves." Mel set the boys down and worked an open palm into the small of his back. "Will you be back this afternoon to teach your grandma and me what you learned today?"

"Yes." All three children spoke at once.

"Good, we'll be looking forward to it." Grandpa Mel waggled his knobby index finger forward in constricting circles until it collided with the tip of Martin's nose. Martin smirked, pleased to have earned the attention of the kind old man. "Pay close heed to your teachers today, will you?"

"We will." The children said good-bye and left their grandparents standing arm in arm on the porch.

Emma lagged behind, but Martin overheard her comment to their grandparents. "Sometimes . . . I wish you two were our parents."

Martin turned. Grandpa and Grandma stared at the girl as if she'd spoken in a foreign tongue. After a long silence Grandma Pearl spoke. "Bye-bye Emma, have a good day at school."

Martin wasn't certain if he felt more upset by Emma's comment, or the response she'd received. He shuffled along, and surprised even himself when he said, "I'm going to climb to the top of that mountain one day."

Joseph stopped. He gazed up at the gigantic pinnacle, Mount Olympus, which had loomed over them for their entire lives, then he regarded Martin. "Why would anyone, least of all a pip-squeak like you, ever want to do a useless thing like that? I can tell you without looking, there isn't anything up there worth seeing. You can see all you need from right here."

"Maybe I want to go there because there isn't anything. It might be nice and lonely. I'll bet you can see forever, too."

"Why would you want to be lonely?" Emma asked.

"What's so bad about being alone?"

"You're talking nonsense. Can't you see it's nothing but a huge cliff?" Joseph asked.

Martin felt insulted. He started to respond, then stopped himself.

Joseph didn't let the silent moment last. "I bet you never climb that mountain. It's too far to walk, there's no reason to do it, and you're too little. You're always bragging on things you'll never do."

Martin scowled at his brother, but he couldn't think of anything to say. Why couldn't he ever fire off great comebacks? Joseph made it look so easy. Martin pursed his lips and turned to the mountaintop. He didn't take his eyes off his objective until he walked into school and the door swung shut behind him.

After school the three children met at the flagpole to walk home. They weren't two blocks into their journey when Mother wheeled around the corner in her little car. She pulled over, and they ran to her.

"Get in," she ordered.

They clambered into their usual spots. Mother manipulated the gear lever, then grabbed the steering wheel with both hands as the car jolted forward. Without any explanation Mother headed north, away from their home, and soon they were in farm country.

"Where are we going, Mom?" Emma asked.

Mother faced Emma, and for the first time Martin noticed she'd been crying. "How could you?"

Martin wondered what she meant. Emma looked confused as well.

Mother stepped harder on the accelerator. When they reached the community of Sugarhouse she made a left hand turn down the main corridor, then veered onto a side street and stopped.

"Get out right here."

Martin climbed from the car behind his sister and brother, and stood on the curb awaiting his mother. She didn't leave her seat. Instead the car revved and sped away. Martin watched in disbelief as the automobile disappeared into the distance. Behind them loomed a tall red brick building, church-like in design. It lacked the familiarity of their neighborhood church, though. Martin didn't want to look at it. It seemed to have a foreboding presence. He stared back down the street in the direction the car had vanished.

"Salt Lake City Children's Orphanage," Emma read aloud. She remained staring at the letters standing in relief above the door of the red brick building.

"Orphanage?" Joseph's cool demeanor broke. He stepped into the street and bent his neck in the direction the car had gone.

"She'll be back. Don't worry." Emma bit her lip and looked thoughtful.

"What makes you think that?" Joseph asked.

"She will. She's our mother," Emma answered.

"That doesn't mean she'll ever return," Joseph said. "Martin will probably like it here, though. This place is nice and lonely. As lonely as it gets. I guess you won't have to climb that mountain after all."

Martin reached for his sister and cried. Emma toted him to a bus bench. Joseph followed, taking his seat on the curb a good distance away. He pulled a candy bar from his pocket and unwrapped it. Martin watched enviously as his big brother licked away chocolate to reveal a caramel base.

Martin looked away. He rocked in his sister's arms, trying to battle his emotions. He never liked change of any kind, and he hated this. A sense of abandonment overcame him. It felt like being suspended by a coathanger in an ever-expanding void.

Normally, when Martin got home from school he took a nap. Today, though he wanted to, he couldn't change his routine. His eyes were determined to close, and close they did.

He had no idea how long he'd been sleeping on his sister's lap when he woke to the sound of his mother's voice. "I hear you'd like to find new parents. Well, this is where you do it."

Martin looked up to see the little car with its door swung open toward them. Mother sat in the driver's seat, looking impatient. Martin didn't wait for permission. He scrambled from Emma's lap and got into the passenger seat.

"Grandma Pearl told you we wanted new parents?" Emma asked.

"She gave me a lecture on how children should be raised. Don't you think I have enough on my hands just trying to keep your father happy? Why would you make your grandmother angry with me too?"

"Grandma Pearl never gets angry, nor gives lectures. You've misunderstood."

"Don't you sass me, young lady. Why did you tell her I'm a bad parent?"

"If that's how she took it, it's not what I meant. It's just that they seem so happy. I want our family to be that way. Can we please go home now?" Emma spoke contritely as she climbed into the car.

"What sort of trick is Joseph playing now?" Mother asked.

"Trick?" Emma asked.

Martin looked out the window to the spot where he'd last seen Joseph sitting on the curb. A discarded Black Cow wrapper lay in the gutter.

Mother groaned. "You kids are going to be the death of me." She turned off the engine, stepped out of the car, and slammed the door. Emma climbed back out of the passenger side.

Martin gripped the seat, fearful of being pulled from the car and forced to assist in the search. He'd been tricked into getting out of the car at an unfamiliar destination once today. It wasn't going to happen again.

Mother and Emma searched on foot up and down the street. Martin watched them check alleyways, around corners, even into the orphanage. Eventually they returned to the car.

"It would be just like him to get himself kidnapped," Mother said.

Martin's heart fluttered, even as he told himself that Mother's fear wasn't possible.

Mother drove the car around the neighborhood, from one block to another. Martin peered into every cubby hole in sight, sure he'd see a sign of his brother. He figured he knew the kind of hiding spot Joseph liked best. After a half hour of searching they pulled up to a police station. Again Martin stayed in the car while Emma and Mother went inside. Mother came out sounding exhausted. "He's lost. Serves him right. I've had it with his pranks. Had it."

Martin felt sick. He couldn't believe how easy it was to lose a person, especially one who'd seemed so permanent. Sure, lots of people came and went in life, but family? Not them. What would it be like without a big brother around? Life wasn't worth living. Then he foresaw even bigger trouble. The thought of facing Father with such news felt more terrifying than the loss of Joseph itself.

A somber mood filled the car on the ride home. Martin went straight to his room. He'd gladly stay there all night, even all week, if it would keep him out of Father's way. He heard voices and phone calls throughout the evening. Every once in a while either Emma or Mother would look in on him. But mostly he just stayed curled in bed, shivering.

It was after eleven at night when the doorbell rang. What could that mean? Martin could stand it no longer. He had to know what the news was. He crept from his bed and cracked the door open a tiny bit. There, standing at the front threshold with a policeman by his side, was Joseph. Martin's feet grew wings. He rushed to his brother and embraced him, squeezing with all his might and looking up to the heavens at the same moment.

The smiling police officer nearly filled his field of vision. "This boy seems to resemble the one you're missing. Will he do, Brother Crump?"

Father pulled Joseph into the home by the ear. "I'm sorry he caused you so much trouble. It won't happen again."

"Who, Joseph? He wasn't any trouble at all. He's well mannered and intelligent, a great kid. All the guys at the station loved him. I wish there were a lot more like him."

Father eyed his son skeptically. "I guess he forgot it was bad manners to nearly give his parents heart failure by running away."

"He didn't exactly run away. He was headed toward your home when our patrol car came across him. He said he just wanted to get to bed."

"Well, he went about that the hard way, didn't he?" Father said.

The policeman looked ready to say more, but Father stopped

him with a raised palm. "Thanks again, Officer." And he shut the door.

Martin watched the policeman's back-lit silhouette through the drapery as he stood in front of the porch light. It looked like he might ring the bell again, then he shrugged his shoulders, replaced his hat, and jogged down the porch steps.

As the shadow of the officer disappeared Father removed his belt. "This is going to hurt me a whole lot more than it will hurt you," he said in a hoarse whisper. "Drop those britches."

\* \* \*

The alarm on my wristwatch shrieked. All four of us jumped—Martin, me, and both dogs. I switched it off. Eight o'clock seemed like such an easy deadline to meet when I made it, but now that it had arrived I wished I hadn't promised to be home so early. "I've got to go. When can we do this again?"

Martin looked dazed. "You're leaving this very moment?"

"I promised my wife."

"You're sure you'll be back?" He sounded suspicious.

"I'll be back. I can return tomorrow night."

"I'd prefer to meet on the 24th of each month," he said.

"You want to meet on a specific day of the month. Are you serious?"

"We met in the park on November 24th. You showed up here last week on April 24th. I've thought about that. It can't be coincidence. Let's stick with what's worked. Besides, getting ready to meet with you on a week's notice was very difficult."

I glanced around, wondering what he'd gotten ready. "How in the world did you ever notice the dates matched up like that?"

He ignored my question. "Can you be here on the 24th of May?"

I opened my day-planner to the date. It was a Saturday and

Sara's relatives would be in town to meet our newborn baby. "No, I can't. Normally, I'm sure, the 24th would be fine. It's usually one of the better days on my calendar," I said sarcastically, "but not next month. Can we pick another day?"

"I'd really prefer if we stuck with the 24th. Why can't you come?"

"Personal reasons." I didn't even try to suppress a groan, still uncertain any event in my life mattered to him. I had to stand for something. As ridiculous as it seemed, it was a relevant issue.

"I guess we'll have to skip a month," he reasoned, if you can call it reasoning. "How's the 24th of June?"

I hoped my grunts and gestures told him how annoying I found this. I flipped to the page, realizing it would be impossible to win. How had I become party to such a bizarre decision-making process? "June is fine."

"Okay, but my schedule's busy. Are you sure you can make it? I can't wait around."

"I'll make it," I reiterated, jotting a note in my day-planner. "Tuesday, June 24th, six in the evening." I separated myself from the milk crate and offered a handshake. Martin reached out. He held my hand limply. I fought to hide the sensation it triggered within me, like handling a dead fish.

# Chapter 13

Sara grabbed at her abdomen and moaned.

I rose on my elbow and reached across her to turn on the bedside lamp. I'd been unable to shut my eyes, having already risen three previous times for the same reason on this night. "Are you all right?"

She blew puffy breaths as the contraction continued, just as she'd been instructed in birthing class.

I noted the time on a pad of paper, 1:03 a.m. lasting 25 seconds, and computed the interval since the last event. Still no pattern.

"I'm fine now. Go back to bed." She swung her feet to the floor in preparation to wander the house, just as she had for most of the night.

The baby could come any day, and her anxiety kept growing as the due date neared. After she left the room I sat on the edge of the bed, listening to her roam around. Her aimless wanderings took her to the kitchen, closet, nursery, laundry, and every other corner of the house. Earlier in the evening I'd given up following her. She had no real objective, therefore I couldn't be of any assistance. Still, it felt wrong for me to consider sleep.

It continued like this through the night. Finally, starting at 2:38 in the morning the pains began making some sense. A one-minute contraction had become the norm, and when it was followed by a respite of just fourteen minutes before the next spasm started at 2:53 I dutifully reported the results. I planned for the future, adding the known interval to the time the most recent cramping had begun, then subtracting a small amount to anticipate our progress. I correctly predicted events at 3:07, 3:23, and 3:37. I became a combination mathematical genius/sorcerer, arranging my wife's timetable of discomfort and extreme discomfort. I fancied she was somehow impressed with my skills each time she would nod, teeth gritted, to inform me her womb again convulsed according to the schedule I'd set.

At 7 a.m. the intervals finally reduced to the magical seven minute mark, the point at which the doctor promised to take action. I'd already loaded the Cherokee, called Dr. Lowrey, and spoken to both our mothers. I helped Sara into the passenger seat, and we left for the delivery room. It felt more like a trip to the dry cleaners than the rushed scene I'd been anticipating.

Inside the brightly lit hospital the nauseating smell of antiseptic assaulted me. An orderly with a wheelchair pushed me aside as he eased Sara down. A nurse helped transfer my wife to a bed. A candy striper delivered paper cups full of ice chips for sucking. It went on and on. I felt more like an unused IV pole than a participant in the process.

I forced my way to the bedside and took Sara's hand in mine. "You ready?"

She gritted her teeth and gave me the thumbs up.

"Okay, here comes a contraction," Dr. Lowrey said, looking at a monitor. "You're fully dilated so let's go."

Sara began the puffy breathing.

"Push, Sara," the doctor said.

She squeezed my hand as she bore down, grunting mightily.

"Good. Now again," the doctor said.

The first contraction passed. Sara gathered strength during the gap before the next onset of heavy labor. Again it came time to push, and again we were unsuccessful. We repeated the process over and over. Each time we went through the routine Sara became weaker. Dripping with sweat, she gasped for air during the breaks.

Finally, after hours of work with no progress, the doctor said, "It's time to make a choice. Sara's not strong enough to push this baby out. I can give her some assistance with forceps, or we can do a c-section."

I looked at Sara.

Her eyes pleaded. "I don't want to be cut open."

"I guess we should try the forceps," I said.

The doctor nodded, looking pleased, and one of the nurses left the room at his signal.

She returned pushing a cart covered with a sterile green cloth. She lifted the cloth, and there in the midst of a number of other instruments, sat the forceps. They were at least twice as large as I'd imagined they would be, huge chrome salad tongs.

"You'll be doing most of the work," the doctor told my sweat soaked wife as he inserted the two pieces of metal into her and twisted them into place.

I tasted bile.

The forceps made a slight clang as the doctor fit them together at the hinge. "Ready to push? My job will be just to guide," he said, as if he didn't think we believed him.

We shouldn't have. At the critical moment where the obstetrician recognized that we'd passed the point of no return, that the initial pull had lodged the baby's skull between Sara's hips, he did what he had to do. He did it automatically. He did what I, for I love my wife, could never have done. Nothing I'd heard in our monotonous six week birthing class prepared me for this. The doctor put his foot on the table. Then he leaned back like an overweight slalom water-skier plowing along behind an underpowered boat. He gritted his teeth; tendons and veins stratified his neck. Sara screamed. She hit and held a high pitched and relentless note, the sound like metal on metal in an engine on the verge of seizing. Her spinal anesthetic was entirely insufficient to cover the sensation of bones being rearranged, of flesh ripping. If I weren't mute with terror in that moment of ultimate confusion I might have pled, "The baby isn't worth this, for God's sake, Doctor, stop!" But I couldn't.

"Again," the doctor yelled. Sweat soaked his face. "Push with everything you have, Sara! Give it all you've got!" With that he put his foot back on the table and arched away a second time. It took three terrible pulls to free the head. After that our baby's body slid effortlessly into the outside world.

That event occurred at 2:07 p.m. on May 2, 1997. That moment, nondescript as any other to the world at large, is when Courtney Ann Lewis took in her first lung-full of oxygen. Her cries silenced pandemonium. No one said a word.

The doctor placed the tiny girl on my wife's breast, and I leaned down so all three of our faces touched, and our tears mixed. It took a long time for the baby to stop crying. When she did I moved back to see her features more clearly. She cuddled against her mother. I memorized the little face, bruised and battered by the metal grabbers that had hauled her from the comfort of the womb. The eyes melted me. I'd expected them to be sealed shut, but they were open wide. Had the trauma of her birth caused this? Her gentle gaze spoke of trust and dependence more purely than any carefully crafted string of mere words ever could. I wondered how she could seem so certain of her place in the world after such a rude entrance.

"Let me see her," whispered Sara hoarsely. It took all her strength to get the words out.

"We need to clean her up, then you can take a good look," a nurse said.

The doctor handed me a pair of scissors, and I cut the umbilical cord. The nurse lifted the now unfettered baby. She carried her to a corner of the room for a quick cleaning and examination. Sara would have to wait another moment for her first good view. I looked at my wife, her eyes damp, her body sopping, and I could still hear the echo of her screams.

It wasn't long before the nurse brought the child to me. "She's beautiful," I said as I took the small bundle. She was worth everything, and I knew Sara agreed even though I hadn't asked her. I didn't need to. I could see the embers of that emotion burning in her weary eyes. Sara's features brightened as she looked at the infant. I turned my attention back to the child, checking that every part was as it should be. I counted each finger and toe aloud for my wife's benefit. I imagined she could find comfort once I'd completed the inventory. But when I looked back at my wife she indicated her satisfaction in a more thorough way. She'd fallen asleep. I carried the child to the other end of the room, sat down in a rocking chair, and swaddled her.

The doctors and nurses worked on Sara. They seemed busy, but in control. Someone turned up the volume on the EKG. A beep accompanied every beat of Sara's heart. The anesthetist hung a unit of blood. My attention remained focused on our beautiful child.

Martin claimed there is no such thing as a good father. I held in my arms the chance to prove him wrong. I smelled her. I'd never tasted a more comforting odor. My thoughts went to the world that awaited Courtney, and I dreamed of her place in it. How big a part would parenting play in her success? To me it seemed crucial.

Sara's convulsion rattled the room. I sprang to my feet. Just as swiftly a nurse forced me out the door into the hallway. Incomprehensible messages echoed over the PA as medical personnel and their carts flooded past me.

Someone grabbed my shoulder. I turned to see Irene's face. She didn't seem to notice the baby in my arms. "What's going on in there?"

"I don't know." I'd forgotten our mothers would be in the waiting room. I shared a look of concern with Mom.

"What do you mean, you don't know? What have you done to my daughter?"

\* \* \*

The diagnosis was a grand-mal seizure brought on by overexertion and blood loss. All I could do was be there for Sara. I'd been sitting by the bedside in intensive care for more hours than I could count, trying to imagine anything but the possibility of losing her. Friends, relatives, nurses, and doctors wandered through our vigil, but made little impression on me. Patrick, my boss, offered to take care of my files until I could return. A neighbor promised to see after Ranger. Mom brought me trays of food now and then.

Sara's hand felt cold and non-responsive. I tickled her arm and kissed her forehead. I didn't know what day it was, nor did I care. I'd seen Courtney, but only briefly. She seemed healthy and I figured that, for the time being, the nurses understood her needs better than I.

I heard Irene's voice before I realized she stood at my side. "I want custody of my grandchild."

I pushed back my chair and headed for the door. There was no way I'd be drawn into an argument that presupposed Sara's death while she lay in the same room.

Irene spoke again before I could get out of hearing distance. "I know Sara better than you. She would want me to raise her child."

Ranger would need a walk, and so did I. I headed home, fed him, then attached a leash. He seemed lonely and bewildered. We walked side by side down the railroad tie steps that led into Brigham Park. He had no enthusiasm. Even though we were in a target-rich environment, dogs everywhere, when I unclipped his leash he remained at my side. I realized it was Saturday only when I noticed how many men accompanied their families and pets at high noon.

For the first time, I really considered the terrible possibility of losing Sara. What would it be like to watch sunsets without her by my side? How could I go on? Would I ever be able to love my daughter? It wasn't that I felt these circumstances were Courtney's fault, but ever since everything had been altered so drastically I'd become oblivious to the baby, and I didn't know if I could change that. I couldn't remember who'd taken her from my arms as the trauma carts rolled into Sara's room, and she hadn't been in them again since that time.

Bits and pieces of Martin's story came back to me: the sense that he'd never felt important in his father's eyes. I wondered how early the dynamics of that relationship had been laid, and I realized in that moment that no matter the outcome of Sara's problems, Courtney held no blame. We needed one another.

When I returned to the hospital I went to the nursery first. An attendant took my I.D. and traded it for my child. I carried the tiny girl up the elevator and across the big hospital to Sara's bed. Irene had apparently left. My tangled thoughts felt even more disorganized than the tubes, cords, monitors, IV drip lines, and everything else connecting Sara to life.

I reintroduced Courtney and Sara, let the infant's hands explore the mother's face. I imagined the baby's gentle cooing sounds making it through my wife's ears and into her awareness. I held the baby close to Sara's nose so she couldn't help but inhale the aroma of new life.

"I wondered what had caused this." I turned to see a nurse standing in the doorway. "Your wife's vital signs have improved dramatically in just the past few minutes."

The remote equipment at the nurses station gave them the ability to look in on her without leaving their desk. After that first time, a nurse would bring Courtney to me every two hours or so. I'd hold the bruised but intact infant in front of Sara's closed eyes and try to sound positive as I spoke about our family's wonderful future. After five minutes or so the same nurse would take the baby away.

I slept in a chair, my head flopped against the bed, when I felt fingers run through my hair. I opened my eyes and gazed into Sara's. Her warm expression sent my spirits soaring. For the first time in two days, I knew she'd live. From that point her recovery followed a gradual arc.

To our eyes, Courtney smiled nearly non-stop. Others told us that wasn't possible, then changed their minds when they saw for themselves. Her forceps shaped bruises hadn't disappeared, but she seemed oblivious to the injury. She had strength and determination. She would often bow her spine backward and throw her arms above her head, stretching. Sara said, "Aha. So that's what you were doing in there once an hour for the last month. It hurt, little girl."

Soon they transferred Sara back to the maternity ward. We began keeping Courtney in the room full-time, and formed an unbreakable bond. Things had improved sufficiently a week after the birth that the doctor said both mother and child could be released from the hospital, provided they would be watched and cared for around the clock. Mom offered her home as a temporary residence, but we knew it was far too small for three visitors. The only unused bedroom, the one I'd grown up in, was now filled to the ceiling with medical billing records.

When Irene made the same invitation we had to accept. Where else could we go? Besides, Irene had no job. From that standpoint she had more ability than anyone else in our lives to offer the care we needed.

It took a full day of grueling work situating Sara, Courtney, and all of their belongings into the spare room at Irene's house. When I finished I called Patrick and thanked him for covering for me so willingly. I could hear his joy when I told him I'd be in to take things over the next day.

At seven in the evening I finally found time to use Irene's kitchen phone to check my messages. The electronic attendant informed me I had sixteen new messages and my mailbox was full. My resolve to get back on top of things sagged. I punched the required digits to play back the recordings and poised my pen above my day-planner.

"Tom, Jeff Sharman here. Congratulations on the birth of your daughter . . . I guess. Fact is, there couldn't be a more inconvenient time for this to happen from my standpoint. You see, you recently took an application from a David and Crystal Shaw. They dropped by an open house I held Sunday and have decided to put in an offer. Unfortunately we can only accept their terms if I can talk to you immediately about some contingencies. Call me as soon as you get this message."

I felt my blood pressure rise. "What's he got up his sleeve?" I wondered aloud as I scribbled a note in my planner. I pressed the delete button and listened to the next message.

"Hi Tom, this is Crystal Shaw. I hate to leave you a message like this when I know you're overwhelmed with personal matters, but we're very upset and hoping you could call to let us know what we should do. We found a house we're in love with, but the listing agent says if we can't prove we're qualified within the hour he's going to accept a different offer. Our agent is out of town, but the guy we met at the house, his name is Jeff Sharman, said he could save us money if we used his in-house lender and let him handle both sides of the transaction, anyway. That makes sense to Dave and me. I'm sure we can do that since we found the house on our own, right? Bottom line, he talked us into making an appointment with his mortgage guy this afternoon so that we can get all the obstacles out of the way. Since I can't get hold of you, I guess there's no other option. I'll talk to you later."

"Damn it." I slammed down the receiver and dialed.

"Hello, Jeff Sharman, your real estate connection," a polished voice answered.

"What are you trying to pull?"

"Who's this?" an unruffled voice asked. He'd long ago become accustomed to angry clients.

"This is Tom Lewis, and I want to know why you've talked the Shaws into dropping me as their lender and Doug as their agent."

"Tom, congratulations on the baby. Is it a boy or a girl?"

I knew him too well to be fooled into thinking he cared. "I know you're paid a kickback whenever you send a deal through your in-house lender. The real estate board doesn't look too kindly on actions like yours."

"I just wanted Dave and Crystal to have a chance at the house. They got a real bargain," he said.

"I bet. Beat out another offer at the last second, did they?"

"As a matter of fact, they did. Things worked out great for them, Tom. I'm sorry it's not what you wanted, but ultimately we're in this business to satisfy the client, aren't we. That's what makes it all so worthwhile, making people's dreams come true. I'll tell you what. I'll send a referral your way to make it up,"

"Don't you dare."

"Suit yourself."

"By the way, who represented the clients that brought in the other offer? I'd like to speak to them."

"Oh, them," he said slowly. "The actual offer uh . . . never materialized."

"Really? The Shaws narrowly beat out a non-existent offer? I'll give them a call so we can have a good laugh about that."

"Tom, Tom, Tom. What are you so upset about? If the Shaws want to go with you, what is there to stop them?"

"One thing. I don't want to be anywhere near a transaction you're involved in. Had I known before they signed I would've warned them, and I can guarantee you they would've fallen out of love with that house."

"Be careful what you say," he said, threateningly.

I hung up feeling angry and defeated. I began to dial the Shaws, then thinking better of it, replaced the receiver on the hook. At this time of night all I could do would be deliver the Shaws a sleepless night. These things could be dealt with in the morning. I realized I hadn't missed my job at all during my unintended week's absence.

Over the next two weeks the Shaw transaction was just one of many that didn't go well. I entered Irene's home every day after work, a freshly defeated man.

She seemed to sense it. One night she intercepted me at the back door. "How was work today, Tom?"

"Just fine. How was your day, Irene?"

"Doesn't look like it was fine to me. You look stressed, worse by the day."

"I'm fine."

"You should really do something about your appearance. Who's going to want to do business with someone who looks like a failure? It's obvious to anyone that you don't get enough sleep. My daughter and granddaughter deserve your very best. You know that, don't you?"

I seethed, but bit my tongue. If I gave Irene the satisfaction of an outburst, I knew Sara would be forced to spend the next day listening to in-depth analysis. I wouldn't put her through that.

We'd been here a couple weeks, but Sara remained far from recovery, still needing help with the simplest of chores. I prayed the next week would bring rapid progress. I squeezed past my mother-in-law and into the house. I hurried through the lace-filled floral-print living room and hallway toward the guest room, craving the simpler decor of our own home.

I opened the bedroom door, and there stood Sara. I stared at her in surprise as I shut the door behind me. She moved stiffly about the room, for the first time in weeks wearing clothing other than a nightgown. "You're up on your own. That's great, Honey. I can't believe it."

"Courtney just woke. While she napped I realized I couldn't sit around for another second."

As I kissed Sara on the cheek I noticed two gently swaying arms in the bassinet. Sara pointed to the foot of the bed, and I helped her to a seated position there. It felt almost like we were in our own room and things had returned to normal.

As usual, on the way home from work I'd swung by our home

to get the mail and visit Ranger at the neighbor's. Irene had been very specific that the dog was not welcome at her house. I handed the day's bundle of envelopes to Sara. I never went through the mail because she looked forward to that job. For her it was like Christmas every twenty-four hours. She loved personal letters, but she liked the junk mail too. "Look how they try to make this look like a government document to get you to open it," she said in disgust as she unsealed an envelope, but I knew she wasn't disgusted. "It's a used car sale. Can you believe the tricks these people try to pull? I tell you."

I walked over to the bassinet and looked down at the baby. Courtney's injuries were, for her, nothing but a distant memory. The faint outline of bruises remained, but she'd never noticed them, anyway. I marveled at the progress she made daily, and could never get home quickly enough to quench my need to see her. The time I spent alone with these two was far and away the highlight of my day.

I picked up my daughter, then and laid her on the changing table. I'd become pretty good at this stuff. As I finished taping a new diaper shut Sara let out a gleeful yell.

"Tom, you'll never believe what came today! I almost overlooked it."

"What?" I asked.

"A postcard from Daisy. Look at it." She held up a 4"x6" glossy photo of a pair of climbers suspended in the center of an enormous cliff. One man stretched for a hand-hold while his partner eyed him intently. The edges of the card were tattered, and I couldn't help thinking it must have undergone harrowing tribulations on its journey around the globe and into our mailbox.

"What does it say?" I asked.

"It's dated May second. The exact day Courtney was born. It took almost a month to get to us. Let me read it to you."

> Dear Sara, Tom, and baby,
> At least, I hope the baby has arrived safely by now.

> I couldn't quit thinking about the three of you today. I picked out this postcard because I thought the picture might be of Tom. Is it? How's teaching at the university going? I'm sure you're following your dreams and have quit that stupid mortgage gig. I thought about it some more and I wanted to tell you, banking doesn't fit you at all. You're far too cool. Anyway, I love you both. Life is great!
>
> Kisses,
> Daisy Love

Sara handed me the card. The usual colorful decorations embellished it, evidence she must have taken a supply of those colorful pens on her trek. Across the top was a row of exotic stamps and postmarks.

I flipped the card over. Is that me on the cliff? Very, very funny. I'd been religious about my Thursday workouts until Courtney arrived. She'd certainly put a quick stop to that. "I can't believe Daisy actually did it. Just picked up and moved to India. Good for her."

"You should do it too." Sara's expression sparkled.

"Move to India? Do you want to get rid of me?"

"You know what I mean. We have plenty in savings. We can cut back on our expenses. I'm certain, in the long run, we'll be better off than we are now, if not financially, at least in every other way. You think I can't tell things are getting worse at the office? Daisy knows what she's talking about. She's connected somehow. She practically predicted Courtney's birth. Listen to her advice."

"It's a huge stretch to say she predicted Courtney's birth," I said, but Sara wasn't listening to me. Her eyes glittered. We stared at each other. After a long pause I said, "You're serious this time, aren't you?"

"Tom, I don't believe you. Is it testosterone that causes your ears to gum up every time we talk about this? I've been serious since the first time I brought it up, since even before then. I see what's going on with you and it breaks my heart. Let me see how succinctly I can state it. Quit– your– job– today!"

I kept my eyes on hers. "This is unlike you, Sara. Where's your caution?"

"Where's your sense of adventure?"

Thoughts whirred through my head. For a moment my spirit felt like it would lift me into the air above the bed. I'd accumulated quite a nest egg in the last few months. This might be the last good opportunity to quit. Rates had recently risen even farther, and business was very slow. I spent most of my work day fighting an unlimited number of competitors for a limited number of clients.

But as I thought further, reality intruded. We had unexpectedly large medical bills, and the insurance left much to be desired. The insurer tried to squirm their way out of paying our hospital charges over every technicality they could find. I'd continue fighting them, but I was becoming less certain I would win. Also, how could I overlook the obligations of raising a family? I already felt an awareness of impending expenses clear through college, let alone the day-to-day costs of an extra mouth. "I'll think about it. That's the best I can do for now."

At my words, Sara deflated. I told myself that such disappointment would pale in comparison to her emotions if I quit and couldn't find new work. Mortgages were the only thing I could be certain anyone would pay me for.

Sara grabbed a magazine and leafed through distractedly.

I crossed the hall to the bathroom and shut the door. I studied my image in the mirror. In that reflection I realized that something had disappeared. My eyes held no fire. What had extinguished it? I'd once been able to see my own potential, and energy, and purpose, and vitality, . . . but no more.

I flipped open my cell phone and dialed Uncle Joe. I wouldn't impose upon Irene by making a long distance call on her line, and I couldn't be certain of privacy anyway. It would be just like my mother-in-law to pick up another extension and listen in at the most inopportune time.

Joe's soothing tones calmed my ulcer-ridden stomach. "Tom, how are you?"

"Hanging in there. Yourself?"

"Well, I'm glad you asked. You couldn't have phoned at a better time. Two years ago, you may recall, I co-sponsored a bipartisan bill to redirect federal funds to teacher salaries. It died when my own party shot it full of holes. Education's always been my pet project, so I stayed on as a lobbyist for this one. We pushed it through again this session, and I just received word we have the necessary votes."

"Congratulations."

"Thank you. At this very moment, Heather and I are toasting our success with glasses of cranberry juice." I heard the pleasure in his voice. "Why did you call?"

"I need advice."

"Shoot."

I'd long ago decided to handle the Martin situation without Joe's help unless I couldn't make progress on my own. Things were going reasonably well on that front, and I didn't want to change strategies. The career problem was entirely separate. "Okay. I went into mortgage banking on your recommendation, but I've never enjoyed it. Fact is, I hate my job."

"You do? I didn't know that. How long have you felt this way?"

"Basically, ever since I started."

"That's not good. In the immortal words of Kalil Gibran, 'Work is love made visible. And if you cannot work with love but only with distaste, it is better that you should leave your work and sit at the gate of the temple and take alms of those who work with joy.'"

I let the words sink in. "I knew you'd have a quote. It sounds pretty bad when it's put that way."

"It is bad, but you'll straighten everything out. You've got character."

We discussed the topic further, and by the time I hung up I felt energized. Joe usually had that effect on me. I'd send out resumes in the morning while still employed. Then I'd look into completing my philosophy degree as well. I could pick up where I left off with joy, provided I could find time.

\* \* \*

On June 24, I went to Martin's home. I arrived at the ramshackle house about five minutes late, and found Martin pacing in the front yard. I felt relaxed. "How's it going?" I said with a smile when our eyes met.

His brow furrowed like a freshly plowed field. "You're late, Tommy." He pointed to his watch.

"Sorry about that," I apologized, feeling far more comfortable than on my previous visits to his weed-filled lot. "Hey, do you happen to have a lawn chair I could use? I don't think I can survive sitting on that milk crate again."

He scowled. "I hadn't planned for that. You'll have to sit on the crate."

I headed toward the junk filled garage. "What are you talking about? Here's one right here." I pulled a flimsy aluminum framed chair webbed with weathered yellow nylon bands out from under a pile of odds and ends.

"Get out of there. You're messing everything up. I would prefer it if you would sit on the milk crate. That's the way I planned it."

I looked at him, wondering if he could be serious, and saw that he was. Agitation shone through his reddened face. Reluctantly, I handed him the chair. He accepted it as if I were returning a kidnapped child. Then he replaced it in the garage, even rearranging the items I'd disturbed to approximate their previous location.

"How about if we go inside the house where we can both sit on chairs with cushions?"

"No," he yelled too forcefully. "No one is ever allowed inside my home."

What in the hell did he have in there? An exasperated feeling came over me. "Martin, I don't need to take up any more of your time. I'm sorry for all of the bother I've put you through."

His eyes darted to me, and I read panic. "You can't go. I've been getting ready for two months. Why don't you just sit on the milk crate the way you did before and I'll tell you what you need to know. Nothing has changed. This is the way we do it." He looked at me urgently, then swept his head toward the porch in a wordless plea for me to join him. He headed for his easy chair, re-enacting the past as he took the same route in the same way he had at six in the afternoon on the twenty-fourth day, two months past. The dogs also played their roles to perfection. I watched the exact performance I'd forced myself not to laugh at on that previous spring day, but this time I had to fight to keep myself from crying.

# Chapter 14

I watched from my spot near Martin's garage. I glanced at the flimsy aluminum chair. Then I shuffled toward the porch. If it weren't for the sudden ache in my heart I'd be headed to my Cherokee. Any fantasy about having a normal relationship with this man was simply that, a fantasy. I remained curious about his stories, but no longer desperate to hear the tales at any cost. "Do you think I could use a chair next time?" I asked, kicking the crate forward.

He continued his preparations, not bothering to answer, apparently satisfied he'd gotten his way. Finally he settled into what must have been the perfect position, and looked up. "It will be easier to talk to you if you sit over there." He pointed to the exact spot I'd kicked the crate from.

I scowled at him, muttering an insult under my breath. How I could ever have taken him for a submissive man? He paid no attention. "Next month I'm bringing my own chair." Such an unplanned deviation would probably set his fragile little world on its ear. I shoved the crate back to the spot he'd pre-ordained, and sat. As if I'd hit the play button on a tape deck his story began. He– the audio cassette, his Barc-O-Lounger– the Walkman. In the right conditions he had no alternative but to divulge his contents.

* * *

As usual, the Sunday School lesson was boring. Martin raised his hand. "Can I go to the bathroom?"

"Only if you'll promise to come back," Sister Jacobs said. "I don't like it when I let you out of my class and you disappear for the rest of the lesson."

"Yes ma'am." Martin went out the door and shut it behind him. He headed for the restroom then went into a stall. He backed toward the toilet and heaved himself up. The door squeaked as someone entered the room.

"We did have some times down there in the Southern States Mission, didn't we?" a voice said.

"We certainly did," came the answer. Martin turned to stone. It was Father. He lifted his legs high so they couldn't possibly be seen beneath the stall.

He looked down and saw a familiar brown wingtip tapping the gray and white checkered floor. He could have reached down and touched it. The men stood at the urinals adjacent to his stall. Father would be furious if he found Martin outside of class.

"It's great to see you again LaVar. I'm glad I looked you up on my way through town. Back in our Louisiana days I'd never have believed it if someone tried to tell me you'd stick with The Church."

"Life is full of little surprises," Father chuckled.

"Now you're the bishop, of all things. Boy, did I ever peg you wrong. I mean, was there a rule you didn't break in the mission field? And to top it off, you didn't get a single baptism the entire two years."

Father spoke softly. "Could you say that a little louder? There are people down the block who didn't hear you."

"I've missed your sense of humor. You could always crack me up."

"I'm not joking."

"You've lost me."

Martin strained to hear Father's whisper. "It looks like I'm going to have to let you in on a little secret. I doctored up some of the documents that got sent home about me. My dad would have fried me on a spit if he'd known I wasn't making conversions, so I made it look like I got about a dozen."

"You're kidding?"

"At my Homecoming the ward sort of gave me a hero's welcome. It was embarrassing. I felt terrible, but what could I do? I went along. Had no choice but to play the part when they kept giving me higher and higher church callings."

The men crossed the room to the sinks. Martin had hardly breathed since they'd entered.

The man laughed. "LaVar 'Back-Seat-of-the Car' Crump getting a dozen baptisms. That's a good one. You did get a dozen or so of the prettiest belles in the South into the missionary position. That should count for something. Maybe that's what the hero's welcome was really for."

Father chortled. "Yeah, well I messed up. I went crazy on my mission because it felt so great to be out of my dad's reach, but my conscience is going to force me into spending the rest of my life making up for my lies. So I'd appreciate it if you—"

The sound of the bathroom door swinging shut was the most welcome noise Martin could have heard. He jumped from the toilet, washed his hands, and headed for the door. He eased it open. Ten feet down the hall in the direction of his classroom stood his father and the man he'd been talking to. Martin had no choice. He hurried down the hall in the opposite direction. When he reached Emma and Joseph's class he stepped inside. Every head turned toward him.

"Well, hello there," Brother Pratt said with a chuckle.

Martin glanced at the teacher, then looked to the children. First he noticed his brother sitting at the rear of the class, then he saw his sister in the middle row. He hurried to her and scrambled onto her lap.

"I need you to hold me," he whispered.

"Shhh," Emma said.

"Father told a man that—"

"Shhh, be reverent."

Martin nodded. What was he to do with this information?

"Very well. Back to the lesson at hand. Why is it important that we live the teachings of the Gospel, even when others aren't looking?"

Mary Beth Eldridge sprang from her chair, hand raised in the air. She jumped excitedly. "I know . . . I know . . . I know . . ."

"There's no right or wrong answer, Mary Beth. What do you have in mind?"

"It would be embarrassing if someone saw us doing something we shouldn't," she said, still apparently certain she'd identified the most important point.

Brother Pratt smiled softly. "Embarrassment is born of arrogance, but God's example teaches us that we should be humble. So fear of embarrassment isn't really a reason for us to behave as we should, is it?"

"But maybe someone will see you and you won't realize it. Then they might tattle on you," Mary Beth continued.

Brother Pratt nodded. "That could happen, but don't you think fear of being tattled on is a poor reason to behave as we know we should? For me, there's almost nothing I like less than tattle-tales anyway. It often means they're hiding something even worse themselves."

Mary Beth's lips fell into a pout.

Brother Pratt scanned the room. "Can anyone think of another reason to live the teachings every day?"

Emma tentatively took an arm from around Martin's waist and lifted it.

"Yes, Emma, why do you think it's important we follow the teachings at all times?" Brother Pratt asked.

"Because it does honor to our parents, our teachers, and those we love when we truly follow the example they have set for us. If we say one thing and do another, how much value does our word have, even if we're the only one who knows what sins we've committed?"

"Very good. No wonder your little brother is unwilling to stay in his own class. He and I both love to hear the way you interpret things."

Martin smiled.

"Well, we're out of time for today. Let's have Joseph give the closing prayer, then we'll adjourn," said Brother Pratt.

Joseph walked to the front of the room and crossed his arms on his chest. Brother Pratt and the children folded their arms, bowed their heads, and closed their eyes.

"Our Dear Heavenly Father," Joseph began, "Thank Thee for the lesson Brother Pratt prepared for us today, and please help us to remember his teachings in the coming week."

Martin opened an eye. He'd often wondered what would happen if he peeked during a prayer, but he'd never done it. He looked first at Joseph, then at Brother Pratt. The teacher looked straight back at him. Martin's guts tied themselves in a knot. He squeezed his eyes shut, embarrassed at his sin. He tried to concentrate on the prayer.

". . . and please help us to lead our lives humbly. These things I say in the name of Jesus Christ, amen."

"Amen," the rest of the children said in unison. Then they filed from the room.

As Martin and his sister reached the exit Brother Pratt pulled them aside. Martin's stomach churned. When Joseph tried to leave the teacher stopped him too. Was peeking during the prayer really such a serious offense?

Brother Pratt shut the door, then assembled the Crump children around him. He squatted and looked at them seriously. Martin felt a bead of sweat roll off his brow. Why hadn't he stayed in his own class? Feeling fearful, he concentrated on gazing straight back into the Sunday School teacher's eyes.

Brother Pratt smiled warmly— genuine and caring. "Your bright expressions are a gift from your father, a sign of your leadership ability," he said. "LaVar Crump is a rare spiritual giant who will eventually take his place near The Church's helm. I'm honored to be in the presence of such a man, and look forward to watching him rise through the upper echelons of Mormon power."

Relief flooded through Martin. Now, though, he wondered whether he should let the others know what he'd overheard in the restroom. Martin stood between his brother and sister. He squeezed both their hands to tell them how much he loved them and decided against passing on his story. After all, he didn't want them to think he was saying it to hide something about himself.

He looked left then right, noticing both Joseph's and Emma's expressions as the teacher placed a thin hand on their shoulders. Martin knew his sibling's eyes didn't always twinkle the way they did in Brother Pratt's presence, and he wondered if the teacher realized that.

"I'm so proud of you Crump children. I can't express the joy it gives me to watch as you mature and take on responsibility. You'll make a huge difference. I'm certain of it. What a world you'll inherit. A universe of limitless opportunity. Keep setting such shining examples for all of us to follow. You'll go so far!"

Martin tingled as Brother Pratt's words seeped in. The message overwhelmed him. He wobbled from the room, dizzy with enthusiasm. He'd never heard anyone mention such possibility. The reason seemed obvious. How could a man in Brother Pratt's position overlook something so basic? The earth was hurtling toward the apocalypse. Destruction would soon be the order of the day, and even the righteous would suffer as the world was cleansed.

Still, Martin sensed hidden magic in the Sunday School teacher's message. Hope pervaded the words. Hope for the future, hope for redemption. He had always thought it unlikely that he would survive the coming turmoil. This notion that tomorrow would be worth living for felt delicious. The moment the taste touched his tongue, he craved it, longed to understand it. What might such a world be like? He twirled down the hallway not caring which way chance took him.

He bumped into Joseph and fell on his rump.

His big brother looked down at him. "What are you so happy about?"

"Didn't you hear what Brother Pratt said?" Martin got back to his feet.

"Sure, I heard it."

"There's limitless possibility in the world. We'll make a huge difference. You, me, and Emma."

Joseph laughed. "He wasn't talking to you, Pip-squeak. His hands weren't on your shoulders when he said those things, were they?"

Martin thought back. Was that important?

"You're not even in that class, and you didn't participate, anyway. Emma and I did."

Martin couldn't deny that. His heart sank as he watched Joseph stride down the hall. Martin recalled what he had done in class, opened his eyes during prayer– and gotten caught. Surely that sealed his fate. How he wished he'd been able to control his curiosity.

* * *

"I'm not pessimistic, darn it, I'm realistic," Father's voice boomed. His footsteps thundered as he moved about the house.

"I'm just suggesting I take the kids somewhere while your John Birch Society meeting is going on in the house."

"Delilah, how many times do I have to say it? I need you here. Who's going to take care of the refreshments if you leave? Do you see any other women?"

"The kids don't want to go to their rooms."

"I'm telling you, I've heard enough. What does it matter what the kids want? That's where they belong. Why did I let you talk me into building this house if we're not going to use it? Now, get those children into their rooms and make sure they take all of these toys with them. I told you a week ago I didn't want to see a single sign of anyone under eighteen years old once the men got here. Well, the men will arrive any moment, and I still see signs of children." Father stood in the living room, but his voice filled the house.

Delilah gathered the children. "You heard what your father said."

"But it's not even seven o'clock. It's still light outside," Joseph said.

"We all have to do things every day we don't want to. This meeting could go late. Your father doesn't want you wandering through the living room on your way to bed. Why can't you follow the example your little brother set?"

Martin heard everything even though he lay on his bed with the door shut.

"I'm not going," Joseph said.

A commotion followed, then Joseph stumbled into the room with a satisfied expression. He shot a good-natured smile at Martin before he turned and yelled, "You can't treat me like this."

"How did she get you?" Martin asked.

"Drug me by the hair," Joseph said.

The doorbell rang.

"Delilah, the door," Father yelled.

Martin watched Mother lean into the bathroom to check herself in the mirror, then scurry to the entry to greet visitors.

Martin peeked through the curtains, watching the stream of men moving up the walk. Their dark suits made them look like funeral goers.

They arrived in rapid succession. Martin could see there were more men than seats. The latecomers would be forced to stand. By the time the last visitor stepped inside, the house audibly strained under the weight. The floor creaked, the walls twisted, even the ceiling moved. In the living room the dull mumble of conversation might have masked the sounds of the groaning structure, but the quiet bedroom felt haunted. It felt nothing like the safe sanctuary it was meant to be. Martin sat imprisoned within the walls, listening to the otherworldly complaints of the uncomfortable lumber surrounding him.

He shivered in a corner, while Joseph sat in the open without fear. The older boy strode to the dresser, opened his pajama drawer, and pulled out two drinking glasses. He handed one to Martin. "If I hadn't complained about getting sent to my room they would've known I was up to something."

Joseph leaned against the wall common to the living room, a drinking glass between his ear and the barrier. Martin watched, and once curiosity got the better of him, moved to the wall and did the same. He could hear mumbling through the wall without the aid of the glass, and he didn't have a real desire to hear anything more. But using the glass was sort of fun, and the distraction made it easier to ignore the creaking timber, so he tried to understand the discussion.

"So, what are we to do about it?" Martin didn't recognize the raised voice. "The menace of communism is spreading like wildfire around the globe. They've even infiltrated the upper reaches of our own United States Government, and when a good man like Senator McCarthy tries to do something about it, tries to expose these traitors for what they are, he's attacked by his political enemies."

Applause filled the home. Martin eyed Joseph, wondering what the words meant. Joseph looked mesmerized. He pressed his glass hard to the wall, apparently determined to hear right through the cheering voices and clapping hands. When a single individual could again be distinguished it was none other than the commanding baritone of Father.

"Gentlemen, you make eloquent arguments, and I have listened to your opinions with great interest. I appreciate your passion. I must tell you, though, I called this meeting with a higher purpose than merely discussing the deteriorating state of affairs in the world. I contend we must do something about it. At the very least we must prepare our families and ourselves for change."

Father cleared his throat. "I know in my very sinews, with every fiber of my being, that this nation, the United States of America, was created under God, by God, for God's chosen people. God the Father guided the founding fathers. The words they put down are none other than those of God Himself!"

Martin wondered why he always had such a hard time understanding Father? It must be that he didn't listen intently enough, because adults always seemed so impressed.

"Have you stopped to consider that God's one true church had been absent from the earth for centuries at the time the Constitution was signed? Does it seem an odd coincidence that the Angel Moroni guided Joseph Smith to restore The Church and the powers of the priesthood less than fifty years later? Do you recognize the awesome responsibility that lies upon those of us who now hold that priesthood? Gather your families around you, and protect them, but never forget your loyalties must also remain with the men in this room, your church, and your God."

The speech went on and on. Those ideas Martin could understand seemed to lead in big circles. He wondered if he were less intelligent than everyone else.

Sudden silence jolted Martin's wandering thoughts back to the living room. It didn't seem possible so many men crammed into such a small space could make so little noise.

Then Father continued. "Brethren, I want to challenge you tonight. Set this question into your subconscious mind and let it work to find an answer. What are our highest and best purposes as servants of God at this crucial point in history? Do we redouble our missionary efforts? Do we work to put our own into positions of political power? Do we amass provisions against famine or enemies? I don't know the answers yet, but I can tell you this. Any man who is not obsessed with the urgency of these issues is, in my opinion, not worthy to call himself a man."

Martin tapped Joseph's shoulder. "I never think about those things."

"You're not a man."

"I don't ever want to think about those things."

"You'll never be a man."

Martin crept away from the wall. "I don't understand what they're talking about, anyway."

"You don't understand?"

Martin shook his head. "What?"

"Big things! Big, huge, gigantic, enormous ideas." Joseph walked over to the bed and threw himself onto it carelessly. He clasped his hands behind his head and stared at the ceiling, as if imagining the possibilities of what he'd heard.

"What ideas?" Martin asked.

"I can't even believe I have to explain it to you. You heard every word I did, didn't you?"

Martin shrugged.

"They were talking about power. Who should have it, and who should be under its control. They were talking about scandal. Who's cheating, and who's getting cheated. They were talking about manhood. Who's red-blooded and who's a coward."

"Didn't they say something about the Second Coming of God?" reminded Martin.

"Yeah, they said that too, but they didn't mean anything by it."

At that moment Martin heard the knob rattle, then turn. He hid his glass beneath his pillow as the door swung open.

There stood Emma, her face ashen. "I feel so alone in my room. I hate these meetings. I hate thinking about how hopeless the future's going to be. I don't want to live through it."

"You and my wimpy little brother," Joseph said.

"You won't be so calm when the things they're talking about start to happen," Emma said.

Before he could answer, a violent gust of wind parted the curtains and swirled about the room.

Martin rushed to his sister. "What was that?" he asked.

"It could have been anything," she said in a wavering voice. Martin felt certain she didn't mean it might be a good thing.

"Now you're scared of the wind?" Joseph asked incredulously. But Martin detected a slight tremble in his big brother's voice as well.

\* \* \*

I flinched when my watch alarm went off. The sound surprised me more than it did my host this time.

Martin looked up casually. "Is it time for you to go?"

I nodded. "But I wish I didn't have to. What happened next?"

He'd already shaken off his role of storyteller. He ignored my question. "Same time next month?"

"That's fine. How long did it take after Grandpa's meeting for the three of you to recover from those terrible feelings?"

"July 24 at 6 p.m.," he said.

"Martin, quit thinking about our next meeting. How long did it take for things to get back to normal after the meetings in your house?"

He stared. I became aware of a warm breeze rustling the hair on my arm as I awaited his response.

"How long?" I repeated.

His eyes glassed over. Finally he asked, "Normal?"

"When did you next play games, have fun, act like kids?"

"That might have been normal for your childhood. Normal for us was worrying about the dark days to come. I grew up terrified of the future, thinking I'd never reach adulthood. The Second Coming seems farther off now than it did in those days, but I still believe there's a good chance it will occur in my lifetime. God will return in the latter days to cleanse the earth of sin. The signs are everywhere."

I strolled to the edge of the patio, wary of a religious debate. I figured our opinions differed greatly, and an argument might end our relationship. I wanted to continue hearing his stories. When I felt I'd moved far enough away that he couldn't draw me back in, I turned. "Martin, I've been thinking, would you like to go on a hike sometime? We might just start off at the Mount Olympus trail-head and see how far we could get."

"Standing on that peak used to be important to me, Tom, but it doesn't matter anymore."

"You ought to consider it. We could turn around whenever you wanted. You don't need to make it on your first try. It's beautiful up there. Anybody who loves this valley as much as you, should see it from that perspective." I sensed a glimmer of his childhood interest in the goal, and I decided to add a little more motivation. "Joseph was dead wrong when he said you could see everything from down here. Not even close, but he'll never know that. He'll never reach that place. He lacks curiosity. I'll tell you something else. He was also wrong when he said you could never make it. You can. Wouldn't that be satisfying to prove?"

His eyes were now fixed on the magnificent peak— at that very moment bathed in the last golden light of day. "More satisfying than you can imagine. Okay, Tom. It's a deal."

"Great, do you know how to get prepared?"

He shrugged.

"Let's attempt the hike in September. By then the weather will be cool. That gives us a little over two months. In the meantime you need to walk— every day. Take it easy at first, then build up slowly, all right?"

"I think we should go on the 24th of September," he said.

"Let's not make it so rigid for now. If the weather isn't good we need to be able to adjust."

"If the weather isn't good on that day, it will be a sign I

shouldn't go," Martin said. "There could be a reason I've never made it. It may not be meant to be."

The reason you've never made it, I thought to myself, is that you come up with too many excuses not to. "Let's play it by ear, all right? If the 24th turns out to be a good day we'll go. If not we'll try at another time. Do you have my phone number just in case you have any questions?"

"No. I don't use phones."

"Can you find somewhere to write this down anyway? It couldn't hurt." I waited while he grabbed a pen from beside his chair. He wrote on his hand. "It's 555-LOAN. That's my mobile. It's the easiest way to reach me."

He nodded almost imperceptibly.

I gave him the thumbs up signal. "I'm looking forward to this, Martin." Then I headed toward my Cherokee. I drove home, my enthusiasm for Martin and his story not merely rekindled, but burning at bonfire proportions. I realized that if my host were to require it, next time I would listen to the session while hanging by my knees from the rafters. If the precise positioning of my body had anything at all to do with his ability to unravel the past, then at the very least I could assume the required pose. A couple of hours on a milk crate seemed the smallest of prices to pay, and I felt embarrassingly delicate to have complained.

He spread my family history out for my inspection like cotton sheets on a clothesline, exactly what I'd hoped for. And I now understood that Martin was the best qualified to do it. What's more, his eccentricities weren't a hindrance, but the means behind his incredible ability to re-create the past.

In addition, I'd discovered a way of repaying him. I liked that idea, not because I owed him anything for talking to me, but because I wanted to show him I appreciated it now that he had. I also wanted to prove to Martin that he was capable of following through on a difficult goal. I looked forward to helping a man who needed it.

It wasn't until I'd driven halfway home that I felt fear. What were our chances of success, of reaching the peak? Given Martin's condition, they were pretty poor. Even if we encountered incredible luck, they weren't good.

# Chapter 15

Sara, Courtney, Ranger, and I arrived at the Ensign Peak Trailhead just before seven in the morning on July 24th. This day brought with it an unusual event, a mid-week holiday. I could have worked, of course, but the market had turned bad and it was unlikely I'd scare up any business.. I might as well enjoy the vacation.

In Utah virtually everything, including the night classes I'd enrolled in to begin completion of my philosophy degree, shut down for Pioneer Day. This one was a particularly big deal because it marked the 150th anniversary of the entry of the Mormon Pioneers into the Salt Lake Valley, the Sesquicentennial. Upon his emergence from Emigration Canyon, Brigham Young is said to have surveyed the land before him and stated, "This is the right place." The story would be re-told many times on this day.

Martin would be telling me more of his story that evening, but for the moment my mind was on my wife and daughter. Sara had regained much of her strength, and we were excited for our first family hike. Ensign Peak, a small promontory near downtown Salt Lake City, wouldn't be too much of a strain.

"What a beautiful day," Sara said as she stepped outside.

A cool breeze brushed against my cheek. Birdsong filled the air. In the city streets below we heard a kettle drum then a tuba as a marching band tuned up for the Pioneer Days Parade.

"Tell me the moment this outing feels too strenuous. We'll turn around immediately," I said to Sara.

She smiled. "I'm going to be just fine. Save your concern for the baby."

I lifted the hatch for Ranger and he sprang to the ground. Then I rigged the snuggy sack, a sort of backpack in reverse, over my shoulders and around my waist. Sara slid Courtney into the pouch. I looked down on the infant cuddled against my chest. "I love you so much."

Sara started off and I followed her up the narrow trail.

Courtney was nearly three months old. Her awareness of the outside world had been steadily increasing. She wore a wide grin. She bent her neck this way and that, struggling to take in everything.

Ranger charged off through the low-lying brush. His passing stirred the smells of sage and wildflower. Tiny dust clouds rose at each of Sara's footfalls. I floated in a cloud of euphoria. Sara's health had returned and Courtney thrived. What more could I ask for in a family?

Sara spoke casually as she climbed. "Your mom has an opportunity to visit Europe next month with a group of girlfriends. Someone backed out, and she'd like to buy the ticket."

"Really? I wish she could go, but she's not one to do anything on a moments notice. Besides, Delilah would come unglued, and what would Mom do with Jill?"

"It's unfair of your grandmother to be so emotionally dependent on your mom. Delilah owes Emma a break, and I offered to take Jill."

I felt a wave of love for my wife. I grabbed her hand as it swung back, turning her to face me. "You mean my mom's really considering it? You're right about Delilah, although that won't change her reaction. I can help with Jill in the evenings, and I'm always available on my mobile if there's an emergency. Are you sure you're up to it, though?"

"I think I am. Jill loves watching Courtney so in some respects it will give me a break, not having to keep my eye on the baby so much. I can lift Jill in and out of the chair if I have to, but mostly you can help me with that."

"Of course I can. What did Mom say when you offered?"

Sara smiled. "She asked me to talk with you about it first, and if you thought things would be all right she said she'd go. She sounded pretty excited. It's a Mediterranean Cruise. It should be incredible."

"This is wonderful! She's always talked of Europe. I never thought she'd make it there."

Upon resuming our hike, visions of Mom exploring Italy filled my imagination. Progress up the hill came easily. Soon we reached the top.

A thirty-foot stone spire commemorated the historic event that had taken place on this site. A series of plaques gave the details. Most Utahns are familiar with what went on. Two days after Brigham Young and his followers arrived in the valley, he and a group of counselors climbed to this spot to lay out their new settlement. They imposed a grid-like system of roads emanating from the plot they'd chosen for their temple. Streets were to be 132 feet wide, oriented to the axis of the compass, and define square ten-acre blocks. Homes must be 25 feet back from the street and be of brick and stone.

"They left little to the imagination," Sara said.

"Mormons love rules."

The brass band struck up "You're a Grand Old Flag". I lifted my binoculars to see what I could of the Pioneer Day Parade. Mostly I saw the corridor of humanity that delineated the route. "I'm glad we're not in the midst of that. Do you want to take a look?"

I handed the field glasses to Sara. She scanned the city streets. "There's a float made to look like the Wasatch Front."

I looked toward the real thing, the wall of rock that loomed over the eastern edge of the Salt Lake Valley, vastly superior to a papier-mâché replica on a flatbed truck. Maybe I harbor an unreasonable bias toward rugged terrain. Whenever I visit areas without mountains I find myself wondering how the locals avoid insanity. Ordinary earth curves away, not merely unobtrusive, but compliant. It waits to be farmed, or traveled across, or built upon. A mountain, on the other hand, is defiant. It resists all of those things. In the time I've watched large tracts of flat land in the Salt Lake Valley go from fallow field, to farmland, to shopping center parking lot, I haven't seen the rugged peaks of the Wasatch change in any way. More than mere monuments, though, the mountains define civilization in Utah. Salt Lake City's shape, water supply, and major recreation are all created by the mountains.

Sara's attention also must have wandered. She pointed toward Mount Olympus. "It's like a sailboat."

I loved Sara's appreciation for nature. She paid attention to momentary things, and reminded those around her to enjoy them as well. She treasured full moons, cloud formations, sunsets, snowstorms and all the rest of the natural wonders.

I looked at the summit. A wispy cloud clung to its apex. From our vantage Mount Olympus' dominant characteristic was a two-thousand-foot high triangular cliff. It did resemble the tightly rigged mainsail of a great yacht on an upwind tack. The vapor emblem streaming from the zenith formed the perfect embellishment to the impression.

I scanned the green valley. The home Emma, Martin, and Joseph grew up in sat on the lower foothills of Mount Olympus. I'm certain Martin found it easy to imagine that the magnificent elevation in his back yard was indeed, as its name implies, the home of the gods. Four major rocky summits preside like sentinels over the Salt Lake Valley. The lowest in elevation, by far, is Mount Olympus. Yet it has the aura of the highest ranking. Its color enhances that impression. Like Napoleon in his differentiated uniform, the rocks of Mount Olympus are red, while its towering subordinates are dressed in granite gray.

But there's more to the mystique than that. As many faces as I have seen on Mount Olympus, I know I'll never see them all, because it's visage surprises me so often. Viewed from the once sleepy community of Spring Creek, Mount Olympus has a dual summit, with a rugged canyon sliced between two peaks of roughly equal elevation. Having spent much of my own life under the same unique shadow of the massif, I've always found inexplicable comfort in that particular view. The twin peaks, like properly aligned navigational buoys in a dangerous coral passage, send a signal to my subconscious that I'm sailing safely into home port.

Sara put an arm around my waist. "You'll be seeing Martin this afternoon, won't you?"

I nodded. "Yep. The 24th day of every month, odd as it sounds. Thanks for finding a way to understand."

The gap that had opened between us after meeting Martin in the park had healed. I thought about what we'd gone through: how I'd lied to Sara about my quest to find Martin, how I'd let her down on the night she went into false labor, how she'd revoked her trust. Our relationship reached depths I'd never imagined possible. We'd repaired it through a combination of honesty, compassion, sweat, and tears. The complications of Courtney's birth brought with it unforeseen blessings as we both gained a new understanding of the value of life. Now, the four of us– Sara, Courtney, myself, and even Ranger– were joined by a bond stronger than any I'd ever imagined. We took another long look at the imposing wall of mountains, then headed down.

# Chapter 16

Later that afternoon on the way to Martin's, I thought about preparations for our September hike. It was still a month or more away, but I'd really begun looking forward to it. Knowing it would be up to me to carry everything, I made a preliminary list of equipment in my mind. I'd take a flashlight and a sleeping bag, just in case I needed to leave him behind and go for help. I'd also take lots of food– fruit, high energy granola gorp, that sort of thing– maybe a gallon of water plus Martin's diabetic supplies. I'd carry a camera, binoculars, my cell phone, extra clothing, a knife, matches, and a first aid kit. We'd avoid technical climbing, of course, but there were sections I'd rope us up as a precaution. It would be nice to have the gear in case of emergency, and with all the gym work I'd been doing I felt prepared to use it. I'd pack two hundred feet of rope, harnesses, carabiners, and other equipment. Thinking it through I wondered, did I need to prepare so thoroughly because I hoped to achieve success, or because I must avoid failure?

As I walked up Martin's driveway I thought about fatherhood. Despite my preconceptions, things weren't always good. The night before I'd been unable to quell a two a.m. tantrum. I tried everything: food, diaper, love, logic, sympathy, comedy, anger . . . nothing worked. Sara woke, told me to bring the baby to bed, and the crying stopped. Despite my simplistic preconceptions, I'd quickly learned there was no perfect way to be a father, no limit to the menu of potential mistakes. Just because I couldn't imagine allowing anything to separate me from my child, didn't mean there hadn't been a viable reason for Martin to separate from me.

I realized I'd begun thinking of him as my father. It wasn't that I admired Martin, just that I'd gradually come to accept his role in my life. His many quirks were part of our relationship, something that needed to be dealt with, but not a reason for contempt on my part. Same for his relative absence from my childhood. Just as Courtney had been made partly from me and would remain my daughter no matter what errors I might make, I was made partly of Martin, and would remain his son.

I found him in the garage winding loose nuts onto bolts. The old wall clock he'd been tinkering on so long ago lay in front of him in roughly the same state it had been before. "How are you today, Martin?"

He flinched, glanced up. "It's six o'clock already?"

I tapped my watch. "Quarter to. I'm making up for last time."

"You weren't supposed to be here until six. I've got work to finish."

"I'll wait." I stood silently, feeling uneasy. I watched him assemble a gear mechanism, then disassemble the same part. Then he switched to a different part of the clock and repeated the process. It looked like useless activity. Maybe, to him, this was some sort of jigsaw puzzle.

The silence wore on me. I wondered if we'd progressed far enough in our relationship that chit-chat would be allowed. "Have you been walking?"

He sighed. "You're not going to need to help me with the Olympus thing."

"What do you mean?"

"I can do it on my own."

Not in a million years, I thought to myself. "Wouldn't it be nice to have company? I think you should let me tag along."

"I'm more comfortable alone."

I bit my lip and nodded, wondering how to get the hike back on track. "It's not really safe to go up there alone."

He gritted his teeth. "Tommy, what haven't I made clear? I'm not going on your hike. Now, I've got work to do. I'll be with you when I'm done."

The hike meant a lot to me, the opportunity to host him on my terms, and I didn't want him to give up on it. I'd let his emotions cool down, then devise a new strategy. As I watched him remove the same nuts from the same bolts I resented him, forcing me to stand there while he fiddled around. But I wanted to hear his story, so I'd play by his rules.

At six o'clock he finally looked up. Without a word he followed unseen rails to his place on the porch. The dogs followed. I trailed behind them all. He wriggled and writhed in his recliner by the time I noticed the yellow lawn chair sat where the milk crate used to be.

I smiled gratefully. "Ah, the pleasures of nylon webbing."

He made no indication that he cared for my opinion either way.

\* \* \*

Martin sat cross legged on the living room floor, captivated by the television set. The year, 1957, was Martin's tenth. At thirteen, Father said Joseph had reached manhood and deserved extra respect. Martin wondered about that because Emma was fifteen, yet Father's respect for her hadn't changed.

Community respect for Father had certainly increased. His church calling was now Stake President. That meant he oversaw five bishops and their entire wards. Martin felt particularly happy about Father's new responsibilities because such a workload made him easier to avoid. Despite the admiration he couldn't help feeling for his father, Martin would just as soon spend as little time in the Stake President's presence as possible.

Martin looked at his watch, 8:27. *Father Knows Best* would

come on next. In the short time the Crump family had owned a television set, it became their favorite series. Martin often wondered if Robert Young hit his kids when the camera wasn't rolling. On this evening Martin's feelings were particularly mixed about his father because he couldn't help looking forward to his return. Father had been on a business trip for four whole days, and he'd promised to return with souvenirs. No telling what he might bring back.

For the past fifteen years Father worked long hours for Rexall Drugs. Often the children didn't see him until just before bedtime. Now, because the store Father oversaw near 4500 South and 900 East finished the previous year as the most profitable in the entire chain, Father had flown to Saint Louis to receive a plaque.

"I thought your father would've been here a couple of hours ago," Mother said, "but the next time he lets me know what's going on will be the first. I don't know why you're all so anxious anyway. Hasn't it been nice without him around for a while?"

"He said he'd bring us souvenirs," Martin said just as the phone rang.

Emma lifted the receiver, listened, then squealed with delight. "A collect call from New York City."

Martin sprang to his feet. "New York City?" The announcement supercharged the atmosphere. Every family member became electrified. Could it be possible a wire extending all the way across the country linked the Crump living room with the most important city in the world? Everyone crowded around.

"Hello, Crump residence. Delilah speaking." Mother straightened her dress. She held the receiver far enough away from her ear that everyone could hear the response.

"Will you accept the charges?" a nasal voice asked.

"I'm sorry. In all the excitement I didn't hear who was calling," Mother said.

"Darn it all. Why can't you take anything in stride? You would think this was the first phone call you ever got," complained a far off male voice.

"LaVar?" Mother asked. "Is that you? Are you in New York?"

"I will ask you one more time before I disconnect this call," interrupted the nasal voice. "Will you accept the charges?"

"Yes, yes, of course I will. It's my husband. I can't just go accepting charges without—"

"She is not on the line anymore, Delilah. Some people have better things to do than listen to your yammering."

"Well, goodness. I certainly wasn't expecting you to call from New York. I thought you'd be home tonight."

Suddenly Martin realized Father had gone there to get a Yankee pennant. What a thing to show around the neighborhood!

"If you will give me a moment, you will understand why I'm not home yet," said Father. "I have exciting news. Our family is about to take a very important step. We are going to open our own business, a men's clothing store. I am in New York City meeting with suppliers. I'll be here for another week. When I return I will need all of the help and support you and the children can give me. We have big challenges ahead. Are you ready for them?"

Mother's face turn ashen. "I . . . I don't know. This comes as such a surprise. What about the drugstore?"

"I burned that bridge behind me. I am taking all I have learned about retail and devoting my energy to our new venture."

Mother put a hand on the wall, as if she might tumble over. "Bu . . . but why? LaVar, the clothing business? What do you know about that?"

"For years I've been looking for an opportunity where my influence in the community could be transformed into profit. Take my word on this. I've found the right business. If we can capture just a small portion of the missionary business, we will build a loyal clientele for life. Those nineteen year old men head to parts unknown, knowing they will be required to wear suits every single day for two full years. They step in the door ready to spend money.

If there is a better business opportunity out there than meeting their needs, I can't imagine what it is. Sure, ZCMI dominates this market, but we can provide better service at a lower price while still maintaining a solid profit margin. Believe me, I've put pencil to paper on this. Now, put Joseph on the line," Father commanded.

Mother handed the mouthpiece to Joseph and quickly moved her free hand to Martin's shoulder for extra support. She wobbled.

Joseph eyes went wide. "Hello, Dad?"

"Hello, Son. Do you remember I told you to be the man of the family in my absence?"

Joseph glowed. "Of course. Everything's under control."

"Good. Now I have a real man's job for you. Do you think you can handle the responsibility?"

"Yes sir, I can." Joseph's voice deepened, as if lower tones increased his competence.

"I knew you could. You've probably gathered that we are opening a clothing store. We need to find a place of business. What I want you to do is take the bus downtown and make me a list of all of the locations that could meet our needs. Something already vacant would be best, but make a note of anything that looks good. It must be a ground floor location at least as big as the drugstore, maybe even a little bit bigger, with a large back room for storage. On Wednesday, when I return, I want you to show me the best properties you find. Can you do that?"

Martin felt relieved Father hadn't asked him. He thought about the responsibility of trying to anticipate Father's needs, and the consequences of guessing wrong.

Joseph never cared about consequences, though. "Sure, Dad. Are you really going to start your own business?"

"I am not *going* to do it, I already *have* done it. It is not just my business, either. It is our business. This is your future, Joseph. We are going to build this together. Now, put your mother back on."

On Saturday Martin enviously watched his big brother board

the bus bound for downtown Salt Lake City. How would it feel to be so free? Joseph had everything Martin wanted: Father's respect, no fear, a quick wit, lots of friends. And the irony was he didn't seem to care. Everything came easy to Joseph.

The next Wednesday at four in the afternoon. Father finally showed up. Martin ran to meet him at the door. "What did you bring me?"

"I did not have time for shopping— more important things on my mind."

Martin's shoulders dropped. He'd waited so long, and now nothing.

Father stepped inside the house. "No time to waste with formalities. There are big changes in store for the Crump family. Are you ready?"

Martin, Emma, and Mother stood there, mouths agape. What kind of "hello" was this?

"I am," Joseph said.

"Good. We might as well go downtown and see what you have scouted out. Anybody else want to come along?" Snow began falling as the words were spoken, but inconvenience never stopped Father.

Martin perked up at the irresistible offer. The entire family prepared for the adventure. Martin put on his snowsuit and galoshes. He noticed Joseph stuff the list of stores into his pocket as he grabbed his gloves and hat. They piled into the big Lincoln and headed toward the city, but it took twice the normal thirty minutes because of the weather. By the time they arrived downtown, after six p.m., night had fallen.

While the rest of the family peered like emboldened thieves into one Main Street window after another, Martin watched the snow fall. He stood on the sidewalk tracking lazy conglomerate flakes, an inch in diameter, in their descent through the soothing lamplight. He enjoyed the cold air against his cheeks. He savored the calm storm. Platoons of flakes settled in the street, on bushes and trees, and across the sidewalk, like angels filling heaven. The city light glowed off the snow. Martin watched as flakes appeared in the cone of light below the lamp, and selected the biggest one. He opened his mouth wide, laying his tongue out to his chin. Then he moved this way and that, trying to anticipate the feather-like meandering of the white crystal. With a last-second lunge he captured the fragment on his tongue, but it disappeared into nothingness before it was ever really there.

The storm went on through the night. Together the family would cross an indentation in the snow and know it revealed their previous passage. Measuring the disparity between the depth of snow in the prints and the virgin accumulation beside it could date every trail. Eventually the prints were in an eighteen-inch gutter compared to the surrounding terrain. Martin shivered, stamped his frozen and tired feet, and pulled his collar tighter around his neck, all to no avail. The heavy snow soaked his old jacket and its insulating ability dwindled through the hours of aimless wanderings. Father didn't notice. He obsessively imagined traffic patterns and measured the distances that might give one location a competitive edge over another. That was Father's way with everything.

Martin tried to come up with a way to end the search. He looked into a storefront and said, "I like this place best."

"Good," Father said. "That eliminates it from consideration. You think unlike any of the customers I am trying to attract. Which of the sites we've seen do you like least?"

Martin didn't say another word for the rest of the night.

Finally, Father decided on the location at 117 South Main Street, the same one Joseph already ranked at the top of his list. It stood within a half block of ZCMI. The showroom was smaller than Father wanted, but its large back room and perfect space for a sign above the picture window made up for the deficit. Father contacted the owner the next morning, and before day's end signed a two year lease.

LaVar F. Crump Men's Wear flourished from the day the doors opened. No business ever more perfectly fit the community it served. Father, already a master of speaking in the manner of the highest-ranking members of church leadership, now used the talent to its fullest advantage. His cadence was slow and patient. At the same time his voice sounded authoritarian and precise. He spoke in such moderate tones that the slightest inflection carried great meaning. Mormons flocked to him like hens to a rooster. In many cases he could simply tell his customers what they should buy, and the sale was complete.

While working as a stock boy Martin paid close attention to his father's methods. Father began each morning with a sales training session, and ended every day with an analysis of each employee's strengths and weaknesses. He had an uncanny knack for overhearing everything. When salesmen stumbled, the boss pointed out their error, but he also congratulated them when they succeeded. Under his watchful eye, the salesmen learned to close their deals so smoothly their customers sometimes couldn't thank them enough.

Martin overheard many meetings.

"Joseph, when you worked with the woman in the blue dress and her son, I heard you ask a powerful closing question after the boy tried on the gray pinstripe. Do you remember?"

"I asked, 'How many shirts are you going to need to go with that?'"

"That's the one. They hadn't even decided to take the suit yet, had they? Your comment implied that you had presented enough information and their decision should now be obvious. In the process you also went for a bigger sale. Even if she'd said, 'We don't any need shirts today,' what has she subtly done?"

"She's accepted the fact she can't leave the store without the suit," Salesman of the Month, Boyd Ludlow said.

"Correct. Never forget, people don't like making choices. Your customers are looking to your expertise to make their decisions for them. They respect your experience and desire your opinion. Make certain they are aware that your advice and time are valuable, and they will not walk away without paying for them." Father focused on Joseph once again. "Do you remember how the woman answered your question?"

"Not exactly."

"Well, she didn't. You let her off the hook. When you ask a closing question, shut up. The next person who speaks . . . loses. You became uncomfortable with the silence and said, 'Are you happy with that color?' didn't you."

"Yep, and then she said, 'What else is available?' We spent another 45 minutes looking around, but they eventually bought the pinstripe."

Father nodded knowingly. "So you ended up making the sale, and that's good, but you wasted valuable time. You missed out on the gentleman Boyd here ended up assisting. Do you know how much that fine fellow spent?"

Joseph shook his head.

"Almost one-hundred dollars. That would have been your customer. Take just a moment to calculate the commission you let slip through your fingers. Now, I bet you wish you could have stood about five more seconds of silence. I will lay odds she would have said, 'I think two shirts will be fine for today.'"

In the early days all salesmen riveted their attention on Father, for they knew he was right. They'd seen him in action often, and he'd proven his impeccable instincts time and again. There came a day in every associate's career, though, when he found himself resenting the advice of the master. Losing an opportunity is always disheartening. Being forced to listen submissively while your errors are dissected can be unbearable.

Father closed every meeting with his favorite adage. "There is no more vital activity in the course of business than the act of closing the current sale." He repeated this same phrase at every opportunity. Each time he would present the idea as if the essence of business had never been stated so elegantly, and he seemed overwhelmed with the profundity of it. One day he made Martin paint the sentence on the only unused space in the back room– the ceiling. Father climbed the ladder when Martin finished and signed the phrase as a sort of authentication. After that he added a simpler statement to his repertoire, "Look up." The abbreviation, though, didn't cause him to repeat the entire quote any less often.

Even as the management of the growing business began making it impossible for him to continue in a sales role, he remained obsessed with technique. He established an office in the back room where he installed a one way mirror which he could look through at his leisure to critique the efforts of his staff. Soon the sellers longed for the day their boss had been on the floor amongst them, because now their customers gazed into the full length mirror behind which the store's proprietor lurked. And if a salesman hadn't done his job perfectly, Father would inevitably look up from his work at the most vulnerable moment. He would stare into the prospect's eyes, and know immediately what had been done wrong.

By the summer of 1959 LaVar F. Crump Men's Wear employed the entire family. Martin worked as a stock boy, his sister as a cashier, and his brother as a salesman. Mother and Grandma Pearl labored into every evening making custom alterations on a never ending rack of new suits. Every aspect of Crump life was a model of industrious organization, and it appeared there were no limits to what the family might accomplish.

The combination of a sewing machine placed conveniently in front of the television set, and the great patriotism of Mormons in general and the Crump family in particular, resulted in up-to-the-minute alterations of the family's American flag. Shortly after Walter Cronkite announced on the evening of January 3, 1959, that "the great state of Alaska" had been admitted to the union, Mother held up one of the first banners in the nation to accommodate forty-nine stars.

"I'm very proud of you, Delilah," Father said.

Mother glowed. "All I did was sew a star on the flag."

Martin knew it had taken much more. She'd removed and

rearranged all forty-eight pieces of white cloth in order to add the new one.

On August 21st of that same year, Newsman Cronkite heralded Hawaii's assimilation as a state. Mother, having anticipated such events, had stockpiled white cotton stars. She proudly unveiled a newly altered flag that included a fiftieth celestial body on Old Glory's field of blue. Martin had never felt happier. He didn't even mind that the family business forced him to spend so much of his time at Father's beck and call. In fact, he enjoyed Father these days.

By 1960 the business had expanded so much that Father decided to hire a personal secretary. The line of applicants was long. Father felt it necessary to speak with every single candidate, calling this one of the most important decisions the company would ever make. He planned to call the best back for a second appointment, and make his final selection after a third meeting.

It was fortunate there were so many choices, because most of the prospects wilted under Father's intensity. More than one woman left in tears. It became a game among employees to guess the fate of each applicant as she headed into the back room.

About half way through the first round an attractive woman walked into the store. Martin re-stocked a tie rack as Joseph hurried to assist the customer. "What can we do for you today, madam?"

She cowered. "Oh, sorry, I'm not here to shop."

"Excuse me?" Joseph asked.

The visitor edged toward Emma at the cash register.

"Can I help you?" Emma asked.

The woman moved with her head bent at an odd angle so her long blonde hair filtered across her face like a veil. "I have an interview with Mr. Crump," she said in a near whisper.

Emma checked the schedule. "You must be Beatrice Haney. I'll let Mr. Crump know you're waiting."

Emma hurried to the back room, then reappeared, sticking

her head through the curtain. She motioned for Beatrice to follow.

Martin heard the salesmen make their wagers. Boyd Ludlow intercepted the path of Jerry Smithers. "She's dead meat," he said under his breath.

Jerry whispered back, "It seems wrong not to warn her." They all agreed; the first unanimous verdict. Martin understood why. Beatrice's good looks were worth nothing in this contest. Her insecurity, on the other hand, would doom her.

The interview didn't last three minutes. Beatrice looked neither left nor right as she scurried through the drape and headed toward the front door. It happened so suddenly that Martin couldn't get into position in time to see whether or not she'd cried. Obviously, such a fragile creature could never meet Father's standards.

When Beatrice reappeared several days later for her second interview everyone gaped. Her return was only mild surprise compared to the shock they got a half-hour later when Father led Beatrice around the store and introduced her as the organizations first ever Executive Secretary. Not only was the third round of interviews canceled, Beatrice's first task would be to call three women who's second interviews were scheduled for the next day and inform them of the "bad news."

On her first day, Beatrice went through the suits making price changes. A male customer came up behind her and asked, "Where would I find the thirty-four regulars?"

Beatrice wheeled around startled, knocking him into the very rack he'd been looking for. The poor fellow lay on the floor, dazed. When he scrambled to his feet he immediately left the store. Father must have witnessed it all from behind his one way mirror, but he didn't emerge from the back room. On later occasions Beatrice spilled drinks on suits, disconnected phone calls, made mathematical errors that resulted in inventory and banking problems, and more. For some reason, her incompetence went without consequence.

\* \* \*

The unpleasant sound of my watch alarm broke my concentration.

Martin seemed mystified at the sudden lifting of his spell. He shook his head disappointedly as he rocked forward and dropped his feet to the ground. "I've never known anyone who has given up their freedom as completely as you, Tommy. How does it feel to be under the control of that watch and calendar? Why are you always in such a hurry to get out of here?"

"It's not the watch or the calendar that's controlling me, Martin. I use them because they give me control. The reason I'm in a hurry is that I have lots of obligations. If I were to start eliminating activities, I hate to say, the time I spend on this porch would have to go first. As it is, I'm just happy we can scratch out a few hours together."

He blew out a disgusted breath. "I wouldn't trade places with you for the world."

"And I didn't ask you to."

"Just tell me this, Tommy. Where are you going right now that's so important? Do you have some client that just can't wait? Are you so motivated by the dollar you've forgotten to live your life?"

"Actually, no. I'm going home to my wife and daughter."

His eyes went wide. "You have a daughter?"

"I didn't the last time you asked me anything personal."

He didn't catch my implication. "I wish I could've spent more time with my children. It just wasn't possible."

I sat bolt upright. "Children?"

His face took on the same panicked expression I'd seen on that day in the park. "You Tommy. You're my child. We've been over that."

That didn't explain what he'd said. My imagination raced. Did I have siblings? I fought to maintain a calm exterior. Obviously, he wasn't going to come right out and share the details. Still, there must be a way to find out.

# Chapter 17

Three weeks later on a Sunday evening the four of us, Sara, Courtney, Ranger, and I, were spread out on the family room floor in our basement when the doorbell rang.

Courtney giggled for the first time. The sound amazed her as much as the rest of us and she laughed even harder. Sara and I scrambled onto our knees to see her face. Ranger jumped to his feet and looked down, head cocked.

Courtney's face shone rosy with delight, her eyes squinting to near nothingness, her billowing cheeks and laughing mouth stretched from ear to ear. She produced the most joyous anthem I'd ever heard, the most perfect expression of innocent happiness that could exist. No precious instrument, Stradivarius or otherwise, ever created a sound half as satisfying to my ear. The music went on and on as one giggle fueled the next. I looked at Sara, and knew my own smile must be at least as wide as hers.

I stood, and edged away to answer the door. It was torture tearing myself from the happy scene. How could I be certain, if I didn't take advantage of this moment now, that it would ever recur? I'd gone through my whole life unaware such a pleasant reverberation existed, and now I didn't see how I could do without it. My wonderful experiences with my child made me more confused than ever at how Martin could have abandoned his. How many children had he left behind? I determined to find out who my siblings were.

I hurried to the door, realizing on the way it would be my

mother and sister. The time had come for the Mediterranean cruise. Mom would leave on the red-eye and be gone for eighteen days.

I opened the door, and both women beamed. It surprised me to see Delilah coming up the walk behind them.

"Can you believe the time is here?" Mom asked.

Jill nodded and grunted enthusiastically. Delilah scowled.

I smiled at Jill then looked toward Mom. "No, I can't. It's about time you saw the world, and guess what? Courtney has a going away present for you."

Mom grinned. "What is it?"

"Follow me." I lifted Jill from her wheelchair. She couldn't have weighed ninety pounds, and seemed lighter every time I lifted her. I carried her down the narrow stairwell and into the red brick family room. Mom and Delilah followed behind. I seated everyone on the couch, just above Courtney, then I went upstairs to ring the bell.

No laughter. I rang it again and again, until I heard my mom say, "I don't get it. What's the surprise?"

Sara answered in baby talk, and I could tell before I returned to the basement that she was nose to nose with her daughter. "Coochy, coochy, coo. Doorbells aren't funny any more, are they? We only laughed at ordinary things like that two minutes ago when we were tiny. But now we're all grown up, and ready for adult humor. Isn't that right, little one?"

I descended the stairs saying, "An Englishman, an Irishman, and an Italian stood at the Pearly Gates. Saint Peter asks them—"

"I'd be willing to miss my trip to hear her giggle," Mom said.

"Courtney, giggle. If you keep Grandma from going on this trip I'll never forgive you," I said.

Delilah broke her angry silence. "Oh, so she'd stay home to hear a baby giggle, but she's happy to abandon me."

"Mother," said my mom, "we've been over this again and again. I'm not abandoning you. Besides, Tom volunteered to watch out for you. All you've got to do is give him a call and he'll come running."

Delilah eyed me. "I'll believe that when I see it. The only person I've ever been able to depend on is you, Emma. I don't understand why you're so anxious to rid yourself of me." Tears filled her eyes. She stood up, sniffling, and headed to the bathroom.

When the door shut Mom sighed.

"Outside of that situation," Sara nodded in Delilah's direction, "are you all ready for your big adventure?"

Mom's eyes lit up. "I didn't sleep last night. I don't remember looking forward so much to anything in years."

"Courtney and Jill will have a great time together," I said.

Jill smiled and nodded enthusiastically.

"You're sure you can handle Delilah while I'm gone?" Mom asked.

I knew my grandmother would manufacture one or more disasters I'd have to deal with. She sought attention like an unruly child. "Whatever she comes up with, I'll deal with it. Rest assured, you won't be coming home to an emotional catastrophe on her part. I won't let that happen."

Delilah returned to the couch and sat stoically. The rest of us talked briefly about the sights Mom would see in Spain, France, Italy, Greece, Turkey, and the exotic ports she'd visit over the next two and a half weeks. I kissed Mom as she and Delilah left, then spent the night dreaming of Mediterranean coastlines.

As I prepared for work the next day I again thought of Mom's trip.

Sara's scream destroyed the early morning calm. "Tom! Tom, get in here!"

I dropped my razor into the sink and hurried to the bedroom. Sara sat in bed, hugging her knees as if fighting off a chill.

"What's the matter . . ." My words died when I noticed her gaze riveted to the TV. A news clip showed Uncle Joe handcuffed and being shoved into a police car.

The newscaster's message found it's way into my ears, but not to my brain. I replayed the words in my mind to comprehend what was going on. "When asked for comment, former Congressman Crump responded with an incoherent tirade." Video footage of the interior of my uncle's favorite restaurant, the one he'd treated Sara and me to when we'd visited in November, appeared on the screen. The picture settled on an overturned table. "The Congressman is being held on a number of charges including assault, resisting arrest, public intoxication . . ." The list blurred in my mind.

The camera shifted to his oldest daughter, Rachel. Mascara streaked her face. In her arms she held her two-year-old son. The little boy's confused expression might have been a reflection of my own. "My father has an alcohol problem," Rachel said in a contemptuous voice. "Why is it my job to hide it?"

Her words grated my ears. "Oh, no," I whispered.

"We live in fear of his temper." She waved her arm behind her to indicate the overturned table. "The stupid things he does."

I yelled at the television. "Stop it, Rachel."

"Shhh," Sara said.

Rachel's accusations continued. I grabbed a fist full of my hair in each hand and gritted my teeth. "This is the worst way to handle it. She should know that."

"Shhh."

Rachel calmed, but her words were no less acidic. "I've tried to love my father the way the public does, but he's got no time for me. His long hours earned your respect– the price was our happiness." She battled back a sob. "I've never understood why . . . whenever my dad finally came home . . . he preferred the company of a bottle of Scotch . . . to time with me."

The scene switched back to the news anchor. He wagged his head sympathetically. "Again, those were the scenes recorded last night by our affiliate, KSBC in Santa Barbara, where the popular Utah-born retired California Congressman was arrested."

I couldn't remain silent. "Something's all wrong. He quit

drinking. I don't know what happened yesterday night, but Rachel should know better than to drag alcoholism into this."

"Tom, why can't you see what's going on? Your uncle's fallen off the wagon. Rachel's paid an unfair price her entire life. She has every right to complain, rolling cameras or not."

I turned my back on my wife and walked away. "How can you say that? You weren't there. You don't know. Rachel's always exaggerated."

"Tom, your uncle made an amazing transformation before we last saw him, but you can't deny what she just said."

"She didn't have to say it on TV." I'd felt so positive about Uncle Joe's future when he, Aunt Heather, Sara, and I toasted it with glasses of water.

Sara continued. "What are you trying to accomplish by digging into your family's past? I thought the goal was to understand what went wrong. Now you sound like you're looking for excuses instead."

My head ached. "I thought I was trying to understand."

I fell onto the bed in a seated position. Sara rubbed my neck. "So what happens next?"

Before I could answer, the phone rang. I picked it up.

"Tom, this is Aunt Heather. Something terrible happened last night."

"I've seen the news."

"Then you know. It's over between Joe and me. I can't take it any more."

"Don't say that, Aunt Heather."

"It is. He doesn't love me, or the kids."

I didn't believe her.

"Tom, I'm worried. He needs someone right now, but it can't be me. You don't know how much you mean to him. He's talked on and on of you since you visited last November."

My heart ached.

"I'm taking the girls to my parents' home in Texas. He's been checked into Coastal Rehab, but they can't make him stay and I'm certain he won't be willing to."

I ran a mental estimate of what it would mean if I volunteered to fly out to see him. Uncle Joe might be difficult to deal with, so the time frame for my return would be unknown. Business was so slow that Patrick could easily handle the volume of activity that might take place at work. All I'd need to do was ask. I'd miss a few of my night classes, but they could be made up. I'd probably miss my appointment two days later with Martin. Why couldn't he just have a phone? I'd have to run by his place to leave a message. The biggest concern, though, would be leaving Sara with Jill and the baby. I put a hand over the receiver and spoke to my wife. "Joe needs me."

"Go to him," she said. "I can handle things on my own for at least a few days."

"You're sure? Even Jill?"

"Positive."

I kissed her. Into the phone I said, "I'll board the next flight."

"Thank you so much, Tom," Heather said. "If you can get Joe to stay in rehab for a while, don't hesitate to use the house." She told me the alarm code and where she'd hidden a secret key. She gave me other instructions, then said goodbye.

I replaced the receiver and turned to Sara.

"What can I do to help?" she asked.

"You've done more than enough already. I'm worried about leaving you to care for Jill and Courtney on your own."

She waved it off. "No problem."

The moment I left the house I'd order flowers to arrive the next morning. She loved receiving bouquets, and I loved sending them. It was the least I could do to thank her for helping me out with a messy situation.

I made my plane reservation, realizing as I did so that if Mom was here this would probably be her problem to deal with. She'd always been the one to pick up the pieces when things fell apart, as if changing plans were somehow less inconvenient for her than the rest of us. I thought of her, somewhere aloft between here and Europe, and felt thankful she didn't have to know about the problems at home. I'd fix this situation myself.

I called the office and asked for Patrick. The receptionist connected me. I explained the situation.

"You've been slipping, Tom," he said. "If you leave I expect you to work double time when you get back."

I held the phone away from my ear and stared at it. His heavy handed motivational tactics could be so annoying. I thought about our dwindling savings and disputed medical bills. The last minute plane fare I was about to purchase wasn't going to help matters at all. But high interest rates and a scarce client list made me wonder if there would be significant income in sight. I put the phone back to my ear and swallowed hard. "I quit."

# Chapter 18

An hour later I vaulted up Martin's porch steps and knocked on the door. No answer. I knocked again. No Martin, no dogs. I turned around. The van occupied its usual spot. Where could he be? Rescheduling our appointment was the last thing I had to take care of before I left town.

I walked toward his lounge chair, then noticed a spot where the drape in the front window parted. Every nerve ending tingled as I cupped my hand beside my face to block reflection and peered into the house. All I saw was a wall of cardboard boxes stacked flat against the window. I returned to the door and pounded. Something felt very wrong. Why was the van there while Martin wasn't?

The sound of creaking hinges surprised me. The door slowly swung open. It seemed a beckoning gesture, though such phenomenon must be a common in tilted homes where doors and their casings are twisted. "Martin," I yelled. "Are you all right?"

No answer, just the sound of static. The dogs would have certainly responded by now if he were around. He must be gone.

As my eyes adjusted to the dim interior I gawked at the innards of my father's realm— boxes everywhere and strange little lights, dim deposits of red, yellow, and green neon. I checked my watch. Only an hour and a half until my flight. My hands felt clammy. I looked into the yard again. No sign of anyone. For months I'd wondered why I couldn't go inside this house, and that was before his comment about wishing he could have spent more time with his "children." Now I realized, deep in my gut, that the evidence of siblings might be within my reach. I'd never done anything like this before, but couldn't hold myself back. I stepped across the threshold onto worn pea green shag carpet.

Thick musty air and a rancid smell enveloped me. I froze in the dim light, and tried again to convince myself to leave. I couldn't. Curiosity had firm control. I must continue.

Narrow pathways led through catacombs of cardboard. In many places the stacks reached the ceiling. Where they didn't they were usually topped with clocks. Not the type of clocks collectors gather, but the type people throw out. A gold leafed mantel clock under a cracked glass dome caught my eye. It had a rotating pendulum of cheap crystals. They twirled left, then right, then left again. Some clocks were digital and back lit– the source of the tiny lights. I saw one exactly like the clock radio at my own bedside. Others were more traditional with two and three hands. Some were electric, but the majority weren't.

On the wall beside me was a clock built like a Swiss chalet. A woodchopper, axe above his head, balanced near the bottom deck of the little house. Bavarian dancers stood ready to twirl on the upper deck. Behind a little green door just beneath the eave I knew a cuckoo bird awaited its stage call. I resisted an urge to push the hands forward and watch the action.

Every clock seemed to be running and set to the correct time. I realized the static noise was their ticking. How many man hours must it take to keep them going? What could be the purpose? I took a cautious step, realizing I understood this home no better than I understood its owner. Maybe if I made noise it wouldn't feel so much like trespassing. "Martin?"

A scratching sound behind me. I turned. Nothing but boxes nearly covering the wall and window.

The sound may have been a rat running through a narrow opening, or maybe only a branch brushing against the glass. Even with plausible explanations, I felt growing fear of a trap. Floorboards creaked beneath my weight as I eased forward.

I peered into the kitchen. The cat clock on the wall spied me, looked away, then looked at me again. It's tail swung opposite its eyes. On the kitchen table four vinyl place-mats, remnants of food stuck to them, lay in disarray. Each featured the photo of a different LDS Temple. Dirty dishes overflowed the sink and scattered the water of a dripping faucet. Refrigerator magnets held scraps of paper in place. I edged closer.

A magnet advertising a pizza delivery company suspended a prescription for Insulin and another for Rezulin. Both papers noted the medications were for "control of diabetic symptoms." One sporting the 1989 Brigham Young University football schedule supported a page of typed names and telephone numbers under the headline, Neighborhood Watch. A ripped out newspaper article titled "*Self-Inflicted Brain Injury Ends Man's Mental Illness*" was under another. I noticed my name and cellular phone number penciled in the margin. "Hasn't he ever heard of Post-It Notes?" I said to myself as I pulled the clipping from behind its magnet and read:

Salem, MA– *The case of a man who shot himself in the head to, "put myself out of my misery," is being hailed as a miracle. Wilbur Redding, 22, a diagnosed sufferer of Obsessive Compulsive Disorder (OCD) didn't succeed in the suicide attempt, but he did cure his condition. In effect, he performed an auto-lobotomy. While frontal lobotomy was once commonly prescribed for disorders of this type, modern treatments focus on medication and behavioral modification.*

OCD wasn't widely recognized, even among psychiatrists, as recently as the early 1980's. Nevertheless, it's a tragic mental illness afflicting millions of Americans. Part of the reason it is so often either misdiagnosed or overlooked is that persons under the influence of such compulsive behaviors are almost universally embarrassed about their situation and go to incredible lengths to hide their symptoms from

Continued on Page C-11

I flipped the article over, but the continuation was missing. I looked for a date. There was none. OCD might explain a lot of Martin's behavior. Everything seemed to fit.

I replaced the paper behind its magnet and proceeded down a narrow hallway. Something scurried across my cheek and into my hair. I flailed at the unseen spider. My hand struck a pile of boxes and they tumbled to the floor before I could catch them. An alarm bell went wild.

I fell to my knees and clambered toward the source of the noise, spitting pieces of spider web from my mouth. The racket came from a hand wound clock whose alarm had been activated upon impact with the floor. I held the rapidly vibrating clanger arm between two fingers, found the off switch, and set the clock aside. Empty cans of Arid XXXtra Dry spray-on deodorant had tumbled out of one of the boxes. I hurriedly collected them. Sweat dripped from my brow. I noticed labels on other boxes. "Colgate Toothpaste", read one. "Campbell's Chicken Noodle Soup," read another. Why would anyone file refuse?

I re-stacked the pile of boxes then remembered the clock, fearful that Martin would immediately know things had been moved. I'd already seen him obsess over the order of the junk pile in the garage. I wound the clock and set it atop the stack.

I started again down the hallway and reached what I guessed was a bedroom door. On the knob hung a clock on a rope meant for looping over a showerhead. I opened the door and entered a surprisingly bright room. Sun shone in a south-facing window. A computer sat on the desk. It looked ridiculously out of place in such a hut. Books on COBOL programming were scattered on the shelf. Large stacks of magazines and clippings littered the floor. A receipt book sat open. I flipped backward through the carbon copies. Martin was earning decent income as a freelance programmer. It had never even occurred to me that he might spend his free time productively. As repulsive as everything I'd come across so far was, I felt a wave of admiration over this.

A bank statement from Garment Workers Federal Credit Union based in New York City and addressed to LaVar F. Crump Trust Fund- Martin L. Crump Beneficiary, sat open on the desk. The balance was $35,462.73. The only activity in the account was a small amount of interest earned since the last statement. If he received the same amount my mother had when Grandpa died twenty something years before, that meant, not counting the interest accrued in his favor, there was about $65,000 missing. I imagine his main purchase had been the house. He might also have taken care of unusual expenses, like the computer, with that money. The overall solvency of the account indicated he'd been pretty frugal. Even in its dilapidated condition he could sell the house for at least $100,000 on land value alone.

Another account statement, this one from Zion's Bank of Salt Lake City, was beneath it. The name on the document read Johnny Q. Public, living at this address. I couldn't help but smile. So this was Martin's "new name." It had a certain panache I hadn't expected. What a coincidence that he'd chosen the same first name as the man I'd grown up believing to be my genetic father.

The balance was $203.27. A single deposit of $327.39 had been enough to cover checks written out to the grocery store, a gas station, several fast food restaurants, a bookstore, utilities, and a phone bill! Had he lied to me? I looked around, then noticed a combination clock/radio/phone beside the computer. I picked it up. Dial tone. He wasn't the entirely honest man he'd claimed to be. It disappointed me, but only for a moment. It didn't matter any more. I understood why he hadn't invited me into this house. It made perfect sense he had a phone line in order to run his business. What I wanted to know about were his other children. I looked up. The backing of the clock on the wall depicted the Norman Rockwell painting, "Gossip." The expressive faces of thirteen people told it all, as they passed on an obviously juicy rumor.

I left the office. At the end of a crowded hallway I reached another door. I opened it. Two entire walls were covered in framed photographs. I glanced at the unmade bed as I hurried toward the pictures. An old photo of my own family drew me. There we stood in the midst of enunciating the word, "cheese," never imagining our images would stare for eternity upon Martin's unfolding life.

I moved on through the pictures. Most were faded. I couldn't help smiling when I noticed the number of dog photos rivaled the number of human shots. The gallery seemed to progress in sequential order from left to right. People from his childhood and their descendants dominated the leftmost portion. There were a couple of photos of my family in general, and a lot of just me. In fact, a quick glance across the wall told me there were probably more photos of me than of any other subject. I noticed among them copies of school pictures from every elementary grade, and then more sporadic ones after that. I was surprised to see pictures of my college graduation and my wedding. I wondered how he'd gotten them. There were several pictures of Joseph's family, at least ten of Martin at various stages of his life, a few of Delilah, one of my grandfather, and two of Patty Peatrie. Obviously, there were more surviving momentos of her than my mother thought.

One of the photos was a close up of her face. It was a much better shot than the one I owned. I looked at it closely, and although I've never been good at picking these types of things out, I could see I bore a striking resemblance to her, more than just the color and shape of our eyes. I wondered where she was now.

A photo-montage in a handmade pine frame, ten inches wide and fifteen inches tall, caught my eye. At the top a wood burned title in a clumsy re-creation of graceful script said simply, "The Crump Family." Below, five photos overlapped one another: a shot of Delilah standing on her patio, a shot of Martin with the Wasatch Front behind him, a picture of Moxie as a puppy, a snapshot of a dog I'd never met chomping on a Frisbee, and a studio photo of me taken in fourth grade.

I backed up to scan the rest of the wall. There were photos of men and women working in a cubicle style office, including one of Martin wearing a goofy expression and peering over an enormous pile of paperwork. I inspected pictures of people who I didn't know standing in front of landmarks— sandstone arches in southern Utah, geysers at Yellowstone, and assorted western tourist attractions. Most of these people, I guessed, weren't relevant to me. A photo of Martin in a tuxedo standing beside a dough-faced woman in a wedding dress drew my eye like a magnet. So he'd married the mother of at least some of his kids, or had he? Where was a picture of the children?

Directly below the wedding shot hung a photo of Martin standing proudly beside the same woman. She held an infant up for the camera's view. I removed the frame from the wall and inspected it closely. The baby, not more than a couple weeks old, was swaddled in a light blue blanket. The man in the photo looked so much like the thirty-year-old Uncle Martin I'd known way back on Thanksgiving Day, 1975, that I assumed this incident must have occurred around that time. Besides, the photo gallery was clearly sequential, and my seventh grade yearbook shot hung near this one of the infant. That would mean the baby was now in his early twenties.

"Damn you, Martin. No such thing as a good father! Are you trying to prove that piece of shit theory to as many kids as possible? How did we end up tied to a deadbeat loser like you?" I considered taking the photograph, but quickly realized that act would accomplish nothing beyond alerting Martin of my trespass. A lot of good this picture would do on a milk carton anyway.

I tried to memorize the face of the infant and mother, then set the frame back on its hook and lined it up to cover the unfaded square of wallpaper behind it. I searched the wall for another photo of either the bride or the child. If there were any, I couldn't pick them out.

I wondered what had become of my half-brother. What sort of a life did he lead? Had he made a safe journey through childhood, adolescence, and into adulthood? Did he have any clues to his own past? Maybe I was imagining a situation worse than the reality. It was entirely possible that Martin maintained contact. I didn't know how I would ever ask. I certainly wouldn't consider bringing up the topic until after I'd heard my own history. If he were even suspicious I'd broken in, our relationship would be over.

I looked back to the wall for evidence of more children. From my left came a startling voice. "Gentlemen, start your engines."

I turned to see a NASCAR clock. On the nightstand a train whistled as it emerged from a four inch tall mountain and made a circuit through a tiny town. Chimes and bells started up throughout the house. Where had the time gone? I panicked. I had less than forty five minutes to catch my plane. Could I make it? I hurried to the front door and peered outside to see if the coast was clear. The woodchopper hacked at his log, the dancers twirled, the yellow cuckoo made lunges at my face. I stepped outside and pulled the door shut behind me, took a quick step off the patio, then stopped cold. I turned back, realizing I still hadn't done what I'd come to do.

I knew where he stashed his pen beside the chair. I grabbed it and glanced around for something to write on, then thought to look in the mailbox. The utility bill would serve my purpose; besides, I knew for certain he'd look at it. I wrote:

> Martin,
> As you have probably heard, your brother's gotten into trouble. I've gone to help straighten things out, so I'll miss our appointment this Thursday. See you when I get back.
> *Tom*

# Chapter 19

I ran down the concourse at Salt Lake International, my briefcase in one hand, my garment bag slung over the opposite shoulder. As I approached gate C-12 I yelled, "I've got to get on that plane."

The attendant grinned, and reopened the doors.

I ran down the jet-way, reaching the aircraft door a split second before it locked. "Let me on."

The thick door paused, and a uniformed woman wearing way too much makeup peeked through the crack. "Do you have a ticket?"

I chuckled. It felt like crashing a private party at her trailer home. I handed her my ticket. She inspected it suspiciously, then opened the door just wide enough for me to squeeze in. Short of breath, I reached my window seat near the middle of the fuselage. I stashed my bag in the overhead bin and put my briefcase beneath my seat.

The same cosmetic-covered flight attendant stationed herself beside my row. While an unseen associate spoke over the PA, the attendant mimed safety procedures— Marcel Marceau in the wrong career path, I thought. I didn't pay attention to her message, for I'd seen this act hundreds of times.

My phone rang, and she glared at me. Experience apparently told her she was dealing with a problem passenger. "Airline regulations prohibit the use of electronic devices including cellular phones," she said in a robotic voice, not missing a beat with her pre-programmed gestures.

Embarrassed, I reached into the bag and shut off the phone. It emitted an electronic beep, signaling it had been disabled. The tone changed my state. It brought on a rare sensation, the freedom of being temporarily out of reach. I'd become so accustomed to hearing that single note as final punctuation to a long workday that now, in some Pavlovian way, it relaxed me. Before this moment, I'd never even noticed the tone carried such a soothing effect. I felt so content that I didn't even consider whom I'd cut off.

After taking off to the north, the plane banked sharply east on its route out of controlled air space. I found myself staring down on Martin's neighborhood. I identified the cross streets and quickly found Martin's overgrown parcel. The house looked as ramshackle from this vantage as from eye level. My imagination could now re-create the interior as well. My thoughts drifted through the front door, past the clocks, down the hall, and into Martin's picture-filled bedroom. I zeroed in on the photo of my brother until the image filled my mind's eye. How could it be that the baby's face, no bigger than an inch in diameter on the photographic reproduction, a mere spec in the overall jumble of things, was the dominant image I carried? I prayed for my brother's safety, wondered what he might be like. Did he know about me? Probably not. My gut told me he didn't even know his own father.

What was it with Martin? Sometimes I looked at him and saw an ordinary guy. He had quirks, but being an oddball isn't a unique act. I'm certain he could be a part of the family if he chose. He could blend into most any public situation. As a matter of fact he clearly did. How else to explain his computer business?

Obsessive Compulsive Disorder explained so much. Sure he could join the crowd, but at what cost? As he'd grown comfortable around me, more and more eccentricities surfaced. Now I understood why. He'd hidden them only with great effort. The funny thing was, in acting around OCD he'd given the impression of an entirely different set of problems. He wasn't the mentally deranged hermit I'd pegged him for on that frigid November day we met. Instead, he was a man who avoided the public because he couldn't deal with their misinterpretations. Socially he was the opposite of his brother, the man I was en-route to see. The extrovert and the introvert grew up in the same bedroom.

As for Uncle Joseph, I'd been too prone to sticking up for his actions. Sara was right about that. Those who lived closely with him paid a high price. The reason he got away with heavy drinking was that people like me were willing to look the other way. That made me an accomplice to his failure, as much as to his success.

The sound of air rushing across the wing changed tone as we began the descent. I'd been in deep thought for nearly two hours. We touched ground in Los Angeles. Another short flight brought me to Santa Barbara. A taxi took me to Coastal Rehab. I tipped the driver, then walked into the building with my luggage.

A smiling desk clerk greeted me. "How can I help you?"

"Can I stash these bags with you for a while? I just flew in. I'm here to see Joseph Crump."

"They tell me Congressman Crump just woke up. I'll have an attendant bring him out." She grabbed my luggage and slid it into a cubbyhole behind her desk. Then she nodded toward a couch.

I walked over and sat down. I picked up a sports magazine, but couldn't focus on the words. I tried to imagine how my conversation with Joe might go.

Ten minutes later, a man in a white lab coat escorted me down a long hallway. He opened the door to a large tile-floored recreation room, and pointed me toward a table where an old man sat. I walked to within five feet before I realized it was Uncle Joe. Ragged shocks of gray hair flared out in every direction. Uneven stubble covered his face. I'd never before seen him even slightly disheveled. I tried to hide my shock.

As I sat down I saw that he looked even worse close up. He'd aged considerably. His splotchy skin hung on his skull. His eyes were jaundiced. I shuddered at his decay.

"Hey, Uncle Joe. What happened?"

He looked up, as if from a daze. "Tom?"

"Yeah, it's me. Everything's going to be all right."

"Who sicked you on me?" he growled.

His aggressiveness caught me off guard. "I'm here because you need me."

"No, Grasshopper. I don't need anyone, least of all you."

He hadn't called me that since childhood, and it sounded like he now meant it to demean me, though I couldn't be sure. It hurt that he used the nickname I'd loved as an insult. "What do you mean by that?"

"I mean, get the hell out. You're just here to enjoy the pain I'm going through."

"That's ridiculous. There's nothing I enjoy about this."

"Yeah, right. Everyone enjoys seeing people fall from grace. When the media finds out they'll be salivating."

"That doesn't mean I am." Apparently he didn't know the story had already broken. Had he been too wasted to notice the camera recording yesterday evening's events? I took a seat. "Why don't you tell me what happened last night?"

He glared. "Isn't it obvious? That damn bitch destroyed my life! That's what happened."

I looked away from his glazed eyes. "You can't simply blame Aunt Heather and call that the end of it."

"And I suppose that means you think I'm to blame." He sounded incredulous.

"You're lucky Aunt Heather's stood by you all these years."

"Oh, and you know so much about my marriage. Spare me your advice, okay?"

I had no advice, and I hadn't come all this way to be abused. "What are we going to do about this?"

"I guess I have to rely on you getting me out of here."

"I'm talking about the bigger picture, Uncle Joe. What about that?"

"This isn't my fault. I didn't ask to have the cops called. Lovely Heather, who I'm not allowed to utter a negative word about, is the one who caused this whole thing to escalate. I wasn't doing anything. If you ask the other people at the restaurant they'll tell you it came as a total shock when some cop showed up and slapped cuffs on me at my wife's request. I saw it in their eyes. Their expressions told me they couldn't believe what they saw. I couldn't believe it either. Who wouldn't go nuts at that point? Do you know I've only ridden in a police car one other time in my life? I ran away from an orphanage when I–"

"Uncle Joe, don't do this. I'm not going to sit here with a smile on my face while you try to sidestep responsibility for last night." For too long I'd facilitated his addiction by accepting his excuses.

"And what makes you think you know so much about what went on?"

My patience wore thin. "I guess you missed the morning news."

His eyes opened wide. I saw his alarm, but the expression didn't last long. Years of political experience took over. He understood damage control and spoke calmly. "I was set up. Someone put something in my drink. They had policemen and cameras standing by."

I jumped to my feet. "Damn you. Would you just admit it? You're an alcoholic and not even the fear of death is enough to keep you away from the bottle. Your marriage is history, your life is in shambles. What is it going to take for you to admit you need help?"

"Since when have you had so much fire in your belly?"

I slammed a fist on the table. "You answer my question!"

Out of the corner of my eye I noticed the man in the lab coat staring our way. I sat back down. My uncle and I glared at one another in a silence broken only by the clip-clop of dress shoes on hard tile.

"Everything all right here?" the man in the lab coat asked.

I didn't take my eyes off Uncle Joe. "No. I think I'd better leave."

Joe's eyes narrowed to slits as I rose to my feet. I turned and walked away.

I wished I could ignore my uncle's voice. "When you were young I always believed you'd make something of yourself, Grasshopper. I thought you were a lot like me."

This time I knew he meant the name as a dig. When I reached the exit I couldn't resist the urge to look back. It was what he'd been waiting for. "Too bad you don't have the balls."

The piston at the top of the door prevented me from slamming it. I pulled hard, and it shut gently.

I approached the desk clerk. "What's going to happen to him?" I asked.

"I assumed you'd take him home and he'd be treated as an outpatient. He's made it clear he refuses to stay here long term, and we won't hold him against his will."

"Hopefully tomorrow things will change. Contact me on my cell phone if necessary." I took out a business card, crossed out the office phone number, and circled my mobile number. I handed it to her, then took my bags. "I'll check back in the morning."

I watched her write, "Joseph Crump's nephew," across the face. She nodded toward the business card holder on her desk and I took one and put it in my wallet.

Now what to do? I took a taxi to Joe and Heather's Spanish style villa on the crest of the Santa Barbara Riviera. I would've thought anyone who breathed daily the aroma of orchids mixed with bougainvillea, honeysuckle, wisteria, and an infinite variety of other semi-tropical plants, all of which teemed over the walls of his manicured garden, couldn't help but be happy. Yet this was the air my uncle inhaled almost exclusively, and he was miserable.

I looked from the second floor verandah at his gardens, flowing as they did first down his own hillside, then transitioning into his neighbors' acreage, and farther on appearing to metamorphose with the town. A golden beach, arbiter of the elements, separated the city from the sea. To the north towering cliffs filled the same role. Either way, the contrast between land and water startled the eye. On the horizon, cobalt colored Channel Islands invaded the sea, and man also inhabited the waves on the decks of sporadically placed boats and oil derricks, but water appeared to be the mightier force. At the very least, it was far less tame.

My uncle had been convinced that with such a remarkable backdrop, his retirement would remain a contented one. Looking at the beautiful scene, I admitted its promise could seduce me as well. Now, despite the apparent serenity, everything had come crashing down.

I went to the phone and called home, looking forward to Sara's comforting voice.

"Tom, did you finally get the message I left on your cell phone?" Sara sounded urgent.

My stomach tightened. "What messages? I didn't think to check."

"I figured you were too busy. There's not much you can do from there anyway. When I couldn't get hold of you I decided I'd just have to take Jill to the hospital. It's a good thing I did."

My mind raced. "What's wrong?"

"The doctor says it's not an unusual problem for paraplegics. It started as a urinary tract infection but progressed so far it threatened her kidney function. They're considering putting her on dialysis."

No wonder all our commotion that morning hadn't awakened her. It never occurred to me there might be a health concern. "This sure came on quickly."

"I think she might have suspected something was wrong, but you know how excited she'd been for your mother to go on that trip. Maybe she overlooked it for fear your mom would stay home on her account."

I gazed out over the beautiful California coastline, wishing I was home. "I'm sorry I left you such a mess to deal with."

"How are things going there?" Her change of subject suggested she needed me more urgently than she was willing to admit.

"I'll be home sometime tomorrow afternoon."

"Oh, good," she said with obvious relief, then paused. "By the way, you'll never believe it. I just received a dozen roses and a card from a secret admirer."

"Secret admirer? I'll kill the guy. You're too good to share."

"Before you do too much damage, will you tell him I said thank you? They're beautiful."

"You're welcome," I said.

"I really do love them, but are you sure you should be spending money given your job situation?"

"We'll have to cut down on expenses. We both know that. For now, enjoy the flowers. Let them remind you how I'm looking forward to returning home."

The next morning I pulled the business card from the rehab center from my wallet and dialed the number. I desperately wanted to take care of this situation by noon so I could return home and deal with the problems there. "How's Joseph Crump this morning?"

"He wants to go home."

I hoped he wanted it badly enough to treat me civilly. "Do you have anyone who could give him a ride?"

"Expect him within the hour."

An hour and a half later a blue sedan pulled up. Joe sat in the front passenger seat. A nurse delivered him in her personal car. He'd showered, shaved, and dressed in his own clothes. It helped his appearance a lot.

When my uncle laid eyes on me he smiled ashamedly.

I smiled back. "We may as well forget yesterday. Rehashing won't do either of us any good."

"I fell off the wagon. It won't happen again."

I made breakfast– scrambled eggs, pancakes, sausage, and orange juice. We moved to the sun room to eat. Morning rays streaked in through the curved solarium windows. My aunt's stunning collection of orchids soaked in the ample light. A Persian rug laid over the red ceramic tile gave the conversation area a cozy feel. We each set our plates on antique oak end tables and sat back in comfortable leather chairs.

Uncle Joe barely picked at his food. "All I've ever gotten out of life is a raw deal."

"How can you say that? Look at all you have."

"I don't have a single thing I haven't worked my ass off for, and it's all nothing more than material possessions anyway. Do you want to know why I accumulated all this shit?"

"Why?" I asked.

"Because I wanted to prove to my wife and family how much I loved them. This stuff represents sacrifice. Do you see this vase right here?" He picked up an urn from the end table next to him.

"Yes."

"It's worth $15,000. Do you know why?"

"No."

"Neither do I, but Heather does, or at least she says so. She wanted it, and I wanted to prove how much I loved her so I bought it on the spot. This whole house is full of junk like that– useless garbage for my wife and daughters. You see the doll collection in that armoire?"

I nodded.

"God only knows how much I have invested in that frilly crap. I don't even care. I bought it all for the girls just because they asked."

"It's a beautiful collection, a nice gesture. I'm sure they'll appreciate the dolls one day."

"One day? How about now? Nice gesture? What do I care about that? It didn't work, did it? My wife and daughters are nowhere to be seen. They hate my guts. They're off spending my money while I rot in loneliness. My relationships aren't worth squat. My life's not worth squat."

"You're sounding pretty dramatic, Uncle Joe."

"Do you think so? You spend a day, just one single day, sitting on this patio wondering if your family has any use for you. In my shoes you'd come to the same conclusion."

"Will you consider an idea?" I asked.

He stiffened. "What idea?"

"How about reaching out without your checkbook in hand? How about telling them how much you love them?"

He shook his head. "You don't understand how far it's gone."

"My mom would tell you that the past doesn't matter. It's the future you should be concerned with," I said.

"She had it easy growing up. Dad didn't have great expectations of her— he did of me."

"What does that have to do with anything?"

"The day I told my father I didn't want to have anything more to do with his business he promised me I'd fail. That drove me, but he died before I could prove him wrong. I was required to be the number one salesman in his store, and the only time I ever heard anything about it was on those rare occasions someone beat me out. I put everything I had into that business. No one ever once said, 'Good work, Joseph,' or, 'Great idea, Son.' No one's ever reached out to give me love."

"I loved you," I said.

He looked at me curiously, like he had no idea what I was talking about. "I hated my father. He never gave me a break. He pounded into my head that if I wanted anything in this life I'd have to earn it myself. He constantly told me I'd better not be expecting to inherit LaVar F. Crump Men's Wear because it wasn't my birthright, I'd have to earn it— even while he bragged the opposite to everyone willing to listen. I can't tell you how often he'd point to the accomplishments of someone else, even when mine were greater, and say 'You better watch out, Joseph. This boy over here has initiative and will likely take this business right out from beneath you.' He said it until I got wise enough not to want that piddley-squat operation. Isn't it ironic he ended up giving it to his incompetent little secretary to drive into the ground? Keeping her mouth shut about their little affair certainly did have it's rewards, didn't it?"

"What's your point?"

"When I became an adult and a father, I vowed I'd learn from the past. I knew how it felt for a child to be an outsider in his own family, to not be given ownership in anything."

His thought seemed to dead-end. Eventually I prompted him. "And . . ."

He hurled the $15,000 vase at the wall. It shattered. I wondered whether each fragment was now worth one buck.

"And now I'm a god damn outsider in my own family as well," he said.

I looked at the mess. The thought of destroying something so valuable sickened me. "You've always been a lot more interested in money than the things it can buy, haven't you?"

"It's just a way of keeping score." His voice calmed.

"Maybe you ought to rethink that."

"I'm too old and set in my ways to change how I do anything," he said.

"Does that include drinking?"

"It includes everything."

"When Sara and I visited back in October you were sober. You said you were using a medication that did wonders to help control your drinking. What was the name of it?" I asked.

"It's called Anabuse Naltrexene. It's aversion therapy, makes you sicker than a landlubber in an ocean-going dinghy if you drink. I ran out."

"You ran out and you didn't get more? You let all of this happen rather than take a trip to the drugstore?"

"So what?"

"Is your prescription on file somewhere?"

"Jacobsen's Drug," he said.

"Let's get you some more of that stuff." I looked up the phone number and arranged for a delivery. "You've got to promise me you'll take your medication."

"I'm going to be all right."

"Uncle Joe, I'd like you to come home with me."

He laughed. "I don't need a babysitter."

"I'm serious. Just for a while."

"Tom, I'll be fine. You get back to your family. They need you a lot more than I do."

"We'd love to have you, though."

He considered the options. "I'll tell you what. I've got things to do around here, but I'll visit in a week or two. Why don't you go now?"

It felt just as hard to think of leaving him as it did to stay away from home. I'd done what little I could here, though. Meanwhile, Sara needed me, Jill needed me, I needed a job. I had to go. He'd be okay and I'd get back to Salt Lake and take care of the problems there. I reached for the phone again and made Joe a plane reservation for one week later. As I charged the fare to my credit card I wondered how long it would be before I could pay it off. Still, the gesture felt inadequate to communicate how much I cared for him. I hung up. "That's your ticket. We'll see you in a week."

"Okay, I'll look forward to the visit."

I looked as deeply into his eyes as I could. He seemed sincere. "I'll call a taxi."

The cab and the pharmacy delivery van arrived simultaneously. I paid for the prescription and handed it to my uncle.

He took the bag. "Thank you. I'll get back on them immediately."

"I'll see you next week, right?"

"That's right," he said.

"I'm going to call you every evening."

"You do that, Tom." He winked.

I got into the cab. The driver accelerated impatiently, and I turned to watch Joseph out the back window as we drove away. He stood there, both hands gripping the upper edge of that tiny brown shopping bag the pharmacist had so carefully stapled shut. He looked like a sailor clinging to the last floating fragment of a sunken ship. For a moment I wanted to tell the driver to stop, but I had to get home.

# Chapter 20

Had I done an unpardonable thing? Throughout the flight I was assaulted by one black premonition after another regarding Joe's future. As I stepped off the plane I dialed Uncle Joe's number. He answered on the second ring. "How are you doing?" I asked.

"Don't tell me you worried about me the whole way home."

"No, no. Of course I didn't."

He assured me that everything was perfectly fine, and we said goodbye.

I reached the hospital before three in the afternoon. The antiseptic smell brought back memories of Sara's difficult delivery. I squeezed into Jill's room without opening the door any wider than necessary, not wanting light or noise to enter with me. In the soft glow at the bedside Sara slumped. She rolled her head in my direction, dark circles beneath her eyes. Courtney suckled at her breast.

I looked at the bed. A depressing array of tubs and wires led out of my sister's body. She slept.

I went to Sara's side.

She looked up at me and whispered. "The doctor believes that the worst is over. She'll be here at least another two days, but she's really improved."

My fingers caressed Sara's cheek. She laid her head into my palm. "You done good," I said.

We spent what time we could at the hospital, but there was

little for us to do. Besides, my financial situation wouldn't improve on it's own. I called everyone I knew who might be of assistance in locating a job. I scoured the Internet, local campuses, and the newspaper. One call to my night class professor turned up an interesting possibility. He knew of a history position opening up at Salt Lake Community College. The dean was an old friend of his, and he promised to call him to offer an introduction and recommendation. I hung up the phone feeling reborn.

The following day, hoping my professor had followed through, I called the dean myself. The conversation couldn't have gone better. We scheduled a face to face interview for the next morning. By the time we hung up I felt confident I had a decent shot. About time something went right.

My mind went to other things I'd been meaning to accomplish. I felt anxious to get back in touch with Martin. Once Jill returned to our house I knew that would become virtually impossible. I'd visit him now.

I spoke to Sara about my plans, promised an eight o'clock return, and headed to Martin's. I arrived at his house with two main priorities. First, I wanted to get through his story, and second, I wanted to find out about his other child.

"Martin," I yelled when I saw him working in the garage, "I'm glad you're here. We've got to make up our last meeting."

"What you did was against the law," he said coldly.

A wave of fear coursed through my body. How had he discovered I'd entered his home? I'd left everything exactly as I'd found it. The only way to deal with it would be to confront the situation directly. "I'm sorry. The opportunity was there and I just couldn't help it."

He extended something toward me. I recognized the gas bill I'd written my message on. It was still unopened. "Tampering with the US Mail is a serious crime. I've been trying to decide what I should do about it. I'm glad you came by, because I'd rather take it up with you before I go to any higher authority."

It took me a long time to understand his accusation. "You . . . you want to punish me for writing a message on your envelope?"

"That's just it. I don't want to punish you at all, but it's not my envelope. It belongs to the US Postal Service." His words were heartfelt.

"No, it's yours," I explained seeing a glimmer of hope. I grabbed the envelope from him. "See, it says Martin Cru . . . it says Johnny Q. Public."

"It may be my name," he said, seemingly forgetting it was the secret name I wasn't allowed to know, "but the mailbox is the property of the US Postal Service. It says so right here." He pointed to relief letters on the underside of the black tin container nailed beside his door.

"Who paid for that mailbox?"

"I bought it at the hardware store," he said.

"Then it's yours."

"But it says . . ."

I ripped open the envelope, pulled out the contents, and wadded up the evidence of my crime. I handed him the naked bill. "Now it's my word against yours. I say you opened the bill and lost the envelope."

"You're lying. You're holding the envelope right there."

"I can get rid of that easily enough," I said. Then I did my best to imitate Humphrey Bogart. "Look pal, I'm a desperate man. I don't want to go to prison over this. Please don't make me do something we're both gunna regret."

He looked at me in complete confusion, then started to laugh. His face transformed, and I realized it was the first time I'd ever seen him smile. "I thought I had problems. You're completely nuts."

"You listen here pal. I'm warning you. We've gotta talk about your childhood. Don't go tryin' somethin' foolish," I begged in my Bogart voice.

He headed to the porch without the slightest hesitation,

chuckling the whole way. He plopped down in this recliner without the usual ceremony, and I pulled up the folding chair. It wasn't the 24th of any month, and we didn't have a set appointment, yet he was willing to meet with me in an unprecedented way with no complaint. I wondered if my silly behavior had thrown him off his quirky patterns.

* * *

Fourteen year old Martin lugged his suitcase along, trying to make sense of the map he hoped would lead him to his dorm room. He'd been looking forward to this Youth Conference on the Brigham Young University campus for a long time, but it wasn't starting out well. The Summer of 1962 had been hot, and this day was particularly uncomfortable. He'd never seen such a confusing map. Now he was lost. He wasn't even certain he was still on university property.

"That map's only good for showing you how to get lost," said a soft voice.

Martin looked up, startled. There stood a beautiful girl with almond shaped eyes. Joseph would have called her, top-heavy, and said "Ooh-la-la."

"What're you smilin about?" the girl asked.

Martin felt embarrassed. He hadn't even realized the expression was on his lips. He frowned, setting down the luggage. "Are you from around here? I need to find Helaman Hall."

She giggled. "You're nowhere close."

Martin felt his cheeks grow hot. "Could you please tell me which way to go?"

"I'll do better than that. I'm headed that way."

Before he could object she grabbed his suitcase and headed off. He hurried to her side. "Who are you?"

"I'm Patty Peatrie. I know way more about Provo than I wish

I did, and you know way less than you need to, so it's a good thing we ran into each other. What's your name?"

"Martin Crump."

She stopped and stared at him. "Crump? Like that guy on TV who does the suit commercials? You look a lot like him, only younger."

Martin smiled again. "That's my dad."

She nodded her head slowly. "You must be pretty rich."

"If we are, no one in my family knows about it."

"I'll bet." Patty batted her eyelashes. "I love TV. I'm gunna be a movie star one day."

"You'll make it. You already look like one," Martin said.

Patty stuck out her hand and grabbed Martin's even though it lay by his side. She shook it vigorously. "Good to meet you Marty. I s'pose you're here for Youth Conference."

"How did you guess?"

"What did I already tell you? I know all there is to know about Provo. You will too after a couple hours of being surrounded by these predictable people. This is gonna be a difficult conversation if you don't listen any better than that."

Over the next three blocks Martin got to practice his listening skills. Patty hardly took a breath. "I'll turn sixteen in two and a half months. Dad transferred to Utah from Los Angeles almost a year ago. Man, I wish his company would send him back to civilization. I can't hardly wait til we return to California, but that may never happen. Anywhere but Provo would be fine by me, though. This has to be the most boring city on the planet. Have you ever been here before? Salt Lake can't be half this bad, can it? I assume that's where you're from with your dad owning that business and all. You don't have to answer. People in this valley have no sense of adventure and being a Gentile— that's what they call me you know— I may as well have leprosy anyway. If you're not Mormon they treat you that way."

When Martin noticed "Helaman Hall" printed above the door

of the building ahead he squeezed in a couple of words. "Thanks Patty. You've been real helpful." He reached for his suitcase.

She swung it to her opposite hand with more strength and agility than he ever could have. "I'm walking you to your room, not dumping you off on another sidewalk."

Martin gaped. He'd never met such a bold female. "You don't understand. Girls aren't allowed inside."

She looked at him with mild disdain. "Oh, I understand all right, and I think this place would be a lot better off with a few more broken rules."

Patty walked right past a group of gawking boys and into the dorm. "What's your room number?"

Martin shuffled through his registration papers. "One-thirty-four."

"Good. I hoped it would be on the ground floor."

The presence of a female in the dorm proved distracting to everyone except Patty. Martin watched jaws drop open ahead of them then turned to see envious ogling eyes in their wake.

When they reached the room she stepped inside and tossed the suitcase on the bed. "What do I get for bringing you here?"

Martin shrugged. "I can't pay you."

"Silly boy. I don't want money." She kissed him on the forehead twice, on the nose once, and then for a long time on the lips. "I'll be seeing you later, Marty."

Martin's knees buckled and the room did a 360. When she left, he crumpled onto his bunk. He'd dreamed of his first kiss many times, but it hadn't been anything like that. It was so unexpected, so unusual, so exhilarating. He could still feel where her tongue had licked his lips.

Martin wandered around the campus the rest of the day thinking of little else beyond Patty Peatrie. Everywhere he went he looked for her. Every thought that crossed his mind related to her in some way.

He didn't see her again, though. He fell asleep that night imagining her almond shaped eyes.

He woke to the real thing. Her long fingernails tickled his toes. Anxiety exploded within him. He nearly screamed, but instead bolted upright, pulling his feet beneath the covers. "What are . . . Where is . . . How did you get in here, Patty?"

She flicked her head toward the curtains. They blew into the dark room on a gentle breeze.

"You've got to go right back out," he whispered urgently.

"Slide over," Patty said, not even in a whisper. She climbed under the covers.

"Man alive, what are you doing? You're going to wake my roommates. You'll get us killed." Martin climbed out over the top of her.

"Marty, did you think about me at all today?"

He felt himself blush. "Whisper, please. You've got to get out of here."

She whispered. "Only if you go with me."

His mind raced, then he said, "Okay, let's go." He pulled a pair of Levi's on over his pajama bottoms and decided his pajama tops would be a good enough shirt. He skipped shoes entirely.

Martin headed for the window, but Patty pulled him toward the door. "There's a rose bush right where you have to drop down." She pointed out a cluster of scratches on her leg.

His heart pounded as they ran down the hall hand in hand. "Where are we going?"

"I'm gonna show you what it's like to live dangerously. You'll love it!"

They turned a corner and there stood two men, fortunately with their backs turned. Martin froze. Patty bumped into him and giggled. They retreated just as the men turned around.

"In here," Patty said, opening a door marked "Custodian."

Martin hurried in. When the door shut, the closet went absolutely dark. He bumped into brooms and mops leaning against a wall. The place smelled of detergent. Martin tried to control his breathing. He felt certain the men would hear. He listened to their approaching footsteps, tried to make out their conversation.

Warm wet lips covered his. What was Patty doing? The men were just outside the door. Any noise at all would be disaster. He wanted her to stop, but couldn't risk pushing her away. She probably didn't care about getting caught. At the same time, he began experiencing sensations beyond anything he'd ever felt before. Thoughts whirled through his mind: guilt, pleasure, clumsiness, lust.

He began to kiss her back. His lips slid against hers, his tongue ran along her teeth. In that total blackness he could feel her, but couldn't see her. He could hear her heartbeat, but couldn't utter a sound. Dizziness enveloped him. What a strange and wonderful game. Martin preferred it to anything else he'd ever done.

Patty took Martin's hand and guided it beneath her shirt. She wore no bra. The texture of her smooth breast was more than he could take. Shuddering uncontrollably, he exploded into his pants.

"That's okay," Patty whispered. "We'll have lots more chances to get this right."

Martin crumpled to a seated position on the floor. Patty dropped beside him. He knew anything that felt so good had to be very, very wrong. He suddenly understood why Father forbade the mention of sex under his roof. But more than that, Martin looked forward to "lots more chances to get this right."

They stayed in the closet for another ten minutes, then Patty stood and opened the door. She peered out, then pulled Martin into the hallway behind her. Soon they were out of the building and running toward the undeveloped land up the hill from the university. They reached a trail and followed it to a meadow.

Patty sat on a fallen log. Martin gazed at the shadowy mountain. The girl took something from her pocket. She struck a match and held it to something between her lips, then sucked hard.

The ember glowed a brilliant orange. She offered the cigarette to Martin.

"What is it?" he asked.

"Weed."

"What's it for?"

"Just do like I do. You'll understand."

He took the offering between his thumb and index finger. He held it to his lips and inhaled, then coughed uncontrollably.

Patty laughed. "You've got a lot to learn, rich man's son."

"What's that supposed to mean?"

"It don't mean a thing. It's just one of the ways I like to think of you." She pulled her shirt over her head. Moonlight caressed her breasts. A bright glow glinted off the pendant on her necklace, an image of Jesus nailed to a cross. Martin handed the cigarette back. She held it between her lips with the thumb and forefinger of her left hand. Then, as she inhaled, she took his hand in her right, and lifted it to her breast.

His penis grew hard.

She took the joint from her mouth, and with her free hand pulled his head to hers. He opened his mouth as she parted his lips with her tongue, then felt his lungs fill as she exhaled. The cooler smoke was easier to bear. He held it in for a long time.

When he exhaled every nerve ending tingled. His senses seemed more acute than ever before. Patty unbuttoned his pajama tops and pulled them off. She placed the marijuana cigarette between Martin's lips. He inhaled as she removed his pants and the pajama bottoms beneath them. By the time he exhaled, she'd started on her own zipper. Then she took a final hit and extinguished the cigarette.

She held both his hands as she sat down in the grass, then lay back. Martin knelt between her legs. She pulled him forward, and guided him inside. The scents of green grass, blooming flowers, fertile soil, and willing female mixed themselves in intoxicating patterns. She writhed beneath him. He kissed and caressed her as he began accepting her rhythm. Together they moved faster and faster, more and more as one until he couldn't tell where his body ended and hers began. Then she let out a moan, and another, and another– each time higher and more urgent. Her nails clawed into his back and he too moaned loud and hard. Together they climaxed. Again, Martin felt pleasure beyond any he'd thought possible. After a while he collapsed, rolled onto his back beside her, and gazed at the starry sky.

* * *

Martin thought of his adventures in Provo constantly in the weeks after he returned home. He and Patty had had sex seven times over the weekend. He'd remember each time . . . forever. He could still imagine the sweat glistening on her skin. He longed to see her, hear her, smell her, touch her, and taste her. Provo might be boring to Patty, but he would never see it that way.

He happened to be the only one in the house one hot Thursday afternoon in August when the phone rang. It amazed him to hear Patty's voice; but that was nothing compared to the things she said.

He hung up the phone and went to his room. He shivered while he sat and stared out the window. Patty couldn't possibly be telling the truth. She claimed to be pregnant, and she wanted to see him– wouldn't take no for an answer. She would hitchhike and, depending on her luck, arrive in an hour or so.

The hands of Martin's bedside clock seemed to accelerate. When her earliest possible arrival time drew near Martin gathered himself and headed for the front door. At least he might meet her at the bottom of the street and get things under control before anyone in his family became involved.

He eased through the living room trying not to disturb Father or Joseph who were seated in front of the TV. As he reached for the doorknob he heard Emma and her husband John call from behind him. They'd been married for three months, and had converted the basement storage space into temporary living quarters until John completed his final year of medical school. Normally, Martin liked having the two of them in the house, but this wasn't a normal moment.

John ruffled his fingers through Martin's hair. "You're not going anywhere, pal. Get your mother in here so we have the whole family together. Emma and I have something to tell everyone."

Martin sagged. "It has to be right this moment?"

"Five minutes ago might have been better, but now will have to do. Get 'em in here."

Martin went to the kitchen and brought back Mother, hoping to get this intrusion over quickly. If they only knew what they were interrupting.

"Sit," said John.

Mother and Martin sat down near Joseph and Father.

John walked in front of the television and turned it off.

"You better have a good reason for doing that," said Father.

Emma walked up to John and took his hand. Martin looked nervously at his watch.

John lifted his wife's hand to his lips and kissed it. "Emma and I have an announcement to make." He stood there as if he'd never finish.

Martin couldn't take it. "Then make it already."

A wide grin crossed John's lips. "You're going to be grandparents!"

"And uncles," Emma added.

Mother screeched, then grabbed her daughter in her arms. Father and Joseph stood up and congratulated John. Martin sat in a state of shock. Then the doorbell rang.

Mother, who wasn't two feet away, reached out and swung it open. "Come on in. We're celebrating the announcement of the first Crump grandchild."

There stood Patty in the doorway, awestruck. To Martin, she

looked more beautiful than she had the month before. Her neckline swooped low. A golden pendant on a narrow chain lay in the cleft between her breasts. The medallion depicted a weary Christ, suffering on a cross of thick timbers.

Martin purposely ignored the pendant during his relationship with Patty, but he felt very aware of it now. He wondered if Patty knew that Mormons consider such symbols idolatrous, but then again, what did that matter. The signal her cleavage sent was more than enough to create the worst kind of trouble with Father.

"You told them I'm pregnant?" Patty gawked at Martin. "I assumed you'd want to keep it a secret. I'm sure your dad does, right?"

# Chapter 21

Martin's blood froze. He stared at Patty, dumbfounded, gripped by terror. Father would kill him. That much he knew for certain.

"Young lady, who are you and what are you talking about?" Father demanded.

Patty looked at him. "Hey, you really are the guy from TV! The suit commercials."

He looked from Patty to Martin and back again. Normally Father loved being recognized. This time it angered him. His spoke sternly. "How do you know my son?"

Patty looked baffled. "How much has he already told you?"

Martin scanned the faces of the others in the room. Their attention was riveted on Patty.

The girl swept her hair behind her ears. "He must have said we met in Provo, right? I'll keep quiet about this for the right price. I'll even have an abortion."

"You believe my boy has impregnated you? This is ridiculous," thundered Father. He looked at Mother. "Close that door."

Patty's brow formed a vee. She clamped her jaw shut, straight-armed the door, and barged into the house. Martin cringed as she entwined her arm in his. "I missed my period a week ago, and I'm always very regular."

There was no immediate response. Each person in the room needed a moment to absorb the impact of an open discussion of feminine hygiene.

Finally Emma spoke. "Mother, are you going to allow this . . . girl . . . to talk like that? I've never heard such vulgarity in mixed company."

Mother looked at her daughter helplessly.

"Being a week late on a period isn't enough evidence to be certain you're pregnant," John said.

Patty glared at him. "I know my body, and I tell you I'm gonna have a baby."

"Why, you're so much bigger than little Martin. He's just a boy, and you're a woman," said Mother.

"We're in love. Right, Marty?" Patty said.

They'd never discussed anything like that. Martin couldn't speak. His face burned with embarrassment.

"Marty, tell them what you told me all the time. Tell them how much you love me. Tell them what you think of my body?"

Sweat saturated Martin's palms. His mind spun frantic circles. He couldn't speak.

"I've heard all I need to." The room shook as Father crossed it. Martin saw the big hand swing toward him, heard the ringing as it connected with his ear. He crashed into his girlfriend. Patty lost her balance and stumbled over Martin in the opposite direction, tumbling against Father's chest. She broke her fall by throwing her arms over his shoulders. The big man made no effort to push her away, but instead allowed her to lean against him for the moment. Then he looked into her eyes and spoke in a compassionate tone that didn't match his words. "You are an unclean thing. Never cross my threshold again."

Patty spoke softly. "I'm carrying your grandchild." She pushed herself slowly away.

The element of compassion in Father's voice disappeared, as if it depended upon their physical contact, "You carry nothing of mine. Do you understand me?" Father opened the front door, lifted Patty under her armpits, and extended his powerful arms to their full length. He toted the girl to the curb like a stinky trashcan. Martin hurried to the door. He saw her face clearly.

She gaped at Father for the entire journey, apparently unable to utter a sound. Once at the street, Father set Patty down and warned her again. "Do not come back. Do not cross that property line. Disappear."

Father returned to the house and slammed the front door.

John put a hand on Father's shoulder. "Brother Crump, think about what you're doing. You can't treat her that way."

Father pushed him aside. "You are not a blood member of this family. Leave. We have business to attend to." Father strode through the room pulling each curtain shut. Shadowy gloom drove the recent joy away.

"Your daughter is my wife. I'm family," said John.

No one stood up to Father this way, thought Martin. He liked John, and feared the consequences.

Father glared into his son-in-law's eyes. "You're not blood and you never will be."

"We've got to bring that girl back in here and talk this thing through," John said.

"That girl is nothing but a gold digger. If I hadn't chosen to appear on the television ads I assure you we would never have known of her miserable existence. She would not have been familiar with our family name when she met Martin, and therefore, I am certain, wouldn't have given him a second look. She is fishing for trouble; you can tell by the bait, and darn it, she has found it."

Martin pushed the drape aside with an index finger. Patty wasn't in sight. He let the curtain fall shut.

Father paced the room. He continued mumbling, "Furthermore, she is from a Gentile family. She would like nothing better than to embarrass me and my church."

He wheeled on Martin, and his voice became powerful again. "Do you see what you have done by allowing that vixen to be near you? She's playing you for an idiot, but you are just a pawn. In the end it's sure to be me who will pay the price for your stupidity and weakness."

"What on earth are you talking about?" John asked.

"I thought I told you to leave my house," boomed Father. He pointed to the door, but didn't bother to watch his son-in-law's reaction. Instead Martin continued to feel his father's full attention. Sweat trickled down Martin's back.

"Do you have any idea by what process a female becomes pregnant? Of course you don't. You are a fool. You are just an incompetent little sprig. Satan has many tricks, young man, and he has certainly put one over on you."

"I'm responsible for—" began Martin.

"You still believe she is pregnant, don't you? You have been taken in by this preposterous little joke. Have you stopped to consider what that would mean?" Father's laughter started in broken segments, like an engine turning over under a weak battery. It might have quickly died out, except he looked at the other family members. The mixture of confusion and concern seemed to fuel his chuckle, convinced him of the magnitude of the prank. With great difficulty he composed himself and asked the family a question. "You all believe it, don't you? You actually accept the idea that such a ridiculous little boy would be capable of planting his seed. I don't for a single second, and I am willing to call the bluff."

He let out one last chuckle, left over from the previous joke, then became very serious. "I don't want any of you seeing or talking to that girl ever again. Do you understand me?" He used his most authoritative voice as he stabbed his stubby finger toward each person in the room. "She will make attempts, of that you can be certain. I want you to direct her, or anyone else who has an interest in this topic, to me. The last thing I need is one of you getting even more deeply involved and messing things up."

"That sounds like a good idea," agreed Mother.

Father rolled his eyes. "Of course it's a good idea, Delilah. Maybe from now on you will heed my words when I explain the dangers of modern society. You people don't have much experience in the world beyond Zion. I do. The things I have seen . . . let's just say the Lord's influence is not nearly so strong in the outside world. You don't know how fortunate you are to have been born into God's chosen . . ." A ray of light shot across the room and ended at Father's feet.

Martin looked up to see where it had come from. John held the door open. "Come on, Emma. We've been excused. Besides, I've heard this speech before."

Father's glare needed no clarification. Martin feared that John would never regain Father's respect after this. John stepped outside, as if to avoid Father's penetrating eyes. As a result, Emma became the unwilling center of attention. She blinked, the way someone would beneath an interrogator's bright light. It seemed unclear where her true preference lay as she fought the attraction of two competitive magnets. Eventually she eased toward the door. Once within reach, John extended his hand and pulled her outside.

"I just wanted to tell my family I was pregnant," Emma said helplessly as she disappeared from view. The door swung shut.

\* \* \*

Martin lay on his bed, staring at the ceiling, his left hand in his underwear. It was almost two in the morning, and he still couldn't sleep. Could it really be four long months since Father had carried Patty to the curb? In that time summer's heat had given way to winter's chill. Through it all, Patty remained nonexistent— no calls, no letters, no nothing.

It would have been something to become a dad, to move away and start a family of his own; but clearly, Father had been right. Patty wasn't pregnant. She'd made the whole thing up planning to embarrass the Crump family and get her hands on some of their money. That had been her plan from the first. How could he have been so gullible? The entire incident now seemed like some bizarre dream.

Martin thought about the wicked things he'd done with Patty. He despised himself for his weakness. He lay there, fondling his penis, alternately cursing it for the problems it caused, and dreaming of using it again. He knew that even this behavior was contrary to word of God, and forced himself to withdraw his hand. He asked the Lord to forgive his many sins. He prayed fervently, and thought he felt the spirit within him. Exhaustion overcame him, and he finally fell asleep.

He woke in mid-orgasm, the image of Patty riding atop him as clear as the real thing. He looked at his nightstand clock. Less than an hour had passed since the last time he'd looked. Cautiously, not wanting to rouse Joseph, he pulled a plastic bag from between his mattress and box springs. He removed his soiled underwear and put it inside with the three previous pair. He shoved the bag back beneath the mattress and put on the dry pair of underwear he'd stashed in fear that this would happen.

He closed his eyes. As he'd already done so many times before, he'd soon have to smuggle the offending briefs from the house and wash them in the creek. Afterwards he'd hang them in a bush to dry while he stood guard. Fortunately, he hadn't yet been caught in the act. How much longer could such luck last? He must truly have a foul mind, that he could rarely make it through a night without succumbing to Satan's temptation.

He didn't sleep again that night. Thoughts of Patty whirled through his mind. Early the next morning he went to the phone. He had every intention of completing the call to her Provo home, but when the operator came on asking for the extension he recovered his senses and hung up. The terrifying image of crossing Father brought reality charging back.

He knew it would be easier getting through the next twelve hours, anyway. During daylight there were plenty of distractions Above all else, the entire family was busily preparing the way for the first Crump grandchild. Anticipation surrounding the event electrified every gathering. No conversation felt complete without a discussion of Emma's growing girth. Whenever she spoke of her feelings or moods, everyone, including Father, became attentive.

By becoming pregnant Emma had made herself, at least temporarily, sacred. The torch of life was being passed. Within her womb a new generation prepared to run its leg of the human race, to take a turn as keeper of the flame, and basic instinct compelled everyone involved to volunteer whatever they could.

"A cup of cider would taste wonderful right now," Emma said to John as they warmed themselves at the hearth in the early morning cold.

"I'll get it," said Martin, dashing to the kitchen. He treasured the bond with his sister. He saw her as a saint, and valued her approval above all else. He returned to the room carrying a tray with three steaming cups of cider, half a dozen slices of fresh toast, and a jar of raspberry jam. He set it on the nearby table.

"I sure appreciate the conscientious way you care for Emma," said John.

Martin smiled. "It's nothing compared to what she's done for me. When I need someone, Emma's always there."

One snowy Friday evening in December the Crump family sat enraptured by the television set. Martin sat in his usual cross-legged TV watching pose. Walter Cronkite discussed continuing worldwide reaction to the Cuban Missile Crisis while an aerial view of seventeen missile erectors and launch stands played on the screen.

Father fumed, "It's no surprise to me this would happen once we got a Democrat in the White House. They're weak on Commies and the world knows it."

The doorbell rang. Martin climbed to his feet and answered it. He swung the door wide. "Patty," he blurted.

Tears welled in her eyes.

He felt shock, delight, and fear, in rapid succession.

"What are you doing here?" he asked, his eyes going immediately to her slightly swollen belly. Father had been wrong. Martin reached out and she collapsed into his arms.

"Marty, I can't handle this alone. Nothing's turning out the way I'd expected. My father says it's an embarrassment to live under the same roof as me, and my mother says she's ashamed for the neighbors to see. They want to send me away and put the baby up for adoption. You're my only friend in the whole wide world, and your family hates me."

He wondered how she'd expected things to turn out, but let the thought go. He squeezed her tight, knowing how it felt to be scared and misunderstood. The bond he'd once felt with her rematerialized on contact, and he imagined his fondest dreams coming true. He lifted his eyes toward heaven. "We'll work things out. Nobody's going to an orphanage." Few suggestions had the power to inspire such fervor.

Father cleared his throat. Martin turned toward the man. Terror flooded his mind. He'd forgotten about Father only momentarily, but still for far too long.

"Take your seat, Martin," ordered Father.

He moved to the nearest chair and sat.

Patty stepped into the house and shut the door.

Father gestured with his chin, beckoning her forward.

Patty understood. She crossed the room and stopped in front of him, still sniffling.

Martin read the fury in his father's face, the lips pulled back, the nostrils flared. He feared the worst. Father shut his eyes and drew in a long breath. When he reopened his eyes he seemed to have mastered his emotions.

"Young lady, I didn't believe you when you told your story before. Now, you've demonstrated that I was at least partially wrong. You cannot prove to me the child you carry is of my blood, but I will not disbelieve your word if you swear to me on the Bible that Martin is the father beyond any shadow of a doubt."

"He is." Her voice didn't quaver.

Father nodded his head in a gesture that revealed both solemnity and defeat. "Very well. I abhor you. I abhor my son. What you have done is a far worse thing than a mere lie. You have violated the laws of God, and any punishment I can mete out will pale in comparison to the one that awaits you in a future life."

Father's tone gained fervor as he spoke. "I am speaking to the two of you, Martin, so pay close attention to what I have to say. The easy portion of your life is over. You are soft, and you must now become hardened to the realities of the world. Adults, and this includes anyone who chooses to behave like an adult by doing what the two of you have, must fulfill adult obligations and responsibilities. They pay for their own housing, food, clothing, and other needs. In order to do this they have jobs.

"Neither of you has much value in the workplace because neither of you has yet earned a high-school diploma, let alone a college degree. I doubt you could get a decent job on your own. You will not have to find out. I will employ both of you, Martin, continuing as a stock-boy but with hours increased to full time, Patty as a cashier. I will accommodate your schoolwork. It should continue, even if it is on a limited basis. I will also rent you each a bed, separately, in my home, at a below-market cost. In return I expect you to abide by every one of my rules."

Martin felt Patty glance at him, then look back at Father.

"First are your spiritual obligations. You will attend church– Mormon Church," he glared at Patty. "You will repent of your sins, the first step being a full and humble admission to me, your Stake President. I will then help you to construct an apology, which you will make in front of the entire ward during Sacrament Meeting. Martin, I see no reason you can't take care of that this coming Sunday. You and I can meet in private tonight. Patty, as you have never attended our services before–"

"Yes I have. I've been to the ward near my house, two times."

"Don't interrupt me, young lady. You haven't attended the services in our ward. That's what I meant. As I was saying, we will set a date for you to speak to our congregation once you are better prepared to behave in accordance with their customs. Delilah will drive you home tonight. Return next Monday. Bring what clothing and supplies you need to move into your new room. The first order of business will be to find time for the two of us to meet privately. Do you understand?"

Patty hesitated. Martin prayed she'd respond correctly. "Yes," she said in a resigned tone. "I can return on the bus."

"Good. You have much to learn. Idolatrous symbols, like that cross you wear around your neck, have no place in the true church. Allow me to remove it."

Patty hesitated, then lifted the symbol and kissed it.

Father's spoke thunderously. "Young lady. I will warn you only once. I will not tolerate insolent behavior."

Martin prayed she would obey.

The girl hesitated, then turned. Father swept her hair away to reveal the golden clasp lying on her bronze neck. He lifted the hair and put it in front of her left shoulder, then placed both hands on her neck and back. He rested them there a moment, looking content.

"Won't the clasp work?" Patty asked.

"Yes, I'm sure it works fine," Father said in a tone reminiscent to the one he'd used on the only previous occasion they'd been in physical contact. "Yes, it works just fine." He maintained his hold on the ends of the chain, and slid both hands across the nape of her neck while bringing it forward. Finally, he broke contact with her skin when he lifted the pendant in front of her face.

He handled it carefully, like a toxic snake. One would have thought he'd defeated a powerful and evil force. He released one end, then lowered the strand into his now free palm. There, the impotent metal viper curled. Father closed his palm over the souvenir, but jiggled his hand as he continued speaking. He seemed to enjoy the feel of the chain and the tiny golden image of Christ as they jostled against his flesh.

* * *

Sunday arrived at its usual determined pace. Time for Sacrament Meeting came all too quickly for Martin. He stepped into the chapel with head bowed, not looking left or right as he sidled his way to his usual spot among family on the third pew from the front. When they sat, Emma patted his leg supportively, but he didn't acknowledged her. He simply stared at his toes.

Halfway through the meeting Father approached the podium. Martin knew what would come next, though no one outside the family could have guessed that Father had anything out of the ordinary in mind. "My beloved Brothers and Sisters, it is my solemn and sorrowful duty to report to you that we at the Crump household have been brought to our knees this past week by a devastating circumstance."

The whole community of Spring Creek gasped. Gossips looked at one another in baffled astonishment, apparently wondering how a piece of such worthy sounding news could have circumvented their ears. Father handled the crowd masterfully. He labored to make his lips work while the congregation settled, and by the time words came out it was so silent the crowd could practically hear itself straining to hear.

"Brothers and Sisters, my youngest son, Martin . . ." Tears rolled down his cheeks. Father struggled, as if trying to imagine a way this terrible thing could be said. "My baby Martin, has yielded to the temptations of Satan. Over the past several days I've asked myself, again and again, what I should have done differently. I know there must be something, but I cannot find the answer.

"Martin has done a despicable and unchristian thing. My son shared his bed with a woman, a girl actually." He halted and thought over something for a moment. "Forgive me, I don't say it this way to offend, but unfortunately it must be said. We can't try to pretend nothing happened by using pretty words. He communed with her as if they were tied by the sacred bonds of marriage. That alone would be enough to break a father's heart, but there is more. The girl has become pregnant."

The sound of a hundred whispers, like a tiny tornado rustling autumn leaves, spun through the room. Father had obviously anticipated such a reaction, probably knew it was unavoidable, so he stood quietly and appeared to be thinking of what to say next until eager ears again waited for details.

"I guess it is in a small way a fortunate thing this girl was not one of our own, that there is not a second family in our midst equally devastated by these events. She is a transient Gentile living for the time near Provo, but that fact does not in any way abate the sadness that has stricken our humble home.

"Martin, as you can imagine, is still quite overwhelmed with the events. I'm encouraged, however, because he has already demonstrated a clear and sincere desire to follow the path of repentance as urgently as possible. He has requested he be allowed to address you, his neighbors, and to ask first for your forgiveness so he might become worthy of the same in the eyes of the Lord. Martin?"

Father backed away from the microphone. Martin watched for an uncomfortable moment before realizing it was now his turn. He rose, then moved down the aisle, pushed forward as much by the repellent stares of the worshipers as by any other force.

He climbed the four stairs, stepped to the microphone, and cleared his throat, hoping to imitate his father. Instead he became more uncomfortable than ever.

"My beloved Brothers and Sisters, I stand before you this day in the utmost shame and humility," his voice cracked and warbled. He looked back at Father, hoping the dignified man could somehow assist. Father's scowl told him he'd looked in the wrong direction. In that moment he forgot the words his father had penned, the words he'd practiced so many times.

"I . . . I'm really sorry for what I did. If I've embarrassed you I didn't mean to. I mean, you're my friends . . ."

Then Father was at his side. The big man unfolded a sheet of paper onto the pulpit— the speech. Father's chubby finger pointed to a spot near the top of the page.

"You deserve better repayment for the favors you've done me and my family and for that I am most peni . . . tent, penitent." Martin read the words on the page, reciting, but not hearing them. He felt a great sense of relief as he neared the end. "I know that this is God's true church, and that we are living in the latter-days. I say all these things in the name of Jesus Christ, amen."

As Martin finished he felt the weight of the staring crowd, every eye upon him. He heard the buzz of conversation, and knew he was the only topic. He left the stage, and like a traveler pushing into a heavy headwind, was only able to retreat to his pew by keeping his head bowed and his eyes on his feet.

When the service ended, Father took his traditional place by the lobby exit, but this time he held Martin at his side. The Stake President kept his big right hand on the boy's shoulder. It may have looked to others like sign of support, but Martin grimaced under the uncomfortable pressure of the grip. As neighbors filed by, nearly every one of them offered either a pat on the back or a hug to each Crump. Martin knew they comforted the man out of affection, and the boy out of condescension. What an enormous hole he'd dug in his persuit of a few moments pleasure with Patty. It may as well have been his own grave.

On the way home from church, Martin slumped in the back seat of Father's brand new Cadillac. He knew he'd never be the same. He deserved this emotional pain, and worse. He cursed himself for his many shortcomings, then bit into the inside of his cheek until he tasted blood. Every trace of optimism he'd tried for so long to harbor must be extinguished. Such Pollyannaish thoughts were only illusions that ultimately made the big, tough, messy business of life just that much more unbearable. Time to face facts. He was nothing more than an impotent pawn who'd be squashed by greater forces soon enough.

# Chapter 22

On Monday afternoon Martin spotted a girl stepping off the bus at the corner. She struggled up the street with two heavy suitcases. She'd almost reached his house when he realized it was Patty. Her clothes were more modest than he'd thought possible. She wore a loose fitting knit sweater with long sleeves and a tight collar. It completely hid the bulge in her stomach. Her skirt reached her ankles. With her hair pulled into a bun she looked like a teenager trying to imitate a middle aged woman.

He walked toward her to help. "I didn't recognize you. You look . . . Mormon."

"I'm here to make the best of things. Do you think there's a place for me in your family?" She smiled.

Martin assessed her. "Is that what you want?"

"For now. Why shouldn't I?"

He shrugged, recognizing a difference in the way they approached life. He drifted, she adapted. His main goal hadn't changed for as long as he could remember. Stay on Father's good side. Hers might well change every morning.

Martin and Patty reached the house and stepped inside. Before the suitcases were on the ground Father said, "It's time we had our meeting Patty."

"I'm ready."

"Let's go to my office at the ward house where we can talk in a more spiritually conducive environment."

Patty nodded and followed Father to the car.

Martin watched them leave, wondering how the conversation would go. He thought about the pattern of the annual "Bishop's Interview" he and his friends underwent. Lots of embarrassing questions: "Are your thoughts pure?" "Are you worthy of the Lord's blessings?" "Do you have a problem with masturbation?"

Last year Martin had wanted to answer that one by saying, "Nope, works every time," but he didn't have the guts.

As the Cadillac backed out of the driveway Martin bowed his head in prayer. "Dear Heavenly Father, please don't let this get any worse."

\* \* \*

The next afternoon Martin entered the house to find Patty there all alone.

"We need to talk," she said.

Martin followed the girl into the living room. Patty moved toward Father's recliner.

"Don't sit there," Martin said.

She turned to face him, a hint of fire again in her eyes. "I'll sit where I want."

"That's Father's chair."

"I don't see him using it. Has he got you that intimidated?"

"A man must demand respect in his own home." Martin couldn't believe he'd just recited Father's oft repeated words.

Patty shook her head. "LaVar isn't what I expected."

"Oh, shit!" He paused, surprised that a cuss word had escaped his lips. "Don't start calling him by his first name. Do you want him to burn you on a stake?"

Patty looked half amused. "You're a better man than he is. You talk about him like he's some infallible being. He's nothing of the sort." The lilt returned to her voice.

"You don't know what you're talking about. My father's a great leader. I'm not even a man."

"You're a man, no matter what he's convinced you of. He's the one who's not what he appears."

Martin covered his face with his hands. "I don't want to hear this."

Patty laughed. "I'll tell you anyway. Haven't you wondered about the little talk your father and I had yesterday?"

Martin shook his head. "What goes on in the Stake President's office is private."

"LaVar kept saying the same thing. All I can say is that confession is handled quite differently in my church."

"It doesn't matter how things are handled in your church. The Mormon Church is the one true church. If you want to reach the highest kingdom of heaven you must be Mormon."

Patty glared at him. "That's an arrogant thing to say."

"It's true."

Martin felt her reassess him. Her expression turned cold, as if he were now an adversary. She strode toward him. His knees gave out, and he dropped into Father's recliner. It surprised him that his honest words made her so angry. Everyone he'd ever discussed this topic with agreed with him.

Patty put one hand on each arm of the chair then leaned her head close to his. "Here's what happened hours ago in the Stake President's office."

"Please don't tell me," begged Martin.

"But I'm bursting to tell someone. Who should I pick? Your mother? Your sister?"

Martin swallowed. It felt like he was trying to get a medium sized dirt clod down his throat. "No. Don't tell either of them. I'll listen."

She smiled. He felt her sweet breath on his face. "LaVar pointed to a chair, and I sat down. Then he walked to the other side of the desk and sat in his leather swivel chair. He said, 'There's no reason to feel rushed. Tell me everything sexual that went on between you and my son,' Then he sat there, waiting for me to speak. I tingled with excitement. LaVar would be the most dangerous man I'd ever seduced."

Martin tensed. "You didn't seduce my father."

"I made sure I sounded nervous when I answered, 'Well, I'll do my best.' I told him about my attraction to you, your beautiful blue eyes, your soft lips. I said the traits that drove me wildest were even more prevalent in him. He smiled at that. Then I told the story of the janitor's closet. Remember it? The absolute darkness, the fear of getting caught, the danger . . . wasn't it exciting?"

Martin frowned.

"Well, I thought it was. The thought made me hot. 'Do you mind if I take off my sweater?' I asked LaVar. 'No, make yourself comfortable.' He smiled ever so slightly when I pulled the sweater over my head to reveal nothing more than a lacy lavender camisole."

Martin cringed. "You're lying!"

"His lust was obvious. But if he thought he was in control he was wrong. He wanted to know what happened? I'd show him. I got up and walked around to LaVar's side of the desk. He just sat there, staring up at me. I moved closer, closing my teeth and opening my lips slightly. 'Shhh, I think someone might be coming.' I leaned into him, just like I'd done with you, and covered his lips with my own."

Martin fell back into the chair and waited for the story to end, knowing there was no escape. Father had been right about this girl, and about the outside world. Evil abounded.

"I slid my tongue through his lips and felt him shudder. 'How does that make you feel?' I asked. I cupped his crotch in my hand. 'That's what I thought.' He let out a helpless moan. I straddled his leg, then leaned back, pulling the Stake President onto the floor on top of me."

Martin turned his head away. He couldn't stand seeing the truth in Patty's eyes. "I don't believe you. Now, let me out of Father's chair. That's his car that just pulled up."

Patty moved aside. Martin scrambled from the seat, and she dropped into it. Father walked into the room and glared at her.

Patty gave Father no time to react. "I've thought about it all day. I want no part of your church."

Sweat rose on Martin's brow.

"Are you going back on your word?" Father asked.

"I could discuss our meeting with my priest."

Martin saw Father flinch, then his face reddened as his focus shifted. "What are you gawking at, Martin? Get out of here. I need to have a word with Patty."

Martin was halfway out of the room before Father finished talking. He hurried to his room and shut the door. He stayed there until Mother called everyone to dinner several hours later.

"Where's Patty?" Mother asked as everyone took their seats around the table.

"We have made new arrangements," Father said. "She will be staying with Grandma Pearl. It is too crowded here, and Pearl has lots of extra space since Mel passed away. I have changed my mind about bringing the girl into the store as well. She would be a distraction to the salesmen. I have my doubts she would be of any use anyway. I have paid Pearl room and board out of my own pocket. In the end, this whole mess will cost me less that way."

When he finished eating Martin went straight to his room to think. He lay back on his bed. What a disappointment to find out Patty would seduce anyone, even Father. The thought sickened him. He could never look at her the same way again.

After a while the door creaked open. Father stepped through and shut it behind him. Martin recoiled involuntarily. The man seemed extra large in the small room, looming above the bed. "Martin, you have a bad habit of seeing and hearing things that are none of your business."

Martin's voice came out squeaky. "I don't mean to."

"Sit up."

Martin hesitated, then swung his legs to the floor.

Father sat down on the bed beside him. The man placed a warm hand on the boy's knee. "I told you that girl was trying to get to me through you, and now you have seen it with your own eyes." The unexpectedly friendly tone took Martin by surprise. Their eyes met. "I don't know what lies she told you, but I'm certain she will continue trying to turn you against me. These are the times family is most important. In your darkest hour you need to be surrounded by people you know you can rely on. I can count on you, can't I?"

Martin stared at Father, then nodded.

Father put his hand on Martin's cheek and looked into his eyes. "That's my boy."

Father's affection felt good. Martin threw his arms around the man's neck for the first time since childhood. When he felt Father hug back a wonderful feeling of belonging surged through his veins. He couldn't restrain a few tears.

As the weeks passed, Martin wondered how Patty managed to stay so hidden. He'd visited Pearl's, and though he avoided Patty, he knew she was there. The neighbors didn't seem to, though. As Patty's body changed she avoided all outside contact. From a community perspective, she didn't exist. The "problem," had it not been aired in church, would never have even been suspected by the ward members, and since none of them was bold enough to bring up such a touchy subject, Martin began believing the crisis might blow over.

One Saturday afternoon Emma and Martin walked to Grandma Pearl's house. They entered through the kitchen door and, before they stepped around the corner, heard Grandma and Patty talking at the quilting frame. Martin turned to leave, but Emma held his arm.

"I never anticipated the two of us would become such fast friends. I haven't been so close to anyone since I lost my husband," they overheard Pearl say.

"I'll always love you with all my heart, but you don't need to say such nice things to me. I realize what a burden I am," Patty said.

"Now Patty, I want you to stop talking like that. How many

times have we had this conversation? It's a pleasure to have you and your child, my great grandchild, as guests in this home. If you tried to go elsewhere I'd find you and bring you back. I love having you here."

"I wish I could believe that's true. I know how people feel about—"

"It is true. I wouldn't say it if it weren't. You've become so self-conscious; I don't know what I'm going to do with you."

"No one has ever treated me the way you do, Pearl." Patty sounded on the verge of tears. "What is it you really want from me?"

"You silly girl. I don't want anything but your love."

"But you must want something else. Everyone wants more."

Martin and Emma looked at one another. Martin again retreated to the door, feeling bad to have intruded on such a private conversation.

"Knock knock," Emma yelled, as if they'd only just arrived.

Reluctantly, Martin took his sister's arm and escorted her where she wanted to go. Grandma Pearl's expression was expectant as they stepped into the living room. A smile spread across her face. "Well, if it isn't my other favorite pregnant lady, and my favorite grandson, too. Come on in here and sit down."

Emma waddled forward.

"These two young ladies look like they're getting ready to burst, don't they Martin?" Grandma said.

He glanced toward Patty, then away. Their figures had become similar. "They sure do."

"What brings the two of you over here?" Pearl asked.

"I'm doing some walking to help bring the baby down. Martin's keeping me company and watching out for me," Emma said.

"She's due any moment," Martin added.

Patty spoke up. "I've decided to have my baby, when the time comes, right here. Pearl says she's delivered plenty of children including both of you, and I want her to deliver mine."

Grandma smiled. "It will be an honor. I can't wait to meet my great grandchildren. It won't be much longer now."

On February 16, 1962 Emma gave birth to a healthy seven and a half-pound baby girl. Two Sunday's later, in a traditional Mormon ceremony, John and other men of the priesthood blessed the infant and christened her Jillian Rose Lewis. All the while, Patty remained hidden away in Pearl's house.

Despite the confusing circumstances with Patty, it was a wonderful time for Martin. Ever since he and his father had hugged, their relationship changed, almost as if Father considered Martin a confidant. Father sought Martin out all the time, even to the exclusion of Joseph. Martin loved the close relationship.

One day Father brought him a Yankee's cap and a baseball signed by the team.

Martin found Mickey Mantle's and Roger Maris' signatures side by side. "The World Champs! Wow, Dad! Where did you get this?"

"I had a supplier in New York ship it. I thought you'd like it."

On Saturday, March 31, virtually the entire neighborhood emigrated to downtown Salt Lake City. The occasion was LDS General Conference, an event held twice a year at the Mormon Tabernacle on Temple Square.

At the last moment Martin decided to stay behind. He knew Patty must be getting awfully close, and Grandma wasn't as young and healthy as she seemed to think.

"I am disappointed, Son," Father said. "I really wish you would go with us."

"I've got to stay, Father. I have a funny feeling that Grandma will need me around."

"We'll drop by her house on the way home to check in on you," Father said.

When everyone left, Martin headed to Grandma's house. He hopped fences through the yards of neighbors he knew would welcome his passage. Soon he reached Grandma's back yard. He spotted her hanging laundry out to dry. At seventy and despite her increasingly frail frame, she refused to slow down. She clearly didn't have the strength she once did. "Hey, Grandma."

Grandma Pearl looked up. "What are you doing here? You're going to be late for Conference."

"I'm not going." Martin noticed Patty through the open kitchen door. She lay on the floor in the fetal position. He sprinted past his grandmother and into the house. A broken plate lay at the girl's side. She squeezed a dishtowel in her hand.

"Pearl. Pearl, help me," the girl moaned.

"What's happening?" Martin asked.

Grandma Pearl arrived. "Oh my. Contractions?"

"I've felt them before, but never so violent. What's gonna happen to me?" Fear permeated her voice.

"You're going to be all right, Patty. Let me check how things are coming along." Grandma slipped her hand between the girl's legs.

"Is everything all right?" Martin asked.

"I never guessed she would progress this quickly. I figured we still had about a week to go. It looks like it's a good thing you stayed behind, Martin."

"Oh, Pearl, I think the baby's coming soon," cried Patty.

"Darling, I'm sure you're right. Everything's going to be just fine. Let me help you to your bed. Martin, can you run to the hall closet? You'll find two plastic sheets there. I need you to spread them out, one atop the other, before I lay Patty down. After that I need you to boil all the water you can. We have plenty of fresh towels. Bring them into the bedroom, too. Oh, I'd planned on more help than this. If I had a car, or even a telephone . . . but I don't and that's just the way it is."

"I can run home to use the phone," suggested Martin.

"We can't risk it. Even with you at my side I'll be busier than a one armed paper hanger with the hives. If you leave for even a moment and things get complicated I could have real problems on my hands."

Grandma Pearl was a flurry of activity. When contractions

came she went through breathing drills with Patty and showed the girl other ways to deal with the pain. Biting on a wet towel seemed most effective. Martin fought off queasiness at the sight and smell of blood. He pulled a chair to the head of the bed and sat down.

Grandma kept reaching between Patty's legs and calling out measurements. Martin wrote them all down along with the times, but he didn't know if his efforts served any purpose. She called out temperatures from a thermometer, and he wrote those down too. She measured pulse rates and timed intervals. Martin recorded everything.

Between contractions Grandma fluffed pillows, organized and reorganized supplies, and leafed through books that apparently told her what to expect next. She gave Patty all sorts of instructions Martin couldn't even understand. Sweat poured from the old lady's forehead. Her damp hair stuck to her cheek. Martin wished he could be of more help, but he couldn't even stand. Each time he thought he'd try, another wave of nausea washed over him.

The delivery seemed to take forever. He looked at his notes. Over three hours had gone by. Martin sat beside Patty, allowing her to hold his hand, and to squeeze it when the pain became great. He found it increasingly difficult to keep his eyes off the mess where Grandma worked. There seemed nowhere in the room he could comfortably rest his gaze. Finally, he allowed himself to look into Patty's eyes.

She stared back at him, her expression pleading and vulnerable. Her eyes glistened with moisture; her brow beaded sweat. When she mouthed, "I'm sorry," he thought his heart might break. She was so confused, in such pain. How could he remain cold to her? Sure, she had schemed against him and her plans had gone awry, but if it weren't for his actions she wouldn't be in these trying circumstances.

His thoughts went to their time together in Provo. How was it possible that the consequences of such pleasure had been so great? Surely she'd suffered punishment enough to atone for whatever sins she'd committed. With Father's new friendly attitude they could all be friends, live happily ever after.

"Now Patty, we're approaching the end." Grandma's words intruded upon the moment Patty and Martin shared.

Patty looked toward the foot of the bed and gritted her teeth.

"Work with me, dear. It will be over soon. I need you to give me another push. The biggest one you can," Grandma said.

"Aaahhh!" Patty yelled as she bore down.

"You're doing great Dear, give me another."

Patty moaned. Sweat glistened over her entire body.

"All right. The head's all the way out. This will be your last push if you can make it a big one."

She bore down a final time.

Grandma worked frantically. After a tense moment she spoke. "Patty dear, you've done it. A gorgeous baby boy."

Grandma lifted the child by his feet and smacked him on the rear.

The room filled with the baby's angry wailing.

Martin couldn't control his tears. He wanted to behave like a man, to provide emotional stability, but when he looked at the two women and saw that they were both crying as well, he really lost it. "I never imagined this. Is that little boy my child?" Fear and excitement blended.

"What's his name going to be?" Grandma Pearl asked as she snipped the umbilical cord and tied it off.

"If it's all right with Marty, I decided on Thomas Martin Crump for a boy."

"That's a beautiful name," Martin said.

"Well, Tom, it's a pleasure to meet you," Grandma said. She set the infant on Patty's breast. He immediately began to suckle. Then Grandma went to work again between Patty's legs. "Raise up a smidge, Dear. I need to pull one of these plastic sheets from beneath you."

Grandma gathered the sheet by the corners and carried it from the room.

Tom stayed at Patty's side. He wanted to speak, wanted to know what she felt, but words failed him. They stared at one another in silence.

After a moment Grandma returned. "Now I need to give that little boy a bath. Hand him over."

Patty reluctantly gave the baby to Grandma.

Martin kept his eyes on the new mother. She looked so content, so beautiful, so complete. They gazed at one another for a long time.

Grandma returned, cradling the tightly swaddled infant and saying, "Tom, why don't you help me move Patty to my clean bed. There's more sunlight in that room anyway. It will be a pleasant place for mother and child to recover." She set the infant in the corner of the room on the floor.

Martin wanted to rush over and pick the boy up, but he had to obey Grandma. Patty draped an arm over each of their shoulders and they moved down the hall. The moment Patty lay down, Martin rushed back for the infant. He picked the tiny package up and cuddled the boy close to his heart. Slowly, he carried the infant down the hall, trying to extend this moment of first contact as long as possible.

Patty called, "Where's my baby?"

Martin stepped into the room and gave the infant up.

The little boy's lips began working the moment he was in his mother's arms. She exposed a breast and the infant took to it immediately.

"I'll clean up in the other room," Martin said.

Grandma let out a sigh. She put a hand to her face and leaned on a chair.

"You're exhausted, Pearl. Lie down for a moment." Patty patted the large open space beside her in the bed.

It surprised Martin that Grandma didn't argue the point. He'd sensed how tired she'd become, but suddenly she looked exceedingly frail. She climbed into bed and let out another long sigh, then she shut her eyes.

Martin closed the door and shuffled down the hall to start the cleanup. He pinched his nose in preparation for the blood.

At four in the afternoon just as Martin finished cleaning the big Cadillac pulled into the driveway.

"You missed an inspirational meeting," Father said as Martin ran to the car.

"You missed the birth of a baby boy," Martin answered.

Everyone spoke at once. Mother and Emma clambered from the car. Joseph grabbed tiny Jill and toted her in a wicker bassinet. Father trailed behind.

Martin hustled beside his brother. "Where's John?"

"Left for Idaho right after Conference. His mom's not doing too well."

As they crowded into the bedroom the commotion woke mother and child. They lay there, groggily, trying to focus on the gathering crowd.

"Pearl, did you deliver this child all by yourself?" Father asked.

Grandma lay silently. Martin answered instead. "She did. I tried to help, but there wasn't much I could do."

Father stepped to the bedside. He put a hand on Grandma's forehead, then lifted her wrist and felt it. He looked at the faces surrounding him, his expression dark. "Pearl's dead."

"No, she's not dead," chuckled Patty. "She's just exhausted. You should have seen how hard she worked." The girl turned to her companion in the bed. She rocked her at first, then shook harder and harder. "Pearl, wake up," she cried. "Wake up. Wake up! You can't die. You're my best friend in the world."

Emma screamed and burst into tears. Mother wailed. When Patty joined in, the chorus reached a ringing crescendo. Martin knew this sound of ultimate sorrow would remain with him for the rest of his life. He dried his eyes with his hand and noticed Joseph doing the same. Father stood stoically. After a while other family members took turns feeling the wrists for a pulse– listening to the chest for a heartbeat— holding a hand above the mouth and nose to sense breath— but there were no signs of life.

"Most likely had a heart attack as a result of all the exercise and stress," Father said.

The baby cried. Patty turned to the infant reluctantly. Martin assisted the pair from the bed to the rocking chair, which sat in the corner of the room.

"If only I hadn't asked so much of her," cried Patty.

Emma lay a reassuring hand on Patty's shoulder. "She gave you what she wanted to give, Patty. That was her way. You couldn't stop her by asking for less. She loved you and wanted to prove it to you through her caring."

Slowly the cries diminished. Eventually the loudest sound in the room was Tom suckling. The sound of life being gathered so eagerly in the presence of death must have angered Father. He glared toward the rocking chair and said, "That child is destined to bring nothing but bad luck to this family."

Patty pulled her baby closer.

"How can you say such a thing? He's a lovely child," Emma said. She looked toward her mother for confirmation.

Mother remained silent for a long moment. "Emma, be realistic. Your father's right. It can't be denied. Think of all the trouble he's already brought."

"You can't be serious. None of this is that little boy's fault," Joseph said.

All eyes turned toward Martin. He dropped his gaze to the floor.

Father sounded authoritative. "It is time I make a decision for the good of this family. I am going to tell you the reasons, not because I want to argue them, but because I know if each of you were able to examine the facts with a clear head you would come to the same decision."

The big man looked around the room, then cleared his throat. "Patty and her son are still invisible as far as this community is concerned. They are nothing more than a pair of rumors. No one outside of this family yet knows of their presence here, or of the birth. If we act quickly, no one else will ever know. We have experienced all the misery we need in this life over one event. Let's not put ourselves through more.

"I've had the form for some time now, I carry it with me, and I've filled in all of the necessary information. We must act quickly, because once the baby is found out, everything will change for the worse."

He pulled a piece of paper from his inside suit coat pocket and unfolded it on the table. Everyone gathered around. Their eyes were drawn to the bold title. "Application to Deem Minor as Ward of the State- Salt Lake City Orphanage."

"The remaining blanks are for the signatures of the parents." He handed a pen to his son.

Martin looked at the ashen faces of his brother and sister. The plea in their eyes could not be missed.

Father cleared his throat again, apparently fully aware of the deference it inspired in his youngest son. He put a hand on Martin's shoulder. "The decisions we make out of the purest love are the most difficult to follow through with. You must do this for the sake of the child."

Martin clung to that simple idea. Father loved him and had his interests in mind. Martin wanted to look at Patty, but he knew the risk was too great. He must prove his love for the child before he lost his nerve. He inked his name to the document.

"No," wept Patty. "Marty, this is our baby, our own flesh and blood. You and I made him. Think of what we've gone through for him. We can't give him away!"

"Be reasonable, young lady," Father said.

"But . . ." Patty said.

Father leaned over her and forced the pen into her hands.

"I won't sign your document," the girl said. "You can't make me."

Martin spoke. He felt like he'd aged years in the past few months. "Patty, I've thought about this as well. Don't think I haven't. Father's right. There's no other choice. You and I can't give this baby the care he needs. For his own good we must give him up."

Patty gazed out the window, and her expression changed. The muscles in her face relaxed. She looked back at Martin.

Father tapped his finger on the signature line. She seemed to accept the futility of fighting the inevitable. Then she lifted the window and yelled toward the street at the top of her lungs. "Hey mister! Come over here! Hurry!"

Martin looked out the window. Brother Pratt walked down the street. The Sunday School teacher turned to face the shouts, "Who's that calling?" He walked toward the bedroom window.

The moment he stuck his head inside, Father's plan crumbled. "What's this?" the neighbor asked, oblivious to how he'd just altered a child's destiny.

"The second Crump baby has been born, Brother," Father said in his controlled tone.

"So, the blessed event has occurred, and what a beautiful child. And here's the mother. What's your name, dear?"

"Patty."

He extended a hand through the window. "It's a pleasure to meet you."

"The pleasure's all mine," Patty said.

"A boy or a girl?" Pratt asked.

"A healthy son. Nearly eight pounds I'd guess," Patty said.

Wonderful news," Brother Pratt said. "I'd begun to wonder why we'd heard nothing more. I worried some harm had come."

"Fortunately, no. Not to the baby, anyway," Father said.

"Well then, let's get the word out. It's time to celebrate," Brother Pratt said.

"No, it's not the time for celebration, either. You are already aware that the circumstances surrounding this birth are less than ideal, but now there is more. With life has come death. Today we lost our beloved Mother, Grandma Pearl."

Brother Pratt grabbed the windowsill for support and looked

to heaven. "No, not Pearl." He pulled a handkerchief from his pocket and wiped his eyes. "Not lovely Pearl. She was dancing jigs on soap bubbles last time I laid eyes on her. She wouldn't tell me what was up, but I thought to myself, 'With that sort of energy she'll outlast me.'"

Father spoke somberly. "It's a great shock to all of us."

"So the entire family is gathered around. The love you Crumps show one another is a glorious thing. When did she die? When was the baby born?"

"It's a long story, my friend. Martin . . . Joseph . . . Emma, could you step outside and fill our neighbor in on the details? I need to ask a favor of your mother. I'll be out in a moment."

Martin went outside with the others and began telling Brother Pratt what happened.

Father joined them less than a minute later and cut the story short. "Brother Pratt, will you excuse us. Delilah will stay behind to care for Patty. I need to take my children home for a family meeting."

"Of course. If there's anything at all I can do to help you in this trying time, please don't hesitate to ask."

Father nodded. "Come with me kids."

The family loaded themselves into the car and Father drove them home.

Half an hour later Martin wandered through the rose garden in front of the house. His thoughts were on his grandmother when commotion down the street distracted him. Mother ran into view holding a small bundle in her arms. What could be going on?

Martin hurried toward her. "What's wrong?"

Mother looked feint. Her face was pale.

Father stalked into the street and took the child in his arms. "What is it, Delilah?"

She barely choked out the words. "I left the room for only a moment. When I returned she was gone. I looked everywhere. She just left her poor baby on the bed, and disappeared."

Father held the baby like a wad of laundry and growled. "I

cannot say I am surprised, although I didn't expected her to turn her back on her responsibilities quite this soon. I saw the weakness of her moral composition the moment I laid eyes on her."

"That doesn't make sense," Martin said. "Why would she do such a thing? We've got to find her."

Father laughed. "Do you actually believe it would be worth the effort? What would you do if, by some miracle, you did track her down? Bring her back and put her under our roof again? Shackle her to the wall and make her take responsibility for her actions? There will come a day when you will look upon her disappearance as one of the most fortunate turns your life ever took, Martin. It may be far off, because you lack intelligence, but mark my words, the day will come."

Martin looked at Father disbelievingly.

Emma stepped between them. "You have no right to talk to Martin that way."

Father glared at her. Rage flared in his eyes. He slapped his daughter across the cheek. "That husband of yours is soft. I raised you right, and already he is ruining you. You never would have spoken to a man in such a tone while you answered to me. Don't even consider starting now."

"I hate you," Emma said.

Father put his face inches from his daughter's. "Out of my house." He pointed at the door. "And don't come back. Obedience to my authority has been overlooked around here lately, but that is going to change right now. This episode is going to be put behind us. I want every reminder of Patty's existence gathered up and loaded into the trunk of my car immediately. That means every photograph, every piece of clothing, every possession. Don't try to hide anything, because I know what is here, I will be looking for it, and I can disown the rest of you as quickly as I have Emma."

"Dad, don't do this. I spoke without thinking. You know I respect you," Emma said through a curtain of tears.

Father switched the baby to his other hand. He looked at

Emma skeptically. He spoke in a cool tone. "I am willing to give you one last chance. Go with Joseph to your grandmother's home. Gather up Patty's things, and put them with those that your mother and Martin collect from this house. Be back in no less than fifteen minutes. I need to call the morgue. You wouldn't want to be seen disturbing things over there once they arrive to take the body."

The day after Grandma Pearl's funeral Father pulled into the driveway at midday. He never left work early. Martin and Mother were pulling weeds at opposite ends of the yard while Emma tended both infants on the porch. Martin looked up. Mother rose to her feet, wiped her hands on her apron, and headed toward the Cadillac. Father stepped from the car and strolled toward Mother with a benign expression; then he extended a manila envelope in her direction. Martin moved into the shadows.

As Mother took the package, Father spoke in a matter-of-fact tone. "You've brought me all the bad luck you ever will." He turned on his heel and strode away. The big car backed out the driveway and was gone.

Martin hurried to his mother's side. She wobbled as she handed him the envelope. Martin glanced at the name of the law firm, then bent the metal clasps and opened the flap. As he drew the papers out, a single word flew off the page and entered his consciousness. He read the word aloud. "Divorce." Mother finally had what she never dared to ask for.

"After all I've given him, how could that man do this to me," she screamed.

\* \* \*

Martin looked into my eyes. "So now you know. Is that what you wanted?"

Facts and allegations swam through my head. "I need time to think about what you've said. I never came close to imagining such circumstances."

"Do you see why it broke my heart when you told Joseph you loved him like a father?"

"I don't remember doing that."

"You did it all the time."

I understood why it hurt. "How was I to know any different?"

He nodded sympathetically.

"Uncle Joe's not doing too well these days. He's very sick," I said.

"What makes you think I care?"

I stared at him, even right through him. How could he be so callous? What made him this dead set on being difficult, on ruining a meaningful moment? My disappointment only increased my determination to flesh out the rest of his story. Many unanswered questions remained. The key would be getting him into my element.

The mountain, an environment where pretense required too much valuable energy to uphold, was where I'd find out who he really was. And I believed I knew something about him he didn't understand about himself. "Thanks for letting me off the hook for that Mount Olympus hike, Martin."

He looked puzzled. "Letting you off?"

"Yeah, I was wondering how I'd find the time, especially with all that's gone on recently. It's been a relief I don't have to."

He stared blankly.

"Well, same time next week? We don't have to quit meeting, do we?" I jogged down the steps.

"Wait just a minute, Tommy."

I turned back.

"You misunderstood. I've always wanted to hike Mount Olympus. You promised you'd help."

"But I thought . . ."

"I was just frustrated by the way you interrupted back then.

I never meant you to think we wouldn't go at all. I've been walking all summer."

I sighed, trying to convey the opposite emotion I experienced. "If you're sure that's what you want I won't go back on my word."

He smiled like he'd won a battle of wills; then his expression softened. "Give your daughter a kiss when you get home."

"I'll do that. Thanks for thinking of her."

"By the way, do you prefer to go by Tom?"

I thought a moment, then nodded. "Yeah. Actually, I do."

# Chapter 23

A nightmare jolted me from sleep. My pulse raced and my breath came rapidly. The dream had a loose connection to my first day on earth. I imagined my grandfather tossing me from one hand to the other, like a lump of pizza dough. He gloated over his prediction that I'd bring bad luck, said that facts were already proving his premonitions correct. Then he said he'd do the world a favor, and he dropped me in a ditch.

Sara mumbled something incoherent in her sleep as she cuddled closer. I lay, staring at the ceiling. I believed Martin's stories. They seemed to fit the facts, but at the same time they raised more questions than they answered. Where had Patty gone, for instance? I'd been getting the impression she'd grown more mature, more attached to the idea of motherhood, as the pregnancy progressed. After all, she refused to sign the adoption papers. Then she just disappeared . . . forever. Had she been acting? I tried to tell myself that she couldn't be so disingenuous, but I knew she could. The story proved it.

On the other hand, maybe there was more behind her disappearance. If so, Delilah might be the only one who knew the truth. She'd been there when Patty disappeared. Unfortunately, the chances of her telling me anything were nil. She'd begged me from the first not to look into the past.

My thoughts drifted to Martin's reaction toward Joe's bad fortune, and also his dislike of my mom. Throughout Martin's story, he seemed to love his siblings. When had that changed?

I could still recall his words in the park, "Emma wanted to gloat, okay? She's certain if I'd followed her advice things would've turned out better." Whatever this advice had been, he'd either left it out of the story or it came later. Obviously, responsibility for me had been transferred from Martin to Emma. It was safe to assume the circumstances were traumatic. It's likely Joe was part of the decision as well.

I knew from his story that Martin felt pretty connected to me immediately after the birth. Having gone through a similar experience with Courtney I could relate. Maybe Martin crossed that fragile line between love and hate as a result of this issue. He assigned my care to Emma while he tried to get his life back in control. Instead things worsened. He turned to drugs and who knows what else. Then Emma and others topped it all off by refusing to tell me about my past. In their minds they did this for my own good, but from Martin's perspective they further wrestled management of his life away from him. As a result, he retreated to the smallest corner he could find, fighting to control every element. I couldn't be sure things had gone according to my theory, but it made sense.

Other thoughts assaulted me throughout the night. They ranged from Jill's health to Courtney's future, from Joe's circumstances to Mom's trip. When my alarm went off I still hadn't fallen back asleep.

Groggily I showered and dressed, then drove to Salt Lake Community College for my interview. Halfway there, I noticed my socks didn't match. Just as I convinced myself it wasn't a big deal I noticed a stain on my light blue tie. I looked in the rearview mirror and bloodshot eyes stared back. Dreams of an impressive interview dimmed. I struggled to find the positives, but failed. I was right for this job. I'd felt it in my bones the moment I heard about it. I had to land it.

My cell phone rang. "Hello, this is Tom."

A panicked voice came over the line. "I'm so glad I reached you. I need your help."

"Hi, Delilah." I'd dreaded this type of call since Mom decided to go on her trip. I'd known all along it would fall to me to deal with at least one of Delilah's emergencies, but why did it have to happen now?

She spoke sharply. "Can you help me or not? Your mother promised you would while she was out of town but I told her, 'We'll see when the time comes!' Well, now the time's come."

Delilah seemed determined to suck dry those who helped her. Most people ran the other way. She went through boyfriends like cold sufferers go through Kleenex. No one put up with Delilah's behavior for long except my mother, her only constant. "You haven't told me what you need."

"If I tell you it will be very embarrassing, and I'm worried you'll make fun of me," she said.

"Okay. I'll guess. Have you checked the pilot light? Sometimes they blow out."

"Tom, are you making fun of me? How can you treat an old grandmother this way?"

I laughed. "This must be some kind of sick prank call. You can't be my grandmother, because my grandmother isn't old. I believe she's several years younger than me."

"Why won't you listen to me?"

"You're not saying anything I can do anything about."

"Tom, I'm in jail."

I laughed and shook my head, distracted. I nearly rear-ended a rusty yellow pickup truck as it braked for a red light. A weathered bumper sticker on the tailgate read, "I'd rather be fishing." My sentiments exactly.

"Tom, did you hear me?"

"Yeah. Who are you visiting?"

She began crying. "I'm not visiting. I've got to get out of here immediately. Please, Tom. This place frightens me."

I checked my watch. Only fifteen minutes until my appointment. "I'll be there in about an hour and a half. I'm on my way to a job interview right now. The hospital has threatened to repossess Courtney if I don't pay my bill immediately."

"What? Tom, you have a good job. I'll never forgive you if you turn your back on me at a moment like this. You promised your mother you'd help if I had even the tiniest problem. She assured me of it." Her voice trembled with apparent terror.

It wouldn't be worth explaining. I didn't doubt she could permanently withhold forgiveness, and the consequences would fall upon my mom. I steered reluctantly toward the courthouse, but didn't mention my change of plans to Delilah. Maybe it was a blessing in disguise anyway. I'd call to reschedule my interview, and I'd certainly be able to spiff up my appearance. I might also be able to get my grandmother to answer some questions about the past. "Delilah, tell me what you're in for, or I won't pick you up."

"Just a silly misunderstanding. This gentleman friend of mine called the police because he heard something in his bushes."

"And they arrested you?"

"Well . . . they found me in the bushes."

I laughed so hard I could barely get my next question out. "What were you doing there?"

"Tom, please don't entertain yourself at my expense. I wish I could've called your mother. She wouldn't blow this out of proportion. Just come down to the police station and help me explain my side of it."

"I don't know your side." I'd never bailed anyone out of jail or detox or anything before this week. Now I would do it for a second time.

"I thought he might be cheating, okay?"

"Cheating at what?"

"Why are you making this so difficult, Tom?"

"Why did Floyd have you arrested? He's your boyfriend, right?"

"Floyd didn't have me arrested. Edwin did."

"So . . . you were cheating on Floyd with this Edwin character, and spying on Edwin to make certain he wasn't cheating on you."

"You're making this sound worse than it is."

"When Edwin saw the cops drag you out of the bushes in handcuffs, why didn't he say, 'Wait a minute. That's my lover you've got there?'"

"Because I'm not his lover. He pressed charges saying I needed to learn a lesson. Now are you going to help me or do you want me to hang up?"

"Delilah, how old are you?" I asked.

"That is the most impolite question I've ever been asked," she groaned.

"I ask because your story sounds like something that might happen to a sixteen year old."

"It does, doesn't it?" The realization seemed to sooth the wound my previous comment inflicted. "I've always prided myself in being young at heart."

"You are that, Delilah. Really young. I'll be right there."

After we hung up I called the college and apologized for having to reschedule at a moment's notice. The secretary told me she saw no problem with that, but that the dean's schedule for the rest of the week was up in the air. She'd have to check with him and get back to me. That would give me the time I needed to regain control. I let out a relieved sigh as I disconnected the call.

I parked my Cherokee and walked into the jail. Abundant incandescent light filled the building. The walls, ceiling, and floor were blinding white. Even in the lobby I could hear the echoing and belligerent voices of the prisoners. A burly woman looked up from the reception desk with a disinterested expression.

"I need to see Delilah Crump," I said. "I'm her grandson."

She broke into a grin. Without even consulting the blotter she called out, "Hey, this guy here's come for the granny."

Smiling cops appeared from all sides. Clearly Delilah's caper had been the highlight of the day for the precinct. Now everyone had an opportunity to associate my face with the saga. I wondered how many versions of the story would be shared with officer's families and friends over the course of the next week, and hoped that what they saw in me didn't somehow make their tales better.

One of the officers escorted me down a short hallway and pointed out a seat. I sat nervously on the edge. Ahead of me a series of iron gates with impressive locks separated the good guys from the bad. A horse-faced officer stationed in a little room nearby kept staring at me. Finally he asked, "Do you wanna hear a poem I made up about your granny?"

"Not really." I saw less humor in the situation now that jail bars were in sight. The echoing voices in the background became much louder. Were the prisoners sharing Delilah's story too?

The officer disregarded my objection:

> "Little Miss Crumpet
> Sat in a closet
> Watching a geezer undress.
> Along came a copper
> And he had to cuff her
> And lead her away in distress."

"Wonderful," I said with a forced smile. "Don't quit your day job."

He looked hurt. "She's ready to see you. Go through the first door on the left.

I did as instructed and found myself in a room where I could look at my grandmother through thick Plexiglas and speak to her over a phone.

I picked up the line, feeling suddenly protective. "How have they treated you?"

"I just want to get out of here."

We filled out papers and signed forms, and I wrote out a

check that seemed a high price to pay for my involvement in the matter, but I didn't complain because I knew Delilah was always strapped for cash.

We walked out of the courthouse and across the parking lot in silence. I opened the passenger door for Delilah, then went around to my side. As I started the engine Delilah spoke. "Thanks, Tom."

I looked at her twice surgically tightened facial skin. It helped her remain a surprisingly attractive woman for her age, whatever that age was. "Can we laugh about it now?"

She chuckled. "It is sort of funny, isn't it?"

I laughed with her, feeling that the price of bail entitled me to smile about the situation. My wallet still reeled with the pain. As far as I was concerned, I'd also purchased the right to ask her some questions. "Delilah, what was Grandpa like?"

She seemed pleased with my question. "He was a very difficult man. You're perceptive to see he's a big part of the reason this happened today."

She'd imagined a way to blame him for her arrest so many years after his death? I knew her habit was to nebulously tag all sorts of unfortunate situations on her former husband, but hadn't expected this. I'd paid little attention to her opinions in the past. I'd always sided with Mom who often told her mother that she'd blown things out of proportion. "I wasn't implying tha–"

"LaVar made me do bad things for him. He was a wicked man."

Maybe I could trick her into saying more. "I'm sure 'wicked' is an overstatement."

Her eyes flared. "It's no exaggeration."

"I've never seen anything to back it up."

"That's only because you never got to know him. He'd go to any length if he thought it might protect him. I can give you an example." She thought for a moment. "Your grandfather conned me into the most terrible favor of all by convincing me it was for the good of the family. 'We're in a crisis,' he said. 'You must do this because it's the only way the family can be kept together.' I did exactly as he asked, and everything came out just like he wanted. Then, he divorced me."

My ears perked. This sounded like the same favor LaVar asked of Delilah right after Grandma Pearl's death. "What did you do for him?"

"That's not the point, Tom. I'll never tell a soul what he made me do. I'm only trying to give you a sense of who your grandfather really was. If you look up hypocrite in the dictionary you'll find his picture."

"So, you're better off without him. You should've been glad to be divorced."

"After all I gave to that relationship? Are you kidding? He worked me to the bone before he ran off with that floozy secretary of his. I gave him, his damn business, and his damn church everything I had to give. When I didn't have any more he wadded me up and tossed me out the window like a used candy wrapper."

The logic was vintage Delilah. Her contradictions covered territory I didn't care to tread. I tried to redirect her thoughts, to learn more about the favor. "Tell me about your divorce."

"He hired himself a Cracker Jack lawyer and they rigged it so I would hardly get anything for the years of pain I endured. I guess I've never learned to be wary of people, but I can tell you, that's one lesson I don't intend to learn. If you let someone take away your innocence they'll rob you of your youth."

I herded her back on track. "Didn't Grandpa's leaving you affect his standing in The Church? What could convince him to risk it? They take divorce seriously."

"He dragged my name through the gutter. He said I'd been mentally abusive and disloyal. It was a lie. Church authorities granted him an almost unheard of temple divorce, anyway. He even gloated to me about it.

"That's why I went to those same men and dumped evidence on their tables that I'd been collecting for years. LaVar's affairs started early on in our marriage, and I knew about them from the first. I had letters, photos, and witnesses. It destroyed his standing in The Church. The way I see it, the whole thing was his choice. I'd have been willing to stay silent forever if he'd treated me fairly. The truth is, I actually preferred his affairs to having a physical relationship with him of my own. I found him repulsive."

"How'd he react?"

"How do you think? He'd gotten away with saying one thing and doing another for so long he thought he'd earned a right to live his secret life. I learned a surprising thing about your grandfather soon after I married him."

Delilah unknowingly verified Martin's stories by describing the same man in the same way. "What surprising thing did you learn about Grandpa?"

She lowered her voice. "He was a lot more fearful of the judgment of his neighbors, and a lot less fearful of the judgment of his God, than he'd ever admit."

I thought about that for a while. "Why do you think he had affairs?"

"I guess the pleasures of this life were a greater temptation than the rewards of the next."

"Delilah, I wouldn't have guessed such thoughts kicked around inside your skull. You never cease to amaze me." I tried to imagine what her life had been like. Maybe I could take the first step in bridging the gulf between us. I was trying to think of a way when my cell phone rang. "Yes, Tom. I'm calling from human resources at the community college. Unfortunately, the dean has asked me to inform you that he's decided to hire a different candidate."

# Chapter 24

The ringing cellular phone, sitting in its charger stand atop my dresser, woke me.

I strained to open one stinging eye. The alarm clock said 2:13 a.m. "You must be joking."

"Are you going to answer it?" Sara asked groggily.

"Hell no. What sane person would call at this hour?"

The ringing stopped, but I kept wondering who it had been. It might have been Martin. An hour later, still unable to sleep, I stumbled out of bed and went to the phone. A back-lit icon indicated a message waited. I dialed in and entered my password.

"This is Sergeant Barry Lang of the Santa Barbara Police Department."

I forgot my exhaustion and scrambled to my nightstand to find a pen and paper. I stubbed my toe as I rounded the foot of the bed, then switched on my reading lamp.

The voice continued. "Your business card was found in the file of Joseph Crump. There was a notation indicating you are his nephew. We're attempting to locate Mr. Crump's next of kin in a matter of extreme urgency. Please return my call as soon as possible." He repeated a phone number twice. I wrote it down.

Sara stared at me without lifting her head from the pillow.

"There's more trouble with Uncle Joe." I dialed the number.

"Santa Barbara Police, how may we help you?"

"Sergeant Lang, please," I said.

I heard a series of clicks, then, "Lang here."

"My name is Tom Lewis. I'm returning your call about my uncle."

"He didn't make it."

"Didn't make what?"

"He didn't make it to the hospital. I called you right after we dispatched the ambulance, but there was no answer on your mobile."

"So, where is he now?"

"You're misunderstanding me. Joe Crump died tonight."

I couldn't respond. This couldn't be real. Weren't they supposed to be experts at breaking this sort of news gently? "Died?" I finally asked.

Sara's eyes went wide. She covered her mouth with a hand and sprang to her feet.

"A neighbor became concerned for some reason, went by to check on him, and found him unconscious on the bathroom floor."

"But I saw him just the other day. He was going to visit us this week. Uncle Joe can't be dead."

No response on the other end of the line.

Eventually I asked, "What did he die from?"

"It appears to be alcohol related."

I sat on the edge of the bed and ran a hand through my hair. This couldn't be happening. "Only last week I bought him some drugs to help control his alcoholism."

"Anabuse?"

"Yeah, that's it."

"I found Anabuse at the scene. I've got it right here. It's evidence."

"How much had he taken?"

"What I have is an unopened bottle in a stapled bag from Jacobsen's Drug. The prescription was filled August twenty-third of this year."

A stapled bag— prescription filled on the day I'd left Santa Barbara. I felt as if I'd been blindfolded and spun. I wanted to vomit.

"If you can give me a phone number where Mrs. Crump can be reached I'll do the rest."

"I need a moment to think." I tried to imagine in what order things must be done. I couldn't find my bearings. The only thing I felt certain of was that my uncle had committed suicide. He'd turned his back on every effort to save him and poisoned himself with alcohol. I should have figured out his plan and forced him to return with me to Salt Lake.

The sergeant continued jabbering details into my ear. I interrupted. "I'll call his wife. I'll call the whole family."

"I can take care of—"

"I'd rather do it myself."

I hung up the phone, then slumped onto the bed. Sara put her arms around me. I turned to face her, and together we cried.

I found the listing for Aunt Heather in my day-planner and scanned to the entry I'd made for her mother's home. I waited until six in the morning, Texas time, to call. She answered on the fifth ring.

"Hello." A voice cracked. Fortunately it was my aunt, and not her mother.

"Aunt Heather, this is Tom."

"Do you know what time it is?"

Sara hugged me from behind, one arm over my right shoulder, the other under my left arm. She kissed me on the cheek.

"I'm sorry to call you like this, but I have terrible news. A neighbor found Uncle Joe late last night. He was unconscious."

"Drinking?"

"Probably."

"How is he now?"

"They couldn't wake him." I couldn't tell if she understood, so I added, "Neither could the paramedics."

She broke into a spasmodic cry. I listened to her sobs, wondering what to say. Eventually the sounds became gentler.

"I'll help any way I can," I said.

She told me about the plans he'd previously discussed with

her. Joe wanted two funerals, one in Santa Barbara and a second in Salt Lake City. He'd long ago purchased a gravesite in the Spring Creek Cemetery. Heather asked if I'd take responsibility for the Utah arrangements. I agreed immediately.

As the sun rose, instead of scheduling job interviews I met with morticians. I contacted my mother. She cut her cruise short. I assisted incoming guests with travel arrangements. I wrote an obituary.

\* \* \*

The pasty-faced funeral director moved about the chapel tending to details— straightening flower arrangements, replacing the pen in its stand at the guest register. He could maintain his somber expression no matter what the task. Mourning was his forte, and he excelled at it. In fact, I'd never seen it more professionally done.

With only three days' notice people from every phase of Uncle Joe's life converged on Salt Lake. Some went to incredible lengths to attend the funeral. I wish Uncle Joe could have been alive to witness it. I stayed near the outside edge of the ward house lobby with Sara and Courtney as it filled with mourners. With Delilah and Jill on either side, Mom greeted one group after another. Heather, Rachel, and the rest of Joe's family milled about the room.

Delilah appeared more comfortable in the role of bereaved mother than she ever had as ordinary mother or grandmother. She held a small handkerchief in her left hand and reconstituted herself at regular intervals by dabbing at her eyes.

I peered into the crowd, then out to the parking lot. Still no sign of Martin. I'd stopped by his house; neither he nor his dogs were there, though the van occupied its usual spot. All I could do was leave a copy of the obituary and a note, begging him to attend. Even if he'd somehow missed my letter, Congressman Crump's death was big news in Salt Lake. He couldn't have missed that. Highly successful Mormons typically remain well known in Utah, wherever else their lives might take them.

When Delilah spied me on the fringe of the room holding Courtney in my arms, she floated toward us. "Coochy coochy coo," she said tickling the baby's tummy.

Courtney turned her face into my chest, afraid of this stranger.

"How are you doing, Delilah?" I asked.

"Not well. I hate funerals," she lied. "Why don't you come on over and join the reception, Tom? There are some people here you ought to meet."

"That's all right. I'm not in the mood to socialize."

She looked hurt, probably sensing my excuse implied something negative toward her. "Who says that I am? I'm doing it for Joseph. It's taking everything out of me, but it's what he would want. A mother has to give up so much for her children."

She waited for me to compliment her. I didn't.

She focused on Courtney, and tears came. "You can't imagine what it feels like to lose one of your own children, Tom. I'd always hoped I'd be lucky enough to die before any of them."

"You'll outlast us all, Delilah."

She dried her eyes with the hanky. "Oh, you don't have to be so nice. You know that won't happen. My day can't be far off. Now, come on over here and meet these people."

I shook my head. "I'd prefer not to."

"Tom, normally I wouldn't mind. I wouldn't mind at all and you know that, but there are many people here from the old neighborhood I haven't seen in years."

"In other words, you're going to keep asking until I say yes?"

She smiled. "I just didn't think you understood how much it meant to me."

"I'm tired of saying no."

"That's better. How about if you be my escort? I need someone to lean on. That baby should only take one of your arms. Let me have the other. Take me over to speak with that gentleman. Oh, and by the way, please call me 'Grandma.'"

I shook my head and couldn't hold back a chuckle. "You're kidding."

"Just for tonight Tom, please. And you're so much more handsome when you smile." She put an index finger on each corner of my mouth and pushed a grin onto my lips.

I looked squarely into her eyes, and understood her intent. She wanted to show her friends from the old ward that she'd completed the primary task expected of every Mormon woman—to raise a large and happy family. My daughter and I provided the best available evidence of her compliance, if only we would act the part. If we would dote over her for just one evening, do everything she'd begged me for a lifetime not to, then she could avoid the embarrassing questions. Appearances, after all, were so much more important than reality.

While I hesitated, a tear formed in the corner of her eye.

"Whatever you want, Grandma." I forced a smile. I don't know that I've ever said anything that brought her more joy.

She pointed across the room with a black gloved hand, then lifted my elbow and wrapped her fingers around it.

As I crossed the room in the way I least wanted to, I hoped we could somehow escape notice.

"Enoch Pratt, how nice of you to come," Delilah blurted toward the crowd in general. We were less than half way to the gathering, but she'd attracted the attention of everyone in the room.

Why did she have to make me a part of her spectacle? I felt my face turn hot with humiliation.

A lanky old gentleman with a head of hair so thick any thirty-year-old man would be envious, looked our way. His face lit up with recognition. With the aid of a cane he toddled around ninety degrees. It took him at least half a dozen tiny steps to make the rotation. He waited until we arrived to begin the conversation. "Delilah, how are you dear?"

Delilah had the hanky prepared for just this opportunity. She worked at her eyes and sniffled. "I don't think you can ever imagine how difficult it is to lose a child. I'd always hoped I'd be fortunate enough to die ahead of mine."

Enoch looked sympathetic. "I'm sure that's true. As you know, I wasn't fortunate enough to have children myself. I lost my wife, though, and that was quite difficult."

"Minnie died? I didn't know that." Delilah unwrapped her fingers from my elbow and placed them consolingly on his hand. "What happened?"

"Cancer. It's been ten years."

"I'm so sorry to hear that. It must be hard to lose a spouse."

"You lost LaVar." His feeble voice carried a comforting, almost relaxing quality.

"That doesn't count. He left me first."

"And now you've lost Joseph. What a shock. He was an exceptional young man. I always had great expectations of him, and still he exceeded my wildest dreams. Whenever I saw him on television I'd think of your family, and I'd feel very proud. I can understand why you're so heartbroken."

I felt happy I'd finally met the Sunday School teacher.

My grandmother dabbed at the corners of her eyes again. "We bear what burdens we must. "

"Well, you're bearing them wonderfully. You look well."

"You know, Enoch, we really should get to know one another again. It's tragic how we lose track of our best friends as life goes on."

I stood there like a discarded accessory while my grandmother and her friend caught up on the past. Delilah's hand remained atop the widower's.

I felt a shoulder brush against mine. With it came the slightest scent of rose, and I knew, without looking, that my mother was at my side. "Oh, I don't believe my eyes. It's been so long since I've seen you."

Brother Pratt took Mom's smooth hand in his wrinkled and

splotchy one, then pulled her to him and kissed her on the cheek. "I'm old enough to get away with that now. I'm so happy to see you as well, Emma. You're still my all time favorite."

They reminisced about old times, and I enjoyed the feeling of being present as friends reunited. After a while the old man extended a hand in my direction. "I don't believe we've met."

"I'm Tom," I said, shaking his hand.

His eyes lit up, and his grip tightened. I felt like another of his long lost acquaintances. "You're Tom. You won't remember this. We met when you were a baby. You weren't even as old as this infant in your arms. In fact, it was the very day of your birth."

I smiled. "You're right, I don't recall that."

"I always knew the Crump look was strong, but you have an equal portion of your mother in you as well."

It occurred to me, if I hadn't found out about the family secret that day in the park, I would be discovering it at this moment instead. Truth resists burial.

"I'm glad I got to meet your mother the one time. I wish I'd seen her again, but I guess it's for the best I never did." He turned toward Delilah. "It's too bad she was so difficult. I overheard that terrible spat you two got into on the day of Tom's birth."

My grandmother looked fearful. "I . . . I . . . never got into a terrible argument with Patty."

"Why, of course you did." His brow furrowed. Had he misinterpreted her panicked expression as an odd sort of selflessness? He prattled on, apparently determined to award her the credit she deserved. "Shortly after LaVar and the kids left Pearl's on that day she died, I returned to offer a hand. I overheard you—"

"Now, now. There's no need to bore others with this rusty old story." Delilah put a hand on each of the old man's shoulders.

"No, it's not boring. Go on Brother Pratt," Mom said.

"Well, let me see here." He looked at Delilah, but concentrated on the recollection so intently he remained oblivious to her desperate expression. "I heard you say to Patty, 'My mother died for you, and this is the way you repay her memory? She was right all along. You'll never be a fit mother.'"

"I never told her any such thing," Delilah said.

The old man nodded his head vigorously. He looked like a marionette– suspended by strings, capable only the simplest expressions. "Those were your words, or close to them. It broke my heart as you explained to her how Pearl visited you daily over the last four months and asked how much longer she must put up with this atrocious girl under her roof."

I looked from Mom to Delilah, trying to understand how this story fit.

Brother Pratt continued. "The realization that the stress had robbed your mother of her health, and ultimately her life, must have been more than you could bear. In that moment I understood why so much secrecy surrounded the birth, what difficult circumstances you Crumps must have been living under. What a favor to keep a girl like that out of your neighbor's lives. Of course, I never meant to eavesdrop. I left when I realized I'd intruded."

Like a lightning strike I realized this was the "terrible favor." To drive my birth mother from the family by whatever means necessary. To tell whichever lies must be told. To strike at her Achilles heel, her insecurity about the trouble her friend, Pearl, had gone to on her behalf. And to be done with her.

I moved away from Delilah, repulsed by her mere presence. She'd told a lie so blatant as to force my birth mother, a confused and emotional girl in supremely vulnerable condition, to abandon her newborn son and take to the streets in shame. I now understood Delilah's Thanksgiving Day intimidation.

There must have been a delay, though I don't know for how long. My thoughts returned to the present when I heard Brother Pratt saying, "I didn't mean to have such an effect on everyone. I guess Delilah was right; I shouldn't have told that story. Let's talk about something happier. Who's this splendid little girl in your arms, Tom?"

I couldn't bring him into focus. I must have just stared dumbly. Neither Delilah nor Mom spoke either.

He encouraged me. "She's a beauty, has that unmistakable Crump look. I want you to know, it's as great a compliment as I can give anybody. In case you couldn't tell, to me the Crump's have always been the very essence of perfection. How I've loved your family. It's a pleasure to see you again, Tom."

I wandered away. I'd nearly reached the chapel exit when I realized Mom was walking at my side. She took Courtney from my arms and passed her off to Aunt Heather.

"I think I better explain what all that meant." Her voice quavered. "Much of it I didn't understand until this very moment."

"I understood everything. I need fresh air." We stepped out the door.

"I need to find a way to believe my mother had no choice but to do what she did to Patty," Mom said.

"You want to tell yourself a lie? Will that improve the situation?"

She ignored me. "My father controlled our family. She feared crossing him. What might have happened if she hadn't done as he asked?"

I stared at her, mouth agape. "Is this the secret to your sanity? You reconstruct terrible events according to your liking and then shove them away in a shoebox never to be reopened? No wonder you couldn't tell me your family's history. You don't know it."

She wore a blank expression.

I put an arm around her shoulder and pulled her to me. "You're as damaged as the rest of your family. You're just unwilling to admit it."

"I'm no worse off than anyone else, Tom. Everyone has to choose what they're going to focus on."

"I admire you, Mom . . . more than I can ever express. I admire your strategy, because now I understand your past. The events of your youth devastated everyone in their wake, even you. Despite it all, you found a way to ignite hope and optimism in the souls of your children, both Jill and me."

We sobbed. My tears joined the first unrestrained ones I'd ever seen my mother allow herself. She'd cried briefly before, but she always quickly to wiped the evidence away. Now our clothes became wet with emotion.

After a long time we sat down, side by side on the curb. I looked around the parking lot as I spoke. "I could never have comprehended the journey life's taken me on over the last several months. I wonder if a happy ending is possible."

Mom must have noticed my wandering gaze. "What are you trying to find?"

"I'd hoped Martin would show. Maybe he'll turn up at the gravesite."

"I don't want to be pessimistic, but don't hold your breath for my little brother," she said.

I hadn't noticed the door open behind us, though it must have because Delilah's voice came from that direction. "Why are the two of you talking about Martin every time I come upon you?"

We turned and looked at her, then we looked away.

"Of course he's not here," Delilah said. Was she trying to make an issue of this to distract us from what Brother Crump said?

"This is his brother's funeral," I bellowed.

My mom answered. "That's just it. He can't even bring himself to face his own family. There's no way he could show up here and confront his entire childhood all at once. He wouldn't be able to understand that what happened to him way back then isn't all that important to these people. They moved on long ago."

"But it is important, Emma. Listen to what you're saying," Delilah said.

"It's not. I didn't believe our friends held anything against Martin when it all unfolded. I'm certain they don't hold anything against him now. To me it's nothing more than small town gossip of which too much was made. As far as I'm concerned, Tom, if you can forgive him, what should it matter what anyone in the old ward thinks?"

Delilah stared at me, ignoring Mom. "Tom, don't bother trying to understand your mother. Emma believes if you have a bad memory you should simply let it go. Her goal is to be happy, and her strategy is not to think about sad things. She'll never understand what life is all about. She lives everything only once, while the rest of us relive it a thousand times."

"You enjoy your misery?" I asked.

"My misery is who I am. Do you know who I really admire? Martin. His response to life is the sanest of anyone in our family, and I envy him for walking away. If I didn't have to face those people in there, I wouldn't be here either."

Mom rose to her feet. Her seething expression was unlike any I'd ever seen on her. "I can't believe it's taken over fifty years for you to mistakenly tell me what your problem really is. I can't believe I never recognized it on my own."

Delilah frowned. "I don't know what you're talking about."

"You know exactly what I'm talking about. It's obvious you've known why I couldn't bring you happiness since the first time I tried. You've been very careful not to let me know this, haven't you? But just a moment ago you were so busy trying to cover one set of tracks that you didn't realize you were revealing another. You've known since I was a small girl trying to console your tears that I could never succeed. Why didn't you ever tell me?" She walked toward her mother.

"Don't say something we'll both regret," said Delilah.

Emma stopped within arm's length of the older woman. "I could never solve your dilemmas for you, no matter how hard I tried, because you always managed to be so vague. I've labored for longer than I can remember. Each time I took care of your difficulty, you responded by adjusting the problem. No matter what efforts I made it's always been impossible for me to affect your mood. Now, for the first time, I know why."

I moved to her side in a show of support.

"What's going on with you, Emma? Can't we have this discussion later? We're at your brother's funeral," Delilah said.

"All this time the only problem has been the one in my most basic assumption. For my whole life you've been telling me happiness is what you desire most in the world, and now you confess it's a lie. You don't want to be happy at all. You love your misery."

"Emma, stop," Delilah pleaded.

But she couldn't stop herself. A half century of dammed up emotion flooded through the breach. Her eyes were liquid with passion. "I've spent my lifetime trying to make you happy, and you've spent my lifetime trying to use me up. Your greatest failure is that you haven't been able to bring me to your level, isn't it? All of my efforts, my endless efforts, to console you have been for naught, because the only thing you've ever really wanted was a daughter to commiserate with."

"That's not true," Delilah said.

"Since you couldn't have that, you settled for one who would cater to your emotional whims. You've been using me since childhood. Now that I see it in this light, all the terrible times we've been through make perfect sense."

Delilah looked like a goldfish peering through the bent wall of its bowl, her features unnaturally wide, her mouth opening and closing in near silence. Every few seconds it re-opened with a pop. I waited to hear her excuse, but then her mouth closed again, as she apparently recognized some weakness in the new argument.

Mom and I returned to the chapel for the service. We sat beside Sara. Delilah eventually slid in beside Mom. My awareness throughout was only at the vaguest level. The shuddering cries of others should've awakened me to the power of the ceremony I attended. Instead they only enhanced the private vigil in my mind. I felt myself soaring atop Joseph's shoulders, the wind in my hair and a smile on my face as we ran down some California beach. I remembered with disturbing clarity how passionately I'd wished he were my father. The irony of reality was a difficult blow to endure. I didn't even try to hold back tears.

Afterwards, in a slow procession, we followed the hearse to

the gravesite. I stepped from my Cherokee into the warm and placid air. Birds chirped. The smell of freshly cut grass filled my nostrils. I went to the hearse and helped pull the mahogany box through the rear door. The metallic hum of the spinning rollers echoed in my ears. I bore one sixth of the weight, wending our way around headstones the final few yards to the grave. We set the coffin down in its intended location beneath the boughs of an enormous oak. I removed the rose from my lapel, kissed it, and set it on the box. Then I stepped back. Alongside my mother, daughter, and wife, I watched the coffin descend. The nylon cables creaked under the shifting weight of the big rectangular load. Then silence.

I looked across the wide lawn and into the trees. Finally I turned to Sara. "Martin didn't show up."

She shrugged. "Courtney and I will ride home with your mother. Go to him."

# Chapter 25

I sped across town to Martin's house. Stepping from the Cherokee, I loosened my tie against the afternoon heat, then strode up the driveway. The moment the house came in view I noticed Martin's familiar form in his usual spot on the cluttered porch.

He wore a suit and tie. "How was the funeral?" he asked like a neighbor yelling a friendly question across the fence.

I gritted my teeth. His nonchalant demeanor irritated me. Rather than heading to the porch steps as usual, I walked directly toward him, tromping through tall weeds. I stopped when I reached the wooden railing surrounding him. I appreciated the barrier because I didn't feel entirely in control of my emotions. "If you knew about the funeral why the hell didn't you come?"

"I couldn't," he said, seemingly unrattled by my anger.

"We just planted your big brother in the ground. All you can say is 'I couldn't?'"

"I planned on being there. I even started out several times, but eventually I realized I'd have to say good-bye in my own way. That doesn't include facing rooms full of people I don't want to see again in my life. I can't help it if that explanation isn't good enough for you, because it's all there is."

"So how do you plan on saying good-bye?"

"Through prayer. I've prayed all day." He smiled. "When are we going on our hike, Tom?"

How dare he change the subject. "Please tell me you're kidding."

He didn't seem even slightly distressed by my reaction. "I'm not kidding. When are we going? I need it more than ever. I think you do too."

His last words took me by surprise, for I immediately realized he was right. I hadn't even considered the hike for over a week. Now I thought quickly. Time in the wilderness always cleared my head, and if my head ever needed clearing, this was the time. "We're going tomorrow."

"Such short notice?"

"You've had months of notice."

"That's fine. Tomorrow works for me," he said.

"Good. I'll be here at six to pick you up. Now, I need to go home and pack. Get to sleep early tonight."

\* \* \*

At six the next morning I pulled up to Martin's house. Amber light glowed from within. I walked up the patio steps and knocked. He answered, opening the door only a crack. His feet were bare, but otherwise he looked nearly ready. I'd more than half expected him to bail out at this point. He didn't invite me in, and I knew full well he wouldn't no matter how long I waited.

"I need to go adjust some things," I said, offering him the excuse he needed.

He grinned. "I'll be right there. I've just got to inject my insulin."

I went back to the vehicle and inventoried the contents of my pack one last time. Besides the sleeping bag I'd tied to the top of the frame, the pack contained a flashlight, fruit, gorp, water, a camera, binoculars, a sweatshirt, extra socks, a knife, matches, a first aid kit, rope, two harnesses, lots of carabiners, and a belay. My cell phone fit into the oversized pocket of my pants, a pair of khakis with zip-off legs.

He walked up swinging a large duffel. "Here's my stuff."

I unzipped the bag and rifled through it. Among the items were several changes of clothes, a computer magazine, a large book, and a pillow. "You realize I have to carry everything on my back? We aren't strolling down an airport concourse, we're climbing to the top of a mountain peak. I can't take anything that isn't absolutely necessary. The only things I see here fitting that description are your diabetic supplies, one of these sweatshirts, and an extra pair of socks."

He peered into the bag. "I can carry this myself." He pulled out a small packet I didn't have time to identify and stuffed it into his front pocket.

Whatever it contained, it certainly wasn't big enough to endanger the expedition. I removed the items that made the cut and set them beside my pack, then I zipped the bag shut and tossed it over the seat back where it would be out of the way.

"Here Bailey, here Moxie," he yelled.

The dogs nosed their way out the front door and came loping into the yard.

"No. I don't have Ranger. We're not taking your dogs either. I have enough to worry about just trying to get you up that hill."

"But I promised them," he said.

The dogs stood at our feet. "Well, I didn't promise them anything, and I'm not about to."

Martin squatted on his haunches and spoke into the dogs' faces. I climbed behind the wheel.

A moment later, as Martin got into the cab, he asked, "Can we listen to KSL on the way there?"

I tuned in the talk radio station. A too nice man spoke to a too sweet lady. It sounded like a relief society president giving a progress report to her bishop. Maybe that explained the station's popularity, it resembled eavesdropping on a power lunch, Salt Lake City style.

They covered an array of news and gossip, bantering playfully through each topic in a manner so uniform I could hardly distinguish the transitions. In the twenty minutes the drive took us, the radio hosts updated us on traffic conditions twice– uncrowded– and the weather forecast three times– sunny and mild for the next five days– though they couldn't bring themselves to describe either so succinctly. Airtime needed to be filled, and their expertise was turning nothing into something. Their prattle made it impossible for me to think.

Neither Martin nor I said a word all the way to the trailhead. When we got out of the vehicle, he waited as I lifted the rear hatch and pulled out the pack. I looked at his feet for the second time this morning. He now wore an inadequate pair of canvas boat shoes.

"What size is your foot?" I asked.

"Eleven and a half, why?"

I sat on back bumper and removed my shoes. "I always wondered who I'd inherited these big boats from. I'm the same size. Let's trade."

He didn't move. I looked up at his puzzled face. "I'm beginning to worry about you," he said.

I pulled the lace end on each shoe. "Step out of them."

He used the toe of one foot to hold down the heel of the opposite shoe, and soon stood in stocking feet.

I handed him my sturdy hiking boots, and put on his ragged old sneakers. "How do they feel?" I asked.

"They fit."

"Good, let's go."

"Where does this path lead?" he asked.

"What do you mean? Haven't we been talking about it for months?"

"I mean, to which summit does it lead? North or south?"

"Everyone goes to the south. The north is too difficult."

He looked concerned. "I always wanted to climb the north summit."

I glared at him. "They're the same elevation. We're going to the south."

"My dream is to stand atop that huge cliff overlooking the city."

"Well, we can't," I said flatly.

He became silent again, and I went back to my work.

I hefted my pack and locked the Cherokee. "You set the pace. Take it as easy as you can. We have a long day ahead of us."

"I'm not going." His tone spoke of finality.

I faced him. "Martin, don't do this . . . please."

"The south summit isn't my goal."

I removed my pack, unlocked the rear hatch, and tossed the gear inside. I'd already learned arguments with this man on pointless topics were unwinnable. "Get back in."

He got in the vehicle and shut his door without complaint.

I backed out of the lot and headed toward his home.

"Do you want to know why your life includes so much failure, Martin?"

He stared out his side window.

"You don't even care, do you? You'd rather spend eternity analyzing your childhood than spend a millisecond in the present."

I saw his face reflected in the window. It spoke of placid resignation. He'd given up that easily. "The north summit was always my goal, not the south," he whispered.

"Don't make me laugh. What a waste of a beautiful day this turned out to be."

"Are we going home?" he asked.

Why should I speak to him? For once I held the cards. I wasn't certain of the answer anyway. While waiting at a stop light I leaned forward. I put my head low, near the dashboard, the only angle from which I could see the north peak which now loomed above us. I thought about the route to that second summit I'd seen overlaid on a photograph in my well worn guidebook. About halfway up the trail the book claimed an amazing thing, and ever since I read about its existence I'd wanted to see it for myself. Supposedly, a hidden couloir ran diagonally through the cliff from that point to the summit ridge. Couloir is a French word skiers and climbers have adopted to describe a geographic element for which there's no adequate English substitute. It's the earliest beginnings of a canyon suspended at a precipitous angle on the side of the mountain. Normally it's an obvious feature from below because it's the course water carves from the hillside. This one must be very strange, because its route was somehow hidden within the rock. From the valley floor I'd studied the apparent crack in the cliff where the draw was said to have been, but it seemed more like a fabulous exaggeration than reality. If such a feature existed, suspended like a staircase to the summit on the side of that forbidding mountain face, I had to see it. I may as well not waste the day. Martin could spend the morning lolling around at the bottom of the hill for all I cared. If I traveled light I might make the round trip to the entrance of the couloir in about five hours. So, the north summit it would be after all.

Without a word to Martin I turned into the Cove and headed uphill. When we reached a gate on the highest street I set the parking brake, hopped out, slung a canteen over my shoulder, and started walking up the road. I enjoyed Martin's confused expression, then listened to his rapid steps as he hurried to catch me from behind.

"Don't you need your pack?" he asked.

"No."

"Why not?"

"Because if this trail is half as tough as my guidebook says, you won't make it a mile. It's a 'difficult.' You don't have a prayer of crossing it. I prepared for a hike today, and I'm taking one. Everything you need, your diabetic supplies and all the rest, are in the back of the Cherokee."

The road switched back on its course up the mountain. The air smelled of pine. Many of the scrub oak leaves had already changed to brilliant red, while others remained vivid green. Yellows, golds, and ambers mingled. They resulted in a dazzling display of color all the way up the mountainside. In my mind this one stunning view made the trip worthwhile.

At the top of the road we reached a water tower. From there, several trails diverged. I selected the most traveled. I could soon tell its purpose was the maintenance of a buried water line. It inclined only slightly, but I knew the elevation would be made up eventually. At that point the man at my heels would have to return to the vehicle. I'd left it unlocked, and he could wait for me.

"This is easy," Martin said.

I smiled. His comment proved his obliviousness to the terrain on all sides. The walls of our small canyon rose sharply on either side. Unless someone had done an admirable job of trail building we'd soon hit a very tough section. We turned a corner and crossed the stream, and there it was. A slippery dirt pathway aimed impossibly up the western slope of the canyon. "Yeah, piece of cake. Do you want to break trail?"

He stared at the foreboding hill. Skid marks showed where downhill travelers simply let gravity take its course. He took a few steps forward and his foot slid from beneath him, like trying to go up the down escalator. There didn't appear to be any way he could hold traction on that hard dust-covered surface.

When he looked back at me I shrugged. I expected him to give up at that moment, but he moved over to the edge of the passage and grabbed onto a scrub oak branch. He hauled himself up to it, then grabbed a second, a third, a fourth. He made significant progress before he sat down in the weeds just off the path to rest. I couldn't believe my eyes. It was the first hint of useful determination I'd ever seen him show. He'd proven he could be stubborn, but about inconsequential things. This was different. After a short breather he stood and repeated the process.

"Great job, Martin. I'm going to run back and get my pack," I said. "Stay on the trail and just take it at a moderate pace."

He nodded.

I added two unnecessary miles to my trip, but I felt happy to do it. This adventure would provide me with a workout of sorts after all. I was breathing heavily by the time I returned to the slippery hill and followed Martin's example to reach the top. Here the slope became much more moderate. I went on for another half mile up the ridge-line, aware of the subtle signs the pathway had been freshly trod, before I caught sight of Martin.

"Need a drink?" I asked.

He looked at me with a dusty and beaten face. I handed him the canteen. He drank thirstily before pouring some on his brow.

"Depending on how far you plan on going I wouldn't be too wasteful with that. You already crossed the only running water you're going to see on this route, and it's a long way to the top." I pointed to the pinnacle which now loomed at a significant angle above our heads.

He looked the other direction and pointed at the valley floor. "We've already come a long way."

"Remember, we drove most of the way up this hill," I said, handing him a bag of gorp.

He took it gratefully. "I need to test my blood. Will you hand me the kit?"

I removed the pack and found the small container he'd given me. I watched as he pricked his finger and measured the blood for its sugar content.

"Remind me to test at least every couple of hours. Increased activity puts me at risk of becoming hypoglycemic," he said.

I felt content to mirror his slow pace, recouping the energy I'd spent at the base of the hill. The incline gradually increased. It wasn't anywhere near as steep as the treadmill we'd taken to get out of the ravine, but it made for hard work. The floppy and treadless sneakers I wore didn't make my going any easier.

The aroma of fresh sage filled my nostrils. I felt content to be on the mountainside. Sometimes our feet brushed against the dry leaves of the low lying sunflowers I'd always known as Golden-Eyes. The foliage scraped together making a sound like thin glass shattering. Bird songs filled the air. I relaxed, despite the load on my back.

"So, here we are on our first father and son outing," I said.

He looked at me apologetically. "Sorry for being such a lousy dad."

"You weren't a lousy dad," I said. "You weren't a dad at all. You were nothing but a sperm donor, and Patty was simply an egg donor. The sister you hate so much is the only one who stuck around with me to be a parent. She had no obligation to do that, so I consider myself lucky."

I thought he nodded, but I wasn't sure. Even if he did, it could've meant anything.

The trail narrowed as it wound through a thicket of scrub oak. Somehow, either our honest conversation or his stoic effort at the climb made me feel close to him. "I wish you'd become a part of our family again. I know everyone would welcome you."

I watched beads of sweat roll down his brow as he thought. Large wet circles stained his tee-shirt. "It's not as simple as that. The old hour hand's done an awful lot of pirouettes since I exchanged kind words with those people. I doubt we could forgive one another."

"You're making it more complicated than it has to be, but I won't try to force you. I won't bring it up again."

"I don't know all that much about you," Martin said.

"If you're willing to listen I'll tell you some things," I offered, thinking that idle banter would take Martin's mind off of the hard work of climbing the hill.

"So, tell me. You're going to have to do most of the talking. I need all of the oxygen I can get."

"The shoe is on the other foot, isn't it," I said.

He laughed an oxygen conserving laugh as he looked at my boots on his feet.

"What do you want to know?"

"I know very little about your life since 1975. You used to love school."

"Yes, I still love learning, but until recently my job's taken up most of my time. I once had ambitions of becoming a teacher. I'm looking for a way to fulfill them now."

"You were active in church back then. It surprised me that you didn't go on your mission," he said.

"It surprised a lot of people. Everybody was hot on my trail, trying to herd me back to the 'straight and narrow,' when the date for my departure came and went. But many of my friends went on missions because they didn't dare not to. Most of them thought their parents would make their life a living hell if they stayed home. My mom allowed me make up my own mind."

"You shouldn't have passed it up. I would've cherished the opportunity to serve the Lord."

What an irony that he longed to embrace the organization—the Mormon Church— run by and populated with the very type of people he couldn't stand. For the first time I comprehended the paradoxical life Martin had constructed for himself, or rather, the life he'd allowed others to construct for him. His existence was that of an acrophobic tightrope walker. Daily he balanced upon the imagined commonality between a theology he couldn't question as essential to his salvation, and a distrust of his fellow man he couldn't doubt as essential to his mortal life. He'd learned in his distant past to scoot forward only when forced, imagining with each movement the penalties that awaited him if he made a minor error on either side. He lacked the courage to look down, the vision to look forward, the faith to look up, and the creativity to look to the side. Paralyzed by fear, his only alternative was looking back, and so he passed his lifetime examining the short length of frayed line that led from the platform of his birth.

"You wouldn't have wanted to find yourself in a foreign land trying to convince strangers of something you don't believe yourself," I said.

"How can you say you don't believe in The Church?"

"It's a long story."

"I want to hear everything." He breathed laboriously, and I knew he'd last much longer if I did the talking.

As we wended our way up the ever fainter trail I filled him in on the details of my life. I told him how much more satisfying I found scientific inquiry than religious doctrine, how I'd met my wife, what I'd done for a living. I talked for over an hour without stopping.

Martin put his hands on his knees and leaned over, sucking oxygen as hard as he could. "You were right. This is a pretty steep trail."

I took off my pack. "If the guidebook is correct, that won't last much longer."

He looked at the terrain ahead. "It gets less steep?"

"Nope. The trail disappears, then it gets a lot steeper. Let me feel your pulse."

He offered his wrist. I counted thirteen beats in six seconds. One-hundred-and-thirty beats a minute, right within the target range for a man his age. Impressive. "Great job, Martin. You're doing just fine."

We'd climbed only a small increment up the face of Mount Olympus, but I reminded myself how low my expectations had been on this difficult trail. He'd already covered terrain I thought he had no shot at.

After a brief rest we started again and soon found that the book had been correct. The path evaporated within our first few steps. No proper trail had ever been built beyond the end of the water line at the bottom of the canyon. From there the path gradually dissipated as the infrequent hikers either picked their own routes or turned back.

Martin led the way. He bushwhacked through the dense scrub oak. Suddenly a doe and her yearling fawn sprang from their hiding places five yards ahead of him. Martin took a startled step back, then relaxed as he watched the graceful creatures bound effortlessly away. At each leap their entire bodies, even the tips of their hooves, were visible above the changing foliage. They seemed to float, somehow procrastinating their landing while they surveyed the ground for suitable footing. Then they would disappear beneath the leaves for a heartbeat only to vault forward again. Finally, after one long leap they didn't reappear. They simply drowned in the leaves.

Martin looked at me reverently. "Did you see that?"

I nodded.

"That's the most wonderful thing I've ever seen."

I smiled.

"I could almost touch them. Did you notice the expressions on their faces? The slightest trace of a smile, and no hint of fear at all in those big beautiful eyes. How about those lashes? Women would kill for eyelashes like that."

"They were very pretty," I agreed.

"Pretty? They were gorgeous. I've never seen anything more beautiful. Now aren't you glad we came up this side of the mountain?"

"Except for the fact that we're not going to make it to the top. We've been on the mountain since seven-thirty. It's eleven o'clock now, and I figure we have to turn around by three at the latest in order to reach the trailhead by sundown."

I felt his pace surge, but knew it couldn't last, and I felt fine with that. It contented me to see so many of the barriers he'd constructed about himself come crashing down over the last few hours. It felt so satisfying to see childlike enthusiasm replace his fatalistic outlook. I didn't feel so bad that we'd be forced to amend our goal. In fact, I felt proud. He would leave the mountain better off than when he'd come.

The trail may still have existed somewhere, but we'd lost it. We battled through a briar of oak. I was often forced to crawl on hands and knees just to get the thick load on my back through the available gaps. Martin didn't have quite as difficult a time since he bore no load, but he struggled nevertheless. I felt envious of the deer's athletic way of dealing with the tangle.

Within a hundred yards we encountered the rocky slab of the lower cliff face. It was tilted at an angle of about forty degrees, and crisscrossed with convenient hand and foot-holds.

There were periodic trees, growing somehow in the solid rock, which would have aided our climb. It wasn't technical terrain by any means, but I knew we'd reached our limit.

"Ready to turn back?" I asked.

"What? Are you kidding?" He spoke incredulously. "You said you'd take me to the top."

"You're serious about this, aren't you?"

"I thought you were, too," he said.

"I was, until this morning when you made us change hikes. I've been pretty much a skeptic since that point. The top of the south peak, a point to which hundreds of people a day sometimes climb, is entirely different than a trip to the north. I doubt it sees a hundred people in a year. This route is becoming too difficult for you."

He looked emotionally injured. "It wasn't a change to me. Remember that day in the park with the dogs? You couldn't even see the south peak from there. You can't see it from my home in the Avenues, either. Of course I thought we'd agreed to climb the north."

"So, now we're doing the one you wanted, but you have to admit, we can't continue over terrain like this. Remember, whatever you go up, you must come down." I eyed the base of the cliff below us.

"So far, so good," he said, not bothering to follow my gaze.

"Enough is enough. You're obviously unwilling to admit it, but we can't continue."

"This isn't the trail, is it? I didn't see how we could get up that cliff." He sighed as if he'd found me out.

"No. This is the trail. I've read about it, but never hiked it. Supposedly, if we could get past this very difficult stretch we'd have a long hike up a tree-filled talus slope. That would put us at the midway point. Beyond there we'd climb into a diagonal hanging valley that runs from right there at the base of the cliff, to over there on the summit ridge. Once we're on the ridge you can guess the rest."

"It's not one huge cliff?" he asked, backing up to the middle of my description. He seemed stunned, and I knew why he felt that way. It was like finding out your best friend had kept lifelong secrets from you.

"It's not even two," I said. "Look around you. It's a jumble of small cliffs tilted at various angles, and divided by deep canyons. The rocks somehow produce the illusion of continuity when viewed from a distance. Up close it's a different story. You haven't had to pay much attention because you're going where I tell you to. Finding your way through those monoliths would be like entering a vertical matrix. If you take one wrong turn, not only will you end up spending a huge amount of unnecessary energy, but you could get into a very dangerous situation."

"Tom, you have no idea how hard I've trained for this. All summer long I've been walking long distances, up and down the Avenues. I can do this."

So that's where he'd been on those two occasions I'd visited his house without an appointment and been unable to find him. He'd really taken this seriously. Pride in his determination filled my heart. He deserved my best effort.

I removed my pack and dug through for the emergency climbing gear. "All right. We'll start out and see how it goes. I need you to wear this climbing harness for safety." I tossed it to him.

He watched as I put mine on, then he did the same. "This big loop is supposed to go on my belly?"

"It's meant to be as close to your center of gravity as possible. I can tie a rope directly to it, or tie a rope to one of these aluminum carabiners and hook it on."

"I feel safe with this."

I tied the rope securely to his harness and left a twenty foot length between us. "Let's go."

The route wasn't too difficult, but both arms and legs were needed to get up the slope.

After a short distance the angle increased to forty-five degrees. "Are you ready to turn back?" I asked.

"Can we really reach the summit this way?"

"It's right in front of us." I said, opening my arms as if to reveal the enormous cliff which now filled our entire field of vision.

"Then I don't want to turn back. I'm doing fine." His chest heaved from exertion, but then again, so did mine. "I want to see if there really is such a secret pathway to the top."

I swung my pack from my back. I felt agile without the gear weighing me down. Of course, I already understood Martin's reaction. I looked down to where we'd come from, and up at where the separation in the cliff face appeared to be. Maybe if we ate lunch quickly and hiked until four in the afternoon we could reach the valley before turning back. I'd always been a sucker when it came to adventure, anyway, and it clouded my judgment as usual. "I'll make you a deal. You sit down right here and have lunch. I'll climb on ahead and see if we can get through this, and what's beyond. I'm going to take the rope with me." I disconnected it from his harness and stuffed it in my pack.

He found a rock where he could sit and survey the valley. He took off his boots and wiggled his toes, then leaned back and let out a long sigh.

I left him with water and food, hoisted my pack, and picked my way up the slope. I retreated nearly as often as I moved forward, looking for safe passage up the rock. After I'd gained six hundred feet I stopped to survey the remainder of the route. What I saw ahead brought to mind an optical illusion sketch I'd come across in a high-school textbook. It was a bizarre three-pronged-bolt drawn in three dimensions. At first glance it looked like a useless, but physically possible invention. Upon closer inspection, that wasn't the case. It turned out the threads circled the gaps between the bolts, instead of the bolts themselves. The escarpment ahead produced the same effect on my eye. It was impossible to tell where an impassable canyon might separate any two monoliths, and even more difficult to imagine which course led most efficiently to the top.

I felt the sensation of looking into a gigantic house of mirrors. I finally decided I may as well navigate the easiest course available as long as it led uphill. From this point the choice was obvious. The forbidding v-shaped canyon to our north that at lower elevations appeared impassable, now became a pine tree filled drainage. I found a small gap in the cliff that would lead us into that zone.

Martin's balance couldn't be trusted on the steep ramp that brought me to this elevation, though. I felt thankful for the rope in my pack and the harnesses we both wore. I had only one-third the amount of line necessary to reach this point, so I removed the pack, fished out the rope, and descended four hundred feet.

"Do you still want to continue?" I called down.

"I feel fine, now."

"Good. I'm throwing down a rope with a carabiner tied to the end. Attach it to your harness, then start climbing."

He climbed the first two hundred feet and arrived by my side, very winded but ready for more. I detached myself from the rope, flipped the coil over so it would play out as I climbed, and told him to yell when the slack ran out.

"That's it," he called as I reached a point two hundred feet above him.

I found a spot to sit and re-rigged the line, then I yelled, "Okay, start climbing."

"This is a lot of fun," he said when he reached my position. "Aren't you glad we came this way?"

"Yes, I am," I admitted. "However, if we'd gone the other way I'm sure we would've experienced a different great adventure, and we'd be approaching the top about now to boot."

"If we'd gone the other way we wouldn't have gotten to use the climbing gear. I'm enjoying seeing how skilled you are with it. I'd love to watch you go up a real cliff like the one over there."

I looked at the imposing wall he indicated. The cliff looked so sheer I doubted there were sufficient handholds. "Let's just get up this slope. We still have a slim shot of reaching the entrance to the couloir before we turn back, but that's just halfway to the peak."

"What about all those camping supplies you're lugging up here?" he asked, pointing at the burden on my back.

"Those are in case of an emergency. If you break your leg and I can't get you down, at least I have a way to make you comfortable until I find help."

He looked hurt, as if the notion I didn't have complete confidence in him was too much to bear.

I stood, and without speaking climbed the last two hundred feet. This section was the most awe inspiring. The rock we climbed resembled an enormous domino, toppled forty-five degrees against a solid barrier. We scaled its gently tilted face, but on either side it dropped off in sheer cliffs. At one point on the ascent, because of the placement of a group of hugh boulders, the only convenient route took me within feet of the edge on the right hand side. Unable to resist, I moved toward the drop off and looked over. My stomach roiled. An enormous void yawned beneath. I eased away from the precipice and resumed the climb.

When I reached my pack, I sat down amongst small boulders and prepared to belay Martin. I took a swig from my canteen then looped it over my shoulder. "Okay, take this section extremely easy. Stay as far from the edge as you possibly can!"

Even though I couldn't see him I knew where he was, because I could hear the clickety-clack of rock on rock as he dislodged the same stones I'd been careful not to disturb. I imagined if someone crossed below him, their reward would be several dents in the head.

"Martin, try not to be a bull in a china—" the rope screamed backward through the belay. Valuable line retreated, burning my hands as it left. My right hand dropped instinctively to a position beside my buttocks. The mechanism locked, and the line went taut. The sudden brake jolted my spine. I leaned back with all my strength, but slid forward.

# Chapter 26

I wedged my right foot against a two foot tall rock. It made a sickening grating sound as it slid several inches under the pressure. I pulled my foot away, not wanting to risk sending the stone down atop Martin, and braced my toe against a slight ridge,.
"Martin! Martin, what happened? Are you okay?"
A crow drifted overhead and cawed. The city hummed far below. No response from Martin.
"Martin! Are you all right?"
My ears strained. The guitar-string tight rope vibrated with a low tone. I figured less than ten feet got away. Ten feet too many.
I needed to change position, to move to a spot where I could tie the rope. But where could I possibly grab solid hold?
A gnarled pine clung ferociously to the cliff face thirty feet down slope. It would be too dangerous to ease my way down there, though. Immediately below me the rock sloped away, smooth and steep. If I tried to cross that section Martin's weight would easily pull me over and send us both careening off the cliff. I wracked my brain for a better plan.
I twisted my neck to look up slope. A boulder, five feet behind me, looked big enough to bear the load. I struggled to crab-walk up slope. Every movement brought excruciating pain. Blood trickled through my fingers where the rope had ripped my skin. There's no way I'd make it up the hill with Martin's weight pulling me down. I fought for air, gasping from the exertion.
I needed another plan. I tried to envision the cliff where

Martin had gone over, the place where I'd peered into the void on my own ascent. It started with a bit of an overhang, then sloped back out. That meant he might be suspended in midair at this moment. That would account for the great tension on the line. If I could lower him to touch the cliff face, maybe he'd find some way to support his own weight and take the weight off the rope. That assumed he was conscious, that I had enough line to lower him far enough to reach the cliff, that there was an available ledge near where he'd end up, and that he'd figure out what to do on his own once he came within reach. The odds of such luck weren't good, but I saw no better alternative. I played out fifteen feet of line.

The rope tension remained.

"Martin!"

Silence.

I let another ten feet retreat through the belay device, then five more. I looked at the woefully short coil that remained by my side. "How much more do you need to reach the cliff face?" I yelled.

"Caw-caw-caw," the crow answered.

Reluctantly I eased another five feet through, but it had no effect. The moment I dreaded had arrived. I could see only one remaining alternative, and it terrified me. I looked at the rugged old pine, thirty feet below and ten feet to my left down the angled slope. If I tied the end of what line remained to my harness, and rushed to the opposite side of the trunk, I could serve as a counterweight to Martin dangling off the cliff. Then I'd tie off the rope, and move over to the cliff to take a look. If I didn't make it around the pine, Martin's weight would drag us both to our deaths. And, even if I did make it and save my own skin, who could tell what effect the sudden release in tension would have on Martin?

He might smack into the cliff head first and be killed. I thought everything through again. There was no other choice. Could the tree withstand the strain? Everything hinged on that.

Only one way to find out. I edged forward in preparation. As I did I felt the slightest release in tension. "Martin?"

He may have heard me and been yelling back with all his might, but the alcove would've pushed the sound in the wrong direction.

I might as well give up my last six inches of slack. The rope slid away and the tension decreased a bit more.

"Hold on to whatever you have with everything you've got," I yelled, willing myself to believe he heard me.

I shut my eyes tight and said a quick prayer, then opened them. "Here goes nothing." I vaulted from my perch, hurtling toward the gnarled conifer. Immediately the line became slack. That meant Martin wasn't sliding, but it also meant I'd have no resistance to check my speed. My momentum would take me far beyond the tree, then I'd stop violently, rocking myself and Martin. I changed my course so that I'd collide with the boughs on the left hand side.

The limbs exploded on impact. Green needles flew everywhere, branches cracked, twigs scratched my face, and I stopped. The canteen flew off my arm and skittered down the slope, but stopped just before going over right above Martin's position.

I gathered in slack as I scrambled toward the trunk. I detached the rope from my harness and noted with satisfaction that the roots braided their way deep into the rock. This tree would hold a lot of weight. How could I feel anything but confidence in the tenacious grip of a creature able to draw life from solid stone? "Thank you," I said, kissing the trunk as I cinched my knot around it. I'd never felt so beholden to a plant. I tasted blood. My shoulder ached. I felt a welt rise on my forehead.

I grabbed the rope, and followed it to the spot where Martin went over the edge. The line danced and jiggled, as if it had hooked a leisurely fish. I lay on my belly, and inched forward. My stomach felt even more queasy than when I'd peered over out of curiosity on my way up the slope. I stopped when my eyes were just far enough over the edge to see Martin. He sat on a narrow ledge nearly fifty feet down. The sheer cliff extended at least 150 feet below him. I couldn't be certain I had enough line to lower him all the way to the bottom, and there didn't appear to be sufficient hand-holds to climb either up or down. The overhang prevented me from climbing down to his position, anyway. No plan for rescue came to mind. I wanted to yell, but not to surprise him.

He didn't notice me. He seemed to be working— but accomplishing nothing. I recalled the way he tinkered in his garage. When I saw him move each hand and foot, relief surged through me. He must not be badly injured. I listened a while longer, and thought I heard him whispering.

"Martin, are you okay?"

His face tilted toward the heavens, but his eyes didn't find mine. "Tom, is that you? I thought I was dead. How will I ever get off this cliff?" His tone was calm, serene.

"Don't worry about that. You're safe. I have everything taken care of," I lied. I tried to devise a plan, but couldn't yet imagine what it would be.

"Oh, good." It seemed such an understatement. "I can't even describe to you what's gone through my mind."

"Try," I challenged, buying time to survey the situation before he panicked.

"It wasn't fear. Not until my feet touched this rock and I regained hope did I feel fear. When I started to slide, then went over the edge, my thought was, 'So, this is how it ends.' A thousand images rushed in behind that, but it wasn't my life flashing before my eyes. I thought about projects I hadn't finished, laundry I hadn't done, stuff like that. There were also things from the past, bits and pieces I haven't remembered in ages. It's strange that they all made perfect sense in the moment I saw them. I could understand exactly why I relived those particular scenes. Then I stopped in mid air with a jolt, held as if by the hand of God, looking straight up at the deep blue sky." He swallowed hard and concentrated on the firmament. "I'd never dreamed a moment like this could exist, not while I lived and breathed. Have you noticed how blue the sky is today?"

"Yeah, I noticed." His tone held such passion I wished I could to take another look at the heavans, but lying on my belly I could only see the cliff, Martin, the slope below, and the city at the bottom of it all.

"I didn't know why I hung there at that moment, then I saw the world more clearly than I ever have before. I said, 'Please God, give me a future, and I promise it won't be like my past. I'll take responsibility for my life from this day forward. Forgive me for the kind of father I've been and I'll do everything I can to make up for it.'"

He searched for me with his eyes, but didn't stop speaking. "Emma told me thirty-five years ago that I must stop blaming others for my misfortune. It made me so angry I walked out on her and never returned, but I realize now it's the solution to most of my problems. Ever since I can remember I've made as much as I could of the mistakes of others to free myself of the responsibility. Isn't that a terrible admission?"

He finally figured out where I was, and looked straight at me. "Clinging to this rock I've already begun to repent for the blame I've assigned my father, mother, sister, and brother. I thought I'd been asking for forgiveness of sin my whole life. Now I realize I haven't, this is different. God knows I'm sincere this time."

How could I be positive we'd ever again have the chance to speak at close range? I had to say what I felt now, in this moment. "I'm proud of you, Dad."

"What?"

Shouting would ruin the intimacy, but there was no choice if I wanted him to hear. "I said, I'm proud of you, Dad." The last word echoed through the canyon.

He turned toward me. I couldn't read his expression. "You don't have to say that."

"I want to. I am proud. You're my father. I'm a part of you, and I'm grateful to be who I am."

He looked down briefly, then stared up at me again. "Thank you, Son."

I felt paralyzed, glued to this spot of permanent change. The circumstances were strange for intimacy, but it was intimate. We stared into one another's faces across that large gap in that unreal moment. A lump formed in my throat. I struggled to yell past it. "You think you're the only one who can have great revelations up here?"

He chuckled, or at least his shoulders bobbed. His hands went to his face, then he turned back to me. "Are you trying to horn in on my near-death experience?"

"Well, I'd prefer not having one of my own if I can avoid it. You ready to get out of here?"

"I am."

"I'll remember my revelations if you'll remember yours."

He nodded. "I will."

"Can you hold on right where you are a little bit longer?"

"I don't want to stay here, if that's what you're asking."

"That's why you need to get comfortable. Just leave the rope hooked to your harness, but don't put any resistance on it until I tell you it's okay. I've got to untie the other end and move it to a place where it will be useful to us."

"Do what you have to do," he said. "I trust your judgment."

If only I trusted myself. My injuries, while numerous, didn't seem serious. My plan, on the other hand, seemed sketchy at best. I returned to the tree and untied the rope. Then I descended to a spot down-slope from where Martin went over where one of the enormous boulder that forced us to climb near the edge sat.

"Okay Martin. Hold on. I need to take all the slack out of the line between you and this rock."

He nodded.

I pulled the line tight, and tied it around the boulder. I took the loose end of the rope another twenty-five feet down the angled rock face and fastened it around a tree that hung out over the abyss. I proceeded twelve feet farther down the slope with the remainder of the tether. I was now just below my Dad's elevation, but nearly fifty horizontal feet north.

I attached two carabiners, one at the twelve foot mark, one seven feet below that. The remainder of the rope I coiled and tied at my hip so it would stay out of the way. I yelled to Martin. "I need you to keep two things in mind. First, you trust my judgment entirely. You just told me that. You've got to do exactly what I tell you, even if it doesn't make perfect sense. Second, you've got nothing to lose."

"Okay," he said, without the usual argument.

I clipped the higher carabiner into my harness, and held the lower one in my right hand. I now stood at one end of the rope, twelve feet below the tree to which it was tied. Martin waited at the other end with approximately thirty feet of line angling up to the boulder. "We have one shot at this. If we fail, we've got real problems. Now, shinny away from me. Move as far to the south as possible."

He did as I asked.

Here came the moment of truth. I yelled, "When I count to three I want you to stand perpendicular to the cliff. Lean against the rope and run toward me as fast as you can. Follow the arcing path the rope takes you in. Climbers call this move a pendulum. I'll be doing the same, but running toward you. When our paths intersect we need to grab one another, and hold on tight. Are you ready?"

"Yes," he said without hesitation.

I wished I felt so sure. I'd purposely neglected to mention that if we missed on our only opportunity, we'd swing to the apogees of our respective arcs with little to do but wait for death, he— hanging directly below the boulder, me— twenty feet away below the tree. I also didn't mention that my geometry was only intuitive. I couldn't be certain our arcs would even cross.

"One . . . two . . ." I took a step back from the face of the cliff. "Three!" I hoped he'd taken me seriously. "Four," I whispered, then launched myself onto the vertical wall. I ran toward him in exactly the way I'd instructed him.

At first I couldn't focus, then I saw him. He'd already reached the bottom of his arc and charged like a man possessed. I passed the lowest point in my swing a moment later, but since I traveled a much smaller circumference I rose more quickly. I focused on his eyes as we neared the intersection of the circles. Each step was slower than the last as thirsty gravity consumed our momentum.

"Lunge," I screamed.

He sprawled face first. I thrust forward, left hand extended. For a moment our fingers touched, but we'd misjudged. His hand found my arm. The weak grip held only for a heartbeat. Then we began swinging toward the bottom of our semicircles. Our "tick" was about to be followed by a fatal "tock."

I threw my right arm toward Martin's belly, carabiner extended. Because of my body position I couldn't even watch where it went. But I heard the tinkley-twang of aluminum on aluminum as the carabiner gate flipped open, then shut.

Martin sprawled backward. He let out an aggravated moan to conclude the slow motion moment, certainly unaware of what the high pitched sound meant to me. He probably hadn't even heard it.

We didn't swing back to center. Instead we hung side by side, the ends of our triangulated piece of nylon rope held together by two tiny aluminum carabiners. Laughter poured from my lungs. Martin gaped. It took him a long moment to understand what had happened. Then he began laughing as well. Our duet echoed through the canyon.

"This is definitely a more difficult hike than I had in mind," I said.

"Things are going well, though, don't you think?" He wore the widest grin I've ever seen, willingly oblivious to our peril. He'd already faced death— and enjoyed it. What could possibly rattle him now?

"You've got every reason to be happy. Your position just improved dramatically. As for mine, I was a whole lot better off before I ran out here to join you."

"How do we get back on top of the ridge?" he asked.

"I'm still thinking about that. Are you a good dancer?"

He answered my question without questioning my sanity. I knew he'd handed his destiny over to me. "I've got some rhythm."

"That's going to help, because this time we need to run while attached a single rope, and we can't afford to step on any toes. You'll be seven feet below me, and you've got to keep up."

"I will. I believe in you."

"Good." I removed the Swiss Army knife from my pocket, extended the serrated blade, and reached toward him. "Take this. You need to cut through the rope that's running up the cliff to your right. Start by sawing slowly, but as soon as the rope starts tearing cut through as quickly as you can. The moment it's severed we'll both fall down the cliff face, swinging back in the arc I followed out here. You'll be below me. Run like last time, only harder. Use the initial fall to get your speed up, but keep your balance. We must stay in unison. When we reach the top of the arc grab hold of anything you can find."

"All right," he said. He adjusted his position so he could cut the rope, then pivot quickly to run with me. It wouldn't be easy, but he didn't seem concerned. He began sawing. I marveled at his unquestioning trust. "When I get close to cutting through, count to three. That worked before," he said.

"Why not." I tried to calm my breathing while listening to the saw chewing into the line. The sound of over-stressed nylon ripping apart is something any sane climber dreads, but it's the noise I now felt anxious to hear. "One . . . two . . . three!"

We remained in place for another breathless moment. Martin sawed frantically. The line screamed as it finally tore. We fell. From the first step our strides became unified. I didn't look at Martin, but felt his presence, charging along beside me. Something more perfect than coordination carried us toward the spot we must reach. I focused on my destination. We slowed as the goal neared. I reached atop the cliff, looped my arm around a small boulder, and felt a moment's joy. The rock slid toward me, then over the edge. I twisted my body just enough to prevent the stone from landing directly on top of me. It went by with a whoosh of air. The critical moment had come and gone. This time I'd failed.

We began swinging back to center– then stopped. I looked at Martin. He'd folded his arms around a small tree growing out of the side of the cliff. He scrambled to entwine his legs through its twisted branches as well. I don't know how he accomplished the latter, but it halted our return swing. It produced enough stability to stop my descent, to change my momentum. I slammed face first into the cliff wall. The impact hurt my cheek and jaw, but I found hand-holds, and clung like a spider to a waterspout. My left foot wedged its way into a crack. Had I been wearing my hiking boots as planned, it would never have held, but Martin's flexible sneakers worked perfectly. I smiled at the irony. I searched blindly with my right foot, but could find no firm placement.

Then the boulder I'd dislodged earlier exploded on the rocks below. The world trembled, and for a moment my muscles froze. I steadied my nerves, and realized I couldn't go anywhere while tethered to Martin. My only option was free-climbing. I reached toward my belly with my left hand and unclipped the carabiner from my harness. I hung two hundred feet above the ground by nothing more than five toes and ten fingertips. I inhaled deeply.

# Chapter 27

My fingers slid in the grit filled indentations.

Images of Sara, Courtney, Mom, Jill, Uncle Joseph, Aunt Heather, Delilah, Daisy– zipped through my mind. It couldn't end this way. Not now that I'd finally found my father.

I adjusted my grip. I clung two feet from the top of the cliff, but I saw no adequate hand-holds higher up. When I tried to look down, my fingers began sliding again. I couldn't analyze the situation any longer. I saw no solution to the puzzle of this cliff, and time had run out. I could only pray there were hand-holds beyond where I could see.

I sprang upward with every ounce of my strength, my hands reaching over the top edge of the cliff. The fingers of my left hand blindly clasped a clump of grass growing from a crack. My pull on it delayed my fall for a gigasecond, then the roots ripped loose. But at that same moment my right hand seized an irregularity in the rock. I pulled myself up until my right toe found my original right hand-hold. My left hand grasped a ridge and I scrambled higher. A moment later I clambered atop the cliff. I jumped to my feet.

Martin clung to the little tree more tenaciously than ever. I extended my arm. "Martin, grab my hand. I'll pull you up."

I grasped his wrist and he grasped mine. I leaned back with everything I had, pulling him between the tree and the cliff. I don't know how I did it, or if he did, but somehow he sprawled face-first onto the less perilous rock at the top of the cliff. I fell to my back a bit farther from the edge.

"Thanks." Martin gasped for air. "Thank you for saving my life. Several times."

"Thank you for saving mine."

We lay there, sucking in oxygen for a long time, then Martin spoke. "That was an amazing plan you came up with."

"Yeah. Pure luck."

"Not pure luck. The pendulum's path," he said.

"What do you mean?"

"We followed the pendulum's path, falling, but using that motion to lift us again. Life follows the pendulum's path, don't you think?"

I recalled the grandfather clock on Martin's porch. I remembered the other clocks, the ornate wall clock he worked on in his garage, the cuckoo clock inside the entrance to his home, the others with their swinging pendulums throughout the house. He'd surrounded himself with them.

"Down, then up," Martin said. "The high would be less without the low. The low is tolerable because you can see the next peak, and you know one day you'll climb to it." He turned to me and smiled. "And reaching the top will be even grander than you imagined. Are we ready to continue up?"

I gaped at him. I couldn't believe he still wanted to hike. We were well past the turn-around time. We'd never make it to the base by dark. My body ached from an assortment of injuries, and his condition couldn't be too good either. "Let's rest a minute while I come up with a plan. Can you see your neighborhood over there? Your house is deep within those trees."

Martin squinted.

I fished my cell phone from my pocket and dialed home. "Hi, Sara."

"Tom. I was just thinking about you. How was the hike? When will you be home?"

"We're not going to make it home tonight. We ran into some

trouble and will have to camp out. I'm just calling to tell you not to worry about us."

"You're both safe, right?"

I looked at Martin, his eyes wide. He seemed amazed that a phone call could be made in such a place. "Yeah, we're safe. Kiss Courtney goodnight for me and I'll see you in the morning." I hung up.

"That thing even works up here?" Martin asked.

I nodded. "Would you like to make a call?"

"I would. I need to speak to Emma."

A satisfied sensation flowed through me. I entered Mom's number. "Just press send," I said, handing him the phone.

He stared at the device in confusion, turning it in his hands, looking at the buttons and display screen. I recalled the same feeling the first time I'd used a phone in a place I thought telephones couldn't be. He pulled his knees beneath him, then pressed the button. I heard only his side of the conversation.

"Hello, Emma. This is Martin. I'm on the side of the mountain with Tom." He listened for a long time.

"I've screwed things up pretty badly, haven't I? Can I get a second chance?" He cried. Soon spasms wracked his body and tears poured from his eyes. I knew she'd told him, "Yes."

"I'm glad you ended up raising my boy for me, big sister. You did better than I ever could have . . . I love you, Emma. I've always loved you so much. Can you ever forgive me for the way I've treated you?" His shoulders convulsed again, and he wiped the back of his hand across his eyes.

I put my palm on his shoulder. "I'll give you privacy. Don't move until I get back." He looked at me and nodded. I rose, then walked up the hill.

As I moved away I overheard one more comment. "I compounded my mistakes with pride. I've always known I wasn't handling things the best way, but I felt so sick and tired of being wrong I couldn't bear being around anyone I knew was right."

I headed to untie the rope from the boulder and tree. Martin's voice became an incoherent mumble from this distance. The conversation showed no sign of stopping.

The mountain, by that time, was drenched in the peculiar light they call alpenglow. Low angled rays of the setting sun hit high-angled surfaces of the cliff, and momentarily illuminated them from below.

No way would we be sleeping in our own beds on this night. I thought wistfully of my usual night-time spot, cuddled beside Sara in our warm house. Tonight would be nothing of the sort. I feared how low the thermometer might drop. I'd brought a sleeping bag for Martin, but I'd be in the cold. I surveyed the neighborhood for camp sites. On such a steep slope I knew I wouldn't find anything too posh. The nearest possibilities were uphill, at least as far as the place I'd left my pack.

I searched to that point and found no suitable spot. I put the pack on my back and went farther. Finally I came upon a landing created by the sheltering elbow of a tree root. It was level, but only the size of a doormat laid lengthwise across the grain of the slope. Another tiny spot looked just large enough for feet. I tried it out. My legs were suspended in midair, but it worked. Below me a five foot drop-off ended in a pile of jagged boulders. It wouldn't be an easy balancing act for an entire night, but there weren't options. In this vicinity, the location looked like a homesite. Still, I'd have to find something much less perilous for Martin.

I discovered a spot about twenty yards away on the uphill side of an enormous pine. The land sloped at about twenty degrees, but the area was large enough to accommodate a man's entire body. It was much safer than the first location because the tree and its undulating roots created a barrier on the downhill side. Their position would make it virtually impossible to take off on a slide for life in the middle of the night.

I spread out Martin's bag. Nearby I noticed a place I could build a campfire on a little peninsula of land. Two boulders on the uphill side served as perfect seats. I broke branches from a dead tree and stacked them for kindling.

Then I headed down the slope to get Martin. He sat right where I'd left him, trying to revive the phone. "I hope I haven't busted this somehow. It quit working." He extended it toward me.

I grinned as I took it, and handed him his sweatshirt. He pulled it over his head while I put on mine. The temperature sank with the sun. Then I handed him his diabetic kit. I watched him prick his finger and run the tests. "I doubt I'll need insulin with all this exercise. Probably sugar instead."

I sliced up an apple with my pocket knife in preparation. He finished the test and grabbed several wedges of the fruit. He ate them eagerly.

We roped together, and I led him in the half light of dusk up to our campsite. It took a long time because Martin adopted a much more cautious approach to climbing. He tested every hand and foot-hold, twice.

"Have a seat on that rock and I'll build a fire," I said.

While Martin situated himself I brought the blaze to life. Once the fire caught, I took my place on the other rock. We sat with the little beacon before us, like a lighthouse balanced on the edge of nothingness. Visually, it separated the untouched wilderness at our backs with the unrestrained civilization at our feet. Below us spread humanity, and everything mankind brings with himself. Roads and cars and homes and factories and shopping centers and office buildings and skyscrapers, each object outlined in its own distinctive sort of light.

Incandescence from a billion bulbs filled the basin to the measuring cup mark left by the recession of ancient Lake Bonneville. The commotion in the city couldn't be escaped even at this altitude in this absolute wilderness. A thousand humming metal engines and spinning rubber tires on asphalt and concrete roads melded into a constant drone. My consciousness eventually ignored the sound. I enjoyed the unparalleled beauty of the city viewed through the gaps in the cliffs.

I handed Martin an orange and set the canteen and an open

bag of gorp between us. "It isn't much, but I bet you'll remember it as one of the finest meals you ever ate. What we lack in variety we can make up for in quantity." I peeled myself an orange. The zesty smell filled my nostrils.

Martin sifted handful after handful of the granola based trail mix into his mouth. He washed it down with water from the canteen. I'd been concerned about his sugar level, but now that he'd eaten he should be safe.

The air felt motionless, then we heard a great commotion below. It came rapidly nearer, until all at once it surrounded us. A broiling storm of spinning air rattled through the trees. The flames disappeared for a moment as the tempest passed. Complete stillness followed, though the violent little storm made a racket as continued on up the hill.

Martin looked at me for explanation. I shrugged it off. It felt eerie, as if something meant to push us off the cliff. I hoped nothing like it would visit again. Then far above we heard a crash. For a moment I thought it might be a deer, but no deer would be this high on the slope. The noise continued and intensified. "Duck," I yelled as I realized a boulder, dislodged somewhere up-slope, was hurtling in our direction. I knew it would cast off razor-sharp shards at each bounding step.

We crouched behind our rock seats long after the sound passed somewhere to the east of camp. My heart raced.

Martin's voice quavered. "This is a dangerous place. Maybe we should leave."

"That's not an option. All we can do is stay alert."

A bat zigzagged through camp. It flitted against a sky filled with stars, far more than were ever visible in the city. Something rustled in the underbrush, and an owl hooted nearby. I stoked the fire. The flames climbed higher.

Martin, I'm sure, would've been prone to divulge his most private thoughts in response to the afternoon's first near-death experience. The continuing peril combined with the warm campfire made such confessions inevitable. Campfires affect men in funny ways, as if there's something in the release of carbon that causes forgotten brain synapses to reconnect. A man situated such that his feet are overheated by flame and his head is cooled by outdoor air is vulnerable to revealing truths he'd otherwise consider absurd. It's as if a crackling flame serves as the second simultaneously turned key to open the safety deposit box of memory.

Whatever the reason, it came as no surprise to me that after a few minutes of warming his toes, Martin began talking. "Did you know I was married once?"

I shrugged, not wanting to lie, or to say anything else that would alter his train of thought.

"I was. I guess I still am. We never bothered to get a divorce. It was July 4, 1976, the Bicentennial. We eloped. Got hitched in Vegas. Betsy Evans. A fine woman, a good marriage. Bet you wouldn't have expected that. Even today I don't have a single bad thing to say about her. Me, in a stable relationship. Preposterous." He spoke in staccato bursts, completely unlike the practiced tapestries he wove for me on his porch.

"It's safe to say both of us had already hit our fair share of bumps in the road by the time we hooked up. We thought we would continue for a while longer with our experimental lifestyles, but eventually settle down. What I'm saying is, neither of us were exactly Temple Marriage material at the time, but even that was a goal for both of us. We had everything in common. They were good times, the best of my life. In 1977 we even had a kid. A daughter."

My pulse quickened. I thought of the picture on his bedroom wall of the infant wrapped in blue. Not a half-brother, but a half-sister. My ears poised to pick up every inflection.

"We named her Isabel."

Then, just like that, he stopped talking. I waited a long time, vacantly watching the automobiles on the Interstate far below as they followed one another nose-to-tail like an ant colony on the scent-line to a feast; but no burst of information followed. Eventually, I looked up. Molten tears, filled with the glimmering reflection of the camp fires light, rolled down his cheeks. I knew his thoughts were on his daughter, obviously a painful and private memory, but I had to pry. I wanted to know what had happened, so I did what I had to do. I tossed another log on the fire, and waited for his feet to sufficiently warm.

"Have you ever heard of SIDS?" he finally asked.

In an instant I found myself re-evaluating many of the conclusions I'd come to about this man. "Your child died of Sudden Infant Death Syndrome?"

"You have a daughter. Can you imagine the terror of walking in to pick her up one morning, looking forward to spending another Saturday introducing her to the world . . . and finding she's gone?"

I shuddered, then shook my head.

"I loved everything about being a dad. I'd never been one before. That, if you ask me, is the biggest blemish on my record. You called me Dad today, but I was no dad to you. I failed. When you said that word to me I understood what a magical title it could be. When I meet my maker he'll ask me, 'What sort of a dad were you?' How should I reply?"

"Tell him you eventually made up for your mistakes."

"When you were born I was nowhere near ready for such a responsibility. That's why I stayed so involved with Isabel. I thought if I did a good enough job I could erase the past, but I couldn't. I didn't know how to face you. I owe you such an enormous apology that I don't know how I can ever get it out."

"You're doing fine."

He nodded. "I guess I wouldn't have made it up this enormous mountain without taking that first step."

I smiled. "Whatever happened to your wife?"

"She stayed in Anchorage. That's where we lived. After Isabel died, we just couldn't look at one another the same way anymore. We'd both overcome damaged pasts, and then to have our future ripped out from under us that way . . . it was more than either of us could bear."

"Do you ever hear from her?"

"Letters. Not many."

The flames slowly lost their enthusiasm, and as they tired, so did Martin. "I think I'm going to try to get some sleep, if you don't mind. It's almost 11:11. I already missed 10:01." He lifted himself from his seat on the boulder.

"What are you talking about?"

"The times I can go to bed. Those two I mentioned, and also 12:51. Those are the only times the reflection of a digital clock looks exactly the same as the face. I like to get into bed at those moments and no others."

I smiled. "Sounds logical." I handed him the flashlight.

"It's worked for me for a lot of years." He moved away from the campfire.

"Martin. One last thing. Sorry about how I behaved when you made us change hikes. I felt frustrated and angry."

"You had the right to be," he answered. He turned and wandered toward his spot under the tree.

He moved slowly through the dim light, then crouched down beside his sleeping bag. I turned away, focusing on neither fire, nor cliffs, nor city— just thinking about the odyssey this day had turned out to be. I'd been so close to canceling it time and again. What great fortune that I hadn't.

I stood up. My teeth chattered. It must have been in the low forties. I'd been so enthralled at the fireside I'd forgotten this earlier concern. I couldn't sit by the fire all night, though. There was no place to lie, and my fatigue was too great to sit. I couldn't build a fire near my sleeping site. My body would occupy the only flat spot.

I went to my pack, drew out the coiled rope and set it on my bivouac ledge. "Worse than the pillows at the old frat house," I said. But a damn site better than my non-existent blanket.

# Chapter 28

Despite my exhaustion, sleep eluded me. I shivered, my various injuries throbbed, and I couldn't find a comfortable position on the hard ground.

Looking toward Martin's sleeping site, I knew he was having the same sorts of problems. Because the boughs of his tree touched the ground on the uphill side, each time he adjusted his position he sent a shiver through the lower branches. I guessed at his main challenge. His nylon sleeping bag must be slippery as an inner-tube on a snowy hill. At the angle Martin lay I'm sure just remaining in a semi-prone position required constant effort. His tired feet would get little relief spending the night carrying at least part of his weight.

I looked up at the uncountable array of stars, and began counting, then let my eyes fall shut.

I saw Sara's face. "What is happiness, Tom?" she asked.

I recalled the question from the freezing November walk in the park. I thought of Martin's words, "When I meet my maker he'll ask me, 'What sort of a dad were you?' How should I reply?"

I remembered Uncle Joe's words when we last talked on his porch. "My wife and daughters are nowhere to be seen. They hate my guts. They're off spending my money while I rot in loneliness. My relationships aren't worth squat. My life's not worth squat." What words could more perfectly describe sadness?

I spoke in my dream. "I know the answer, Sara. Relationships. Not money, not fame, not status, not health. Just meaningful relationships with those you love."

She put her hand on mine. "I love you."

"I love you, too."

I lay there, barely able to fight off the chill. Long before dawn a light rain began falling on my face. Hadn't the weather report said sunny and clear? Without opening my eyes I grabbed at my crooked neck, massaging. I tried to locate a part of my body that didn't ache, but failed. I'd become far too accustomed to my soft bed.

I wriggled around for a moment, trying to find comfort, but to no avail. Reluctantly I opened my eyes, and beheld a strange world. Everything was bathed in white light on its uphill side, and buried in black shadow on the other. Objects shone the colors of a 1930's motion picture— a thousand shades of gray. I looked at the sky. The unusual light came from a waning harvest moon. It rose just high enough to be visible over the mountain peak. The moisture streamed from an unlikely wispy strand of clouds.

I lay there— cold clear through. The thought of cuddling beside Martin for warmth seemed inviting, but there wasn't any extra space. My chilled body needed activity to generate warmth. Since the light seemed sufficient, I wanted to hike to the saddle and look into the hidden valley. When I noticed the gray pine tree rustling, I went to tell Martin my plan.

"I can't sleep either. Let me go with you."

Argument would be pointless. I couldn't expect him to stay in such an uncomfortable place. We packed our things and left. I glanced at my luminous watch. It read 3:10 a.m. We moved into the talus-filled valley we'd been on the verge of reaching more than twelve hours earlier. The climb was steep and uneven, but not too difficult. No need to rope up.

Shards of rock were strewn everywhere. I imagined massive boulders crashing down this drainage, an intimidating thought. There wasn't a tree without major wounds on its uphill side. Many had knife sharp rocks buried in their woody flesh. Other forest giants lay toppled by collisions too severe to stand.

We trudged upward, the cool air making it easier to push hard for long distances. I selected my pathway based on ease for Martin's sake, and my own. He stayed near my heels. We hardly spoke.

Finally we reached a spot where the slope ahead appeared to be disjoined from the cliff beyond. The hidden valley must lie between; either that or it was an unbelievable optical illusion. On either side of the narrow saddle that must serve as the entry to our goal, a rock monolith towered. I pushed forward, energized by the prospect of seeing this sight.

We reached the saddle. Ahead the terrain dropped steeply. It must be the couloir, but I'd never imagined it could be so deep. Because of the angle, the light of the gibbous moon didn't fall into it at all. Everything within hid in a sea of black. The stark white moonlight landed high on the opposite wall. I'd guess it stood at least two-hundred feet away.

I removed my pack and retrieved the flashlight. We moved forward and peered down. I shone the light toward the bottom, but the beam wasn't strong enough to penetrate the dark. I surveyed the terrain. It confused me that there appeared to be no safe way into the void. The guidebook made getting into the couloir sound quite easy. This didn't look easy at all.

I inched toward the edge, wondering if I'd somehow missed an obvious spot. My toe pushed a stone into the chasm. A trail of cold blue sparks traced the path of the rock down the incline. Martin looked at me, his expression asking if I'd expected the electrical looking result.

"I've never seen anything like that in my life," I admitted. I picked up two more stones and struck them together. Sparks flew. I touched the stones together gently, and even that produced a small charge.

Martin heaved a large rock behind the one I'd kicked. A trail of light followed both it and the shards that broke off at each impact as it tumbled into the abyss. "Is this mountain made out of flint?" he asked.

"I don't know what's causing it."

Martin heaved more rocks into the darkness. Each time the phenomenon repeated itself, and each time he mumbled in amazement.

For me, exhaustion returned. I sat on the ground beside the pack. "Do you want to rest until the sun comes up?"

"No, I have too much on my mind."

I removed the sleeping bag. "I'm going to use this until you're ready for it, all right?"

He nodded.

I climbed in and lay down, happy to be on the level ground of the saddle, and especially thankful for the warmth. If this location was as uncomfortable as the previous spot, I was too tired to notice. I wanted to remain alert until Martin settled down, but cobwebs filled my mind. I shook my head clear, trying to concentrate on the mysteries we'd come across on this journey, but didn't have the mental alertness to understand any of them before I drifted off to sleep.

When the morning sun warmed my cheek, I woke. All about me I heard bird songs, punctuated by the echoing caws of crows. I opened my eyes and looked for Martin. I couldn't see him, so I stood up and looked more diligently. No sign.

I hurried to the spot where he'd been releasing his rocks. He hadn't left a trace. A shudder went down my spine. I peered down where the rocks went. Seventy feet below lay a fertile valley. It looked cool and comfortable, entirely unlike the terrain we'd traversed so far. Grasses, ferns, flowers, and berries grew. I could also tell I'd been correct when I figured the valley wasn't easily accessible from this spot. The transition ahead was one I wouldn't consider without a rope. I must have taken a wrong turn in the moonlight. This clearly wasn't the route the hiking book recommended, but Martin wouldn't have considered that. Had he been lured toward the edge by the whispering seductions of the beautiful valley?

"Marrrtinnn," I yelled into the hole.

"tinnn-tinn-tin," came the echoed reply. I waited for a long moment.

Then I heard, "Heelllloooo– elllooo– elo."

"Are– you– all– right?" I yelled over the edge, trying to keep my message clear by separating the words from their reverberations.

"I'm– fine," the voice returned.

For some reason I looked up, and there I saw a man taking the last strides toward the top of the sub-pinnacle bordering our camp on the east. The radiant sun directly behind him blurred his profile.

I lifted my hand to shade my eyes, peering through the gaps in my fingers. Even then, I could hardly make out his form. I could see enough, though. The knot in my stomach came loose. Martin hadn't fallen off the cliff. Instead, he'd gone exploring on his own. With overwhelming relief I picked my way up the difficult slope. It took me quite a while to reach the apex.

As I climbed I overheard Martin speaking in a quiet rush. "Dear Heavenly Father, thank Thee for watching over me and bringing me to this place. Thank Thee for creating a spot such as this. Thank Thee for answering my prayers. Thank Thee for sending me, at last, a friend who believes in me. Please forgive me for the spite I've felt in my heart for all of those who wouldn't believe in me, for now I realize the real error was that I'd failed to believe in myself. I never truly wanted harm to befall my father, mother, Joseph, Emma, Bishop Jacobs, Brother Steele, Sister Shephard . . ." He listed a long litany of names, mostly unfamiliar to me. "Show me, please, how I can better serve Thee, and make up for all of the time I've wasted. Thank Thee again for my many blessings, and I say these things in the name of Jesus Christ, amen."

Once he finished, I climbed the last few feet. He turned to

me. "This is the greatest experience of my life. You were right. Joseph didn't know what he was talking about."

The view from the top exceeded three hundred and sixty degrees, it was spherical. The only direction without an expansive panorama was directly down, and because of the rough terrain even that was a sight worthy of attention. "This is an incredible spot," I said, trying to take in the hidden couloir, the jagged cliffs, the azure sky, and the city far below. The vastness and beauty humbled me, made me feel I had all the consequence of a dust mite; yet I felt favored to be balanced atop the hungry flames of this inferno frozen in stone.

No one but those who'd been here, and there must be very few, could possibly imagine the existence of this sanctuary. The spot hid itself masterfully, even though it stood in relief from everything around. Its blatant obviousness served as camouflage. Yet once seen, it must be impossible to imagine the mountain in any other way.

I looked west, and saw the enormous shadow of the mountain blanketing the eastern half of the valley floor. In concert with the jagged shadows of other peaks, there was the illusion of teeth— a giant dinosaur gradually opening it jaws. The awesome Wasatch gave up, in the most miserly way possible, the penumbra of night cast across the valley below.

"I want to thank you for getting me here, Tom. I couldn't have made it without you." In that way he told me he would never stand atop the northern summit of Mount Olympus, the peak he'd dreamed of for a lifetime, the elevation he no longer needed to attain. I looked up and noticed a lone eagle soaring along the ridgeline of the true summit, at least one-thousand feet above. For the man Martin Crump had become, there was now something better than conquering the absolute acme, something superior to standing alone against a cobalt sky, from the perspective of the city below. No one down there could possibly see him from such a distance anyway. He now understood that. His image had been merely childhood imagination. Reality, as it's prone to do, revealed a more perfect spot.

Martin touched my arm. "Open your hand."

I did.

He lifted his fist above my palm. "I carried a good luck charm in my pocket. Now I want you to have it."

Out of his hand sifted a single golden strand. The chain sparkled as it grabbed the morning light and refracted it randomly. I watched it settle into my palm, wondering what it meant, and then the image of Christ nailed to a cross appeared. It spun in disorganized circles as it neared my flesh, and I knew what it was.

"How did you get this?" I asked.

"Patty convinced Father to give it back to her, I guess. It arrived one day in the mail shortly after she disappeared. With it I found a note asking me to remember her by it, and to pass it along to you when the time felt right."

I held the crucifix at eye level and examined it. The edges were rounded. I guessed the metal had been worked by hours upon hours of rubbing between Martin's fingers. As far as I knew, this cross might be the only thing I'd ever see that once belonged to the woman who gave me life.

"Thanks," I said, as I traced its shape with my thumb. Then I strung the chain around my neck.

Out of the corner of my eye I saw him reach into his pocket and pull out several small pieces of cloth. They were white, and cut with many sharp angles. He didn't even look at them before letting them slide from his grasp. I watched with satisfaction as the stars that never found a home on the Crump family flag floated down to find secret spots among the jumble of boulders. There they would decompose, like the marriage they'd been designed to save, so long before.

We turned wordlessly, and made our way from the summit my father and I will forever know as Crucifix Peak.

The End

# Endnotes:

The song, *We Thank The O' God for a Prophet*, is copywrited by the Church of Jesus Christ of Latter-Day Saints.

# Afterword

Thanks for reading my novel. I hope you enjoyed it, and that you'll recommend it to friends. Maybe you'd even be willing to visit your favorite on-line bookstore and write a review. Please visit me on the Web at www.daveshields.com. In the moment you're reading this I hope I'm at work on another novel. I'm full of ideas, and I'd love nothing more than to share them with you one day.

Until next time,

David Shields
me@daveshields.com
July 24, 2001

# Acknowledgments

Over the years of working on this novel, I've thought often about the people I want to thank once it's in print. Now that the day I've dreamed of has finally arrived, the list has grown so long that I know I can't do an adequate job. My apologies in advance to the many helpful people I'm forced to leave out.

Early readers input shaped my story in dramatic ways. Thank you Mom, Dad, Debs, Candi, and the rest of my family, plus the Morris family, Fred, Sue, Zane, Amy and the others— all members of Humanities 1000. In many ways, you are the people who started me on this journey. Thank you also Mike Hooper, Louis Bohannan, Alan Ahtow, RBR, and Robyn Mendenhall. Each of you provided encouragement when I needed it in order to continue.

In the process of researching and refining I've turned to the Internet often, and I've always come away in awe both of the power of technology, and the willingness of people to lend a hand. Experts of all sorts shared detailed information with me. Whatever lapses in logic or logistics remain, they are entirely my fault. Among the cyberspace group, I especially want to thank Jilla Lankford and the members of her incredible organization, Noveldoc.com. These people are truly dedicated to the storytelling craft, and are certain to make a lasting impact on the literary world. I want to extend my special gratitude to three Noveldoc members, each of whom went above and beyond the call of duty in critiquing various drafts of my manuscript. Joylene Butler patiently taught me more than I'd ever imagined there was to know about novel writing technique. Keith Pyatt showed me how to make my descriptions and dialogue more vivid than I ever could have on my own. On numerous occasions, the words you've read in my novel are really his. Gloria Piper understood my characters and their motivations better than I ever will. How she accomplished this, I don't know, but her suggestions elevated my story to a new level. I thank all of these people for their meticulous attention to detail.

There are so many others. Anne Lemmon and Michael Kayser went over the manuscript a final time with a fine tooth comb. William Brian Tatafu brought imaginary events to life with his extraordinary artistic ability. Frank Barry, Pat Brown, Michael Jensen, Paul Zane Pilzer, Tony Robbins, Leonard Driggs, Brad Brown, David Lake, Drusilla Campbell, Sol Stein, Ben Bova, Rick Evans, Karen Kindred, Gary Strand, and others provided encouragement and motivation beyond anything they are aware. Participants in conferences including The San Diego State University Writers Conference, Writers at Work, and Rocky Mountain Fiction Writers Colorado Gold Conference, are all responsible in various ways for what my manuscript has become. Special thanks go to my wife, Elle, for doing everything she possibly could to help me reach my goals.

Thank you, one and all, for transforming my journey into my reward. I can't wait to see what the future holds.

Dave Shields